THE MACHIAVELLI COVENANT

THE
MACHIAVELLI
COVENANT

ALLAN FOLSOM

A TOM DOHERTY ASSOCIATES BOOK / NEW YORK

Fol

THE MACHIAVELLI COVENANT

Copyright © 2006 by Allan Folsom

This book is printed on acid-free paper.

A Forge Book
Published by Tom Doherty Associates, LLC
175 Fifth Avenue
New York, NY 10010

www.tor.com

Forge® is a registered trademark of Tom Doherty Associates, LLC.

ISBN-13: 978-0-765-31305-8 (hardcover)
ISBN-10: 0-765-31305-7 (hardcover)
ISBN-13: 978-0-765-31839-8 (trade paperback)
ISBN-10: 0-765-31839-3 (trade paperback)

First Edition: January 2007

Printed in the United States of America

0 9 8 7 6 5 4 3 2 1

For Karen and for Riley

SUNDAY

APRIL 2

1

The slow pound of Nicholas Marten's heart sounded like a drum buried somewhere inside him. His own breath, as he inhaled and exhaled, resonated as if it were a movie sound track. So did the sound of Caroline's labored breathing as she lay on the bed next to him.

For what seemed the tenth time in half that many minutes he looked at her. Her eyes were closed, as they had been, her hand resting gently in his. For all the life in it, it might as well have been a glove. Nothing more.

How long had he been in Washington? Two days? Three? Flown there from his home in Manchester, England, almost immediately after Caroline's call asking him to come. He'd known the minute he heard her voice something was terribly wrong. It had been filled with dread and fear and helplessness, and then she'd told him what it was: She had a very aggressive, untreatable staph infection and was expected to live only a few days more.

For all the horror and shock of it, there had been something more in her voice. Anger. Something had been done to her, she told him, suddenly whispering as if she were afraid someone would overhear. No matter what the doctors said or would say, she was certain that the infection killing her had been caused by bacteria that had deliberately been given to her. It had been then, judging from sounds in the background, that someone had come into the room. Abruptly she'd finished with an urgent plea for him to come to Washington, then hung up.

He hadn't known what to think. All he knew was that she was terribly frightened and that her situation was made all the worse by the very recent deaths of her husband and twelve-year-old son in the crash of a private plane off the coast of California. Considering the physical and emotional toll the combination of these tragic things would have had on her, and with no other information, Marten found it impossible to know if there was any basis at all for her suspicion. Still, the reality was that she was desperately ill and wanted him to be with her. And from everything he'd heard in her voice he knew he'd better get there as quickly as he could.

And he had. Within the day flying from Manchester in the north of England to London and then on to Washington, D.C., taking a taxi from Dulles International directly to the hospital, and later getting a room at a hotel nearby. That Caroline knew who he really was and the risk she dared subject him to by asking him to come back into the United States had not been brought up. It wasn't necessary. She would never have asked if something wasn't terribly wrong.

So he had come hurriedly back to the country he had fled four years earlier in fear for his life and that of his sister. Come back— after so many years and the differing paths their lives had taken— because Caroline had been and was still the one true love of his life. He loved her more deeply than any woman he had ever known and in a way that was impossible for him to describe. He knew too that even though she was happily married and had been for a long time, in some unspoken, even profound way, she felt the same about him.

Marten looked up sharply as the room door was suddenly flung open. A heavyset nurse entered followed by two men in dark suits. The first was broad-shouldered, in his early forties, with dark curly hair. "You'll have to leave, sir, please," he said respectfully.

"The president is coming," the nurse said curtly, her manner abrupt and authoritative, as if she had suddenly become commander of the suits. A member of the Secret Service.

At the same instant Marten felt Caroline's hand tighten around his. He looked down and saw her eyes were open. They were wide and clear, and looked into his the way they had that first day they met, when they were both sixteen and in high school.

"I love you," she whispered.

"I love you too," he whispered back.

She looked at him for a half second more, then closed her eyes, and her hand relaxed.

"Please, sir, you have to leave, now," the first suit said. At that same moment a tall, slim, silver-haired man in a dark blue suit stepped through the doorway. There was no question who he was— John Henry Harris, president of the United States.

Marten looked at him directly. "Please," he said softly, "give me a moment alone with her. . . . She's just . . ."—the word caught in his throat, "died."

The men's gaze held for the briefest moment, "Of course," the president said, his words hushed and reverent. Then, motioning to his Secret Service protectors, turned and left the room.

2

Thirty minutes later, head down against the world, barely aware of the direction he was going, Nicholas Marten walked the all but deserted Sunday-night streets of the city.

He tried not to think of Caroline. Tried not to acknowledge the pain that told him she was no more. Tried not to think that it had been little more than three weeks since she had lost both her husband and son. Tried to put out of his mind the idea that she might have been intentionally given something that caused her fatal infection.

"Something has been done to me." Her voice suddenly echoed inside him as if she had just spoken. It resonated with the same fear and vulnerability and anger it had had when she had first called him in England.

"Something has been done to me." Caroline's words came again. As if she were still trying to reach him, trying to make him believe without doubt that she had not been merely ill, but murdered.

What that "something" was, or at least what she thought it was and how it had begun, she'd told him during the first of the only two lucid moments she'd had since he arrived.

It had happened following the twin funerals of her husband, Mike Parsons, a well-respected forty-two-year-old congressman from California in his second term in office, and their son, Charlie. Certain she was strong enough to see it all through, she had invited numerous friends to their home to join her in a celebration of their lives; but the shock of what had happened, coupled with the almost unbearable strain of the funerals and the crush of well-meaning people, had overwhelmed her, and she'd broken down, retreating in tears and near-hysteria to lock herself in her bedroom, screaming for people to go away and refusing even to answer the door.

Congressional chaplain and pastor of their church, Reverend Rufus Beck, had been among the mourners and immediately sent for Caroline's personal physician, Lorraine Stephenson. Dr. Stephenson had come quickly and with the pastor's help convinced Caroline to open the bedroom door. Within minutes she had injected her, as Caroline said, "with a sedative of some kind." When she woke up she was in a room in a private clinic where Stephenson had prescribed several days' rest and where "I never felt the same again."

Marten turned down one darkened street and then another, replaying the hours he had spent with her in the hospital. With the exception of the other instance when Caroline had been awake and talked to him, she had simply slept, and he had stayed by her side keeping vigil. Throughout those long hours health care personnel monitoring her condition had come and gone and there had been brief visits by friends during which Marten simply introduced himself and then quietly left the room.

There had been two other visitors as well, the people who had been immediately involved when Caroline had broken down at home. The first had been an early-morning call by the woman who had given her the "sedative" and prescribed her stay in the clinic, her personal physician, Dr. Lorraine Stephenson: a tall, handsome woman in her mid-fifties. Stephenson had exchanged a brief pleasantry with him, then read Caroline's chart, listened to her heart and lungs through a stethoscope, and left.

The second had been congressional chaplain Rufus Beck, who visited later in the day. A large, gentle, soft-spoken African-American, Beck had been accompanied by a young and attractive dark-haired Caucasian woman with a camera bag slung over one shoulder who'd stayed pretty much in the background. Like Stephenson, Reverend Beck had introduced himself to Marten, and they'd had a brief exchange. Afterward he'd spent a few moments in prayer as Caroline slept before telling Marten good-bye and leaving with the young woman.

A light rain began to fall and Marten stopped to turn up the collar of his jacket against it. In the distance he could see the tall spire that was the Washington Monument. For the first time he had some concrete sense of where he was. Washington was not just the inside of an intensive-care hospital room but a large metropolitan city that just happened to be the capital of the United States of America. It was a place he'd never been, even though he'd lived all of his life in California before fleeing to England and could easily have visited. For some reason just being here gave him a deep sense of belonging, to one's country, to one's native land. It was a feeling he'd never had before, and he wondered if there would ever be a time when he could return from the exiled life he lived in Manchester.

Marten moved on. As he did he noticed a car coming slowly down the street toward him. That the streets were all but empty made the vehicle's pace seem odd. It was late Sunday night and raining—wouldn't the driver of one of the very few vehicles on the street be anxious to get to wherever he or she was going? The car came abreast of him and he glanced at it as it passed. The driver was male and nondescript, middle-aged with dark hair. The car passed and Marten watched it continue down the street, its speed never changing. Maybe the guy was drunk or drugged out or— suddenly the reflection became personal—maybe he was somebody who had just lost someone extraordinarily dear to him and had no idea where he was or what he was doing other than just moving.

3

Marten's thoughts went back to Caroline. She had been the wife of a well-respected congressman who had become an increasingly popular figure in Washington and one who just happened to have been a close boyhood friend of the president, and the sudden, tragic deaths of both her husband and son had seen the political community embrace her with everything it had. It made him wonder why she would think "something had been done to her." Why she would think she had deliberately been injected with a disease that would kill her.

Methodically Marten tried to assess her mental state over the last two days of her life. In particular he thought of the second instance when she had been awake. That time she'd taken hold of his hand and looked into his eyes.

"Nicholas," she'd said weakly. "I—" Her mouth had been dry and her breathing labored. Just speaking took enormous effort. "I was to . . . have . . . been . . . on that plane with . . . my husband and my . . . son. There was a . . . last-minute change . . . of plans . . . and I . . . came back to . . . Washington a . . . day . . . earlier." She had stared at him intently. "They . . . murdered my . . . husband and . . . son . . . and now they have . . . killed . . . me."

"Who are you talking about? Who is 'they'?" he'd pressed gently, trying to get something more tangible from her.

"The . . . ca . . . ." she'd said. She'd tried to say more but it had been as much as she could do. Her strength gone, she just lay back and fell asleep. And she had slept right up until those last moments of her life when she'd opened her eyes and stared into his and told him she loved him.

Thinking about it now he realized the little she had told him had come in two sections, one quite separate from the other. The first had come in snippets: that she was originally to have been on the ill-fated plane with her husband and son but a last-minute change of plans brought her back to Washington a day earlier; what had happened at her home after the funerals; and finally what she had told him when she'd called him in England, saying she was dying from a staph infection caused by a strain of untreatable bacteria that she was certain had been given to her deliberately. "The . . . ca"—what she'd started to say when he'd asked her to explain it, and who the "they" were she was referring to, he had no idea.

The second section had come from utterances she'd made in her sleep. Most had been everyday things, calling out the names of her husband, "Mike," or her son, "Charlie," or her sister "Katy," or saying things like "Charlie, please turn down the TV" or "The class is Tuesday." But she'd said other things too. These had seemingly been aimed at her husband and were filled with alarm or fear or both. "Mike, what is it?" Or "You're frightened. I can see it!" Or "Why won't you tell me what it is?" Or "It's the others, isn't it?" And then later, a sudden fearful blurting—"I don't like the white-haired man."

That part he was familiar with because it was a piece of the story she had told him when she'd called him in Manchester and asked him to come.

"The fever came less than a day after I woke up in the clinic," she'd said. "It got worse and they did tests. A white-haired man came, they said he was a specialist but I didn't like him. Everything about him frightened me. The way he stared at me. The way he touched my face and my legs with his long, hideous fingers; and that horrid thumb with its tiny balled cross. I asked him why he was there and what he was doing but he never answered. Later they discovered I had some kind of staph infection in the bone of my right leg. They tried to treat it with antibiotics. But they didn't work. Nothing worked."

Marten walked on. The rain came down harder but he barely noticed. His entire focus was Caroline. They had met in high school and entered the same college certain they would marry and have children and be together for the rest of their lives. And then she had gone away for the summer and met a young lawyer named Mike Parsons. After that, his life and hers changed forever. But as deep as his hurt, as badly as he had been wounded, his love for her never diminished. In time he and Mike became friends, and he told Mike what Caroline and only a few others knew—who he really was and why he had been forced to leave his job as a homicide detective in the Los Angeles Police Department and move to the north of England to live under an assumed identity as a landscape architect.

He wished now he had gone to the funeral of her husband and son as he'd wanted to. Because if he had he would have been there when she'd broken down and when Dr. Stephenson had come. But he hadn't, and that had been Caroline's doing. She had told him she was surrounded by friends and that her sister and husband were coming from their home in Hawaii, and that, considering the danger surrounding his own situation, it was better he stayed where he was. They would get together later, she'd told him. Later, when things had quieted down. She'd sounded alright then. Shaken maybe, but alright, and with the inner strength to carry on that she'd always had. And then all this had happened.

God how he had loved her. How he still loved her. How he would always love her.

He walked on thinking only that. Finally, he became aware of the rain and realized he was nearly soaked through. He knew he had to find his way back to his hotel and looked around trying to get his bearings. That was when he saw it. A lighted edifice in the distance. A structure embedded in his memory from childhood, from history, from newspapers, from television, from movies, from everything. The White House.

At that same moment the tragic loss of Caroline caught up with him. And against the rain and the dark, and with no shame whatsoever, he wept.

MONDAY

APRIL 3

4

It was still overcast and drizzling.

Nicholas Marten sat behind the wheel of the rental car parked just down and across the street from Dr. Lorraine Stephenson's Georgetown residence. The three-story house, in this leafy, up-scale neighborhood, was dark. If anyone was home they were either already asleep or in a room to the rear. Marten chose to assume neither. He had been there for more than two hours. Someone asleep would have gone to bed about 6:30. Possible, of course, but unlikely. Alternatively, over that same two hours, someone in a room to the rear would most likely have left it for one reason or another: to go to another room, the kitchen, something; and because of the time of day and the dreariness of the weather that person in all probability would have turned on a light to illuminate their way. So common sense told him Dr. Stephenson had not yet come home. Which was why he was waiting. And would continue to do so until she did.

How many times that day had he taken the note from his jacket pocket and read it? At this point he could quote it from memory.

I, Caroline Parsons, give Nicholas Marten of Manchester, England, full access to all of my personal papers, including my medical records, and to the personal papers of my late husband, United States congressman Michael Parsons of California.

The note—typed, signed in a shaky scrawl by Caroline, then dated, witnessed, and stamped and signed by notary public—had been delivered to Marten that morning at his hotel. The day and date of its writing and the timing of its delivery were telling. This was Monday, April 3. Caroline had called him in Manchester late in the day on Thursday, March 30, asking him to come, and he'd left for Washington the following morning. Her letter had been written and notarized that same day, Friday, March 31, but he had known nothing about it until this morning. On Friday she had still been lucid, and knowing her time was short and unsure that he would get there before she died, had called for a notary and had the piece done. Yet he had known nothing of its existence and it had not been delivered until after her death.

"That was as she wished, as I wrote you, Mr. Marten," Caroline's attorney, Richard Tyler, told him over the phone when he called to inquire about it. Tyler's cover letter had informed him that Caroline's letter was indeed valid. Just how far the authority she had given him might go if challenged in a court of law was difficult to say. Nonetheless it remained a legal document and Marten could use it as he chose. "Only you would know her intentions for writing it, Mr. Marten, but I take it that you were a very close and dear friend and she trusted you implicitly."

"Yes," Marten had said, thanking Tyler for his help and asking if he could call on him later if legal questions arose, before hanging up. Clearly Caroline had not discussed her suspicions or fears with her attorney, which probably meant she had shared them with no one but him. That the delivery of the letter had been delayed until after her death would have given Marten an opportunity to reflect and to see how very serious she had been about her allegations that she and her husband and her son had been murdered. The letter and the timing were everything, designed with the sense that Marten might not fully believe her allegations because of her physical and mental state, but knowing too that if he did, he would do everything he could to find out about them.

He would do it because of what they'd meant to each other for so many years, regardless of the divergent roads their lives had taken. He would do it too because of who he was and what he was made of. The letter would help convince him she'd been right. It would also help open some doors that might otherwise have remained shut.

8:25 P.M.

Headlights suddenly reflected in Marten's rearview mirror and he watched a car come down the street behind him. As it drew nearer he could see that it was a dark late-model Ford. The car slowed as it approached Stephenson's home then moved on past, turning at the end of the block. For a moment he thought it might have been the doctor herself, but if it had been she'd changed her mind and kept on going. It made him wonder if maybe she wanted to return to her house but was afraid to. If so, it underscored the reason he was there and went hand in hand with what had happened earlier when he'd tried to get in touch with her.

He'd phoned her office twice that morning. Both times he'd explained to the receptionist that he'd been a close friend of Caroline Parsons and that he wanted to discuss Caroline's illness with Dr. Stephenson. Each time he'd been told the doctor was with patients and would return his call later. By noon there had been no response.

After the lunch hour he'd called again. Still the doctor was not available. This time he asked that Stephenson be told that if she was reluctant to discuss Mrs. Parsons's situation she need not worry because he had the lawful authority to access her medical records. His tone had been wholly businesslike and was meant to ease any professional concerns Stephenson might have had. In truth, despite Caroline's letter and what she had told him, he had no tangible reason to believe there had been foul play. Caroline had been terminally ill and under enormous stress and life would have seemed desperately hopeless and cruel any way she looked at it. Nonetheless, the letter existed and the questions lingered, and so until he was wholly convinced Caroline had been wrong, he would continue to pursue it.

What surprised him, what turned him and made him sit waiting in the dark outside Stephenson's home, had come at ten minutes to four in the afternoon, when the phone rang in his hotel room.

"This is Dr. Stephenson," she'd said, her voice flat and without emotion.

"Thanks for calling back," Marten had said evenly. "I was a close friend of Caroline Parsons. You and I met briefly in her hospital room."

"What can I do for you?" she pressed; this time her voice had an impatient edge.

"I would like to talk to you about the circumstances surrounding Caroline's illness and the cause of her death."

"I'm sorry, these are privacy issues. It is not something I can discuss."

"I understand, doctor, but I have been given legal access to all of her papers, her medical records included."

"I'm sorry, Mr. Marten," she said sharply, "there is nothing I can do to help you. Please don't call again." Abruptly she hung up.

Marten remembered standing there, the receiver still in his hand. Like that, he'd been shut down and shut off. What it meant was that if he wanted to see Caroline's medical records he would have to go through an entire legal process and then months and perhaps thousands of dollars in legal fees later, he might or might not get to see them. Even if he did—especially if Caroline had been right and there had been foul play—how could he be sure that the records he had been given access to had not been tampered with?

From his own past experience he knew that investigators who took no for an answer and went home rarely got any answers at all. The detectives who stayed in the game and pressed it, who sometimes didn't go home for days were the ones who got the resolutions they were looking for. It was why he knew what he had to do next. Get to Dr. Stephenson right away and ask her point-blank if she thought Caroline had been murdered.

It was an approach that more often than not got some kind of concrete response. Usually it came in the way a question was answered, a hesitation or an awkward wording of a phrase, or by the person's eye movement or body language, sometimes by all three. Rarely did someone involved with a crime not somehow give themselves away. Proving it, of course, was something else. But that was not his purpose now, only to get some sense that Caroline had been right, that she had deliberately been given some kind of toxin that had killed her. And if she had, to see if Dr. Stephenson had personally been involved.

5

Lorraine Stephenson had called him at ten minutes to four. By four twenty he had walked the several blocks from his hotel to George Washington University Hospital. At four twenty-five he was in the hospital's medical staff office talking to the woman behind the desk. Once again his experience as a homicide detective served him well. Doctors who regularly work at a hospital are registered with that institution's medical board and their personal records are kept on file in the medical staff office. Because she had visited Caroline at University Hospital, Marten expected Dr. Stephenson would have formal medical privileges there and consequently her personal records would be on file in the medical staff office. Assuming that, he'd simply told the woman at the desk that Dr. Stephenson had been recommended to him as a possible family physician and he would like some professional information about her—where she had gone to medical school, done her residency, that kind of thing. In response the woman had brought Stephenson's file up on her computer screen. As she did, Marten looked around the room and saw a large box of facial tissues on a filing cabinet several feet behind her. Stifling a sneeze and saying he had caught a cold in the rainy weather, he asked if he might have a tissue. It took the woman ten seconds to get up from her desk and walk with her back to him to retrieve the box of tissues. It took Marten seven seconds to step around her desk, look at her computer screen, scroll down, and retrieve what he needed. Three minutes later he left the office with a handful of tissues and the knowledge that Dr. Lorraine Stephenson was divorced, had graduated from Johns Hopkins University Medical School, had done her residency at Mount Sinai Hospital in New York City, kept professional offices at the Georgetown Medical Building, and lived at 227 Dumbarton Street, in the city's Georgetown section.

8:27 P.M.

Again Marten saw lights in his mirror. A car approached and then passed. Where was she? Out to dinner, to a movie, some kind of professional conference? Suddenly he thought of Stephenson's tone and manner, heard her words as she'd ended their conversation.

"I'm sorry, Mr. Marten," she'd said sharply, *"there is nothing I can do to help you. Please don't call again."* Then she'd hung up.

Maybe there was more there than he'd thought. Maybe what he'd heard as cold aloofness had really been fear. What if Caroline *had* been murdered and Stephenson had been involved or had even done it herself? And then he'd telephoned her saying he had a legal document giving him access to Caroline's medical records and that he wanted to talk about her illness and the cause of her death. If Stephenson *had* been involved, what if she had returned his call and put him off simply to buy time so that she could cut and run? What if at this moment she was on her way out of the city?

8:29 P.M.

Another vehicle came down the street behind him. It began to slow as it neared Stephenson's home and Marten saw that it was the same Ford that had slowed minutes before. This time it slowed even more, as if whoever was in the car was trying to see inside the house, to determine if a light or lights had been turned on, an indication that the doctor had come home.

No sooner had it moved past, than it abruptly sped up and drove off. As it did, Marten caught sight of the driver. A chill touched his neck and ran down his spine. It was the same man who had been driving the car that had so slowly passed him near the Washington Monument the night before.

What the hell is this? Marten thought. Coincidence? Maybe. But if it's not, then what is it? And what does he want with Dr. Stephenson?

Marten saw a car turn at the end of the block and start down the street toward him. As it neared he could see it was a taxi. Like the other car it slowed as it reached Stephenson's home, then it stopped. A moment later the rear door opened and Dr. Stephenson got out. She closed the door and the taxi drove off, then she started for the house. At the same time Marten stepped from his rental car.

"Dr. Stephenson," he called out.

She started and looked back.

"It's Nicholas Marten, Caroline Parsons's friend," he said. "I'd like a few minutes of your time."

Stephenson stared at him for the briefest moment then suddenly turned and walked hurriedly down the sidewalk away from her house.

"Dr. Stephenson!" Marten called again and went after her.

His feet touched the far curb and he saw her glance back. Her eyes were wide and filled with the fear.

"I mean you no harm," he said loudly. "Please, just a moment of your—"

She turned back and kept on. Marten followed. Suddenly she broke into a run. So did Marten. He saw her pass under a streetlight and then disappear in darkness beyond. He ran faster. In a moment he was under the streetlight and then in the darkness. He didn't see her. Where the hell was she? Another twenty feet and he had his answer, she was standing there watching him come. He stopped.

"I just want to talk to you, please, nothing else," he said, then took a step forward.

"Don't."

It was then he saw the small automatic in her hand.

"What's that for?" He looked up from the gun and saw her eyes locked on his. If before he had seen fear, he now saw cold resolve. "Put the gun down," he said firmly. "Put the gun on the ground and step back from it."

"You want to send me to the doctor," she said quietly, her stare unwavering. "But you never will. None of you ever will." She paused and he could see her trying to decide something. Then she spoke again, her words deliberate and clearly enunciated. "Never. Ever."

She was still staring at him when she shoved the barrel of the automatic into her mouth and pulled the trigger. There was a loud *pop*. The back of her skull exploded and her body dropped like a stone to the pavement.

"Jesus, God," Marten breathed in horror and disbelief.

A heartbeat later his senses caught up with him, and he turned in the dark and ran from the scene. In ninety seconds he was in his rental car turning off Dumbarton and down Twenty-ninth Street. Stephenson's suicide was the last thing he had expected and it had unnerved him. It had been an act clearly done out of sheer terror and came about as close to confirming that Caroline had been right as you could get, that *she had been murdered.* Moreover, it made him believe Caroline's other allegation was true as well, that the plane crash killing her husband and son had been no accident.

Right now all of those things faded to the background. The important thing was that he not be caught in the middle of it. There had been nothing he could do for Stephenson, and a call to 911 for help could well have forced him into a situation where he would have to identify himself to the police. They would want to know why he was there. Why she had shot herself in front of him on a darkened sidewalk several hundred yards away from her house. Why his rental car was parked just across the street from it.

What if someone, a neighbor maybe, had seen him sitting in the car and then confronting Stephenson when she came home and following her when she ran off down the street? The questions would be nagging and ugly. He had no proof of anything Caroline had said and if he told the truth his story would seem incredible at best and the police would probe deeper. All he needed was for them to begin doubting who he was and look into it. If they did they might well open the door to the past, one that could turn loose the dark forces in the Los Angeles Police Department still hunting him. Men who hated him for what had happened in L.A. those not-so-many years ago and were still trying to track him down and kill him. It meant he had to keep as far away from all this as possible yet still remain close enough to stay on top of it.

In England he had a new name and a new life, one that he had worked hard to achieve and revolved around the design and planting of beautiful gardens. For all the sentiment he might have had about returning to his roots and his native land, staying here and moving back into a world of fear and violence was the last thing he wanted. But he had no choice. In her own way Caroline had asked him to find out who was responsible for her death and for the deaths of her son and husband and the reason why.

The thing was, he would have anyway.

He loved her that much.

TUESDAY

APRIL 4

6

President of the United States John Henry Harris walked side by side with French president Jacques Geroux across the manicured grounds of the Élysée Palace, the official residence of the French president. Both men were smiling and chatting amiably on this bright spring day in the French capital. Keeping pace at discreet distance were plainclothes agents of the United States Secret Service and of the Direction General de la Securité Exterieure, or the DGSE, the French Secret Service. Prominent too was a select contingent of the international media. This was an arranged photo-op following a private breakfast Harris had had with Geroux and was designed to exhibit the cordiality between France and the United States.

Today was President Harris's 369th day in office: exactly one year and four days since, as vice president of the United States, he had assumed office following the sudden death of President Charles Singleton Cabot; 153 days since he had been re-elected president in an extremely close election; 76 days since his inauguration.

As president, the former vice president and senator from California had made it a campaign pledge to lessen the image of the U.S. as a pugnacious, aggressive superpower and make it more a partner in an increasingly complex global marketplace. His mission in Europe was to warm the still-chilly atmosphere created by America's near-unilateral decision to invade Iraq and the long and bloody aftermath following it. His meeting with the French president today was the first in a week-long series of face-to-face engagements with the heads of the European Union before they all met formally at a NATO summit this coming Monday, April 10, in Warsaw where he hoped to announce a newfound unity.

The trouble was, for all the outward signs of openness and the willingness of the heads of state to meet with him, there was the very real sense it wouldn't work. At least not with the two leaders of primary importance; French President Geroux and Anna Amalie Bohlen, the chancellor of Germany, with whom he would meet this evening in Berlin. What to do about it, especially now after his face-to-face closed-door session with Geroux, was something else and something he needed to weigh before discussing it with even his closest advisers. Thinking before talking had long been his habit, and everyone knew it. It was why he knew they would leave him alone on Air Force One when they made the comparatively short hop to Berlin.

Yet now, as he smiled and chatted with President Geroux as they approached a bank of microphones where they would address a larger gaggle of media, his thoughts were not so much on the state of international affairs but on the recent deaths of Congressman Mike Parsons and his son, and the heartbreaking passing of Mike's wife, Caroline.

John Henry Harris and Parsons had grown up within a mile of each other in the dusty California farming town of Salinas. Fourteen years older, and first as a babysitter when he even changed his diapers, and later simply as a pal, Johnny Harris had been a surrogate older brother to Parsons from the time he had been in junior high school until he left for college on the East Coast. Years later he had been best man at Parsons's marriage to Caroline and then helped him in his run for a congressional seat. In return Parsons and Caroline had been hugely supportive of his own senatorial and presidential campaigns in California. And both had been exceedingly kind and supportive of himself and his wife, Lori, during a long and exhausting battle with the brain cancer that took her life just a week before the presidential election. That long personal history made Mike and Caroline Parsons, along with their son, Charlie, about as close to family as people could get and their tragic deaths at such a young age and so hurriedly following each other had staggered him. He had attended the funeral of Mike and Charlie and would have gone to Caroline's memorial service had not this vastly important European trip already been scheduled.

Now, as seemingly a thousand cameras clicked and whirred and he and President Geroux approached the microphones, he could not help but think of the tableau when he had entered Caroline's hospital room that final night to see her illness-ravaged body lying deathly still under the bedcovers and the young man at her bedside looking up at him.

"Please," he'd said softly, "give me a moment alone with her. . . . She's just . . . died."

The memory of it made him wonder just who this man was. In all the years he had known Mike and Caroline he had never met or even seen him until that moment. Yet he was clearly someone who knew Caroline well enough to be the only person with her when she died and be moved enough to ask the president of the United States for the privacy to be alone with her for a few moments longer.

"Mr. President," French president Geroux guided him to the microphones, "this is Paris on a glorious day in April. Perhaps you have something to say to the people of France."

"Je vous remerci, M. le président." I do, Mr. President, thank you, Harris said in French, smiling comfortably as was his nature. It had all been rehearsed of course, as was the short speech he would give in French to the Gallic people about the long tradition of reliance, friendship, and trust between their nation and the United States. Still, as he stepped to the microphones, a part of him was thinking of the young man who had been with Caroline when she'd died, and he made a mental note to have someone find out who he was.

7

Nicholas Marten walked slowly through the wood-paneled study of the Parsons's modest home in suburban Maryland trying to do nothing more than look around. Trying not to feel the gaping hole of Caroline's absence, trying not to let himself think that nothing had happened and expect she would walk through the door at any moment.

Her touches were everywhere; especially in the abundance of house plants intermixed with carefully placed brightly colored ceramic knickknacks: a tiny shoe from Italy, a glazed platter from New Mexico, two small pitchers from Holland sitting back to back, a brilliant yellow and green ceramic spoon holder from Spain. The effect was a cheeriness that was clearly Caroline. Yet for all of it, this was clearly her husband's room, his home office. His desk was a maze of books and papers. More books were crammed every which way into two large bookcases with the overflow stacked on the floor.

Everywhere were framed photographs: of Mike and Caroline and their son, Charlie, taken at various times over the years; of Caroline's older sister, Katy, who lived in Hawaii and took care of their mother who had Alzheimer's, and who had just been in Washington for Mike and Charlie's funeral and who might or might not be returning for Caroline's memorial service scheduled for tomorrow— he hadn't been in touch with her and so didn't know. There were the pictures too of Mike in his professional role as a congressman: with the president, with various members of Congress, with prominent sports and entertainment figures. Many of these people were outspoken liberals, while Mike Parsons, like the president, had been strongly conservative. Marten smiled. Everybody had liked Mike Parsons and which side of the fence you sat on politically meant nothing at all, at least on a personal level. That was, as far as he knew.

Marten looked around once more. Past Mike Parsons's desk and through the open door to the living room, he could see Richard Tyler, Caroline's attorney and executor of her estate, pacing back and forth talking on his cell phone. Tyler was the reason he was there. He had called him the first thing that morning and asked if in light of Caroline's notarized letter giving him access to her and her husband's papers, he might not spend a few hours in the Parsons's home going through some of their personal things. Tyler had conferred with colleagues in his office and then agreed, with the proviso that Tyler himself be present when he did. Tyler had even picked Marten up at his hotel and personally brought him to the house.

The drive through the suburbs had been genial enough but in it there had been something odd, or rather something not discussed, something Marten had purposely left for Tyler to bring up, and he hadn't. The same way no one else seemed to have brought it up either, because it wasn't in the papers or on television or the Internet—the suicide of Dr. Stephenson.

In her own way Lorraine Stephenson had been a celebrity. Not only had she been Caroline's doctor, but Mike's as well. She had also been personal physician to many prominent legislators, men and women, for more than two decades. Her suicide should have been fodder for any number of news outlets, local, national, even international. But it wasn't. Marten had seen nothing about it anywhere. One would have thought that as executor to Caroline's estate Tyler would have been one of the first to know because under the circumstances, where Caroline had given Marten the legal right to examine her medical records, Tyler most certainly would have brought it up. That was, if he knew. So maybe he didn't know. And maybe the media didn't know either. Maybe the police were keeping it quiet. But why? Notification of next of kin? Perhaps. It was as good a reason as any, or maybe there was some other angle the police were working on.

If Stephenson had played it the way she could have and just told him she was sorry but she could not give him access to Caroline's medical records without a court order, he might very well have left it in Richard Tyler's hands and gone back to England. Troubled perhaps, but gone anyway, thinking Caroline had been very ill and in a terrible emotional state, and knowing there was little he could do until and unless Tyler got the court order. But she hadn't. Instead she had run from him and then committed suicide. Her last words about *the doctor* and *none of you*, had been said with icy resolve and were followed immediately by her horrifying final act.

What had Stephenson said to him just before she killed herself? *"You want to send me to the doctor. But you never will. None of you ever will. Never. Ever."*

What *doctor?* Who was she talking about she had been so afraid of that she had to take her own life to avoid being sent to?

And who or what was the group or organization she had apparently taken Marten to belong to? The *you* in *none of you?*

Those blanks were enormous.

Marten stepped behind Parsons's desk and looked at the stack of working files on top of it. Most of it was legislative stuff. This bill, that bill, this appropriation, that. There were more files to the side, labeled *LETTERS FROM CONSTITUENTS TO BE PERSONALLY ANSWERED.* Another stack on a side table were labeled *COMMITTEE REPORTS AND MINUTES.* Taken together the material was mountainous. Marten had no idea where to start or what to look for once he had.

"Mr. Marten." Richard Tyler came into the room.

"Yes."

"I just received a call from my office. One of our senior partners has looked over Caroline's note to you and determined that the firm and myself could be open to major litigation by the Parsons family if we let you continue here without their approval and quite possibly the court's."

"I don't understand."

"You are to leave the premises right now."

"Mr. Tyler," Marten pushed back, "that letter is notarized. Caroline gave it to me for the purpose of—"

"I'm sorry, Mr. Marten."

Marten stared at him for a long moment, then finally nodded and started for the door. Why the message came now, after they were already there and under way meant one of two things. Either the senior partner was more protective of the firm than Tyler was, or somebody else had learned about Caroline's note and wanted Marten's investigation stopped. Marten had known Katy, Caroline's sister, but that had been years before, when he was LAPD detective John Barron, and as far as he knew neither Caroline nor Mike had told Katy what had happened since. That meant she would have no idea who Nicholas Marten was, and to try and explain, especially under the eye of Richard Tyler's attorneys, and/or the court's if it came to that, could reveal his past and make his situation as precarious as it might have been had he been confronted by the police over Dr. Stephenson's death.

Tyler opened the front door and Marten glanced around the house trying to remember it all. It was, he knew, probably the last time he would be in Caroline's home and in the presence of all she had left behind. Once again the reality of her death stabbed through him. It was awful and empty and hollow. They had never spent enough time together. And they never would again.

"Mr. Marten." Tyler gestured toward the door, ushering him out. Tyler followed closely, then closed the door behind him and locked it and they left.

8

2:05 P.M.

Victor stood looking out the window of a rented corner office in the National Postal Museum just across from Union Station. From where he stood he could see taxis pulling into the station from Massachusetts Avenue to disperse or pick up passengers going to or coming from the Amtrak trains.

"Victor," a calm voice filtered through his earpiece.

"Yes, Richard," Victor said as calmly, speaking into the tiny microphone on the lapel of his suit jacket.

"It's time."

"I know."

Victor looked like a middle-aged everyman. Forty-seven and

divorced, he was balding and a little thick around the waist and wore an inexpensive gray suit and equally inexpensive black wing-tip shoes. The surgical gloves he wore were cream colored and available in any drugstore.

He stared out the window a moment longer, then turned to the desk beside him. It was an everyday plain steel desk, its top bare, its drawers, like the bookcases and file cabinets across the room, empty. Only the wastebasket under it held anything, a round two-inch piece of glass he had cut from the windowpane fifteen minutes earlier and the small cutting tool which he had used to do it.

"Two minutes, Victor." Richard's voice was the same steady calm.

"Acela Express number R2109. Left New York at eleven a.m., due in to Union Station at one forty-seven p.m. R2109 is seven minutes late," Victor said into the microphone and stepped around the desk to where a large semi-automatic rifle with a telescopic sight and sound suppressor sat on a tripod.

"The train has arrived."

"Thank you, Richard."

"You remember what he looks like?"

"Yes, Richard. I remember the photograph."

"Ninety seconds."

Victor picked up the rifle-mounted tripod and moved it to the window, adjusting it so that the tip of the gun barrel sat squarely in the center of the circle he had cut from the window glass.

"One minute."

Victor brushed a lock of hair from his forehead, then looked through the rifle's telescopic sight. Its crosshairs were trained on the main entry to Union Station, where a wave of just-arrived passengers was coming through in a rush. Victor moved the gun sight carefully over them. Up, down, back and forth as if he was looking for someone in particular.

"He's coming out now, Victor. In a moment you'll see him."

"I see him now, Richard."

Victor's gun sight suddenly squared to follow a dark-skinned man. He was maybe twenty-five and wearing a New York Yankees jacket and blue jeans and looking toward the line of taxi cabs.

"The target is yours, Victor."

"Thank you, Richard."

Victor's right hand slid forward over the rifle stock until it touched the trigger guard and then the trigger itself. Serpentlike, his gloved index finger curled around the trigger. The man in the Yankees jacket stepped toward a taxi cab. Victor's index finger eased slowly back on the trigger. There was a dull *pop!* as the weapon fired and then a second *pop!* as Victor fired again.

The man in the Yankees jacket grabbed his throat as the first shot hit. The second exploded his heart.

"All done, Richard."

"Thank you, Victor."

Victor crossed the room, unlocked the door, and left the rented office. Just Victor. Not the rifle or the tripod that supported it. Not the circular piece of cut glass. Not the small cutting tool he had used to make the cut. He walked twenty steps down a corridor lined with doors to other rental offices, then opened a door to the fire stairs and walked two floors to the street below. Outside he climbed into the back of a faded orange van marked DISTRICT REFRIGERATION SERVICES, closed the door and sat on the floor as the van pulled away.

"Everything alright, Victor?" Richard's voice spoke to him from the driver's seat.

"Yes, Richard. Everything is alright." Victor could feel the van lean to the right as Richard turned a corner.

"Victor," Richard's voice or the tone of it never changed. It was always calm and direct and because of it, trustworthy and soothing.

"Yes, Richard." By now, after nearly fourteen months, Victor's state of mind was very nearly the same. Trusting, comforted, directed. Whatever Richard wanted, Victor was happy with.

"We are going to Dulles International airport. Across from you is a suitcase. Inside it are two changes of clothes, assorted toiletries, your passport, a credit card in your name, twelve hundred euros in cash, and a reservation on Air France flight 039 to Paris, where you will arrive at six thirty tomorrow morning and from where you will take a connecting flight to Berlin. Once there you are to check into the Hotel Boulevard on the Kurfurstendamm and wait for further instructions. Do you have any questions, Victor?"

"No, Richard."
"You're certain?"
"Yes, I'm certain."
"Good, Victor. Very good."

9

3:40 P.M.

Nicholas Marten was not a drinking man, at least not the kind who sat in the bar of his hotel in the middle of the afternoon drinking whiskey. Yet now, today, this afternoon, still emotionally devastated by Caroline's death, he simply felt like it. He was sitting alone at the far end of the bar working on his third Walker Red and soda and trying to get past the near-crippling wave of emotion that had washed over him the moment her attorney had ushered him out of her house and closed the door behind them.

Marten took another pull at his drink and absently looked around. Halfway down the bar he could see the female bartender in the low-cut blouse chatting with a middle-aged man in a rumpled business suit, her only other customer. The half dozen leather-padded booths across the room were empty. So were the eight tables with accompanying leather chairs in between. The TV behind the bar was tuned to a live news broadcast from Union Station where a man had been shot and killed barely an hour earlier. Not just killed, the on-camera reporter said, but "assassinated," shot dead by a gunman from a window in a building across the street. As yet the authorities had revealed little about the victim other than to say he was thought to have been a passenger on an Acela train that had just arrived from New York City. Nor had there been speculation as to the motive for his killing. Other details were only beginning to trickle in, one suggesting the murder weapon had been left behind. It was a situation that made Marten think again about Dr. Stephenson, wonder again why there had still been no public announcement of her suicide, and made him wonder if somehow her body was still lying on the sidewalk and for some improbable reason had not been discovered. That hardly seemed likely. The only other explanations were what he had thought earlier, that her next of kin had yet to be notified or maybe that the police were working on something they didn't want made public.

"Nicholas Marten?"

A man's voice suddenly crackled behind him. Startled, Marten turned around. A man and a woman were halfway down the bar coming toward him. They were probably in their mid-forties, city-worn and intense and wearing dark off-the-rack suits. There was no question who they were. Detectives.

"Yes," Marten said.

"My name is Herbert, Metropolitan Police Department." He showed his I.D., then put it away. "This is Detective Monroe."

Herbert had a medium build with a touch of belly and gray hair mixed in with natural brown. His eyes were very nearly the same color. Detective Monroe was maybe a year or two younger. Tall, with a square chin, her blond hair cut short and highlighted. She was pretty in a way but too tough and too weary to be attractive.

"We'd like to talk to you," Herbert said.

"What about?"

"You know a Dr. Lorraine Stephenson?"

"In a way. Why?"

This was the thing Marten had dreaded, that someone had seen him outside of her house, maybe even seen him follow after her when she ran off down the street, perhaps even heard the gunshot, and then seen him leave and taken down the license number of his rental car as he drove away.

"You made several calls to her office yesterday." Monroe said.

"Yes." Calls? What is *this*? Marten wondered. This was a suicide and they'd gone over her telephone records? Well maybe. She knew a lot of important people. The whole thing could be more involved than he thought and have nothing to do with Caroline.

"Persistent calls," Monroe said.

"What did you want from her?" Herbert pressed him.

"To talk to her about the death of one of her patients."

"Who was that?"

"Caroline Parsons."

Herbert half smiled. "Mr. Marten, we'd like you to come down to police headquarters and talk to us."

"Why?" Marten didn't understand. So far they'd said nothing about her suicide. Nothing to suggest they knew he had been anywhere near her residence.

"Mr. Marten," Monroe said flatly, "Dr. Stephenson has been murdered."

"Murdered?" Marten said in genuine surprise.

"Yes."

10

METROPOLITAN POLICE HEADQUARTERS,
DISTRICT OF COLUMBIA, 4:10 P.M.

"Where were you between eight and nine o'clock last night?" Detective Monroe asked quietly.

"In my rental car driving around the city," Marten said evenly, working to give them nothing. In a way it was the truth. Besides he had no other alibi.

"Anybody with you?"

"No."

Herbert leaned forward across the institutional table in the small interrogation room where they sat facing each other. Detective Monroe stood back against the door they had come in. The only door in the room.

"Where in the city?"

"Just around. I don't know where exactly, I'm not familiar with the city. I live in England. Caroline Parsons was a close friend. Her death disturbed me a lot. I just needed to keep moving."

"So you—drove around?"

"Yes."

"To Dr. Stephenson's home?"

"I don't know where I went. I told you, I don't know the city."

"But you found your way back to your hotel." Herbert kept working on him while Monroe remained silent, watching his reactions.

"Eventually, yes."

"About what time?"

"Nine, nine thirty. I'm not sure."

"You blamed Dr. Stephenson for Caroline Parsons's death, didn't you?"

"No."

Marten didn't get it. What were they doing? There was no homicide cop in the world who couldn't tell murder from suicide, at least not the way Lorraine Stephenson had done it. So what were they really going after, and why? Was it possible they too were onto the idea that Caroline might have been murdered? If so, had Stephenson been a suspect? If she had been, maybe it was the police who had been in the passing cars keeping an eye on her home. Maybe they had even seen him sitting in his car, then jump out to accost her as she stepped from the taxi and follow after as she ran off down the street. If that were the case, they might think he had been involved in Caroline's death. If they did, he wasn't going anywhere for some time and showing them the notarized letter she'd signed giving him access to her and her husband's private affairs could even make things worse. Suggest that he had coerced her into writing it even though he hadn't even been in the country when she'd done it. Coerced her because he had something else in mind once she was dead, something in her estate or something political her husband had been involved with.

He knew all too well that if the police had any reason to believe he had been involved with Caroline's death or the death of Dr. Stephenson, they would charge him as an accessory and book him. In the process he would be fingerprinted and his prints would be run through the local data bank, the AFIS, the Automated Fingerprint Identification System; and then the National FBI Data Bank, the IAFIS, the Integrated Automated Fingerprint Identification System. At the same time they would query Interpol. If they did they would find he was a former police officer because his prints would still be on file and ID him under his real name, John Barron. After that it wouldn't be long before those on the LAPD still looking for him knew about it. To them he remained a "person of primary interest" on a Web site called *Copperchatter.com*—a chat room of cops talking to cops around the world, in cop vernacular, with cop humor, and cop vindictiveness—with his name freshly posted every Sunday night by someone using the moniker *Gunslinger* but who he knew was Gene VerMeer, a veteran LAPD homicide detective who despised him for what had happened in L.A. those few years earlier and who had created the Web site just to find him. Find him, and then keep him under close surveillance until *Gunslinger* VerMeer or some of his cronies showed up to take care of him once and for all.

"How did you know Caroline Parsons?"

Now it was Detective Monroe's turn, and she moved from where she stood by the door to lean beside what appeared to be a large mirror mounted on the room's back wall. It wasn't a mirror at all but rather a one-way glass with an unseen observation room behind it. Who, or how many, were behind it watching him Marten had no way to tell.

"I'd met her a long time ago in Los Angeles," Marten said calmly, trying to stay as matter-of-fact as he could. "We became friends and stayed friends. I knew her husband as well."

"You fuck her a lot?"

Marten bit his tongue. He knew they were trying to get to him any way they could. That it came from a woman made no difference.

"How many times?"

"We did not have a sexual relationship."

"No?" Monroe half smiled.

"No."

"What did you want to talk to Dr. Stephenson about?" Herbert took over again.

"I told you before, the death of Caroline Parsons."

"Why? What did you expect she could tell you?"

"Mrs. Parsons had become seriously ill very quickly and nobody seemed to know exactly what it was. Her husband and son had just been killed in a plane crash and she was an emotional wreck. She called me in England and asked me to come. She died soon after I arrived."

"Why did she ask you to come?"

Marten glared at Herbert. "I told you, we were close friends. You have anyone who would call you like that? Somebody you'd want to be with in your last hours?"

Marten wasn't playing tough guy, he just wanted them to see he was angry. Not just because of the questions and the way they were asking them but so they would see and hear and feel the depth of his relationship with Caroline, that it had been and still was, genuine.

"And since Dr. Stephenson was her primary physician," Monroe came toward him, "you wanted to hear from her what had happened."

"Yes."

"So you called and called but you never got through to her. It made you mad. How mad?"

"She finally did return my call."

"And what did she tell you?"

"That the things I wanted to talk about were privileged information between doctor and patient."

"That was all?"

"Yes."

"And between eight and nine last evening you were just driving around the city?" Now it was Herbert again.

"Yes."

"Alone?"

"Yes."

"Where?"

"I told you, I don't know."

"Anybody see you?"

"I don't know that either."

"Did you kill her?" Monroe snapped suddenly.

"No."

Herbert kept the pressure on: "You're an American but you live and work in England."

"I graduated from the University of Manchester with an advanced degree in landscape architecture. I liked it there and decided to stay. I work for a small firm, Fitzsimmons and Justice, where I design formal gardens and other landscape projects. I have a British passport and consider myself an expatriate."

Herbert got up from the table. As he did, Marten saw him exchange the briefest glance with Monroe. What it told him was startling. They had not come after him because they thought Caroline had been murdered or because they thought he or Dr. Stephenson had been involved with it or because he had been seen chasing after Stephenson in the moments before she killed herself. No, they had picked him up simply because of the phone calls he'd made to her. It meant they were certain she had been murdered. But that was impossible because he had been right in front of her when she shot herself. So why did they believe what they did?

The only possible explanation was that someone had gotten to her body very soon after he'd left and done something to it to make it appear she had been killed. Maybe taken her gun from the scene and then shot her in the face with a weapon of much larger caliber, destroying the evidence of the suicide and making it look like murder and giving the investigators and the coroner little reason to suspect anything else. But *why?* Unless the motive for the suicide of a woman of her prominence would have been far more carefully scrutinized than if she had simply been killed.

Marten looked to the detectives. He wanted to press them for details about the state of Dr. Stephenson's body when they'd found it, but he didn't dare. Right now it seemed they were still pretty much in the dark about what had happened. Consequently they had nothing they could hold him on, so showing any curiosity at all would only pique their interest, make them wonder why he wanted to know and start in on him again. So best to get off it while he could.

"I think I've answered your questions," he said respectfully. "If you don't mind, I would like to go."

Herbert studied him for a long moment, as if he were looking for something he had missed. Marten held his breath, afraid that this might be when they would ask for his fingerprints just to make certain he wasn't wanted somewhere.

"How long do you intend to stay in D.C., Mr. Marten?" he said, instead.

"Caroline Parsons's memorial service is tomorrow. After that I don't know."

Abruptly Herbert handed him his business card. "You check with me before you go anywhere outside the city. You understand?"

"Yes, sir." Marten tried not to show his relief. For now, at least, they were letting him go.

Monroe walked toward the door and pulled it open. "Thank you for your cooperation, Mr. Marten. To your left and down the stairs."

"Thanks," Marten said. "Sorry I couldn't help you more." He went out quickly. To his left and down the stairs.

WEDNESDAY

APRIL 5

11

The heavy armored doors of the presidential limousine swung closed, the Secret Service agent at the wheel nudged the machine into gear and the car carrying President of the United States John Henry Harris moved slowly away from the German Federal Chancellery, leaving Chancellor Anna Bohlen and a large gathering of the world media behind.

President Harris and Bohlen had met the evening before; had attended a performance of the Berlin Symphony Orchestra; and then, this morning, accompanied by a handful of close advisers had had a long, cordial breakfast where world issues and the long-time German-American alliance were discussed. Afterward they'd preened for the press, shaken hands and then he had left, the whole thing nearly a mirror copy of what had happened at the Élysée Palace in Paris twenty-four hours earlier. In both situations the president had hoped to start smoothing over the still volatile situation concerning both countries' earlier refusal to support the U.S. invasion of Iraq in the United Nations and their continuing concerns now.

But for all the seeming goodwill and cordiality during both visits, little or nothing had been accomplished and the president was clearly upset. Jake Lowe, his portly fifty-seven-year-old longtime friend and chief political adviser sitting beside him and quietly reading text from a BlackBerry nestled into his palm, knew it.

"None of us can afford this damned ongoing transatlantic rift," Harris said abruptly. "Publicly they agree, but in reality they won't move a quarter of an inch in our direction. Neither one of them."

"It's a difficult path, Mr. President," Lowe responded quietly. The president might characteristically be introspective but anyone who was as close to him as Jake Lowe knew there were times he wanted to talk things through, usually when he had come to a dead end in his own reasoning. "And I'm not sure it has an end that will make everyone happy.

"I've told you this before and I'll say it again now, it's a cruel fact of history that more than once the world has been provided with leaders who are the wrong people in the wrong place at the wrong time. And the only thing that corrects it is a change of regime."

"Well those regimes aren't about to change. And we don't have the luxury to wait for the next. We need everybody with us and right away if we're going to put this Middle East Humpty-Dumpty back together again. You know it. I know it. The world knows it."

"Except the French and the Germans."

President Harris leaned back in his seat, trying to relax. It didn't work. He was angry and frustrated and when he was like that and he talked, everything showed. "Those are two steel-jawed, unbendable SOBs. They'll go along but just so far, and when we really get to it they'll pull back and let us dangle in the wind, all the while clapping their hands in glee. There's got to be a way to turn them, Jake, but the damn truth is I don't have a clue as to what it will take. Or after today and yesterday, even how to approach it."

Abruptly President Harris turned to look out the window as his motorcade moved through the Tiergarten, Berlin's dramatic two-mile-long city park, then continued along a widely announced route that would take them down the Kurfurstendamm, the main street of Berlin's fashionable shopping district.

The motorcade itself was huge, led by thirty German motorcycle police with two massive polished black Secret Service SUVs traveling in front of three identical presidential limousines, preventing anyone from knowing in which car the president rode. Immediately behind were eight more Secret Service SUVs, an ambulance, and two large vans, one carrying the press pool, the other, the president's traveling staff. The rear was brought up by another thirty-strong contingent of German motorcycle police.

Since they'd left the Chancellery every street and boulevard was massed with people, as if half of Berlin had turned out for a glimpse of this president. Some applauded and waved small American flags;

others booed or whistled, shaking their fists and shouting in anger. Others held banners reading: U.S. OUT OF MIDDLE-EAST, HERR PRÄSIDENT, GEHEN NACH HAUSE, HARRIS GO HOME!, NO MORE BLOOD FOR OIL!—one banner read simply: JOHN, LET'S TALK PLEASE. Other people simply stood and watched as the giant motorcade bearing the leader of the world's lone superpower passed before them.

"I wonder what I'd think if I were a German standing out there watching us go by," Harris said, watching the crowds. "What would I want from the United States? What would I think about her intentions?"

He turned to look at Lowe, one of his best friends and his closest political adviser, a man he had known for years when he first entered the Senate race in California. "What would you think, Jake? What would you think if you were one of them?"

"I would probably—" Lowe's conversation was abruptly cut short when his BlackBerry alerted him to a voice message from Tom Curran, the president's chief of staff, waiting for them aboard *Air Force One* at Tegel Airport. "Yes, Tom," he said into his ever-present headset. "What? When? . . . see what more you can find out, we'll be onboard in twenty minutes."

"What is it?" the president said.

"Caroline Parsons's personal physician, Lorraine Stephenson, was found murdered last night. The police have held back the news for investigative reasons."

"Murdered?"

"Yes, sir."

"Good Lord." The president's eyes shifted away and he stared off. "Mike, his son, then Caroline, and now her doctor?" he said, then looked back to Jake Lowe. "All dead, just like that, and over so short a period of time. What's going on?"

"It's a tragic coincidence, Mr. President."

"Is it?"

"What else would it be?"

12

"Victor."

"Yes, Richard. I hear you."

"Are you at the window?"

"Yes, Richard."

"What can you see?"

"The street. All sorts of people lining it. A big church is across from me. The Kaiser Wilhelm Memorial Church. At least that was what the porter called it when he showed me into the room. Why, Richard?"

"I wanted to make certain the hotel didn't give you a different room, that's all."

"No, they didn't. The room is exactly as I requested. I followed your instructions to the letter." Victor no longer wore the gray suit he had in Washington but instead was dressed in light brown slacks and a dark blue oversized cardigan sweater. He still looked like an everyman, but now his appearance was more academic. A middle-aged professor, perhaps, or a high school teacher. Someone unremarkable who would stand unnoticed in a crowd.

"I knew you would, Victor. Now listen carefully. The presidential motorcade has turned onto the Kurfurstendamm. In—" Richard paused for the briefest moment, then went on, "forty seconds it will come into sight and pass beneath your window. The president is in the third presidential limousine. He's sitting on your side of the car, the rear seat next to the left window. You won't be able to see him through the tinted glass but he's there just the same. I want you to tell me how long it takes for the limousine to pass and if you would have time to get a clear shot at that window from where you are."

"A presidential limousine has bulletproof glass."

"I know, Victor. Don't worry about it. All I want you to tell me is how long it takes for the limousine to pass and if you would have time to get a clear shot from that angle."

"Alright."

President Harris stared out the limousine's window absently watching the crowds his motorcade was passing, his thoughts on his secretary of defense, Terrence Langdon, in the south of France for a meeting of NATO defense ministers. Langdon was essentially delivering the same message that Secretary of State David Chaplin had a day earlier to his twenty-five NATO counterparts at a working lunch in Brussels: that the U.S. was signaling a new readiness to work more closely with its NATO allies, something the previous administration under President Charles Cabot, had all but refused to do.

In a speech to Congress before he left Washington Harris had promised that he would not make this extensive trip to meet European leaders and "come up empty," and no matter the disappointments in Paris and Berlin, he still had the same resolve. He wanted now to concentrate on the next leg of his trip: Rome and dinner tonight with Italian president Mario Tonti, a man whose position he knew was largely ceremonial but whose job it was to unify factions within Italian politics, which made him a strategically important ally.

Harris considered Italy a friend and both the president and prime minister, Aldo Visconti, men he could rely on, but he also knew Tonti would know the meetings in Paris and Berlin had not achieved the results Harris had wanted. It was a failing that would add an element of awkwardness to their meeting because Italy was very much a part of the European Union, and the European Union's long-range goal was to become the United States of Europe and that was something that always had to be taken into consideration no matter the public deportment of its individual members. So how he would present himself to Tonti, what he would say and how he would say it should have been foremost in his mind. But it wasn't. Lay it to jet lag, to his failures yesterday and today, or to his own personal emotions, the thing foremost on his mind was what had happened to the Parsons family and so quickly afterward, the murder of Caroline Parsons's physician, Lorraine Stephenson. Abruptly he turned to Jake Lowe.

"The fellow who was in Caroline Parsons's hospital room when she died. What did we find out about him?"

Harris could see the crowds lining the street in front of the Kaiser Wilhelm Memorial Church.

"Don't know, it wasn't a priority," Lowe punched some code into his BlackBerry then waited for the information to come up as text.

The president looked to his left and saw they were passing crowds in front of the Hotel Boulevard.

"His name is Nicholas Marten," Lowe read from the text. "He's an American expat living in Manchester, England, and working for a small landscape architectural firm there, Fitzsimmons and Justice." Lowe stopped and read something in silence, then looked to the president. "For some reason Mrs. Parsons signed a notarized letter giving him private access to her personal files and those of her husband."

"Both of them?"

"Yes."

"Why?"

"I don't have an answer."

"See if you can come up with one. This whole thing is increasingly disturbing."

Victor turned from his perch in the hotel room window. "Richard?"

"Yes, Victor."

"The motorcade has passed. It took seven seconds. I saw the limousine window clearly. I would have had a clean shot for three seconds, maybe four."

"Are you sure?"

"Yes, Richard."

"Enough time for a kill shot?"

"With the right ammunition, yes."

"Thank you, Victor."

13

Nicholas Marten had turned the television to the local news channel the moment he got out of bed nearly thirty minutes earlier, hoping to hear something about Dr. Stephenson's "murder." But so far there had been nothing. It made him more curious than ever why that the police were still holding the information back, and amazed that some aggressive reporter hadn't discovered the story and broken it.

He'd left the volume up, taken a quick shower, and begun to shave. Among the trivia, traffic, and weather reports he learned that the man shot down by a sniper at Union Station the day before had been a Colombian national in the country legally as a baseball player for the Trenton Thunder, a minor league team affiliated with the New York Yankees. An unnamed source revealed that investigators had recovered the murder weapon from a rented office in the National Postal Museum just across the street from the station. Purportedly it was an M14, a standard U.S. armed forces training rifle, manufactured in the hundreds of thousands by any number of firearms companies.

It seemed like a rather peculiar murder—a minor league ballplayer "assassinated"—but no more than that and Marten went back to shaving, his thoughts on how he could devise a way to retrieve and examine Caroline's medical files. For no particular reason he thought of what she had said to him in the hospital when she'd taken hold of his hand and looked into his eyes and said in hesitant speech—

"They . . . murdered my . . . husband and . . . son . . . and now they've . . . killed . . . me."

"Who are you talking about?" he'd asked. "Who is 'they'?"

"The . . . the . . . ca . . ." she'd said. But it was the most she could do, and her strength gone, she'd fallen asleep. They had been the last words she'd uttered before she'd woken later and told him she loved him and then—died.

Marten felt the emotion begin to creep up in him and he took a moment to collect himself before he finished shaving. Done, he went into the room to dress, determined to drag himself from his still-gaping sorrow and get on with the problem at hand.

"The ca . . ." he said out loud. "What *ca?* What was she trying to tell me?"

Immediately he thought of the brief time he'd had inside Caroline's home before her lawyer had asked him to leave. What was there? What could he have seen, if only for a moment, that might give him the answer to what she had been trying to tell him? Besides the short-lived walk through, and apart from appreciating her homey touches, the only place he'd been where there had been anything definitive was her husband's office. The little time he'd had spent there he'd seen what? Photographs of the Parsons family, of Mike Parsons with celebrities. Beyond that had been the stacks of working files that covered most of the congressman's desk with more still on a side table. Those, he remembered, had been clearly labeled in felt pen—COMMITTEE REPORTS AND MINUTES. That was it, nothing more.

Frustrated, Marten pulled on his pants and then sat on the edge of the bed to put on his shoes. As he did, the thought hit and he sat bolt upright.

"Committee reports and minutes," he said out loud. "*Committee.* How would a person begin to say the word 'committee' in everyday speech? Not '*com*-mittee' but—'*ca*-mittee.'"

Could Caroline have meant that someone on a committee Parsons was a member of was responsible for their deaths? But then she hadn't said *someone,* she'd used the plural *they.* So if he was right and she had been referring to a *committee,* had she meant several members of it or the entire group itself? But how could an entire congressional committee be involved in the complex murders of three people, not to mention the other innocents on board Parsons's chartered plane? The idea was crazy, but for now it was all he had.

By his watch it was just a little after seven thirty in the morning. At two he was to attend Caroline's memorial service at the National Presbyterian Church. That gave him a little more than six hours to try and dig into the history of Mike Parsons's recent congressional service and maybe find some sort of answer, or at least the beginning of one.

Marten opened his electronic notebook, clicked it on and brought up the Google search engine. In *Search* he typed "Representative Michael Parsons" then hit "Enter."

On the screen popped Parsons's Congressional Web page. Marten breathed a sigh of relief; at least Parsons name was still in the government database. At the top was "Congressman Michael Parsons, Serving the people of California's 17th District. Monterey, San Benito, Santa Cruz Counties."

Parsons's office locations in Washington and California were listed farther down the page, followed by a place to find the committees he had served on. Marten clicked on that and up came the list.

Committee on Agriculture
Committee on Small Business
Committee on Budget
Committee on Appropriations
Committee on Homeland Security
Committee on Government Reform
House Permanent Select Committee on Intelligence

Within those were a number of subcommittees Parsons had also served on. One in particular caught Marten's eye, a subcommittee he was a member of at the time of his death.

Subcommittee on Intelligence and Counterterrorism.

Mike and his son had died on Friday, March 10. The subcommittee's last scheduled meeting had been at 2 p.m. on Tuesday, March 7. Its subject had been "Progress in Consolidating Terrorist Watch Lists" and had been held at the Rayburn House Office Building. Listed were the names of its members. Curiously, as opposed to other congressional committee meetings, this one gave no further information, such as lists of witnesses who were to appear before the committee. It was simply blank. Marten tried several different government Web sites and came up with no more information than he had on Parsons's home page. He was certain there was an answer as to why and blamed it on himself and his inability to understand and navigate the workings of the government Web. Still, the proximity to the date of Parsons's death and that there was seemingly no information available about the meeting troubled him. He wanted to find out more, but he didn't know how.

Richard Tyler, Caroline's lawyer, might have helped if someone in his office hadn't already stepped in and shut down Marten's access to the Parsons's personal information. It meant he would get no help there, and if he tried his attempt would be looked on with suspicion or even worse, especially if that same someone wanted his investigation completely stonewalled. If he pushed it he might very well risk physical danger from an unknown source or another visit from the police. Neither of which he wanted.

There was a time element too. Fitzsimmons and Justice, his employer in England, had very graciously given him time off to come to the states to tend to Caroline's situation, but at the same time he was intimately involved in the design of a large landscape project called "The Banfield Job" for Ronaldo Banfield, a star soccer player for Manchester United, at Banfield's country estate northwest of the city. The project was already behind schedule and needed to be completed by the end of May so that the actual work—the ordering of materials, the grading, the installation of irrigation systems and finally the planting—could begin. It meant that whatever he had to do here in Washington had to be undertaken and completed quickly.

Marten got up, thinking that if he went to the Capitol building he might begin to find some answers in the archives there. He was reaching for the phone to call the front desk for directions when he saw a copy of the *Washington Post* on his bedside table and remembered that several years earlier his close friend Dan Ford had worked for the *Los Angeles Times* Washington bureau—before he was transferred to Paris and subsequently murdered by the infamous Raymond Oliver Thorne. While in Washington Ford had become friends with a number of journalists from other papers. There had been one he'd come to know well but whose name Marten didn't recall. What he did remember was that he'd been a political writer for the *Washington Post*. Whether he was still there Marten didn't know but he thought that if he scanned the paper's bylines he just might see a name he would recognize.

It didn't take long. The name was right there on page one, a byline to a story about President Harris's trip to Europe: "President on Rough Road Overseas." The writer was Peter Fadden.

14

"Peter Fadden." The voice on the other end of the line was abrupt and raspy like leather. Marten had expected to hear a younger man; Fadden sounded seventy or more but with the energy of someone who could beat a thirty-year-old to a pulp in an alley or match him drink for drink in any saloon in town. He also sounded like he had Washington in his blood, and had since the days of Eisenhower or maybe even before.

"My name is Nicholas Marten, Mr. Fadden. I was a close friend of Dan Ford. I was also a friend of Caroline Parsons and her husband. I'd like to talk to you in person, if I might."

"When?" Fadden snapped back. There was no "why," just the gruff "when."

"As soon as possible. Today, now, this morning. I'm going to Caroline's memorial service this afternoon. Afterward would be okay too. I'll buy you a drink, dinner if you like."

Now it came. "Why?"

"I'm trying to find out what congressional business Mike Parsons was working on at the time of his death."

"Look it up. It's in the public record."

"Some of it is, some of it isn't. I need some help getting more information."

"Rent yourself a high school teacher."

"Mr. Fadden, there might be a story here for you. I'm not sure. I'll explain when we're alone. Please."

There was a long silence and Marten was afraid Fadden was going to brush him off. Then the gruff voice snapped at him.

"You said you were a friend of Dan Ford."

"Yes."

"Good friend?"

"His best friend. I was staying at his apartment in Paris when he was murdered."

Again there was a silence and then Fadden simply said— "Okay."

15

AIR FORCE ONE, ALOFT OVER SOUTHERN GERMANY. 2:15 P.M.

The television interview with chief CNN European correspondent Gabriella Roche had long been planned and President Harris sat with her for the first thirty minutes of the flight from Berlin to Rome. The flight had been delayed for thirty-seven minutes because of what Berlin air controllers called heavy traffic at Berlin's Tegel Airport but what Jake Lowe had quietly told President Harris was really nothing more than German chancellor Anna Bohlen's way of "busting your balls a little more. Letting you know her true feelings."

"I know her damn feelings, Jake, but we need her," Harris had said, "so I don't know what we can do about it but ignore it."

"Mr. President," Lowe responded quickly, "what if we needed her right now?"

"What do you mean, 'right now'?"

Lowe started to reply but then his ever-mindful-of-schedule chief of staff, Tom Curran, interrupted, telling him it was time to do the CNN/ Gabriella Roche interview.

A half hour later the interview was over. Harris joked lightly with Roche and her camera crew then thanked them and went directly to his executive suite, where Jake Lowe was waiting. With him, in shirtsleeves, was the towering six-foot four-inch Dr. James Marshall, his national security adviser, who had flown into Berlin from Washington and joined them as they boarded the plane.

Harris closed the door, then took off his jacket and looked to Lowe. "What did you mean when you said 'what if we needed Chancellor Bohlen right now'?" he spoke as if their brief exchange had just happened and there had not been a television interview in between.

"I'll let Dr. Marshall tell you."

Marshall sat down across from the president. "These are some of the most disturbing times we've ever encountered in our history, maybe even more worrying than at the height of the Cold War. I've been increasingly concerned about our ability to act quickly and decisively in a major emergency."

"I'm not sure I follow you," Harris said.

"Suppose something happened in the next hours and we had to take immediate and significant action somewhere in the world. We would need the French and German votes backing us in the UN and right then, and you know now, from personal experience, it's highly unlikely we would get them.

"Let's play a what-if, Mr. President. For the moment forget about the present big-picture politics in the Middle East. Forget about Iraq, Israel, Palestine, Lebanon, even Iran. This is a deeper, simpler 'what-if'. Suppose al Qaeda or some other zealous group of jihadists, and there are hundreds of them, was to strike Saudi Arabia at midnight tonight. With enough fanatical force, by dawn they could wipe out the entire Saudi royal family. The government would collapse and the fundamentalist movement would explode over the entire region. Moderates would fall by the wayside and be slaughtered or join in the religious fervor that would rage like a wildfire. Within hours Arabia would fall, then Kuwait, then Iraq and Iran, Syria and probably Jordan. In less than thirty-six hours al Qaeda would control everything and the flow of oil to the west would stop, just like that. Then what?"

"What do you mean 'then what?'" The president was staring directly at his national security adviser. "Is this a what-if, or do you have something from intelligence and this is real? Don't screw around here, Jim. If it's real I want to know. And right now."

Marshall glanced at Jake Lowe, then looked back to the president. "What it is, Mr. President, is a very bona fide scenario that comes from any number of collective sources and should be taken very seriously. If it happened it would be all but impossible for us to respond quickly or massively enough to contain it. Immediate nuclear response might be our only option. One we wouldn't have time to argue through the Security Council. We would need every member already up and on the same page and moving within hours. It means we have to know beforehand that we have every member nation one hundred percent behind us. And as we well know, Germany might not be on the Security Council but from its influence, it might just as well be."

"What Jim means, Mr. President," Lowe added quietly, "is that we must have an arrangement that will guarantee America instant, ongoing, and unquestioned support in the UN. And as I said before, the way things stand now we don't have it."

President Harris looked from one man to the other. These were longtime members of his inner circle, close friends and trusted advisers, men whom he had known for years, trying to make him understand the importance and relevance of his just-concluded meetings with the leaders of France and Germany. Moreover, it wasn't just the French and Germans they would need, it was also the Russians and Chinese. They all knew that if they had France and Germany behind them, especially if the matter had to do with the Middle East, the Russians would come along as well. So would the Chinese.

"Fellas," he said in the homey style he used in the company of friends, "the picture you draw may be accurate, and God help us if it is. But I seriously doubt the French and Germans haven't considered some version of it themselves and what they would do in response. In the same breath I can guarantee you that suddenly dropping their stance over a scenario without hard intelligence behind it and giving us a blank check overnight for whatever we want to do isn't one of them."

"That's not necessarily so," Dr. Marshall leaned back and folded his hands in his lap.

"I don't follow you."

"Suppose the leaders of those two countries were people who *would* give us a blank check."

The president raised his eyebrows, "What the hell does that mean?"

"You won't like it."

"Try me."

"The physical removal from office of the President of France and the Chancellor of Germany."

"Physical removal?"

"Assassination, Mr. President, of both. To be replaced with leaders who we can trust, now and in the future."

Harris hesitated, then slowly grinned. It was a joke, he knew. "What do you fellas want to do, get in the video-game business? Set up a frightening situation, find the troublemakers who won't cooperate, then hit the 'assassinate' button and afterward insert whoever you want and write your own ending?"

"It's not a game, Mr. President." Marshall's eyes were locked on the president's. "I'm deadly serious. Remove Geroux and Bohlen and make certain the people we want in power are elected in their place."

"Just like that." The president was stunned.

"Yes, sir."

The president looked to Jake Lowe, "I suspect you agree."

"Yes, Mr. President, I do."

For a moment Harris stood frozen in silence as the weight of what had been presented sank in. Suddenly he flashed with anger. "I'll tell you fellas something. Nothing like that is going to happen on my watch. First, because under no circumstance will I be party to murder. Second, political assassination is forbidden by law and I am sworn to uphold the law.

"Moreover, even if you had your way and the assassinations were carried out, what would you expect to gain? Exactly which people would you want in power and how could you make certain they were elected? And even if they were, what makes you think we could trust them to do what we wanted, whenever we wanted and for how long we wanted?"

"There are such people, Mr. President," Lowe said quietly.

"It can be done, sir," Marshall added, "and rather quickly. You'd be surprised."

Harris's eyes darted angrily from one man to the other. "Gentlemen, let me say this one more time. There will be no political assassinations on the part of the United States, not while I'm president. And if the subject comes up again you can both dig out your golf clubs and call for a tee time because you will no longer be part of this administration."

For the longest moment neither Marshall nor Lowe took his eyes from the president. Finally Marshall spoke, and in a tone that rang with condescension. "I think we understand your position, Mr. President."

"Good," Harris held their gaze, giving them no ground. "Now," he said brusquely, "if you don't mind there are a few things I'd like to go over on my own before we touch down in Rome."

16

MR. HENRY'S RESTAURANT, PENNSYLVANIA AVENUE, 11:50 A.M.

Marten and Peter Fadden sat in a back booth in the dark-wood-and-authentic-retro atmosphere of this Capitol Hill saloon where the lunchtime crowd was just beginning to make noise and where decades earlier Roberta Flack was first crooning "Killing Me Softly" upstairs.

"Your friend Dan Ford was a heck of a reporter, a very special kind of guy, and—" Peter Fadden leaned in across the table when he talked. It was a manner, studied or not, that accentuated his presence. "His future was bright as hell. To be murdered the way he was? It was all wrong, nobody should ever die like that. I still miss him."

Fadden, thickset with gray hair and a trimmed gray beard and ruddy complexion, was closer to fifty than seventy and looked even younger. A byline reporter with an old-timer's rough demeanor, he wore brown slacks with a tattersall shirt and worn herringbone jacket. His eyes were sparkling blue and piercing as he watched Marten take a sip of coffee or a bite of tuna sandwich.

"So do I, every day," Marten said genuinely. Nearly five years had passed since Ford's murder in the French countryside, and even now Marten was plagued by the thought that Dan's death was somehow his fault. There was another level too, especially now, because, as with Caroline, they'd been best friends since childhood and all those memories, all their history, compounded his death even more.

It had been Dan Ford the professional journalist with his never-ending string of connections who had made it possible for John Barron to become Nicholas Marten, thereby enabling him to make a new life in the north of England, one far from the reach of the Gunslinger, the deadly LAPD detective Gene VerMeer, and his equally vengeful associates still on the force.

"You said you had a story. What is it?" The sentiment was done. Peter Fadden took a sip of coffee.

"I said I might have a story," Marten said, then lowered his voice. "It has to do with Caroline Parsons."

"What about her?"

"What I tell you has to be off the record."

"Off the record is not a story, period," Fadden snapped. "You either have something or you don't. Otherwise we're wasting each other's time."

"Mr. Fadden, at this point I don't know if there is a story or if there isn't. I'm looking for help about something that's very personal to me. But if it turns out to be true, it's a blockbuster, in which case it's all yours."

"Oh for chrissakes!" Fadden sat back. "You want to sell me a used car too?"

"I want some help, nothing more." Martens eyes came up to meet Fadden's and held there.

Fadden judged, then let out a sigh. "Okay, off the record. What the hell is it?"

"Caroline Parsons believed her husband and son were murdered. That the plane crash was no accident."

"Now we're back to the used cars. Marten, in this town there's a goddamn conspiracy theory in every toenail clipping. If that's all you have, forget it."

"Would it make any difference if I said she told me that on her deathbed? Or that she was convinced the staph infection that killed her in so short a time had been deliberately administered?"

"What?" Fadden's interest was suddenly piqued.

"I realize she'd just lost her husband and only child and was dying herself. The whole thing could have been in her mind, the rantings of a terrified, hysterical widow. And maybe they were, but I promised her I'd do what I could to find out and that's what I'm doing."

"Why? Who were you to her?"

"Let's just say that at some point in our lives we," Marten paused, then went on, "loved each other very much and leave it at that."

Fadden studied him. "She give you anything real? Specifics? Why she believed it?"

"As in hard evidence? No. But she was supposed to have been on the same plane with her son and husband. She told me, or tried to tell me, that 'they' were responsible for the crash. When I asked her who 'they' were, she said 'the ca,' but that was all she got out. She couldn't finish it and never did. In thinking it over and tying it to her husband's death, the only thing that made sense was that maybe she was trying to say 'the *ca*-mmittee.'

"The last committee meeting Mike Parsons attended before he died was the House Subcommittee on Intelligence and Counterterrorism. It took place on Tuesday, March 7, at the Rayburn House Office Building. Its subject was 'Progress in Consolidating Terrorist Watch Lists.' The thing about it is, there are no lists of witnesses who were to appear before the committee. Now I don't know much about how these things work, but scanning the *Congressional Record* for other committees over a two-week period I never found another that didn't have at least one witness to be presented. And that's why I need you, not just to walk me through the high school algebra of how all this works, but because you're a Washington insider who Dan Ford trusted. You know what goes on in these committees even if you don't write about it. Well I want to know what was going on in Parsons's committee. What it was about. Why there were no witnesses. What might have happened there that could have made Caroline's suspicions real."

"You're pursuing this emotionally, you know that," Fadden said quietly.

Marten stared at him. "You weren't there. You didn't hear the fear in her voice or see it in her eyes. In her whole being."

"Did it ever occur to you that you might be pissing in the wind?"

"I didn't ask for your opinion, I asked for your help."

Fadden picked up his coffee cup, held it for a moment, then drained it and stood up. "Let's take a walk."

17

Marten and Peter Fadden came out of Mr. Henry's under a partly cloudy sky. Crossing Seward Square, they started up Pennsylvania Avenue toward the U.S. Capitol.

"Caroline Parsons thought her staph infection had been deliberately administered," Fadden said.

"Yes."

"She say by who?"

"We're still off the record," Marten said guardedly.

"You want my help, answer the damn question."

"Her doctor."

"Lorraine Stephenson?" Fadden was clearly surprised.

"Yes."

"She's dead."

Marten half smiled. So at least somebody else did know. "She was murdered."

"How the hell do you know? That information hasn't been made public."

"Because the police told me. I'd called Stephenson several times to ask her about Caroline's death. She refused to discuss it. The police went over her phone records and found me. They thought I might have been angry enough to do something about it."

"Were you?"

"Yes, but I didn't kill her." Suddenly Marten found an opening. If Fadden knew Lorraine Stephenson had been killed, he might also know something of what the police had found, why they were so convinced it had been murder, and why they were still holding the information back. "Fadden, the police talked to me yesterday. Her murder has still not been made public. Why?"

"Notification of next of kin."

"What else?"

"What makes you think there's anything else?"

"She was a name in this town. She was a longtime doctor to a number of people in Congress. Moreover, she was Caroline Parsons's personal physician. Caroline's memorial service is this afternoon. Maybe someone is afraid someone else might see a coincidence and start looking a little further."

"Who might that be?"

"No idea."

"Look, Marten, as far as I know you're the only one who thinks Caroline Parsons was deliberately killed. Nobody else has even suggested it."

"Then why has the murder of a prominent physician been kept so hush-hush?"

"Marten"—they walked by several people, and Fadden waited until they were past—"Lorraine Stephenson was decapitated. It took them that long to find out whose body they had. Her head was nowhere around. Nobody's found it yet. The police want some time to poke around on the quiet."

Decapitated? Marten was stunned. So that was the reason there'd been no publicity. It also meant someone had been there only moments after he'd fled, saw what had happened and decided to change the makeup of the entire thing. And they had, quickly and efficiently. It made him think what he had before, that the suicide of a woman of Dr. Stephenson's prominence would be far more carefully scrutinized than if she had been simply murdered. The decapitating naturally removed any suspicion of suicide, but to him, the only person who knew the truth of what had happened, it raised the specter of conspiracy. That someone wanted to cover up one crime with another brought the whole Mike Parsons committee thing back in a rush.

"Fadden," he said, "let's get back to Mike Parsons. His subcommittee on intelligence and counterterrorism. What was it focused on? Why no formal witnesses?"

"Because it was a classified investigation."

"Classified?"

"Yes."

"About what?"

"A top-secret apartheid-era South African biological and chemical weapons program long thought to have been dismantled. The CIA had given the committee a checklist of covert weapons programs that foreign governments had previously had in development so in the future, if push came to shove, they wouldn't commit the WMD mistakes we did before the war on Iraq. The South African program was one of them. The committee wanted to be certain it was as dead as the government claimed."

"Was it?"

"From what my sources tell me, yes. They had the top chemical and biological scientist who headed it on the hot seat for three days and finally concluded that the program had been abandoned as officially declared years ago."

"Meaning?"

"Meaning that all the weapons, pathogen strains, documents, and anything else pertinent had been destroyed. That there was no longer anything there."

"What was the man's name, the scientist who headed it?"

"Merriman Foxx. Why, did Caroline Parsons mention him?"

"No."

Marten looked away and they walked on in silence, the domed Capitol looming in front of them, the pedestrian and motorized traffic around them picking up, the daily activity of the seat of the federal government growing exponentially as the lunch hour ended. A moment later Marten thought of two separate things in rapid order.

The first was what Stephenson had said in the dark, icy seconds on Dumbarton Street before she shot herself, apparently taking him for one of the conspirators. *You want to send me to the doctor. But you never will. None of you ever will. Never. Ever.*

The second was what Caroline had uttered in her sleep—*I don't like the white-haired man,* she'd said, fearfully ranting about a white-haired man who had come to the clinic where she had been taken after her breakdown following the funerals of her husband and son and the subsequent injection by Dr. Stephenson.

"This scientist, Merriman Foxx," Marten said abruptly, "is he also a medical doctor, a physician?"

"Yeah. Why?"

Marten took a deep breath and then asked, "Does he have white hair?"

"What's that got to do with anything?"

"Does he have white hair?" Marten was emphatic.

Fadden raised his eyebrows. "Yeah. A lot of it. He's sixty years old and has a mop like Albert Einstein's."

"My God," Marten breathed. Immediately the thought came. "Is he still here? Still in Washington?" he asked with urgency.

"For chrissakes, I don't know."

"Can you find when he first came to Washington? How long he was here?"

"Why?"

Marten stopped and took Fadden by the arm. "Can you find out where he is now and the day and date he came to Washington?"

"Who the hell is he in this?"

"I'm not sure, but I want to talk to him. Can you get that information for me?"

"I do, and you go to see him, you're taking me with you."

Marten's eyes glistened. Finally—maybe—he was onto something. "You find him, I'll take you with me. I promise."

18

ROME, 7 P.M.

The presidential motorcade turned onto via Quirinale in twilight. President Harris could see the huge lighted edifice of the Palazzo del Quirinale, the official residence of the president of Italy, where he would spend the evening in the company of President Mario Tonti.

Regardless of his failures and frustrations with the leaders of France and Germany, Harris was staying the course: the traveling salesman making the rounds of the major capitals of Europe, drumming up goodwill and calling for a new era of transatlantic unity, meeting those countries' leaders on their home soil, where the trees and gardens and neighborhoods were as dear to them as the same things were to him in America.

With him in the presidential limousine were Secretary of State David Chaplin and Secretary of Defense Terrence Langdon, both of whom had been waiting when *Air Force One* landed at the Champino Military Airport outside Rome. These two men were a show of force and assurance: one to demonstrate that the United States was openly courting a better relationship with the entire European community; the other to make clear that the president was not there hat in hand, that he had his own definitive point of view, especially as it applied to terrorism, the Middle East, and countries covertly developing weapons of mass destruction, as well as other pressing issues—trade, protection of intellectual material, world health, and global warming. In all those things, Harris was realistic but also politically and economically conservative, at least as conservative as the man he had succeeded in office, the late President Charles Cabot.

Not forgotten in all this necessary political "forward motion" was the incident aboard *Air Force One* on the flight from Berlin. He could still feel the numbing chill of Dr. James Marshall's proposal to assassinate the president of France and the chancellor of Germany. *To be replaced with leaders we can trust, now and in the future.* Followed by Jake Lowe's bold statement, *There are such people, Mr. President.* And then Marshall's *It can be done, sir, and rather quickly. You'd be surprised.*

These were men he'd trusted for years. Both had been instrumental in his election. Yet in the context of what had happened it almost seemed as if they were people he'd never met before, strangers with a dark agenda all their own, urging him to take part in it. That he had fiercely refused was one thing, but that it had been proposed at all troubled him deeply. And the way it had been left—with both men looking at him almost in contempt, and Marshall's last words still echoing in his ears; *I think we understand your position, Mr. President*—made him think that, despite his outright refusal, in their minds their initiative was far from dead. It frightened him. There was no other way to put it. He'd thought he should bring it up with David Chaplin and Terrence Langdon on the way here, but both secretaries were filling him in on the meetings they had come from, and to bring up something so ominous and far-reaching then didn't seem appropriate, so he decided to hold off until later.

"We're here, Mr. President." The voice of Hap Daniels, his broad-shouldered, curly-haired SAIC (pronounced *SACK*)—Special

Agent-In-Charge of the Secret Service detail traveling with him—came over the intercom from where Hap rode shotgun in the limousine's front seat. Seconds later the motorcade pulled to a stop in front of the Palazzo del Quirinale. A military band in full dress uniform struck up the United States's national anthem, and through a wash of armed men in uniforms and plain clothes, Harris saw the smiling, resplendent Mario Tonti, the president of Italy, step from a red carpet and come forward through the sea of pomp and security to greet him.

19

NATIONAL PRESBYTERIAN CHURCH, WASHINGTON, D.C.,
MEMORIAL SERVICE FOR CAROLINE PARSONS, 2:35 P.M.

Nicholas Marten sat near the back of the cathedral listening to the deep velvety voice and gentle words of the distinguished African-American minister who led the service, congressional chaplain Rufus Beck, who was pastor of Caroline's church and had made the call to Dr. Stephenson when Caroline had broken down following the funerals of her husband and son. A man he had met briefly in her hospital room.

Emotionally Marten had done everything he could to divorce himself from the event and from the official stamp the service itself gave, the awful acknowledgment that Caroline was truly dead. To that end he had created his own distraction, which he hoped would somehow bear fruit. It was to continually scan the mourners packing the church in the hope that the white-haired man, Dr. Merriman Foxx, had not yet left Washington and had instead come here to take some sort of perverse pleasure in the results of his work. But if he was here, if he was indeed as Peter Fadden had described him, sixty years old and looking like Einstein, so far Marten hadn't seen him.

Those he did see—and there were more than several hundred—were political figures he recognized from the press or television, and many others whom he did not recognize but who had to have been friends or at least associates of Caroline and her family. Just the size of the gathering gave him a very real sense of how rich and expansive their lives here had been.

On a more personal level he saw Caroline's sister, Katy, and her husband, escorted quickly to the front of the church as they arrived, once again, and in so short a time, making an unbearably tragic flight from Hawaii to Washington.

Marten had no way to know if Caroline had shared any of her fears with her sister. Or if Katy knew that Caroline had asked him to come to Washington to be with her for the last hours of her life. It would have been wholly in character for Caroline to have been mindful of what Katy was going through caring for their Alzheimer's-debilitated mother in Hawaii and not want to add another level of anguish, deciding instead to keep her beliefs about some kind of conspiracy between herself and Marten. But whatever Katy knew or didn't, the question of what do about her lingered. If he went to her, reminded her who he was, told her a little of what had happened in the years since she knew him in Los Angeles, and then confided what Caroline had told him and showed her the notarized letter she'd had prepared for him, it was all but certain Katy would accompany him to Caroline's law firm and demand that he be allowed access to the Parsons's private papers, thereby breaking the firm's reluctance to give him access to those things.

That was on the one hand. On the other was the idea that his initial investigation had been smothered by someone in the firm powerful enough to be concerned about what he might find. If that were the case, and considering the situation with Dr. Stephenson, and he and Katy showed up to file a protest, there was every chance that before long the same fate the Parsons family had suffered would befall either Katy or himself or both. It made the whole thing dicey, and even now he wasn't sure what to do about it.

"God's love pours out among us. As it pours out for Caroline, and for her husband, Michael, and her son, Charlie," Reverend Beck's voice filtered through the church.

"In the words of the poet Lawrence Binyon—

'They shall not grow old, as we that are left grow old,
Age shall not weary them, nor the years condemn
At the going down of the sun, and in the morning
We will remember them.'—

Let us pray."

As Reverend Beck's prayer resonated through the church, Marten felt someone slide into the pew beside him. He turned to see a very attractive young woman with short dark hair, dressed respectfully in a black suit. A large digital camera hung from one shoulder, and around her neck was an international press pass with her photograph, her name, and her media affiliation, Agence France-Presse. Marten recognized her as the woman who had accompanied Reverend Beck when he'd visited Caroline in the hospital. He wondered what she was doing there, why she had come to the service. And why she had seated herself next to him.

Then Beck's prayer ended, organ music swelled, and the service was over. Marten saw Beck step down from the pulpit and go over to Caroline's sister and her husband in the front row. Around him people stirred and began to stand. As they did the young woman turned toward him.

"You are Mister Nicholas Marten?" she said with a French accent.

"Yes. Why?" he asked cautiously.

"My name is Demi Picard. I don't mean to intrude, especially under these circumstances, but I wonder if I might have a few moments of your time? It's about Mrs. Parsons."

Marten was puzzled. "What about her?"

"Perhaps we could talk where it is less crowded." She looked toward the large open doors behind them, where people were filing out of the chapel.

Marten studied her carefully. She was tense with anticipation. Her eyes, wide and deep brown, never left his. There was intrigue here—maybe she knew something about Caroline he didn't, or at least something that could help.

"Alright," he said. "Let's go."

20

Marten let her lead the way through the crowd as they walked from the dark of the church into bright afternoon light. Outside, police provided a tight web of security as a long string of cars pulled up one by one to collect the VIP mourners. Behind them and to one side was a gaggle of media satellite trucks. Closer in, television cameras taped the activity while stand-up correspondents reported the event. Clips for the early and late news, Marten thought. And then that would be the end of it, the last public interest in the life of Caroline Parsons.

Demi led them away from the church toward a parking area on the church grounds near Nebraska Avenue. As they went, he caught sight of two familiar figures standing back watching as people left: Metropolitan Police detectives Herbert and Monroe, the man-and-woman team who had questioned him about the "murder" of Lorraine Stephenson. He wondered if by now they too had learned of the white-haired South African scientist Merriman Foxx and were there hoping, as he had, that he might show up at Caroline's service.

"Hey, Marten!" A voice cried out from behind. He turned to see Peter Fadden coming quickly toward them. A moment later he caught up.

"Sorry, I'm running late." He glanced at Demi, then handed Marten a letter-size envelope. "My cell phone number's in there along with some other material you might find interesting. Call me when you get back to your hotel." With that he turned and left, disappearing into the throng still lingering outside the church.

Marten stuck the envelope in his jacket and looked to Demi. "You wanted to talk about Caroline Parsons. What about?"

"I believe you were with her in the last days and hours before she died."

"So were a lot of other people. You included—you came in with Reverend Beck."

"True," she said with a nod, "but most of the time you were alone with her."

"How do you know that? How did you even get my name?"

"I'm a writer and photojournalist doing a photo-essay book on the clergy that minister to prominent politicians. Reverend Beck is one of them. It's why I was with him when he visited the hospital and why I came to the service today. Reverend Beck is pastor of the church where the Parsons family were members. He knew you had been keeping vigil over Mrs. Parsons. He was curious about you and asked one of the nurses. I was there when he learned who you were and that you were a close friend of hers."

Marten squinted in the glare of the afternoon light. "Just what is it you want?"

Demi took a step closer. She was on edge and anticipatory, even more than she had been when she approached him inside the church. "She knew she was dying."

"Yes." Marten had no idea where she was going with her questioning or why she had sought him out.

"You and she must have talked."

"A little."

"And under the circumstances she might have told you things she would not have told others."

"Maybe."

Suddenly Marten was on his guard. Who was she and what was she trying to find out? What Caroline knew or had suspected about Dr. Stephenson and what had been done to her? Or what she felt had happened to her husband and son? Maybe even about the white-haired man, Merriman Foxx, if he was indeed the person Caroline had been referring to.

"Just exactly what is it you want to know?" he said flatly.

"Did she mention—?" Demi Picard hesitated.

Just then Marten saw a dark gray Ford turn the far corner in the parking lot and come toward them. He looked back to Demi. "Did she mention what?"

"The"—she hesitated—"witches."

"Witches?"

"Yes."

The Ford was closer now and slowing. Marten swore to himself. He knew the car and the two people in it, and the way it was slowing told him they had no intention of driving past. Quickly his eyes went to Demi. "Witches?" he pressed her. "What are you talking about?"

Then the Ford was there, pulling up and stopping, its doors opening. Detective Herbert got out from behind the wheel, Monroe from the front passenger seat.

Demi glanced at the police. "I have to go, I'm sorry," she said abruptly, then turned and walked quickly back toward the church.

Marten took a breath, then looked at the detectives and tried to smile. "What can I do for you?"

"This." Monroe snapped a handcuff over one wrist and then the other.

"For what?" Marten was outraged.

Herbert started him toward the car. "We let you attend Mrs. Parsons's service. That's the only favor you get."

"What the hell does that mean?"

"It means we're going for a little ride."

"A ride where?"

"You'll find out."

21

BRITISH AIRWAYS FLIGHT 0224, WASHINGTON, DULLES, TO HEATHROW, LONDON, 6:50 P.M.

Marten watched the hardscape and parkland of Washington dissolve to a twilight sky as the plane banked steeply and headed out over the Atlantic. Handcuffs gone, he was crammed into a window seat of three-across seating in a sold-out coach section and arm to elbow with his two companions, a just-married, hand-holding, cooing couple who hadn't taken their eyes off each other since they'd buckled in. And who, he guessed, weighed somewhere in the neighborhood of three hundred pounds each.

There had been a standby line of at least twenty, but intrepid detectives Herbert and Monroe had found a seat for him anyway.

Their entire MO had been quick and slick. Stopping by his hotel, letting him collect his personal belongings, then whisking him to Dulles International with barely a dozen words said between them. The few they used had been simple and succinct. No interpretation needed. "Get out of Washington and stay out."

They had waited with him at the British Airways gate right up until boarding time and then put him on the plane themselves just to make sure he didn't decide to get off and venture back into their fair city at the last minute. The procedure wasn't unusual; cops did it all the time to get rid of people they couldn't charge with a crime but didn't want around either. The process was made easier if that person was from another city, state, or, as in his case, country.

He hadn't been overjoyed with being kicked out, not with his emotions still there and all the questions still unanswered. On the other hand, the "little ride" the detectives had promised could just as well have been back to police headquarters, especially if they'd found someone who had seen him confront Dr. Stephenson outside her house.

By now they might well have found her head and wanted to talk to him about it, maybe even take him down to the morgue to see it and watch his reaction. But they hadn't. Instead they'd simply tossed him out of the country. Just why he wasn't sure, but he suspected they'd learned something about his relationship with Caroline Parsons, the hospital part anyway, and the letter she had written giving him access to her family's personal files. Whether they were concerned that he might become an awkward kink in their investigation into Dr. Stephenson's death, or if word had come from whoever was pulling strings in Caroline's law firm and wanted him as far out of the picture as possible, there was no way to know. Nor was there a way to know if that same someone was connected to Caroline's death, or the deaths of her husband and son, or the decapitation of an already dead Lorraine Stephenson. Of course none of it meant he couldn't just turn around once he got to London and come right back to continue the investigation on his own.

And, police or no police, he might well have if after the plane took off he hadn't remembered the envelope Peter Fadden had given him outside the church and elbowed himself free of the bulging, cooing couple next to him to take it out and open it.

What he'd found inside was what the reporter had promised: his *Washington Post* business card giving his cell phone number and his e-mail address; the day Dr. Merriman Foxx arrived in Washington, Monday, March 6; and some highly interesting background on Dr. Foxx and the top-secret operations he had headed as brigadier of South Africa's notorious Tenth Medical Brigade. Operations that had included covert international shopping expeditions for pathogens, or disease-causing organisms, and the hardware to disperse them; plans for epidemics that could be spread undetected through black communities to devastate them; special poisons that would cause heart failure, cancer, and sterility; and the development of a kind of "stealth" anthrax strain that would be able to circumvent the intricate tests used to recognize the disease. A major aim was to develop devices to kill opponents of apartheid without a trace.

On top of that Fadden had added something else: the date the doctor left town, Wednesday, March 29, and his current whereabouts, or at least where he was thought to have gone following the secret subcommittee hearings in Washington. It was his home.

> *200 Triq San Gwann*
> *Valletta,*
> *Malta*
> *Phone #: 243555*

This last was what had made Marten change his plans. For now, at least, he would not be returning to Washington once he got to London. Nor would he immediately be going back to his pressing work at his landscape design firm in Manchester. Instead, he would be on the first available flight to Malta.

THURSDAY

APRIL 6

22

"Victor?"

"Yes, Richard."

"Did I wake you?"

"No, I was expecting you to call."

"Where are you now?"

"We left Medina del Campo Station about a half hour ago. We are due to arrive in Madrid at seven thirty-five. Chamartin Station."

"When you get to Chamartin I want you to take the Metro to Atocha Station and from there a taxi to the Westin Palace Hotel on the Plaza de las Cortes. A room is reserved for you."

"Alright, Richard."

"One thing in particular. When you get to Atocha Station, I want you to walk through it carefully and look around. Atocha is where terrorist bombs placed on commuter trains killed one hundred and ninety-one people and injured nearly eighteen hundred more. Imagine what it would have been like when the bombs went off and what would have happened to all those people. And if you were there maybe to you as well. Will you do that, Victor?"

"Yes, Richard."

"Do you have any questions?"

"No."

"Anything you need?"

"No."

"Get some rest. I'll call you later today."

There was a click as Richard signed off, and then Victor's cell phone went silent. For a long moment he did nothing, just listened to the sound of the train as it passed over the rails. Finally he looked around his first-class sleeping compartment with its little washstand, the fresh towels on a rack above him, fresh linens on the bunk bed. There had been only one other time in his life when he had traveled first-class, and that had been yesterday, when he'd taken the high-speed train, the TGV, from Paris to Hendaye on the French-Spanish border. Moreover, the Westin Palace in Madrid was a first-class hotel. As had been the Hotel Boulevard in Berlin. It seemed that from the moment he had shot and killed the man outside Union Station in Washington they had treated him with a great deal more respect than they had before.

He smiled warmly at the thought, then lay back against the soft bedding and closed his eyes. For the first time in as long as he could remember he felt truly appreciated. As if finally, his life had worth and meaning.

1:20 P.M.

President John Henry Harris sat in shirtsleeves watching the island of Corsica slide past beneath them, then saw the open water of the Balearic Sea as *Air Force One* flew west against a strong headwind toward the Spanish mainland. After that it would be on to Madrid and a scheduled dinner with the newly elected prime minister of Spain and a select group of Spanish business leaders.

Earlier that morning he had breakfasted with Italian prime minister Aldo Visconti, and afterward he'd addressed the Italian parliament. His grand dinner at the Palazzo del Quirinale with Mario Tonti, the president of Italy, the night before had been filled with warmth and goodwill, and the two leaders developed a bond almost immediately. By evening's end Harris had invited the Italian president to visit him at his ranch in the California wine country, and Tonti had enthusiastically accepted. That the relationship had developed as it had was important politically, because even as the Italian populace was wary of America's moves and intentions in the Middle East, Tonti had gone out of his way to show the president that he had a strong and dependable ally in Europe. This morning

Prime Minister Visconti had assured Harris of the same. The support of both men was a crucial gain for his tour and all the more important after his more painful experiences in Paris and Berlin, and he was grateful for it. Yet it was Paris and Berlin, or rather the leaders of France and Germany, that still hung in his mind. He had dropped his idea of discussing the Jake Lowe–Dr. James Marshall problem with either Secretary of State Chaplin or Defense Secretary Langdon because he knew that if he did, it would become an overriding cause for worry, and the attention to it would take away the focus on their overall mission.

Besides, frightening and unsettling as it had been, it was still only conversation, and neither man was on hand to take it any further. Earlier that morning Lowe had flown on to Madrid to meet with staff members and the advance Secret Service team at the Hotel Ritz, where he would be staying. Marshall had remained behind in Rome to spend the rest of the day in conference with his Italian counterpart.

Harris sat back, fingered a glass of orange juice, and wondered what he had missed in his judgment of Lowe and Marshall that they could be seriously discussing things he would have thought were so alien to their natures. Then he remembered Jake Lowe taking a phone call from Tom Curran during the motorcade in Berlin and being told afterward of the murder of Caroline Parsons's physician, Lorraine Stephenson. He remembered thinking out loud about the very recent deaths of Mike Parsons, his son, and then Caroline, all three compounded by the murder of Caroline's doctor. He remembered turning to Jake Lowe and saying something like: They are all dead over so short a time. What is going on?

"It's a tragic coincidence, Mr. President," Lowe had responded.

"Is it?"

"What else would it be?"

Maybe Lowe was right; maybe it *was* just a tragic coincidence. Then again, maybe it wasn't, especially not in light of the "assassination" business. Immediately he pressed the intercom button at his sleeve.

"Yes, Mr. President," the voice of his chief of staff came back.

"Tom, would you please ask Hap Daniels to step in here? I'd like to chat with him about procedures in Madrid."

"Yes, sir."

Five seconds later the door opened and his forty-three-year-old Secret Service detail leader entered.

"You wanted to see me, Mr. President?"

"Come in, Hap," Harris said. "Please close the door."

23

Nicholas Marten felt the aircraft bank slightly as the pilot swung them southeast, crossing the Tyrrhenian Sea toward the lower boot of Italy. Soon they would drop down over Sicily and begin their approach to Malta.

At seven fifteen that morning his British Airways flight from Washington had touched down at London's Heathrow Airport. By eight he had retrieved his luggage and bought a ticket on Air Malta for a ten thirty flight that would get him to the Maltese capital of Valletta at three that afternoon. In between he had a cup of coffee and some poached eggs with marmalade toast, booked a room at Valletta's three-star Hotel Castille, and tried calling Peter Fadden in Washington to tell him what had happened with the police and that he was on his way to Malta. Fadden's cell phone had been answered by voice mail, so he'd left a brief message giving Fadden his cell phone number, then backed it up with a similar call to his *Washington Post* office, saying he'd try to reach him again later in the day. Then he'd waited for his flight and tried to put together the pieces of what had happened in Washington, the most curious of which was what the French writer and photojournalist Demi Picard had asked him outside the church just before the police arrived. Had Caroline mentioned "the witches" before she died?

Witches?

No, that wasn't quite it. She'd said "*the* witches."

The same as Caroline had said. "*The* ca—"

Whether she had been meaning to say "*the* committee" was still a guess, but it seemed more than reasonable if—and it was a big if—Dr. Merriman Foxx turned out to be not only "the white-haired man" but also the "doctor" Lorraine Stephenson had so feared that she put a gun to her head and pulled the trigger in front of him.

Merriman Foxx and Dr. Lorraine Stephenson aside, there was no doubt Caroline had said "*the* ca." Just as Demi Picard had said "*the* witches." Both had been plural, meaning there had been more than one person involved. And if Caroline had indeed been referring to a committee, she would have been talking about a group.

VALLETTA, MALTA, 3:30 P.M.

Marten took a taxi from the airport to the Hotel Castille and checked into a comfortable third-floor room with a large window that gave him a striking view of the city's Grand Harbor and its massive stone fortress, St. Angelo, which jutted into the sea from an island across from the city. The fortress had been built, his taxi driver told him on the way from the airport, in the sixteenth century at the behest of the Knights of St. John to protect the island from the invading Ottoman Turks. "It might have looked like the Knights of St. John versus the Turks," he'd said loudly and passionately. "But it was really West against East. Christianity versus Islam. The groundwork for today's terrorist devils was put down right here in Malta five hundred years ago."

He was exaggerating of course, but with Marten's first viewing of the harbor fortifications from his hotel window came an immediate, even eerie, awareness of that past. Despite its oversimplicity, what the cabdriver had said might well be true; the great distrust between East and West had indeed been established centuries earlier on this tiny Mediterranean archipelago.

Jet-lagged but energized, Marten took a quick shower and shaved, then pulled on a light turtleneck sweater, fresh slacks, and a tweed sport coat, from the clothes he had so hastily packed when he'd left Manchester on the run to be with Caroline.

Fifteen minutes later, a hotel-provided map of Valletta in his pocket, he was walking down Triq ir-Repubblika, or Republic Street, the city's main shopping venue, looking for Triq San Gwann, or St. John Street, and then number 200, which according to Peter Fadden was the home of Dr. Merriman Foxx.

What he would do when he got there he'd worked out in London during his wait in the Air Malta passenger lounge. He'd found a cubicle with an Internet connection, plugged in his electronic notebook, then logged on and accessed the U.S. *Congressional Record* Web page. There he'd scrolled down to the Subcommittee on Intelligence and Counterterrorism Mike Parsons had been part of, then clicked on the list of its members and found the name of the committee's chairwoman: Representative Jane Dee Baker, a Democrat from Maine, who, as a further Internet search turned up, was at that moment part of a small contingent of congresspeople on a fact-finding tour of Iraq.

If Merriman Foxx had testified for three days as Peter Fadden had said, he would be more than aware of who Congresswoman Baker was. Marten's plan was to call his residence, give his name as Nicholas Marten, a special aide to Representative Baker, and say there were three or four minor ambiguities in the hearing's transcript that the congresswoman would like clarified. Since he was in Europe and would be traveling through Malta anyway, the congresswoman would very much appreciate it if Dr. Foxx would give him a few moments so that the text could be finalized for the *Congressional Record*.

It was a kind of boldness Marten knew was risky. There was every chance that he would get a firm "No, I'm sorry but my testimony has been completed" or that Foxx might first check with Baker's office in Washington to see if there was indeed a Nicholas Marten on her staff and if he had been given such an assignment. But as a former investigator, Marten was going on the belief that the scientist's reaction would be cordial. Cordial, as in guarded, as if he might still be under the committee's scrutiny. Or cordial, as in friendly, if some kind of cooperative venture was going on between himself and the committee and he didn't want to upset it. In either case, cordial enough to at least meet with him face-to-face. And when they met, Marten would begin to "cordially" feel him out for what he knew about Dr. Stephenson and about the illness and death of Caroline Parsons.

Marten walked down Republic Street looking for St. John's Square, where Republic and St. John streets crossed. He passed a small games and toys shop, another selling wine and spirits, and then under a colorful banner stretching overhead across Republic Street. A few paces more and he was at St. John's Square and in front of the massive Church of the Knights, the seventeenth-century Co-Cathedral of St. John. He had heard of its grand noble hall and the magnificent design within, but from the outside it looked more like a fortress than a church, and reminded him once more that Malta, especially Valletta, had been designed foremost as a citadel.

St. John Street was hardly a street but rather a long climb of stone steps. No vehicles here, only pedestrians. It was now a little after five in the afternoon and the sun cut deep shadows across the stairs as he climbed them. His reason for coming here was simple; to find number 200 and hopefully get some sense of how Merriman Foxx lived—a glimpse of him would be a sheer bonus—before he returned to his hotel and telephoned him.

One hundred fifty-two steps later he was there. Number 200 was similar to all of the buildings on the street, a four-story edifice with an enclosed overhanging balcony on each floor. Balconies that he was certain gave a clear view of the street below.

Marten walked up another twenty steps, then turned back to study the building. Without going up to the front door and peering in, it was hard to tell if the four floors were part of one residence or were broken into single apartments on each floor. A lone residence might indicate Foxx was a man of some wealth—an investment of part of his alleged siphoned-off millions, maybe. An apartment on a single floor would be less definitive. The one thing that was certain was that anyone who lived here had to be at the very least ambulatory; the steep stone-step street itself proved that. It made him begin to wonder if, as a former military officer, Merriman Foxx may well have chosen this island domicile not only for its rich military history but because as he aged it would force him to stay in shape physically. It was a personal discipline he should not overlook when they met face-to-face and he began to question Foxx about Dr. Stephenson and Caroline Parsons.

24

On the other hand maybe he was jumping the gun by assuming Foxx was both the "doctor" and the "white-haired man." What if he wasn't? What if he was just a former army commander with white hair who had run a secret South African bioweapons program and then retired after the whole thing was dismantled? Someone who had never heard of Caroline Parsons or Lorraine Stephenson, had told the truth before a congressional committee, and was now back home to whatever his life in Malta was and happy to have everything else behind him?

What then?

Go back to England? Go back and go to work putting the finishing touches on the landscape drawings for the Banfield country estate northwest of Manchester? Get everything ready for the grading, the irrigation people, the nursery orders, and the planting crews? Go back and forget about what had happened to Caroline? Or to her husband and son? Or about the decapitation of the already dead Dr. Lorraine Stephenson?

No, he'd forget none of it because it wouldn't come to that. Merriman Foxx *had* to be the doctor/white-haired man. He'd been in Washington from March 6th to the 29th, the period during which Mike Parsons and his son had died in the plane crash and when Caroline had become ill. He'd been the principal witness for the subcommittee Mike Parsons had been a member of. *And* he knew firsthand about the makeup and covert use of secret deadly pathogens.

There was little doubt Foxx was the man he was after, but even if he was fortunate enough to get the face-to-face meeting with him why would Foxx tell him anything at all about what he was involved in? If Marten persisted and it got ugly Foxx might very well find a way to kill him. Conversely, if what Foxx was engaged in was far-reaching enough and somehow he forced him into a corner, it might be cause enough for Foxx to kill himself. A cyanide tablet under the tongue, or considering his professional background, something more ingenious, prepared long in advance in the event of such a circumstance.

Peter Fadden had told Marten he was pursuing this emotionally, and he was right. It was why he was here. But now, in the shadow of Foxx's apartment building, he realized that what he had been thinking was true and that if he continued on that same path there was every chance either he or the good doctor would wind up dead, and in the process send Foxx's entire operation, whatever it was, underground. Furthermore, and what he should have thought about from the beginning, was that no matter what he uncovered he had no support structure to back him up. Even if he got Foxx to divulge everything, who was he going to turn to?

If this was as potentially explosive as it seemed—the murder of a United States congressman and his son, and later his wife, followed by the decapitation of his wife's doctor, all intertwined with a congressional subcommittee hearing on intelligence and counterterrorism—it was not something an expatriate landscape designer from England should be pursuing alone. That he had once been an LAPD homicide detective meant nothing; this was a national-security issue, especially if it involved congressional-level Washington politics. So far he had no proof of anything. But a trail had opened up and Merriman Foxx was at the end of it. It meant that whatever Marten did and said when he met him had to be done with great care and self-control, and with all his personal feelings left out of it. His objective had to be wholly singular; to ascertain if Merriman Foxx was—or was not—the doctor/white-haired man. If he was, his next step would be to get hold of Peter Fadden and let him turn loose the one organization in Washington that would have no qualms about taking the investigation further—*The Washington Post*.

MADRID, WESTIN PALACE HOTEL, 7:30 P.M.

"Hello, Victor." Richard's telephone voice was calm and soothing as always.

"I'm glad to hear from you, Richard. I thought you were going to call me earlier." Victor picked up the remote and turned down the television, then moved to sit on the edge of the bed, where he had been resting until his cell phone had rung with Richard's call.

"How is the hotel?"

"Very nice."

"Are they treating you well?"

"Yes, thank you, Richard."

"How was your walk through Atocha Station."

"I—" Victor hesitated, unsure of how to respond.

"You did walk through it as I asked?"

"Yes, Richard."

"What did you think when you saw the area where all those people died in the terrorist attack? Did you imagine what it must have been like for them? The bombs going off inside the railway cars. The screams, the pieces of bodies, the blood. Did you think of the cowards who hid the explosives in backpacks and put them on the trains with all those innocent people on board, then set them off by cell phone when they were themselves safely miles away?"

"Yes, Richard."

"How did you feel?"

"Sad."

"Not angry?"

"Sad, and angry, yes."

"Sad for the people who were hurt and died, angry at the terrorists who did it. Is that right?"

"Yes, I was especially angry at the terrorists."

"You would like to destroy them, wouldn't you?"

"Very much."

"I want you to do something, Victor. There is a garment bag in the clothes closet in your room. Inside it you will find a dark business suit and with it a dress shirt and tie. The suit and shirt are your size. I want you to put them on and go out. As you exit the hotel you will see the Hotel Ritz across the plaza. It's where the president is staying while he is in Madrid. I want you to go there and walk in through the front entrance as any visitor would. Inside you will see the lobby and beyond it the bar and lounge. Go into the lounge and sit down at a table where you can see the lobby and order a drink."

"And then what?"

"Wait a few minutes and then get up and go to the men's room. When you come out look around. The president and his staff have taken over the entire fourth floor. See how the other guests are getting to their rooms on the second and third floors. See if there is any reason you could not get to those same rooms. Then see if there is a way for you to get to the fourth floor. Try both the elevator and the fire stairs. Don't do anything, just see if you would have access. Then go back to the lounge, finish your drink, and return to your hotel."

"Anything else?"

"Not now. I'll call you in the morning to learn what you have found out."

"Alright."

"Thank you, Victor.

"No, Richard, thank you. I mean it."

"I know you do, Victor. Good night."

Victor hesitated, then clicked off. He'd waited all afternoon for Richard's call, and with each passing hour he'd become increasingly worried that they'd changed their minds and wouldn't need him anymore. If that happened, he didn't know what he would do. There was no way he could contact them. Except for a tall pleasant man named Bill Jackson who had met him at a shooting range near his home in Arizona and talked to him about joining a secretive patriotic organization of homeland "protectors," men and women who knew how to use firearms and could be counted on to fight as individuals in the event of a major terrorist invasion; and Richard, who he'd talked to almost daily for the last weeks but had never met, he had no idea who they were or, for that matter, even how to contact Richard.

And as the minutes and hours ticked away before Richard finally called, his anxiety level had risen almost to bursting. What would he do if they abandoned him? Go back to Arizona and the meager life he'd lived there before they'd found him? It would be as if he'd been given another chance and failed again, then let go for reasons that were not his fault at all, the same as had happened so many times before. It seemed as if it was his damnation—hard worker, always on time, never complaining, but let go in a few months anyway for reasons never made clear. It had all been hands-dirty sweatwork: warehouseman, truck driver, short-order cook, security guard; in his entire life he had never held a job for more than fifteen months. And then this wonderful opportunity had come along, and with it growing respect and first-class travel to cities he had never dreamed of. And now the thought of losing it. O God! The awful shadow of that possibility burned in his guts. Fear and despair twisted inside him with each passing minute. Too often he looked at the silent phone on the bed next to him. A phone that should have rung hours before but hadn't. Then, finally, mercifully, it did ring, and he snatched it up to hear the comfort of Richard's voice bringing him back into the fold. Afterward, when he'd clicked off, he let out a deep breath and relaxed, even smiled.

Everything, he knew, was still alright.

25

VALLETTA, MALTA, 8:35 P.M.

Nicholas Marten left the hotel and started down Trig ta York. The light fog coming off the Mediterranean was crisp and invigorating for someone still suffering from jet lag as he was. He wore a dark sport coat and gray slacks, a blue shirt and burgundy tie. In his left hand was a hastily bought briefcase he had scuffed up a little to make it appear somewhat used. Inside it were several file folders, a notebook, and a small, also hastily bought, battery-powered tape recorder.

His destination was an easy ten-minute walk from his hotel and he walked it quickly, following the street past the Upper Baracca Gardens to where it turned into Triq Id-Duka.

"The doctor would be happy to meet with you, Mr. Marten," Merriman Foxx's housekeeper had told him when he'd called requesting to see the doctor on Congresswoman Baker's behalf. "Unfortunately his time is short, but he asked if you would drop by the restaurant where he is having dinner. He will take a few moments to give you whatever information the congresswoman requires."

The time was promptly at nine. The place, the Café Tripoli on Trig id-Dejqa, on the far side of the R.A.F. War Memorial, a monument to British fliers who defended the island against the German and Italian invasion forces in World War Two. Walking past it Marten once again felt the history of battle here and with it the strategic importance of this fortress island. Just the feeling of it, of seeing the ancient stone garrisons and thinking of the countless invasions Malta had suffered over the centuries gave him a very real sense of the adage that war never ends, that there is always one in waiting.

It made him think of Merriman Foxx's Tenth Medical Brigade and its efforts to develop covert biological weapons, and made him realize Foxx knew that maxim all too well. If he did and took it to heart, did that mean the projects he had been working on before the program was ended had not been dismantled at all and were still alive and active? If so, was that what Mike Parsons had stumbled onto in the committee hearings? That and the fact that some members of the committee knew it and were determined not to let it become public? If that was true, then the next question had to be *why*? What were they protecting that they had to kill Parsons because of it?

The sharp cry of an alley cat brought Marten back to where he was. He waited for traffic to pass then crossed a wide boulevard and turned down Trig id-Dejqa, looking for the Café Tripoli. He had to appreciate Foxx's openness in agreeing to see him but at the same time knew he had to be wary of him. A public meeting was always circumventive and hardly like being in a hearing room. With others in close earshot one could listen to what was being asked and then answer directly or indirectly or not at all, politely and at choice. The problem for Marten was how to handle the interview because the questions he would ask would have little to do with the hearings and instead focus on Caroline and Dr. Stephenson. It would be tricky and delicate and what would happen as a result would depend as much on Merriman Foxx himself, his character and manner, as on how Marten presented them.

8:45 P.M.

The Café Tripoli was down a narrow stone-step alley, its doorway lighted by a large brass lamp. Marten stopped at the top of the steps, watching as the café's door opened and three people came out and started up toward him. Behind him was a darkened doorway, and he stepped into it and waited. A moment later the three walked past and turned onto the street without ever having seen him. This was what he wanted and why he was early. The doorway was a place to observe Foxx as he passed by on his way to the restaurant. Marten wanted to see him first, if nothing more than a glimpse. See his features and the white hair, to know beforehand what he looked like. It would be an edge up, nothing more.

8:55 P.M.

For a long time it had been quiet, and Marten wondered if Foxx had been early himself and was already inside. He was beginning to wonder if he should abandon his plan and just go down to the restaurant when a cab pulled up at the end of the alley, the doors opened, and a man and then a woman got out. Marten pressed farther back into the doorway as the taxi drove off and the two started down the stone steps toward the café. The woman passed first. She was quite young, dark-haired, and very attractive. The man was right behind. Medium height, medium build, his shoulders back, he wore a gray knit fisherman's sweater over dark trousers. His face was taut and deeply lined. His hair, the massive shock of it, was white as fresh snow and so theatrical as almost to be a trademark. Merriman Foxx was almost exactly as Peter Fadden had described him. "He looks like Einstein."

Marten waited until they entered, then opened his briefcase, took out the tape recorder, and slid it in his inside jacket pocket. He waited another moment, then stepped out of the shadows and walked down to the entrance of the Café Tripoli.

"Good evening, sir!"

Marten was barely inside the door when he was met by a cheerful, balding maître d' in black slacks and starched white shirt. Behind

THE MACHIAVELLI COVENANT • 101

him was a smoky pub-like lounge with the sound of a jazz piano floating out of it.

"I'm to meet Dr. Foxx. My name is Marten."

"Yes, sir, of course. Follow me please."

The maître d' led him down a flight of stairs to the supper club
in the basement. A number of people crowded a small bar near the
foot of the stairs. Beyond it was a dining area with maybe two
dozen tables; all were taken and Marten looked around for Dr. Foxx
and his companion but saw neither.

"This way, sir."

The maître d' led him toward an enclosed area near the back
that was separated from the rest of the club by a wood-and-opaque
glass partition. The maître d' stepped around it and ushered him
into what was essentially a private room.

"Mr. Marten," he announced.

26

Four of them were at the table. Foxx and his lady friend, as he had
expected. The other two were a total surprise. He had last seen them
in Washington little more than a day earlier—Congressional chaplain Reverend Rufus Beck and the French writer-photojournalist
Demi Picard.

"Good evening, Mr. Marten." Merriman Foxx stood to take his
hand. "Let me introduce my other guests. Cristina Vallone," he
nodded to the young woman who had come in with him, "the Reverend Rufus Beck and," he smiled warmly, "Mademoiselle Picard."

"How do you do?" Marten's eyes met Demi's for the briefest moment, but she revealed nothing. He looked back to Foxx. "It's very
kind of you to meet with me like this and on such short notice."

"It is always a pleasure to assist the United States Congress any
way I can. Unfortunately my time is short, Mr. Marten; if our guests
will excuse us perhaps we can go to a corner of the bar and take
care of what needs to be done."

"Of course."

Merriman Foxx ushered Marten out of the enclosed area and toward the bar near the stairs. As Marten went, his eyes again met Demi's. She was watching him without trying to show it. Clearly she was as surprised to see him as he was to see her. Further, and just as clearly, she wasn't happy about it.

Reverend Beck was a surprise too, and like Demi, he had shown no recognition. Yet Marten was certain he remembered him from Caroline's hospital room. Not only had they introduced themselves when Beck came in, but, as Demi had told him, Beck was curious enough about him to have asked one of the nurses who he was.

"Just what ambiguities did Congresswoman Baker want clarified?" Foxx said as they reached the bar. It had cleared out a little now and they stood alone at the end of it.

Marten set the briefcase on the bar, opened it, and took out a folder, then reached into his jacket pocket for a pen. As he did, he clicked on the tape-recorder. At the same time, and without being asked, the bartender set a snifter of single malt whiskey at each man's sleeve.

"There are several, Doctor," Marten said, deliberately reminding himself of the reason he was here, to ascertain as best he could whether Foxx was or was not the doctor/white-haired man. His great disadvantage here, and one he hoped was not fatal, was that he had no transcript of the congressional hearings and therefore no idea of what had been asked or answered. All he had to work with was what he knew about Foxx's history and that of the Tenth Medical Brigade, the bits and pieces he'd learned through a brief search of the Internet when he'd returned to his hotel; what Caroline had told him, and what Dr. Stephenson had said just before she shot and killed herself.

He opened the folder and glanced at the page of handwritten notes he'd prepared in his hotel room as if he had taken them down during a phone conversation with Congresswoman Baker.

"Your biological weapons project in the Tenth Medical Brigade was called Program D, not B. Is that correct?"

"Yes." Foxx picked up the snifter and took a pull at his whiskey.

Marten made a notation on the page next to his notes and went on to the next. "You stated that the toxins you developed, including forty-five different strains of anthrax, and the bacteria that cause brucellosis, cholera, and plague and systems to deliver them, as well as a number of new and unaccounted-for experimental viruses—all had been accounted for and subsequently destroyed. That is correct as well?"

"Yes."

Foxx took another drink of whiskey. For the first time Marten noticed how extraordinarily long his fingers were in proportion to the size of his hands. At the same time too he took stock of the doctor's build. When he'd first seen him in the alley he'd seemed average, neither stocky nor slim, but in the bulky fisherman's sweater, if he was indeed in shape and muscular as Marten had previously thought, it was hard to tell. Either way it was something he couldn't dwell on without drawing attention to what he was doing, so he went back to his questioning.

"To your knowledge has any further experimentation been done on human beings since 1993 when the president of South Africa declared that all of your biological weapons had been destroyed?"

Foxx suddenly put his glass down. "I answered that quite clearly before the committee," he said irritably. "No, no further testing was done. The toxins were destroyed, along with the information about how to create them."

"Thank you." Marten leaned over his file, taking his time to scribble a few more notes. Initially Foxx had greeted him cordially. It meant he had taken Marten's introduction of himself at face value and in all likelihood had not verified that he was with Congresswoman Baker's office. Yet now he was clearly becoming short-tempered, either by the questions themselves or more likely because of his ego. These were things he'd already been over in a closed congressional hearing and here he was standing in public going over the same material with some third-string messenger, one he was showing increasing contempt for. What he wanted was to have it over and done with once and for all.

It was just this display of temperament that told Marten he could be vulnerable if pushed, that with more direct questioning he might give something away he had not intended to. Marten knew too that if he was going to do it, he had to do so quickly because the doctor was clearly not going to give him much more of his time.

"I'm sorry, there are just a few more," Marten said apologetically.

"Then get to them." Foxx glared at him, then picked up his glass once more, his long fingers wrapped around it.

"Please let me explain, as perhaps I should have earlier," Marten said in the same contrite manner, "that some of these clarifications have been made necessary because of the death of one of the committee members after the hearings had closed, Congressman Michael Parsons of California. Representative Parsons, it seems, had left a memo for Congresswoman Baker that only recently surfaced. It had to do with a consultation he had with a Dr. Lorraine Stephenson, who, besides being a general practitioner, was also, I believe, a virologist. She also happened to be the personal physician of Congressman Parsons's wife, Caroline. Are you familiar with Dr. Stephenson?"

"No."

Marten glanced at his notes, then looked up. Now was the time to push, and hard. "That's curious because in Congressman Parsons's memo to Congresswoman Baker, he mentions that you and Dr. Stephenson had met privately more than once over the course of the hearings."

"I have never heard of a Dr. Stephenson. Nor do I have any idea what you're talking about," Foxx said tersely. "Now I think I've given the congresswoman quite enough of my time, Mr. Marten." He put down his snifter and started to turn from the bar.

"Doctor," Marten kept on, "Congressman Parsons's memo raised questions about the veracity of your testimony, particularly in the area of the unaccounted-for experimental viruses."

"What's that?" Foxx turned back, his face flushed with anger.

"I didn't mean to upset you. I'm only doing as instructed." Again Marten played the apologetic messenger. "Now that you know about the memo and since Congressman Parsons is dead, Congresswoman Baker asked if you would state for the final transcript that everything you said under oath was, and to the best of your knowledge, still is, the whole truth."

Foxx picked up the snifter again, his eyes deadly cold. "Yes, Mr. Marten, for the final transcript, everything I said was and is the whole truth."

"The viruses included? That none had been used on a human being since 1993?"

Foxx's stare bore into him, both hands encircling the snifter, his thumbs protruding up and over the rim. "The viruses included."

"One last question," Marten said quietly. "Have you ever been know simply as 'the doctor'?"

Foxx finished his whiskey and looked to Marten. "Yes, by hundreds of people. Good night, Mr. Marten and please give Congresswoman Baker my best wishes." He set the empty snifter on the bar and walked off for his table.

"My God," Marten breathed. It had happened so quickly and inadvertently he'd almost missed it. Yet there it had been, shown to him as clearly as if he had asked to see it. Yes, Merriman Foxx had white hair. Yes, he was called "the doctor." But those two things taken alongside Marten's rather sorry attempt at getting hard information did not mark Foxx without a doubt as the doctor/white-haired man who had overseen, if not administered, the toxin that killed Caroline.

But the other thing did.

It was something he had forgotten completely until he had noticed the unusual length of Foxx's fingers as they circled his whiskey glass. It was what Caroline had told him over phone when she'd first called him so fearfully in Manchester and asked him to come to Washington.

"I didn't like him," she'd said about the white-haired man who'd come to the clinic where she'd been taken following the injection given her by Doctor Stephenson. "Everything about him frightened me. The way he stared at me. The way he touched my face and my legs with his long, hideous, fingers."

Those fingers around the whiskey glass were only part of it. The rest had come when an angry Foxx had held his snifter in both hands with his thumbs protruding up and over the rim. It was then he'd seen it and remembered the whole of Caroline's description: "The way he touched my face and my legs with his long, hideous, fingers; and that horrid thumb with its tiny balled cross."

A faded cross—two straight lines that intersected in the form of a cross with a tiny circle, a ball, at the tip of each of the four ends—had been tattooed on the tip of Merriman Foxx's left thumb.

Marten had almost missed it, but he hadn't. A tiny, faded

tattooed cross described in passing by a terrified, dying woman. At the time it had been part of a jumble of information and had seemingly meant little. Now it meant everything.

It told him he had his man.

27

Marten reached into his pocket and clicked off the tape recorder. There was little doubt that it was Foxx who had overseen the murder of Caroline but there was nothing incriminating in the recorded conversation nor was a lone tattoo the kind of hard evidence Peter Fadden would need to warrant an investigation by *The Washington Post*. Marten needed something concrete and definitive but getting it or even how to approach getting it would be hugely difficult, especially since Foxx had clearly closed the door on him and because there was no doubt the doctor would contact Congresswoman Baker's office to verify who he was. Once that happened he wouldn't get within a mile of him.

"Mr. Marten."

Marten looked up to see Demi Picard alone and coming toward him. It made him wonder what she was doing here. That she was with Beck was no surprise because she had told him the reverend was one of the subjects of a photo-essay book she was doing on political clergy. But that they were both here in Malta and at Foxx's dinner table so soon after Caroline's service in Washington was more than a little disturbing, especially now, with what he'd learned about Foxx.

"Ms. Picard." he started to smile. "How nice to—"

Her eyes suddenly narrowed and she cut him off in a sotto voce charged with anger. "Why are you here? In Malta? In this restaurant?"

"I was going ask you the same thing."

"Dr. Foxx and Reverend Beck are old friends," she said defensively. "We were on our way to meet with a group of Western clergy visiting the Balkans and stopped overnight to visit."

"Presumably you know Reverend Beck quite well."

"Yes."

"Then maybe you can explain how an African-American minister can be the friend of an apartheid-era officer in the South African army, one who headed a notorious medical unit that developed secret biological weapons designed to wipe out the black African population."

"You would have to ask Reverend Beck."

Marten stared at her. "What if I asked *you* about 'the witches'?"

"Don't," she warned.

"Don't?"

"I said, don't!"

"You're the one who brought it up," Marten said quickly. "You came to me, remember?"

"Demi," a familiar voice called from behind her. They turned to see Beck approaching. Cristina Vallone, Merriman Foxx's attractive female friend, was with him.

"I'm afraid Dr. Foxx has been called away. An urgent family matter," he said to them both, then directed the next at Demi. "He asked that I see you and Cristina back to the hotel."

Demi hesitated, and Marten could see she was troubled by the sudden turn of events. "Thank you," she said politely, "I have to use the loo. I will meet you upstairs."

"Of course." Beck looked to Marten as she went off toward the restrooms. "It was a pleasure to see you again, Mr. Marten, perhaps we shall do it another time soon."

"The pleasure would be mine, Reverend."

Five minutes later Marten stood on Trig id-Dejqa watching the taillights of a taxi carrying Reverend Beck, Cristina, and Demi Picard disappear in a swirling fog. He glanced back down the dampened alley toward the Café Tripoli. The door was closed. Nothing stirred. He wondered how Foxx had left without him seeing him, or if he had left at all. In either case there was nothing he could do about it now. He took a breath and then stepped off for the walk back to his hotel, Demi's words still clear as when she'd stopped at the bar on her way from the loo.

"I don't know who you really are or what you're doing here," she'd said forcefully with the same heated tone she used before. "But stay away from us before you ruin everything." With that she'd turned and gone up the stairs to where Cristina and the Reverend Beck waited.

Ruin everything. What did that mean?

And now as he walked, making his way in damp night air toward the R.A.F. War Memorial and after it the Upper Baracca Gardens on the way to his hotel, Demi's words faded in favor of what Reverend Beck had said as he bade him goodbye.

It was a pleasure to see you again, Mr. Marten, perhaps we shall do it another time soon.

See you again—*again.*

It meant Beck knew who he was, and clearly remembered their meeting in Caroline's hospital room. At the time they'd met, the subject of Marten's profession had never come up, so it was possible that he might believe Marten did indeed work in Congresswoman Baker's office. Nonetheless it was a coincidence that would have been pointedly discussed with Foxx when he returned to the table. Couple that with the fact that Marten had not only brought up Caroline's name and that of Dr. Stephenson but that he'd said Mike Parsons had left a memo behind questioning the veracity of Foxx's testimony before the committee—Foxx would have put all those things together in a hurry, which was undoubtedly the reason the evening had ended so abruptly for everyone.

28

The lights of nighttime Madrid flashed by. Palacio de la Moncloa, residence of the Spanish Prime Minister, the dinner there with the newly elected prime minister and the twenty or so top Spanish industrialists he had invited to join them, over and done with and left behind.

Only four people rode in the presidential limousine, the Secret Service agent driving, a second agent riding shotgun beside him, and the two in the back; President John Henry Harris and his Secret Service Special Agent in Charge, Hap Daniels. The interior communications system was turned off. Whatever the president and Daniels said was wholly private.

The motorcade itself had been reduced to the presidential limousine, two black Secret Service SUVs, and the black communications Hummer following behind. This time there was no ambulance, no staff van, no press pool van—just a small presidential motorcade going to a private residence in the wealthy La Moraleja suburb to share a brief drink with an old friend, Evan Byrd. Byrd was a former network news correspondent and press secretary to the late president Charles Cabot. For a time he had been President Harris's press secretary, before he retired to this Madrid suburb. After that it was back to the Hotel Ritz where the presidential entourage had taken over the entire fourth floor and the president looked forward to a sound night's sleep.

"The plane carrying Representative Parsons and his son"—Hap Daniels was reading from notes taken in a small spiral notebook. No BlackBerry here, no chance that the information he had received could have been electronically monitored, just handwritten notes jotted down in an everyday notebook. What he had learned had come over the STU, or secure-line phone, he had as part of his own personal communications equipment—"went down due to pilot error, at least according to investigators from the NTSB. No part of the aircraft was found to have malfunctioned."

"We know the official word, Hap," Harris said, "Is that all you were able to find out?"

"As far as the crash, yes, sir. The thing that no one seems to know about, or at least to have brought up, was that Mrs. Parsons was to have been on the flight with them. Her plans changed at the last minute and she flew back to Washington on a commercial flight. It was coincidental. There certainly was no conspiracy theory behind the crash. No reason to expect foul play. She never made a thing of it, at least publicly. It appears to have been one of those things that just happened."

"One of those things. . . ."

"Yes, sir."

President Harris nodded vaguely, trying to absorb whatever meaning there might or might not be in Caroline's change of plans, then immediately moved on.

"The man in Caroline's hospital room, the one Caroline gave legal access to her and Mike's private papers."

"All we have is what we knew before. His name is Nicholas Marten. He's an American ex-pat living in Manchester, England, and working as a landscape architect. He's seems to have known the Parsons family for a long time; at least that's what he told the D.C. police. Their feeling was that he and Caroline Parsons had had a relationship of some kind. He said they were just old friends. No proof of it. But no sense he was blackmailing her either."

"Why did the police talk to him?"

"He'd made some pretty strong phone calls to Mrs. Parsons's doctor after she died. He wanted to ask her about Mrs. Parsons's illness but she wouldn't talk to him, claimed privileged information between doctor and patient. They thought he might have been involved in her murder. But there was nothing to hold him on so they put him on a plane to England and basically told him not to come back."

"The murder of Caroline Parsons's doctor? What do we have on that?"

"That's a nasty one, Mr. President. She was beheaded."

"Beheaded?"

"Yes, sir. The head hasn't been found, and the police have kept it very quiet during their investigation. The FBI has their own people on it."

"When was someone going to inform the White House?"

"I don't know, sir. Probably they felt there was no need."

"Why a beheading?"

"You're thinking some kind of terrorist act. Some Islamic group."

"It doesn't make any difference what I think. It's what I know. And so far no one seems to know much of anything. Get somebody you're comfortable with in the FBI to keep you on top of it. Tell them I'm interested personally but don't want the media to jump on it and blow it out of proportion. We don't need to stir up the Islamic world any more than it's already stirred up, especially if there's nothing to it and the head business was done by some cuckoo out there."

"Yes, sir."

"Now," the president shifted gears. "Caroline Parsons. I want a report on what kind of infection she had, how she got it, and the treatment for it, from initial diagnosis to death. Again, I don't want to send up a flare, I just want the information and as quietly as you can get it. We've got four people dead here in a very short time. Three from the same family and the last, Caroline's doctor."

"There's something else you should know, Mr. President. I don't know if it means anything but Representative Parsons . . ."

"What about him?"

"He tried to get an appointment to see you privately. Twice. Once during his subcommittee hearings on terrorism. Once again the day they were concluded."

"How do you know?"

"His secretary requested it, but she never heard back."

"Mike Parsons had full access to me, anytime. Chief of staff knew that, my secretary knew it too. What happened?"

"I don't know, sir. You'd have to ask them."

Suddenly Hap Daniels put a hand to his headset; at the same time the limousine slowed and then leaned as the Secret Service driver made a sharp right turn and started up a long private driveway.

"Thank you," Daniels said into his headset, then looked to the president. "We're here, sir. Mr. Byrd's residence."

29

Evan Byrd greeted him at the door like an old school chum he hadn't seen for years, not with a handshake but a bear hug.

"Damn good to see you, John," he said, leading him past an ornate fountain and then inside through a Spanish-tiled foyer and into a small dark-paneled room with a full bar and big leather chairs that faced a fireplace where a warming fire crackled.

"Not bad for a retired civil servant, huh?" Byrd grinned. "Sit down, what can I fix you to drink?"

"I don't know. I've had my share of everything tonight, just water or coffee, black, if you have it."

"Damned right I have it." Byrd winked and pressed a button on an intercom at the bar and ordered coffee in Spanish, then he walked over and sat down in a big chair next to Harris.

Evan Byrd was in his early seventies and dressed casually in cream-colored slacks and a matching sweater. He seemed a little on the heavy side but otherwise appeared in good shape, still favoring the stylish long gray hair and matching sideburns Harris remembered. Byrd had been around network television and Washington politics for nearly forty years before he retired to Spain and still had an active Rolodex that would put most Washington insiders to shame, meaning he knew just about everyone worth knowing and in result wielded considerable influence without ever seeming to.

"Well," he said, "how did it go tonight?"

"I'm not sure." Harris let his gaze fall to the fire. "Spain is in a war with itself. The prime minister's a nice guy, too much of an altruist maybe and too far to the left to get anything done to really boost the country's economy. But the business leaders, the power guys who joined us for dinner, most of them are fiscally conservative, they see the bottom line as part of the national identity. They have money to invest and at the same time want to be invested in. They want to be in the same global marketplace as everyone else.

That puts them at odds with their own leadership. But still the prime minister had the cojones to have them there, so you've gotta give him credit for that. Of course they're all worried about terrorism and where the next shoe will drop. No one's being helped on that count."

"What about France and Germany?"

"You read the papers, Evan. You watch TV. You know as well as I do. Not good."

"What are you going to do about it?"

"I don't know." For the briefest moment the president looked off, then his gaze went to Byrd. "I really don't know."

Just then a voice came over the intercom in Spanish. "Your coffee is ready, sir."

"Gracias," Byrd spoke into the intercom and then stood. "Come on, John, we'll take coffee in the living room." He grinned as President Harris got up from his chair. "I have a surprise for you."

Harris groaned. "Not at this time of night, Evan, I'm too damn tired."

"Trust me, you'll love it."

Seven men waited in the room as they entered and the president knew every one of them. Vice President of the United States Hamilton Rogers. Secretary of State David Chaplin. Secretary of Defense Terrence Langdon. Chairman of the Joint Chiefs of Staff, United States Air Force General Chester Keaton, and the men he had last seen in Rome: Tom Curran, his chief of staff; his chief political adviser, Jake Lowe, and National Security Adviser, Dr. James Marshall.

Evan Byrd closed the door behind them.

"Well, gentlemen, this is indeed a surprise," Harris said evenly, trying not to show his astonishment at their presence. "To what do I owe it?"

"Mr. President," Lowe began, "as you know the NATO meeting in Warsaw is to take place a very few days from now. Before, when we went into Iraq, when we had problems with France and Germany and Russia, our people were not yet in place. Now they are. We have been assured of this by friends of trust. Friends who are in a position to know."

"What friends? Who are you talking about?"

"In order to prevent the kind of unthinkable catastrophe I spoke of earlier"—National Security Adviser Marshall stepped forward—"of terrorist groups taking over the entire Middle East and its oil supply in a very short composite of time, it has become necessary for us to take a full and decisive initiative in that part of the world. To do that we can have no dissent in the United Nations. We have been assured that neither Germany nor France will object this time when we ask for their vote. And, as you know, if they do not object, in all probability neither will Russia nor China."

"Assured?"

"Yes, sir, assured."

The president looked around at faces as familiar as family. Like Lowe and Jim Marshall, these people had been his most trusted friends and advisers for years. What the hell was going on? "Just what is it *we* are going to *do* in the Middle East?"

"Unfortunately, we're not in a position to tell you, Mr. President," Secretary of Defense Terrence Langdon said directly. "The reason we are here is to ask you to authorize the physical removal of the current leaders of France and Germany."

"Physical removal. . . ." The president looked to Lowe and Marshall. They had started it earlier; now they had the whole team with them. He didn't understand. He was a conservative Republican, the same as they were. They had been behind him all the way, made certain he was nominated, then pulled out every stop possible to guarantee his election. "I think assassination is the word you want, Mr. Secretary."

Then it came to him like a thunderbolt and shook him to his core. He wasn't their president at all; he was their pawn and had been from the beginning. He was there because they had put him there. Because they had been certain he would do whatever they asked.

"Who are these 'friends of trust' you are referring to?" he asked.

"Members of an organization who have guaranteed that the people who will be voted to replace the President of France and the Chancellor of Germany will wholly support whatever we do."

"I see," the president said finally. There was no point in asking what this "organization" was because they wouldn't tell him. Instead he put his hands in his pockets and walked over to where a large window opened out onto lighted formal gardens. Through it he could see two Secret Service agents standing in the shadows. There would be more he couldn't see.

For a long moment he stood there with his back to them. They were waiting for his answer. They could wait a while longer while he tried to put it together, to understand how all this had happened and what would happen next. As he did, Jake Lowe's words cut through him.

Before, when we went into Iraq, when we had problems with France and Germany and Russia our people were not yet in place. Now they are.

Our people.

Now they are.

Now they are.

Whatever this organization was, it was strikingly clear that they, all of them, were members of it and what they had planned they had been working on for a long time. And now, finally, they had people in every country that counted in position to execute it, himself included. He looked back and then started across the room toward them.

"Harry Ivers belong to this 'organization'? You all know Harry Ivers, chairman of the National Transportation Safety Board. The man in charge of investigating the crash of Congressman Parsons's plane." Suddenly he looked to Tom Curran, his chief of staff.

"Congressman Parsons tried to get an appointment to see me. Twice. Once during and once immediately following the close of the subcommittee hearings on intelligence and counterterrorism. You knew he had full access to me at any time. Why didn't those meetings happen?"

"Your schedule was full, Mr. President."

"That's bullshit, Tom." The president looked around the room, stopping at each of the eight men in turn. "Congressman Parsons was onto something, wasn't he? It had to do with his subcommittee looking into the supposedly dead South African bioweapons program and the questioning of this Dr. Merriman Foxx. I'm guessing that that program or some offshoot of it is not dead at all. And whatever it is, somehow we, or rather you and your 'friends of trust,' are involved with it.

"You thought Mike Parsons as a strong conservative would go

along with it but he wouldn't and threatened to bring it to me if you didn't back away from it. The result was you killed him."

There was a long silence and then National Security Adviser Marshall spoke. "He couldn't be trusted, Mr. President."

The president suddenly became furious. "And his son and everyone else on board that plane?"

"It was a matter of national security." Marshall was cold and unemotional.

"His wife, too."

"Who knows what he might have told her? Her doctor gave her a little something to take care of the problem."

"Dr. Stephenson."

"Yes, sir."

"Her reward was that somebody cut off her head."

"Unfortunately she became frightened afterward and that put her into the category of 'liability' and she had to be terminated."

The president's eyes left Marshall and swung to the others. Every one of them stared back at him in silence. And that included his long time political adviser and close friend, Jake Lowe, and his dear host, Evan Byrd.

"Jesus, God," he breathed. He had no friends here, none at all. Again he heard Jake Lowe's words. *Before . . . our people were not yet in place.* Now *they are.*

And before *they didn't have the weapons they needed.*

Now *they did.*

"What you are planning is some kind of biological warfare. Against what, the Muslim states?"

"Mr. President." Vice President Hamilton Rogers crossed in front of Marshall. Rogers was blond with dark savage eyes, ten years his junior and far more conservative. The truth was he had fought against having him as a running mate, feeling he was much too conservative, but had finally given in to the pressure of Lowe who had convinced him Rogers was the man to push the vote over. Now he knew why. Rogers was one of them. Whoever *they* were.

"For the security of the nation we are asking you to authorize the physical elimination of the president of France and the chancellor of Germany. Please give us that authorization."

In that instant President Harris knew that if he didn't go along with everything they wanted, they would kill him. And then, by law, the vice president would become president and authorize the killings anyway. Looking at them—who they were, the offices they represented, the vast connections they had—he realized that from top to bottom there was no one he dared trust. No one. Even his private secretary, who had been with him for nearly twenty years, had to be suspect. The same with his Secret Service protectors, and that included his SAIC, Hap Daniels. What he needed was time to find some way out, to find some way to stop them and whatever horrifying Armageddon they were planning.

"Where and when do you want to carry out this 'removal'?" he said.

"At the NATO meeting in Warsaw. When the whole world is watching."

"I see," the president nodded, then once again looked around the room at the faces of the men watching him, waiting for his answer.

"I need time to think about it," he said quietly. "Now, I'm tired. I would like to go back to my hotel and get some sleep."

FRIDAY

APRIL 7

30

Jake Lowe took the call in the dark in his private fourth floor suite.

"Yes," he said, moving up on an elbow in bed, then instinctively glancing around, making sure he was alone.

"I have a mosquito that needs swatting," a middle-aged female voice said calmly. "His name is Nicholas Marten. He pretended to be an associate of Representative Baker. How he found us I don't know. He was asking very 'enlightened' questions. He was also with Mrs. Parsons in the last hours before she died."

"Yes, I'm aware of that."

"I would like to find out who he works for, what he knows, and if anyone is working with him before we call in an exterminator."

"Where is he now?" Lowe asked.

"Malta. The Castille Hotel."

"When are you leaving?"

"Shortly."

"I'll be in touch."

There was a click as the caller hung up. Lowe hesitated for a minute, then turned on the bedside lamp and picked up his Black-Berry. The voice had come over a secure phone and had been altered and then digitally scrambled, making it virtually impossible to identify let alone trace. Only one person had the equipment and the necessary code to use it—Merriman Foxx.

"Come back in five minutes!" Demi Picard barked in answer to a knock on her door. She fastened the last buttons of a blue-striped man tailored shirt, slipped a woven leather belt through her tan slacks, then, one, two, clipped on a pair of small gold hoop earrings.

The knock came again. She sighed in annoyance, then went to the door.

"I told you to come back in—" she said as she opened it, then stopped in mid-sentence.

Nicholas Marten stood there.

"I was expecting a porter," she snapped in the same infuriated tone she'd used the night before. Immediately she turned and went back into the room to take a blue blazer from the closet. Her all-but-packed suitcase was open on the bed, her camera gear in a hard case next to it.

"You're leaving."

"Like everyone else, thanks to you."

"Me?"

She glared at him. "Yes."

"Who is everyone?"

"Dr. Foxx left early this morning. So did Reverend Beck a short while later. So did Cristina."

"For where?"

"I don't know. I found a note under my door from Reverend Beck saying he had been called away unexpectedly and that our trip to the Balkans had been canceled."

"What about the other two?"

"I called Cristina's room to see what she knew about it and was told she'd already checked out." Abruptly Demi went into the bathroom. A moment later she came back with a small bag of toiletries. "I made the same call to Foxx's apartment. His housekeeper said he'd gone as well." She put the toiletry bag in her suitcase and deliberately zipped it closed.

"And you have no idea where any of them went."

She glared at him again. "No."

"Porter." A man in hotel uniform stood in the open doorway.

"Just the one bag," she said, then pulled on her blazer, threw her purse over her shoulder, and picked up her camera case. "Good-bye, Mr. Marten," she said and with that brushed past him and walked out.

"Hey!" Marten said and went after her.

Forty seconds later Demi, Marten, and the porter rode the elevator down in silence. Demi stared at the floor. Marten stared at her. A full minute, two elevator stops, and three hotel guests later, the elevator stopped. The door opened and Demi led the group toward the main lobby. Immediately Marten fell into lockstep with her.

"What did you mean last night when you said to stay away before I 'ruined everything'?"

"Don't you think it's a little late for explanations?"

"Okay, let's change the subject and try 'the witches.'"

Demi ignored him and kept walking. They reached the lobby and started across it.

"What witches? What were you talking about?"

Still she ignored him. They went three strides farther then Marten took her arm and pulled her around. "Please, it's important."

"What do you think you're doing?" she bristled.

"For one thing, asking you to be civil."

"Do you want me to call the police? Because there they are." She nodded toward two black-uniformed, black-booted motorcycle police who stood just outside the front door.

Marten slowly let go of her arm. She fixed him with an irate stare, then walked off. He saw her stop at the concierge desk and chat briefly with a mustachioed gentleman behind it. He smiled knowingly, then reached into his desk, took out an envelope, and handed it to her. She thanked him, glanced briefly back at Marten, then followed the porter to a taxi waiting outside. A moment later she was gone.

31

"What do you mean he's not there?" Six-foot four-inch National Security Adviser Dr. James Marshall abruptly stood from his working desk, his papers and electronic message boards scattered across the top of it.

"I mean he's not there. He's gone. Vanished." Jake Lowe was white with disbelief. "I went into his suite to get his answer to what we talked about last night and there was no one there. Pillows were rolled up under the bedcovers to make it look like he was still sleeping."

"The president of the United States is gone? He's missing?"

"Yes."

"Does the Secret Service know?"

"They do now. But it wasn't until I started yelling. Then they freaked."

"Good Lord."

"What the hell's going on?" Hap Daniels came hard into the room. "Is this a joke? Is the POTUS (president of the United States) having fun? Are you guys? If this is a game, say so. I'm not kidding!"

"No game here, Hap," Marshall snapped. "The president is your charge! Where the hell is he?"

Hap Daniels stared, openmouthed, stunned. "You're kidding."

"Nobody's kidding."

"Jesus Christ!"

Front door closed. Jake Lowe and James Marshall stood in horrified silence waiting while Hap Daniels made a sweep for the second time. Conference room, bedroom, bathroom. Seconds passed and he came out, crossed the room without a word and went into the hallway. A half minute later he came back in with a six-foot one-inch bulldog of a man, Secret Service agent Bill Strait, his deputy special agent in charge.

"Other than Mr. Lowe, only room service has come or gone from the suite since the president entered at 0:20 hours," Daniels said.

"At 0:35 hours the president called for a sandwich, a glass of beer, and some ice cream," Strait said. "A hotel employee brought it on a pushcart at 0:45. The cart had a vase of fresh flowers, the sandwich, beer, and ice cream—vanilla—cloth napkin, and silverware. At 1:32 hours, the president said he was going to shower and then go to bed and asked that the cart be taken away. At 1:44 hours the same employee entered the sitting room here and took the cart away as asked. By then the president had closed the door to the sleeping area. The employee left and no one has come or gone since. That was until Mr. Lowe arrived to see the president at 0:700 hours."

"Well, gentlemen," National Security Adviser James Marshall said icily, "bottom line, 'Crop Duster' has gone missing."

(*CROP DUSTER*—the Secret Service's code name for president Harris.)

"It's impossible," Agent Strait protested in shock and chagrin. "I was right outside his door all night. There are monitored surveillance cameras in every hallway, elevator, and stairwell. We have a dozen agents on the floor with a dozen more stationed at every ingress and egress, not to mention the Spanish Secret Service on the grounds. A mouse couldn't get in undetected."

"Well somehow Crop Duster got out!" Lowe snapped. "Who did it, how it was done, who has him now, and what the hell we tell the rest of the world I haven't the damnedest idea."

"Fuck!" Hap Daniels said loudly and to no one after what had been the longest minutes of his life.

32

Within minutes the entire hotel was under lockdown. A suspected breach of security, hotel and hotel security officials were told, as was the Spanish Secret Service, which, as the host country, was providing the majority of the president's protection. Guests were not allowed in or out of their rooms. Every hallway, closet, room, and possible hiding place was searched. Every employee interrogated, including the room-service waiter who had delivered the president's order at a quarter to one the previous morning.

Yes, he had seen the president, he said. Had been graciously thanked and then left.

"What was he wearing?"

"Dark blue pants and a white dress shirt with no tie."

"You're certain?"

"Yes, sir. You don't forget the president of the United States when you meet him in person in the middle of the night."

"Did you see him when you came back to retrieve the food cart?"

"No, sir. His bedroom door was closed."

"Your food cart is covered with material that goes from the top of the cart to just above the floor."

"Yes, sir. In case we have extra china, utensils, chafing dishes, or the like."

"Is there any way a person could have hidden unseen in that space when you took the cart away?"

"Yes, sir. And no, sir."

"Explain."

"Yes, there is room for someone to hide, if they tucked themselves up. But all I delivered was a sandwich, beverage, and ice cream. I would have noticed the extra weight immediately and checked to see why."

The white dress shirt and dark blue trousers the room-service waiter described matched the white shirt and dark blue suit the president had worn the evening before. His explanation of the extra weight if someone had attempted to hide in the food service cart either on the way into the presidential suite or on the way out of it seemed accurate and correct. His security clearance was verified once again. There was no reason to suspect him of doing anything other than what he had done—delivering room service to a hotel guest.

As the minutes ticked by and the search intensified it became increasingly clear the POTUS was not in the building. At the end of an hour it was confirmed without doubt. Yet no one outside the highest levels of the Secret Service agents present or the men there who comprised the president's closest inner circle knew it.

At 9:20 A.M. those men gathered in a highly secured suite on the Ritz's fourth floor: Jake Lowe, National Security Adviser Dr. James Marshall, Secretary of Defense Terrence Langdon, Chief of Staff Tom Curran, White House Press Secretary Dick Greene, and the president's SAIC Hap Daniels.

The rest—Vice President Hamilton Rogers, Secretary of State David Chaplin, and United States Air Force General Chester Keaton, Chairman of the Joint Chiefs of Staff—were en route back to Washington by private jet and in live communication with the others by secure speaker phone.

"We have to go on the premise of foul play," Hap Daniels told them.

"Yes, of course," Marshall said, and looked to the others. "This is not only a monumental catastrophe, there's protocol here. Our ambassador in Madrid needs to be informed immediately. So do the CIA, the FBI, and probably a dozen other agencies. All we can hope to God is we don't get a tape with him in terrorist custody pleading for his life with some hooded sonofabitch threatening to cut off his head.

"Still, until we learn something, until we see what happens next, we can't afford to have this get out. The world can't think the president of the United States is missing. If that happened God only knows what the hell the financial markets would do and what rumors and power plays would begin and who might try to take advantage of it inside their own countries." Marshall leaned toward the speakerphone. "Mr. Vice President, are you there?"

"Yes, Jim." Vice President Rogers's voice came back clearly.

"You understand what position this puts you in. Until the PO-TUS is found and is safely in our custody, you are put on notice that you may be sworn in as president at any moment."

"I know, Jim, and I take that responsibility gravely."

Jake Lowe crossed the room. "There are a billion questions here," he said. "What's going on? Who's responsible? How did they get in and get out without attracting the attention of any of the Secret Service's rings of security? What power or powers were involved? Which countries do we notify and what do we tell them? Do we set up roadblocks, close down airports? And—how do we do it without the media getting wind of it? As Jim said, we can't have the world thinking the president of the United States has gone missing. We need a cover story and fast. I think this is it." He looked to Hap Daniels. "Tell me if there's a flaw here or why it won't work." He looked to White House press secretary Dick Greene. "You tell me if you can pull it off with the media, or you can't." He looked again to the secure speaker phone. "You still there Mr. Vice President?"

"Yes, Jake."

"Can the others hear me too?"

"We can, Jake." It was the voice of Secretary of State David Chaplin.

"Okay, here we go." Lowe looked to the others. "The hotel's already in an uproar. Everyone knows we feared a serious breach of security. What no one knows is we first got word of that breach, a serious terrorist threat, at three o'clock this morning. At that time we woke the POTUS and took him down a service elevator to the basement garage and then by unmarked car to an undisclosed location. That's where he is now. Safe and unharmed, while our investigation continues," he looked to Dick Greene. "Can you handle that?"

"I think so. At least for a while."

Now he looked to Hap Daniels. "You?"

"Yes, sir. But that still doesn't answer the most urgent question. Where he is and who's got him?"

National Security Adviser Marshall's eyes swung to Daniels. "He was lost on your watch. This has never happened in history. You find him and you bring him home safely. But you keep the doing awful goddamn quiet. You don't and this gets out, the Secret Service is going to look like Little Bo Peep to the whole damn world."

"We will bring him home, sir. You have my word on it. Safely and quietly."

Marshall glanced at Lowe and then back to Hap Daniels, "You damn well better."

33

ROME, LEONARDO DA VINCI AIRPORT, 9:40 A.M.

Nicholas Marten's Air Malta flight from Valletta had landed thirty minutes earlier and now he waited to board an Alitalia flight for the hour-and-forty-five-minute trip to Barcelona, which was Demi Picard's destination when she left Malta.

He'd learned where she'd gone the same way he'd found out where she was staying in the Maltese capital—by bribing the maitre d' at the Café Tripoli for the destination of the taxi he had called for her, Reverend Beck, and the young woman, Cristina—"The British Hotel, Mr. Marten," he'd said quietly.

Marten had done the same with the mustachioed concierge at the British Hotel, approaching him moments after Demi left, telling him Ms. Picard was his fiancée and that they had gotten into a quarrel and she had run off.

"Her mother was supposed to meet us here in Valletta tomorrow. I don't know what I should tell her now; Demi is her only child," he'd lied despondently, playing the kind of game he hadn't played since he'd been a homicide detective in Los Angeles, taking almost any role necessary to get the information he was after. "Do you have any idea where she went?"

"I'm afraid I can't say, sir."

Marten became even more sincere. "She was quite upset, wasn't she?"

"Yes, sir. Especially when she called just after six this morning and asked, or rather demanded, that I do everything in my power to make a hotel reservation for her."

"And did you?"

"Yes, sir."

It was then Marten slipped the concierge a sizable tip and said, "For mother."

The concierge hesitated then leaned forward and quickly scribbled *Hotel Regente Majestic, Barcelona* on a piece of stationery. Folding it, he handed it to Marten. "For mother," he said genuinely. "I understand completely."

Why Demi was going to Barcelona and in such a hurry after everyone in Malta had seemingly abandoned her, or at least left the island, was anyone's guess. No matter what had happened between her and Reverend Beck, she was clearly connected to him, as, it seemed was Merriman Foxx. Once again he thought how curious it was for an African-American minister to be a long-time friend of an apartheid-era officer in the South African army who had headed a medical unit attempting to develop secret biological weapons designed to wipe out the black African population.

There was also something else. Something Marten hadn't really thought much about until he'd come upon Beck at Merriman Foxx's table at the Café Tripoli—that it had been the reverend who called Dr. Stephenson for medical assistance when Caroline had broken down after the funerals of her son and husband, and that it had been Stephenson who administered whatever it had been that had started Caroline's rapid spiral into death. Beck to Stephenson to Foxx, the *doctor/white-haired man*, with *his long, hideous, fingers and that horrid thumb with its tiny balled cross.* Those things taken together made Reverend Beck nearly as interesting as Dr. Foxx himself, and Marten hoped that by following Ms. Picard to Barcelona he would find either or both.

Marten heard his Alitalia flight called for boarding. Carry-on bag with his electronic notebook inside over his shoulder, he started for the gate. As he did, he noticed a slightly built young man in line several passengers behind him. He looked to be in his early twenties and was wearing jeans and a baggy jacket over some kind of campy T-shirt. A student maybe, or a young artist or musician, who knew? The trouble was he had seen him before. In the lobby of Castille Hotel in Valletta as he checked out, and then again on his flight from Valletta to Rome. And now here he was boarding the same flight to Barcelona. There was no reason to suspect that it was anything more than coincidence. Except that he did, and it made him uneasy. It was almost as if the young man had the name *Merriman Foxx* written on his forehead.

34

MADRID, 11:00 A.M.

It was now four hours since Jake Lowe discovered the president was missing. In the United States every top-security federal agency was clandestinely in overdrive, among them the Secret Service, the CIA, the FBI, the NSA, and every branch of military intelligence. Vice President Hamilton Rogers had personally informed the prime minister of Spain and the U.S. ambassador to Spain. It was thought at first he should also inform the U.S. ambassadors worldwide and in turn, the presidents of Russia, China, Japan, France, and Italy, the chancellor of Germany, and the prime minister of Great Britain, but that idea was stopped in its tracks by Jake Lowe.

This was and had to remain an absolute "need-to-know" circumstance, Lowe said. What had happened had taken place only a short while earlier, meaning there was every chance the president was still somewhere close by and could be found quickly and brought to safety in secret. The more people who knew what had happened, the greater the risk of a security breach. If that happened it would only be a heartbeat before the world knew the president was missing. What would follow—he elaborated on Dr. Marshall's earlier worries—would be a sudden perceived imbalance of global power, followed in turn by sharply escalated national security fears, America's as much or more than any other. In rapid succession those fears would morph into raised military tensions and a massive upheaval in the international stock markets, and after that God only knew what else, the possibilities were endless. Such was the power of the office of the president of the United States and accordingly, the person who occupied it, which made it imperative to keep "the need to know" to as few people as possible.

In Madrid and under the order of the Spanish prime minister, the CNI, Centro Nacional de Inteligencia, the Spanish secret intelligence service, was coordinating a top-secret manhunt that included all points of exit from Madrid—airports, railway and bus stations, and major highways, as well as heightened electronic surveillance of communications between known radical political and terrorist organizations operating in Spain, including the Basque separatist group, ETA.

At the Hotel Ritz, Hap Daniels and Secret Service video experts huddled in the Secret Service mobile command post in the building's underground garage examining digital video recordings taken by the scores of surveillance cameras mounted in and around the hotel: the fourth floor presidential suite, the hallways, elevators and staircases nearby, those in the hotel's underground garage, its entryway and public rooms, and those mounted on the roof that gave a 360-degree view of the building's grounds.

On the hotel's fourth floor, Secret Service technical experts were going over the presidential suite itself, treating it as what they believed it was, a crime scene.

On the fourth floor too, and inside the same secure room they had gathered in earlier, National Security Adviser Dr. James Marshall, faced a somber foursome of Jake Lowe, Secretary of Defense Terrence Langdon, White House Chief of Staff Tom Curran, and the president's close friend, Madrid resident Evan Byrd. What Marshall had to say was something that at one point or other had crossed all of their minds.

"What if the president is not a victim of foul play? What if he's not been kidnapped at all but somehow found a way to beat security and get out on his own? If that was his answer to our demand that he authorize the assassinations of the president of France and the chancellor of Germany?"

"How could he beat the Secret Service's impossibly complex circles of security?" Tom Curran dismissed the idea, at least out loud, as if somehow the idea of one man doing it alone were impossible. "And even if he did, how could he defeat Spanish security outside?"

"Tom, assume to hell he did." Marshall was angry. "Assume it was his idea and he got out. How doesn't make any difference except to show that he's smart as hell. What we've got here is a potential disaster. He knows what we requested of him. He knows who was there. The question is what is he going to do with that information? Until we bring him down, we're hanging in the wind, all of us."

"I think, Jim—" Jake Lowe crossed to the window, then turned around to face them. "There's nothing he can do."

"What the hell does that mean?" Marshall snapped. "He's the president of the United States, he can damn near do anything he wants."

"Except tell the truth about this," Lowe looked from Marshall to the others. "What's he going to do, burst into a TV station and say, 'Put me on the air I've got an important announcement to make? Every one of my top advisers, including the vice president, the secretary of defense, the national security adviser, and the chairman of the Joint Chiefs has demanded I authorize the assassination of the leaders of France and Germany'?

"The first thing they'd do is put him in a room and call a doctor, followed by the Spanish police and the U.S. embassy. They'd think he'd gone off his rocker. Hap Daniels would have him back here in no time. And the more he protested the crazier he would seem.

"More than that, if he has done this on his own, it means he doesn't think he can trust anyone. He's in office because we put him there. Everyone he knows, we know, and then some. He'll be very aware of that. Furthermore, he wouldn't have run if it wasn't a last resort, if he wasn't afraid that if he didn't do what we asked we'd kill him and Vice President Rogers would become president. A president whose first act would be to authorize the assassinations. And he'd be right about that, we would kill him. And we will kill him now as soon as he's brought back to us.

"He may be a conservative, gentlemen, but he's far too independent for us. It's our fault we didn't see it from the beginning. But we didn't and now he's out there, a time bomb if he can find a way to expose us. On the other hand there's not a lot he can do. He can't use electronic communications, because he'll know that all cell-phone, BlackBerry, and 'hardline' traffic, voice or text, is being monitored for electronic intercept by every security agency in our arsenal and Spain's. He tries to call anywhere, his location will be pinpointed before he gets ten seconds into his conversation. That communication will immediately be shut down in the event he's being made to do it against his will, and Spanish intel or our guys will pick him up in minutes if not seconds.

"So with no electronic communication. That means he's on the streets looking for a place to hide until he can figure out what to do. Next to maybe a couple of rock or movie stars, his is the most recognizable face on the planet. Where the hell does he think he can go that someone won't recognize him and shout about it one way or another? When that happens, the police and Spanish intelligence will show up in a heartbeat. They'll get him out of sight fast and call us. Then Hap and Jim and I will go to collect him. No matter what he says, within the hour he'll be back here, with everyone believing the death of his wife, the pressure of the campaign, of the office, of the whole thing here, finally just got to him and he lost it. He'll be examined by the medical staff who will recommend a little R and R, a breather in the countryside before Monday's NATO meeting in Warsaw. That's where he will be taken, and then taken care of. A heart attack or something. A sad and tragic ending to a proud and extremely promising presidency."

"All well and good," President Harris's close friend Evan Byrd said. "But what if this is not his own doing? What if he *is* a victim of some terrible foul play?"

"Then we hope and pray for the very best, don't we?" Lowe said evenly. "But don't count on it, Evan. If you'd seen him on *Air Force One* when he turned us down, you'd know what I meant. No, this is his show and he's going to try to crush us. How, I don't know, but he's going to try. We just have to tighten the screws and make sure we get him first."

35

"Good morning, Victor."

"I was wondering when you were going to call, Richard."

Victor paced up and down in his underwear, his cell phone to his ear, his room curtains drawn against the brightness of midday. What was left of his room-service breakfast, coffee, cereal, ham and eggs and toast rested on a tray near the door. The TV was on in silence, tuned to a cartoon channel.

"You don't worry about that, do you? I always call when I say I will. Maybe sometimes a little bit later than you'd like, but I always do call, don't I, Victor?"

"Yes, Richard, you do."

"Did you go to the Hotel Ritz last night as I asked?"

"Yes, of course. I ordered a drink in the lounge just as you said and then took the elevator to the second floor with some other guests. Afterward I went up to the third floor, alone. You asked me to try and get to the fourth floor, where the president was staying. The elevator was blocked from going past the third floor, and the stairs to the fourth were controlled by what seemed to be security people. When they asked what I was doing I said I was just walking around while I was waiting for a friend to meet me for a drink. They said I couldn't go upstairs and so I thanked them politely and left. Then I went down and finished my drink as you instructed and went back to my hotel. That's where I am now."

"The security people did see you."

"Oh yes. But there was no trouble about it."

"Good, Victor. Very good." Richard paused. "I have another assignment for you."

"What is it, Richard?"

"I want you to go to France, to a race track outside of Paris."

"Alright."

"Pack now and go down to the desk and check out. When you do an envelope will be waiting. Inside will be an airline ticket to Paris and instructions on what to do when you get there."

"Is the ticket first-class?"

"Of course, Victor."

"And you want me to go now?"

"Yes, Victor. As soon as we hang up."

"Alright, Richard."

"Thank you, Victor."

"No, Richard, thank you."

11:45 A.M.

A tall, slim, balding man wearing glasses and dressed in a black sweater, blue jeans, and running shoes sat at a back table in a small café in the center of Madrid's old city, a mile or more from the Hotel Ritz. He sipped strong coffee and watched people begin to filter in for lunch. That he spoke Spanish fluently helped because it made him seem more at ease and less foreign than he was. So far, as had been the case throughout the morning as he had walked the streets trying to get his bearings, not one person had given him as much as a second glance. Hopefully it would remain that way and no one would realize that the lone man sitting among them was John Henry Harris, the president of the United States.

Growing up, Johnny Harris had heard his late father's double-barreled admonition often enough. The first part was, "Always think on your feet and never be afraid to act if the need arises." Part two followed immediately: "And just because things seem comfortable don't think things can't change in a hurry because they not only can, they usually will."

If that constant, often grating homily had helped prepare him to take action against the cruel and sudden turn of events here in Madrid, two other pieces of his education had helped almost as well. First, as a young man he had worked on farms and ranches in his hometown of Salinas, California, where he learned to speak Spanish to the point where he shifted easily and comfortably between it and English and where he had a hand in almost everything, including the flying of crop dusters, hence his Secret Service code name. Second, as an adjunct to farming he had been a carpenter and later a building contractor, working primarily in the renovation of older commercial buildings in Salinas and then farther north in San Jose. In result, he was familiar with the nuts and bolts of construction: structural and mechanical requirements; electrical, plumbing, heating, and air-conditioning; and the use of space as it applied to function and design. Older buildings took special care, especially when it came to incorporating central heating and air-conditioning systems into the original architecture and fitting them into spaces not initially designed for them. The Ritz Madrid had opened in 1910. Since then it had been renovated any number of times. When the current heating and air-conditioning system had been added he didn't know. What he did know was that the Ritz was a large hotel, which meant the ducting for central heating and air-conditioning would be substantial—the main ducts themselves might well be four to six feet square, with side ducts probably in the neighborhood of two by three feet. The side ducts would be concealed in drop ceilings in the hallways and in certain individual areas of the guest rooms. The main shafts would, or should, have built-in ladders to access the interior of the system from basement to roof.

He knew the Secret Service advance team would have checked those shafts and made certain they were secure long before the presidential party arrived. It meant they would be locked at the specific points of entry; the access panels on the roof and in the basement. What they would have had no reason to consider was that at both roof and basement those same access panels would have internal safety latches to prevent anyone from becoming trapped inside. Meaning the panels could be opened from the inside and would lock again automatically once someone had come out. Considering any commercial building's need for usable space—and the Ritz, as an old renovated building, would be no different—it was more than probable that the bottom of the air ducts would be incorporated into already existent areas of the basement, a storage area or furnace room, perhaps even the laundry.

It was this knowledge and this assumption that Johnny Harris had counted on to make his escape. It had taken nearly two hours and been considerably more difficult than he had expected. The side ducts had been smaller than he'd anticipated and he'd made a number of turns that led to dead ends that had to be retraced backwards in the dark. He'd used up several books of matches lighting his way and was beginning to think he might be trapped in there forever until he finally found a main duct and started down.

Several knuckles and a part of shin had been scraped raw, and every bit of him was strained and sore from the sheer physical effort, but nonetheless his main sense of it had been right and it had worked—the principal air shaft opened through an access panel into a large supply room in the building's cellar. Once out, the panel had automatically locked closed behind him, and he'd walked down a short, dimly-lit hallway to an area near the loading ramp, where he'd hidden behind a large walk-in freezer until a produce truck arrived at a little after three in the morning. He'd watched carefully, biding his time as two men unloaded it. Then, when they went to the truck's cab to sign the delivery manifest, he slipped into the back and hid behind a stack of lettuce crates until the driver got in and drove off, passing both his own Secret Service agents and Spanish security posted outside. The next delivery stop was another hotel several blocks away. Here he waited until the driver had gone inside, then simply jumped down and walked off in the darkness.

Now, with the time closing on noon, he sat, still unrecognized, sipping coffee in the small old-town café, his wallet in his back pocket—a wallet that held his California driver's license, personal credit cards, and nearly a thousand euros in cash, and minus the toupee no one except his personal barber had any idea he wore—fully aware of the chaos that would have exploded once it had been discovered he was missing and trying to decide how best to get from where he was to where he was going without someone recognizing him and sounding the alarm.

36

The entire fourth floor was a screaming beehive as Hap Daniels had known it would be. White House press secretary Dick Greene was about to make a special statement to the crush of world media who had swarmed the building, adding chaos to the throng of reporters in the White House press pool already following the president on his European tour. Word had been leaked that the president was no longer in Madrid, that he had secretly been taken to an undisclosed location in the middle of the night after a credible terrorist threat was intercepted by Spanish intelligence. As the Secret Service senior official supervising the investigation, Daniels had already been in contact with George Kellner, CIA chief of station Madrid, and Emilio Vasquez, the head of Spanish intelligence, setting up a joint task force that would coordinate their own bureaus with Spanish law enforcement authorities in an all-out, full-blown search for the president; one that would be designated a national security operation, meaning TOP SECRET on every level. Immediately afterward Daniels had been on a secure phone to the special agent in charge of the Secret Service field office at the U.S. embassy in Paris, asking that the Paris office go on full standby alert in the event additional bodies were needed in Madrid. Soon to be added to the chaotic stew was Ted Langway, an assistant director of the Secret Service at USSS headquarters in Washington, who was already en route to Madrid to liaison with Daniels and then to set up a twenty-four-hour communication with the director of the Secret Service in Washington who would in turn advise the secretary of U.S. Department of Homeland Security, under which the Secret Service now operated.

And then there was the rest, the trail that led Hap to the air-conditioning access panel in the drop ceiling of the presidential suite's bathroom.

A painstaking review of digital videos made by the roof-mounted security cameras showed a produce truck arriving at the hotel at 03:02 hours. It had been stopped and searched by Secret Service agents and then cleared to enter the hotel. Security cameras in the hotel's underground parking area showed the same truck coming down a ramp and stopping at a loading dock at 03:08 hours (eight minutes past three that morning).

A hotel worker and the truck driver unloaded several cartons of produce and then went to the front of the truck, where the hotel worker signed the delivery manifest. In that moment a vague shadowlike movement was seen near the rear of the truck. It began near the top of the screen, coming from the area of a walk-in freezer, then approached the rear of the truck and went out of view. A moment later the hotel worker stepped away from the truck, and the driver got in and drove away. Security cameras outside the building caught the vehicle as it left the building, turned onto a side street, and disappeared from view.

"Somebody got into the truck while the hotel worker went to talk to the driver. Whoever it was was still in the truck when it left," Hap Daniels had barked in response to what he saw. The vehicle's driver had since been taken into custody by the CNI and had given them the location of his delivery stops immediately after he had left the Ritz.

Meantime, the Secret Service and hotel officials had traced the phantom's progress backward from the truck across to a large walk-in freezer, then to the dimly lit hallway behind it, searching every room and corridor that led from it. Within minutes they'd found a large closed storage area and inside it a main heating and air-conditioning shaft that led to the roof, with side ducting leading to every room on every floor of the building. That the access door to the shaft was locked and had been checked and verified secure by the advance Secret Service team and then checked and verified once again just before the president arrived seemed to rule out the possibility that anyone had gone in that way—using the shafts to get to the presidential suite and kidnap the president and take him back out the same way—especially when the video cameras had caught a lone shadow entering the truck.

In one moment everyone realized the same thing: their entire approach had been designed to prevent someone from getting *into the hotel without being seen,* not someone trying to get *out of it:* especially someone who had full knowledge of the concentric blankets of security the Secret Service used—someone like the president himself. Moreover, it appeared he had done it with forethought and purpose. An inventory of the clothes the president's valet packed when they left Washington revealed what was missing—a pair of underwear, athletic socks, running shoes, a black sweater and blue jeans. The clothes the president liked to relax in when his official day was over. His wallet was gone as well. Exactly how much money he might have had in it no one seemed to know for certain, but his personal secretary confirmed she had given him a thousand euros before he left the White House for the European trip. Carrying a fair amount of cash wherever he went was a habit that dated back to President Harris's farm days, when he paid cash for almost everything.

As for his use of the hotel's ventilation ducts to avoid Secret Service surveillance, hotel maintenance people had demonstrated how the access panels to the main ducting system could be opened from the inside, and that those same panels would automatically relock once whoever had been inside came out and the panel had been closed behind them. Moreover there were built-in footholds that ran from roof to basement in the main shafts, and the side ducts leading to the guest and public rooms were wide enough room for a man to squeeze through.

As skeptical as Hap Daniels might have been at the start that the president had acted alone and used the ducting system as a means to make his escape from the hotel, the clincher came when the remains of several recently burned wooden matches were found at the bottom of the shaft that opened into the storage area. The president's friend, Evan Byrd, was a pipe smoker and had little collections of small decorative boxes of wooden matches near ashtrays throughout his home. Daniels had seen President Harris pick up several of those boxes as they left Byrd's residence the night before and put them in his pocket. The president didn't smoke and as far as Daniels knew, never had, so what he'd wanted the matches for had been anyone's guess. Now he understood. They had been to light his way through the hotel's ducting system without having to turn on the system's interior lights and thereby take the chance he might trip some kind of alarm.

"Hap?" Jake Lowe's voice came at him from the other room.
"In here."

A moment later Lowe and National Security Adviser Marshall entered the presidential suite's bathroom, where Daniels and two other Secret Service agents were examining an open access panel in the bathroom's drop ceiling.

"This is where he went out," Hap was looking up into the duct area where a third Secret Service agent could be heard moving around in the duct work.

"Anything?" Daniels called up.

"Yeah," the agent's head suddenly appeared in the open rectangle. "For one thing, the maintenance guys were right. You get up here and slide the panel closed behind you. A simple turn of a bolt will relock it. Nobody would know anyone ever used it."

"How did he get it open from down here? It takes a special key."

"You want it, you got it. Catch." The agent dropped a twisted piece of steel into Daniels's hand. "It's a spoon. Bent to operate like a key. Crude, but it works. I tried it."

Lowe stared at the spoon and then looked to Jim Marshall. "Room service. A sandwich. A beer. Ice cream. You need a spoon to eat ice cream. He knew what he was going to do all along." Abruptly he turned to Daniels. "Let's go talk."

37

12:00 P.M.

Sixty seconds later Lowe, Jim Marshall, and Hap Daniels entered the secure room they had used earlier. Lowe closed the door behind them.

"I think by now we can presume the president did this on his own," Lowe looked at Daniels. "You agree?"

"Yes, sir, I agree. The question is why?"

Lowe and Marshall exchanged the briefest glance, then Lowe walked across the room. "Obviously none of us has that answer," he said. "But my sense is that too much has happened too quickly for him. To the point he was pushed to sheer psychological exhaustion. I'm no psychologist, but this trip, the way it's been going, France and Germany in particular, and coming so soon on the heels of a long and enormously draining election campaign, followed almost point-blank by the inauguration, fine-tuning the cabinet and what's going on in the Middle East, has been, strong as he is, exceedingly trying, as it would be for anybody. I know because we've had private conversations about it. He even asked me once if I thought he was really suited for the job. Add the thing he doesn't talk about but that I know still haunts him, the death of his wife—think of him winning the election and then spending his first Christmas in thirty-three years without her and alone in the White House to boot. On top of that we all know how close he was to Mike and Caroline Parsons and their son.

"Maybe if he was the kind of guy to complain or get testy or even get drunk once in a while it would be different, but he isn't. Put it all together and you've got a man who's kept it all inside and is emotionally spent. All of sudden it catches up with him and he does something crazy, just to keep from suffocating.

"The story Dick Greene is telling the media downstairs—that the Secret Service hustled him away in the middle of the night to an undisclosed location following a credible terrorist threat we can't talk about—is the one we'll continue to use even when we get him back. That way he gets enough time for a full medical exam and then, assuming he's alright, to rest and recover before he goes to the NATO meeting in Warsaw." Lowe came back across the room. Before, he had been talking to them both; now he was looking directly at Hap Daniels.

"We know what he was wearing when he went out and the places where the delivery truck stopped after it left the hotel. He's on his own, maybe even disoriented. It's not like he can walk around like a tourist without being recognized. With your people, the CIA, Spanish intelligence, and Madrid law enforcement working together, my guess is he's not going to stay missing for very long."

Daniels said nothing. He just hoped to hell Lowe was right.

"Chief of staff is arranging for a place to take him once we have him. It's up to us—Jim, myself, chief of staff, Press Secretary

Greene here in Madrid and the vice president and secretary of state in Washington—to dance with other governments and the media until we can bring him public again. It's up to you to find him and get him the hell out of here fast and unseen to the marker location. You guys got President Bush secretly to Iraq twice, the first time nobody even knew he was gone until he was back home in Texas." Lowe paused and his eyes narrowed, "Hap we need, we *have to have,* that same efficiency here. The situation is infinitely more critical."

"I understand, sir. This happened on our watch. We'll take care of it."

"I know you will, Hap," Lowe looked at Marshall then walked Daniels to the door and opened it. "Good luck to us all," he said, and Special Agent Hap Daniels left. Lowe closed the door and came back into the room. "He buy it?"

"That the president went off the deep end?"

"Yes."

"I don't think he had any choice. His feathers are really ruffled. The president is gone, it happened while he was in charge and he feels personally responsible. He's not just protecting the man, he's protecting the office. He wants exactly what we want, the president back as quickly and with as little noise as possible. As if he'd never left."

Lowe walked to a mahogany sideboard, turned over two glasses and picked up a bottle of whiskey. He poured a double shot into each glass and handed one to Marshall.

"It seems we have a president who has decided he wants to be his own man and who has very definite ideas of how he wants the country run," Lowe took a stiff tug at his drink. "In all the years I've known him I never had the slightest clue he wasn't a team player all the way. Until now."

Marshall took a drink then set his glass on a table next to him. "It's humbling lesson, Jake. One that's going to cost the president his life. Let's just hope to hell it doesn't get that expensive for us."

38

Nicholas Marten heard the grind of hydraulics as the aircraft's land-ing gear came down. Ten minutes later he was on the ground at Barcelona's El Prat Airport and heading into the terminal. Twenty minutes after that he had collected his luggage and was in line to board the Aerobus for the twenty-five-minute trip into the city, his thoughts—only moments earlier on Merriman Foxx and Demi Picard and the brief phone conversation he'd had with Peter Fadden while waiting to board his flight in Malta—had now shifted to a man three passengers in line behind him. He was about five-foot ten, Caucasian, and maybe forty, with salt and pepper hair. He wore sunglasses and a light yellow polo shirt tucked into blue jeans; a small red traveling bag was thrown indifferently over his left shoulder. He looked like a tourist, one accustomed to traveling casually and lightly. There was nothing about him to attract attention, and Marten probably wouldn't have noticed him at all if he had not seen him nod in passing at the young man in jeans and baggy jacket who had been in the lobby of his hotel in Valletta and then on the flights from Valletta to Rome and Rome to Barcelona. And now that young man was no longer there but this other man was, waiting in line behind him to board the blue Aer-obus into Barcelona. If the first man had indeed followed him from Valletta, then there was every possibility this second man was now tailing him. In essence, one had handed him off to the other.

12:30 P.M.

That second man was now two seats in front of him and on the other side of the bus looking out the window as they turned out of the airport for the drive into the city. Marten watched him for a long moment and then sat back and tried to relax.

Today was Friday, April 7. The day before yesterday the Washington, D.C., Metro Police had escorted him from Caroline's memorial service and put him on a plane to London, where he'd arrived the next day, yesterday, and soon afterward boarded another flight to Malta. Then this morning, following last evening's encounter with Merriman Foxx, he'd hurriedly left the island following Demi Picard to Barcelona. He was jet-lagged, had had very little sleep, and was running on little more than adrenaline. He knew he had to be aware of his own state of mind. In situations like this it was easy to make monsters out of what in reality were only furry little animals. Meaning there was every chance he was wrong about the salt and pepper-haired man in the dark glasses and yellow polo shirt, and that the nod that had taken place between him the baggy-jacketed young man might well have been nothing at all, and in truth that neither man had any design on him whatsoever. So he let it go and thought back to the telephone conversation he'd had earlier with Peter Fadden, reaching him in London shortly after the *Washington Post* reporter arrived on a stop over on the way to cover the upcoming NATO summit in Warsaw.

Marten had quickly briefed him on his encounter with Merriman Foxx at the Café Tripoli the night before, telling him how he had played himself off as an aide to subcommittee chairwoman Baker and how Foxx's initial congeniality had quickly become heated over Marten's questions about the testing of experimental toxins on humans after South Africa's biological weapons had been officially destroyed. He'd become even more heated when Marten told him the made-up story about a memo Congressman Mike Parsons left shortly before his death in a plane crash suggesting that Foxx had consulted in secret with Dr. Lorraine Stephenson, over the course of the committee hearings. Adding separately, that Parsons had questioned the truthfulness of Foxx's testimony. Foxx's reaction, Marten said, had been to fiercely defend his testimony and to deny knowing Dr. Stephenson, after which he'd abruptly ended the conversation and walked off.

Finally he told Fadden about Caroline's fearful description of the *"white-haired man with the long hideous fingers and that horrid thumb with its tiny balled cross"* who had examined her at the clinic where she had been taken following her breakdown after the funerals of her husband and son.

"Peter," Marten had said emphatically, "Foxx not only has white hair, he has extraordinarily long fingers and that same tattoo on his thumb. I can tell you he *was* involved both with Dr. Stephenson and with Caroline's death. One more thing—when I met him he was having dinner with congressional chaplain Rufus Beck."

"Beck?" Fadden had been wholly surprised.

"They weren't trying to hide it either. At least not tucked away the way they were in a café in Malta and thinking Foxx was meeting with a representative of Congresswoman Baker."

"I don't get it," Fadden said.

"I don't either. Reverend Beck and Dr. Foxx should be like oil and water."

"Yet they're both comfortable enough to be around someone they think works for the chairwoman of the subcommittee Foxx was testifying in front of."

"Not just testifying, Peter. Testifying in a classified investigation."

Marten finished with the rest: that the French photojournalist Demi Picard had been with Foxx and Reverend Beck at the Café Tripoli and had privately warned Marten to "stay away" before he "ruined everything"; and that early this morning Foxx and Reverend Beck had left Malta for places unknown and that Demi had left soon afterward, going to Barcelona with a reservation at the Hotel Regente Majestic, which was where Marten was headed now.

"Peter," he'd said emphatically as his flight was called for boarding, "try to find the name of the clinic where Caroline Parsons was taken after Dr. Stephenson gave her the injection and before she was transferred to George Washington University Hospital. She had to have been there for several days. There has to be some record of it and of who treated her and for what."

Marten felt the Aerobus slow and he looked up. The man with the dark glasses and light yellow polo shirt was watching him. Caught, he smiled casually, then turned away to look out the window. Several minutes later the bus made its first stop at Plaça Espanya. Four passengers got off, three got on, and the bus moved off. Then they stopped at Gran Via/Comte d'Urgell, and again at Plaça Universitat where three more passengers collected their luggage and got off. Marten watched carefully, hoping his man in the yellow shirt and salt-and-pepper hair would stand and get off with them. He didn't and the bus continued on.

The next stop, Plaça Catalunya, within walking distance of the Hotel Regente Majestic, was his. The bus pulled to the curb and Marten stood with a half dozen others. Gathering his traveling bag, he moved toward the front of the bus, glancing at his man as he did. The man stayed where he was, sitting back, his hands in his lap, waiting for the bus to go on. Marten was the last off. He stepped around several people waiting to get on and walked off looking for the street called Rambla de Catalunya and the Hotel Regente Majestic. A moment later the Aerobus passed him, moving away in traffic. He walked on a moment longer, then something made him turn and look back. The man with salt-and-pepper hair and the yellow polo shirt was standing at the bus stop staring after him.

39

MADRID, ATOCHA STATION, 1:05 P.M.

A folded copy of the Spanish language newspaper *El Pais* under his arm, President of the United States John Henry Harris walked down a platform in a group of passengers toward the Altaria train number 1138 that would take him on a five-hour trip northeast to Barcelona. There he would transfer to the *Catalunya Express* for the hour-plus ride to the one-time Moorish stronghold city of Gerona.

Everything had been thought through the night before on the ride back to the hotel from Evan Byrd's home following his surprise meeting with "his friends," as he called them. Right off, there had been no doubt that if he refused their demands, they would kill him. It meant he had no choice but to run. And he had. Freeing himself from his Secret Service protection and escaping the hotel had been difficult enough. Carrying out the next piece of action was something else entirely.

Included in his European agenda had been time set aside to address the annual conference of The New World Institute, a think tank of celebrated international business, academic, and former political leaders who met annually for the express purpose of exploring the future of the world community.

An institution for more than two hundred years, the NWI had met in various exotic locations around the globe for most of the last century, but for the last twenty-two years it had made its home the exclusive resort called Aragon in the mountains outside of Barcelona. As the newly elected President of the United States he had been invited to be this year's "surprise guest speaker" and give the main address at its Sunday sunrise service. It was something he had agreed to when prevailed upon by the host clergyman, Rabbi David Aznar, a cousin of his late wife and a highly respected leader in the Spanish city of Gerona's large Jewish community.

That his wife had been Jewish was thought at first to be a political liability to him, but it had proven otherwise. She had been a funny, brilliant, outspoken, and extraordinary life's companion who the public had adored. That she had been unable to bear children was a sadness they both accepted, but as he climbed the political ladder, they found themselves embraced as if the entire electorate were their family. There were nonstop invitations to spend holidays or other special occasions at the homes of private citizens across a broad economic, racial, and religious range, and often they accepted. The media loved it, the people loved it, his political machinery loved it, and he and his wife loved it.

It was through her the president had come to know Rabbi David, and the two had become close when the rabbi had traveled several times from Spain to Washington to be with them during his wife's illness and rapid decline. He had been there when she died and had officiated at her funeral; had been there to embrace him on election night; had been a personal guest at his inauguration; and then had invited him to be the surprise speaker at the convention at Aragon. It was to Rabbi David's home in Gerona he was going now, the only person within physical reach he dared trust and confide in, and the only place he knew, for the moment anyway, he could hide.

Head down, he reached the train and boarded a second-class car in a crowd of other passengers in the same unassuming way he had conducted himself inside the station, when he'd waited patiently in line to pay cash for his ticket. The same way he had all along. On the streets of Madrid and in the café where he'd taken refuge before coming to the station—trying to blend in, not attract attention. So far his luck had held; no one had paid him the slightest notice.

So far.

He knew that by now Hap Daniels would have Spanish intelligence, the FBI and CIA, and probably a half-dozen other security agencies working frantically to bring him back under Secret Service control. He was equally certain that the NSA, would be using satellites to electronically monitor communications across the whole of Spain. It was the reason he'd left his communications equipment behind—his cell phone, his BlackBerry— because he knew any contact he tried to initiate would be intercepted in seconds, and they'd be on him before he could go a half block.

Scant hours earlier he'd been the most powerful, protected man on the planet, with every agency and state-of-the-art piece of technology at his fingertips. Now he was a man alone, stripped to nothing but his guile and wits, and charged with the task of stopping the first genuine attempted coup d'état that he knew of in the history of the United States.

Not just stopping it but crushing it. Whatever *it* was. Assassinating the leaders of France and Germany and replacing them with leaders they could trust to do their bidding in the United Nations, was only the beginning. Part two was putting the Middle East under their control and in the process crushing the Muslim states that comprised it. How they would do that was the real horror: the unknown plan for what had to be a campaign of mass destruction, which he was certain had been devised and developed by the former South African army scientist Merriman Foxx. It was a nightmare beyond anything imaginable.

Uneasy lies the head that wears a crown.
Henry IV, Part 2

1:22 P.M.

There was a lurch and the train moved slowly out of Atocha Station. The car he had chosen was nearly full when he'd boarded and he'd taken the first available seat on the aisle, next to a man about his age in a leather jacket wearing a beret and reading a magazine. In a show of normalcy he unfolded his newspaper and began to read it. At the same time he tried to stay aware of what was going on around him, alert for anyone—young, old, man, woman—who could be a member of the security forces trying to find him.

The one thing he had known from the start was that when the Secret Service realized he was gone not only would a massive and very clandestine manhunt have begun in the search for him, they would also have gone over every inch of the presidential suite trying to put together what had happened. Among those they would call in would be his valet, who would have done an immediate inventory of his clothing and determine that he had worn a black sweater, blue jeans, and running shoes when he left. Those clothes were now in a trash can in a back alley of Madrid's old town and had been replaced by a pair of khaki pants, a blue sport shirt, an inexpensive brown jacket, and brown walking shoes. All paid for with cash and purchased at an El Corte d'Inglés department store. Added to that were the pair of cheap reading glasses bought at a shop near the railway station, and the thing he was certain was helping most of all—he had removed his hairpiece. Hap Daniels and everyone else would be looking for the POTUS as they knew him, not the balding, eyeglass-wearing, Spanish-speaking public school administrator or minor civil servant he appeared to be, one carrying a Spanish language newspaper and riding tourist class on the train to Barcelona.

40

"Do you know if Ms. Picard has arrived?" Nicholas Marten smiled at the attractive female clerk at the front desk. "My name is Marten. I'm with *The Washington Post*. We were told to check in here for room assignments."

"I'm sorry," she smiled. "I don't understand."

"We're in Barcelona for the Newspaper Writers and Photographers conference. Her name is Picard. P-I-C-A-R-D. First name, Demi."

"One moment," the woman's fingers danced on her computer keyboard. "Yes, Ms. Picard checked in about noon," she said without looking up. "You said your name was—"

"Marten. With an 'e'. Nicholas Marten."

"I don't seem to have a reservation for you, Mr. Marten. Is there any other name it might be under?"

"I—" Marten hesitated; she'd given him an opening he would be foolish not to use. "I was to have been registered with the small group that included Ms. Picard and Reverend Rufus Beck from Washington, D.C. Reverend Beck has checked in too hasn't he?"

Again the woman's fingers worked the keyboard. "Reverend Beck has a reservation but has not yet arrived."

Marten was right, Demi had followed Beck here. "And you say you have no reservation for me?" he asked with all sincerity.

"No, sir."

"I was afraid something like this would happen. Never trust a new secretary to do your own work," Marten looked off, as if trying to decide what to do next, then looked back. "Do you have a room? Anything will do," he smiled, "Please, it's been a very long day already."

She looked at him sympathetically. "Let me see what I can find."

Room 3117 was small but with a view of the street below and Marten stood at the edge of the window looking down at it. He hadn't liked using his own name to check in, but he had hardly come prepared with an alias or false documents, so he'd had no choice.

Still, he was reasonably certain he'd lost his salt-and-pepper-haired, yellow-polo-shirted tail—and he was sure the man had been tailing him. He'd followed him at a distance the first five blocks Marten had walked after leaving the Aerobus stop at Plaça Catalunya. Then Marten had deliberately entered a tapas bar on Pelai Street, where he'd had a light lunch and lingered for nearly an hour. Then, playing the tourist and taking his time, he left and walked toward the Plaça de la Universitat, stopping to browse in a bookstore, then a shoe store, and then spending a solid thirty minutes exploring a huge Zara department store before going out a side exit and making his way to the hotel on Rambla de Catalunya. In none of those places had he seen Salt and Pepper.

Who he was or who the baggy-jacketed man who had followed him from Valletta was, he had no idea, except that it had begun in Malta, where the main attraction had been Merriman Foxx. Assuming Foxx had finally done his homework and found Marten had no connection whatsoever to Congresswoman Baker then his displeasure would be greater now than it had been at the Café Tripoli the night before. He would want to know who Marten was and what else he knew and why he was doing what he was, and if he reported to someone. And once he learned enough to satisfy him, Marten could almost certainly be assured the South African would find a way to permanently put an end to his curiosity.

Marten watched a moment longer then turned from the window and started back across the room. As he did, his cell phone rang. Immediately he clicked on, hoping it was Peter Fadden with information about the Washington, D.C., clinic where Caroline had been taken. Instead he heard the familiar voice of Ian Graff, his supervisor at Fitzsimmons and Justice. Marten loved his work and his employers and he liked Graff a great deal. But he needed none of it now.

"Ian," he said, surprised, trying to be pleasant. "Hello."

"Marten, where the hell are you?"

The rotund, widely read, highly educated Graff, normally pleasant and easygoing, became difficult and quick-tempered under pressure. And Marten knew all too well the ever-increasing pressure to finalize the plans for the large and costly Banfield country estate project they were working on.

"I'm in—" there was no point in lying, "Barcelona."

"Barcelona? We tried your hotel in Washington. They said you'd checked out. We assumed you were on your way back here."

"I'm sorry, I should have called."

"Yes, you should have. You should also be at your desk right now."

"I apologize, but this is something very important."

"So is the Banfield project, if you understand what I'm saying."

"I understand, Ian. I do. Completely."

"Just how long is this 'very important' whatever it is going to keep you occupied?"

"I don't know," Marten crossed to the window and looked out. Still no Salt and Pepper, at least that he could see. Just traffic and pedestrians. "What do you need that I can walk you through from here? Is the problem with the plant selection, the grading permits, the ordering, what?"

"The problem is Mr. Banfield and his wife. They have decided the rhododendron woods should be on the south hill not the north and that the north hill should be planted instead with eighty to a hundred ginkgo trees."

"Ginkgo trees?"

"Yes."

Marten turned from the window. "They'll grow too high and too thick and will block their view of the river."

"Exactly what we told them. But that's nothing compared to what they want to do with the forsythia, azalea, and hydrangea placements."

"They approved all those ten days ago."

"Well they disapproved all those this morning. They've agreed to pay for the changes. They just won't have the schedule interrupted. If I were you I would hustle my bum back here on the next plane out."

"I can't do that, Ian. Not right now."

"Are you employed by us or not?"

"Please try to understand what I'm doing here is difficult and very personal. If—" A sudden loud knock on Marten's door stopped him in mid sentence. A second knock followed immediately.

"Ian, hang on a moment, please."

Marten went into the short hallway that separated the room from the front door. He was almost to the door when the thought suddenly hit—what if he hadn't lost Salt and Pepper after all? What if he was right outside in the corridor and Merriman Foxx had decided he wasn't going to play who-what-and-why but was simply going to have him eliminated right then.

The knock came again.

"Christ," Marten breathed. Immediately he brought the phone to his ear. "Ian," he said in a voice just above a whisper, "I need to take care of something. E-mail the changes and I'll get back to you as soon as I can."

He clicked off and the knock came once more, louder and harder. Whoever it was wasn't giving up. He looked around for a weapon of some kind. All he saw was a room telephone on the wall next to him. Immediately he picked it up and rang room service.

A voice answered in Spanish.

"Do you speak English?" he said into the phone.

"Yes, sir."

"Good. Hold on please."

Phone in hand, a lifeline to the room service operator if he needed it, Marten took a breath, then turned the lock and opened the door.

Demi Picard stood in the hallway, hands on her hips, glaring at him. "What Newspaper Writers and Photographers conference?" she spat angrily in her French accent. "How did you find me? What the damn hell are you doing here?"

If she'd been any hotter she'd have burst into flame.

41

It took a very long walk before Marten could get Demi to calm down enough to even talk to him. It took even longer to convince her to join him for lunch. And after that, nearly half a bottle of a good local *cava*—champagne—to become at least halfway civil.

Now they sat at a table in the back room of Els Quatre Gats—The Four Cats—a café on a narrow street in the city's Barri Gòtic section, eating *suquet de peix,* a hot fish and potato mixture, and drinking still more *cava.* Slowly she was coming around.

Demi still wore the navy blazer over the striped man-tailored shirt and tan slacks she had worn that morning in Valletta. Professional photojournalist or not she was clearly used to traveling quickly and light. Which was probably the reason for her short hair too, not a lot to do with it except wash and fluff. She was smart and determined and, as he knew, fiery. But as true as those things were, she also seemed strangely unconnected, as if everything she was about, even her profession, had to do with something else. What that was he couldn't begin to guess, but it gave her a strange air of vulnerability that made her hard to figure out. Her big, deep brown eyes didn't help either because they drew your attention and threw you off, especially when she was looking directly at you, the way she was at Marten now.

"You want me to trust you," she said, "yes?"

"It would help."

"But you don't think you can trust me."

Marten smiled, "I asked you in Malta if you knew where Dr. Foxx or Reverend Beck or the girl Cristina had gone and you said no. Yet you knew all along Beck was coming to Barcelona and to what hotel and—"

Demi cut him off. "The concierge called me shortly before you arrived at my hotel room. He said the reverend had asked him to apologize for his leaving so abruptly. He told me where he had gone and said an airline ticket had been left for me if I wished to follow. That was what was in the envelope I picked up from the concierge as I left."

"The details of how you got here or why doesn't interest me. What does is the fact that you flat out lied. Tell me where 'trust' fits in there."

"Let's just say your showing up in Malta and the way you handled things with Dr. Foxx put me in a very awkward position."

"That's why you told me I could ruin everything."

"What do you want with me?"

The way Demi avoided the question and the way she looked at him when she did told Marten that for now, at least, that was as far in that direction as she was going to go.

"Look," he said directly, "I'm here for the same reason I was in Washington and in Malta, to find out the truth about what happened to Caroline Parsons. Whatever you want to talk about or don't is your business but from where I sit it's clear you came to Barcelona because of Reverend Beck, and that's why I'm here. Beck and Foxx were together in Malta for a reason. They both left suddenly and separately. That tells me they just might get back together as quickly, especially since Beck is still hanging around this part of the world. Beck is a curiosity but it's Foxx who's my real interest and I'm betting the good reverend will lead me to him, and sooner rather than later."

"And you think Dr. Foxx has an answer for you about Mrs. Parsons."

"Yes," Marten's eyes were suddenly intense. "He started to talk to me about it last night, then he realized he was going too far and got upset. I want him to finish what he had to say."

Just then their waiter, a pleasant, delicate-faced man with dark hair, stopped at their table. "May I get you something else?" he asked in English.

"Not now, thanks," Marten said.

"Of course," the man nodded and left.

Demi took a sip of the *cava* and looked at Marten over the top of the glass, "You seem to have cared about Mrs. Parsons a great deal."

"I loved her," he said without embarrassment or apology.

"She was married."

Marten didn't reply.

Demi half smiled. "Then you are here because of love."

Marten leaned forward. "Talk to me about 'the witches.'"

"I—" Demi hesitated and looked down at her wine glass, as if she was uncertain what to say, if anything. Finally she looked up, "Do you know what a *strega* is, Mr. Marten?"

"No."

"It's the Italian word for female witch. I have a younger sister who came to Malta two years ago and disappeared. I found out later that she was a practicing *strega* involved with a very secretive coven of Italian witches. Whether that had anything to do with her disappearance I don't know. What I do know is that Malta is old and filled with ancient places and secretive things. My sister was there for three days and that was the last anyone saw of her. The authorities searched but found nothing. They said she was a young woman and might have done anything.

"For me, that was no answer, so I kept looking on my own. That was how I heard about Dr. Foxx. He has many connections on Malta and knows people and things that others would not, not even the police. But they are things he would never reveal to a stranger. I didn't know what to do, and besides, I had to get back to work. My job put me on a photo assignment in Washington covering the social lives of U.S. congresspeople. It was there I learned about Reverend Beck and discovered he knew Foxx well. This was a huge opportunity to find out what happened to my sister, so through a French publisher I arranged to do a photo-essay book on clerics who minister to politicians. I made Beck a primary subject so that I could become his friend and gain his confidence. Because of that I was able to go to Malta and meet Dr. Foxx personally. But I didn't get to speak with him the way I needed to because—" for an instant her eyes flashed with anger, then she seemed to get over it "—you suddenly arrived and it all fell apart. I followed Reverend Beck to Barcelona because, as you guessed, he is to meet with Dr. Foxx again soon. Maybe even tomorrow."

"You know that for certain?"

"No, not for certain. But Cristina, the woman who was with us at dinner in Malta, told me that the reverend and Dr. Foxx had talked about it just before Foxx left the restaurant. 'Until Saturday,'

Foxx said. Since that took place Thursday night, I would assume he meant this coming Saturday, which is tomorrow. That's why I came here, to continue work on the book with Reverend Beck and because of it, hopefully get to see Dr. Foxx when he meets with him." Suddenly her eyes came up to his and the anger returned, "Maybe I can do that if you stay away."

Marten ignored her outburst. "There's one thing you're leaving out: why you asked me if Caroline Parsons said anything about 'the witches' before she died. What makes you think she would know anything about them?"

"Because—" She looked up. Again their waiter was at the table and topping off their glasses with cava as he had twice before. Now the bottle was empty.

"May I bring you another? Or perhaps something else from the bar?" he asked.

"No, thanks," Marten said for the second time. The man looked at Demi and smiled, then turned and walked off. Marten waited until he was out of earshot, then looked back to Demi, "Because—what?"

"Of her doctor."

"Stephenson?"

"Yes," Demi reached into her purse and took out a pen. "Let me show you." She pulled a paper napkin toward her, then carefully drew a simple diagram on it and pushed it across the table to Marten.

He exhaled loudly when he saw what it was, the same balled cross he had seen tattooed on Merriman Foxx's thumb, the same balled cross Caroline had described in her fearful description of the white-haired man.

"It is the sign of Aldebaran, the pale red star that forms the left eye in the constellation Taurus. In the early history of astrology it was considered to emanate a powerful and fortunate influence. It is also called 'Eye of God.'"

"What does it have to do with Dr. Stephenson?"

"She had it tattooed on her left thumb. It was small, you could barely see it."

Marten was incredulous. "Foxx has the same thing."

"I know. So does the woman, Cristina."

"What does the tattoo have to do with 'the witches'?"

"It's the sign of the coven to which my sister belonged."

"Foxx and Stephenson are witches?"

"I'm not sure. But my sister had the same tattoo. Why else would people so dissimilar have the sign of the Aldebaran tattooed on their thumb, specifically the left thumb?"

"What led you to think Caroline was involved with them? I held her hands for a long time, I never saw that mark or any other."

"She was dying. Dr. Foxx had been nearby and Stephenson had been her doctor for some time. I don't know their rituals but I hoped she might have had some knowledge of it. If she was frightened she might have wanted to share it with someone she completely trusted, and quite frankly that seemed to be you. I had to find out."

"She never said a thing."

"Then I was wrong. Either that or it was a secret she took into eternity."

"Does Reverend Beck have the mark?"

"Have you ever looked at his hands?"

"He has a pigmentary skin disorder, vitiligo. The skin on his hands is blotched," Marten said, then he understood. "You mean that even if he had the mark it would be very difficult to see."

"Yes."

"So you don't know if he's a member of the coven or not."

"I think he's involved, but whether he's a member I don't know."

"Tell me about the coven itself. Is it some kind of cult? Satan worshipers? Religious extremists? Or with Foxx's background some sort of military group?"

"Does the name Nicolo Machiavelli mean anything to you?"

"You mean Machiavelli, the man."

"Yes."

"As I recall he was a sixteenth-century Florentine writer famous for a book called *The Prince* about the ways to gain and keep raw political power, where authority is everything and expediency is placed above any kind of morality. A sort of how-to book for becoming a dictator."

"Yes," Demi nodded appreciatively.

"What does Machiavelli have to do with the coven?"

"There is a story that on his deathbed he wrote an addendum to *The Prince,* a kind of secondary blueprint for gaining power. It was

based on what he called a 'necessary prerequisite,' the creation of a
secret society to be governed by the rule of complicity; a brotherhood of blood where members would participate in an act of *ritual
murder*. It was to be an elaborate, carefully orchestrated human
sacrifice held once a year at a remote and secured spot, a church
preferably, or a temple, that would give the ceremony religious im-
pact. The rules required every member to sign a heavily guarded,
dated journal that included his name, place and date of birth;
name and manner of death of the victim; and a print of his thumb
dipped in the ink of his own blood and pressed in the journal alongside his signature. This was done to confirm his presence there, his
allegiance to the society and his willing involvement in the killing.
The journal was the key to the society's power because public expo-
sure of it would mean ruin, even death, for them all. Once the murder was done, and the participants' presence recorded, the society
could set forth its agenda for the year with the knowledge that what
they did was wholly protected from treachery within thereby freeing it to execute whatever plan was agreed upon.

"Those familiar with the story believe the addendum, if it existed, never reached its intended audience—Florentines oppressed
by the ruling Medici family that Machiavelli hoped he could unite
in blood to overthrow—and instead was smuggled to Rome where
it fell into the hands of an already powerful and influential group
who used it, and have continued to use it over the centuries, as an
ideology to further their own ends. For those who follow such
things the addendum has come to be known as *The Machiavelli
Covenant*."

"And you think that's what the Aldebaran coven is about, a
present-day edition of the Covenant?"

"That, Mr. Marten, is what I have been trying to find out for a
long time."

Abruptly something caught Marten's eye. He picked up his
glass and sat back, casually scanning the room.

"What is it?"

"Get up as if you're mad at me, pick up your purse and walk out
of the restaurant," Marten said quietly. "Go up the street, turn the
corner, and wait."

"Why? What's going on?"

"Just do it. Now."

"Alright," deliberately Demi pushed back from the table, glared at Marten, then picked up her purse and left. He stared after her for a moment then signaled the waiter for the check. Purposely he took another sip of *cava,* then put the glass down and sat back. A moment later the waiter brought the check. Marten paid cash, then got up and walked out, passing without a glance the fortyish-looking tourist who had taken a table near them and was looking at a menu. A tourist with salt-and-pepper hair who now wore a dark-colored sport coat over his yellow polo shirt. If there was any doubt he had been handed off at the Barcelona airport, it was gone now.

42

3:40 P.M.

Marten stepped through the door and pulled on dark glasses against the glare of the sun, then walked quickly up the street. At the corner he glanced back toward the entrance to Els Quatre Gats. If Salt and Pepper was coming after him he hadn't done it yet. Another step and he was around the corner looking for Demi. The sidewalk was crowded and he didn't see her. For a moment he was afraid she might have gone off on her own, that she still didn't trust him and that he would have to find her and fight the same battle all over again. Then he saw her waiting beneath the overhang of a storefront.

"What is it?" she said as he reached her.

"A man with salt-and-pepper hair and a yellow polo shirt. I've been followed, and all the way from Valletta. It's got to be Foxx's doing but I can't be sure."

"You were *followed.*"

"Yes."

"That means we've been seen together."

Marten could see the fire in her start to roar back. "You can dodge the whole thing by telling Beck straight off that I tracked you to Barcelona and insisted you talk to me. In the restaurant I asked you a bunch of crazy questions you knew nothing about and when I kept pushing you got mad and left."

"You're right, I did get mad and I am leaving," she said angrily and abruptly turned and started off into the crowd.

Marten caught up with her. She ignored him.

"Whether you like it or not we're in this together. You want to know what happened to your sister and I want to know what happened to Caroline Parsons." He glanced around and then lowered his voice, "Dr. Foxx seems to be key in both situations."

Still she ignored him, just kept walking.

Marten stayed in stride. "If Foxx is here and Reverend Beck is meeting him—where and when, that's all I want to know. Other than that I'll stay out of your hair, I promise."

She didn't reply. They reached the end of the block and stopped in a crowd waiting to cross a main boulevard. Marten stepped close to her. "You're alone in all this, aren't you?"

Demi said nothing. The light changed and she stepped off with the others. Again Marten caught up with her. "These are not terribly nice people, Foxx especially. At some point you're going to wish you had a friend."

They reached the far curb and she suddenly turned and confronted him.

"You won't go away, will you?"

"No."

She stared at him a second longer, "All you want to know is when and where," she said finally and in resignation.

"Yes."

"I'll do what I can."

"Thank you," he said, then quickly looked up and stepped off the curb to hail a passing taxi. The driver crossed two lanes of traffic and pulled up beside them.

Marten opened the rear door. "Go back to the hotel. Hopefully by now Beck will have checked in. See how comfortable he is with you, if you think the situation has calmed enough for him to actually talk about Foxx and his meeting with him." Demi slid in and he handed her a slip of paper, "The number of my cell phone. I don't hear from you by five o'clock, I'll call you." Abruptly he closed the door, the taxi moved off and Marten started quickly back the way they had come.

43

Marten and Salt and Pepper saw each other the moment Marten rounded the corner heading back to Els Quatre Gats.

At that instant Salt and Pepper realized what was happening and bolted. He ran across the narrow street, then darted down another, turning at the end of the block onto the heavily congested Via Laietana. Marten came after him on the dead run. As he ran, Marten's foremost thought was how the man had tracked him to the restaurant when he was certain he had lost him earlier. All he could think of was their attentive waiter, maybe not so obviously pushing drinks to build the bill as he'd first thought but making sure he and Demi stayed where they were until Salt and Pepper was informed and could get there. If that was the case what was going on had far more reach than he had imagined. Some kind of cult embracing medieval witchcraft that controlled, or least paid, a network of street informers who probably had no idea where their money was coming from. People like Salt and Pepper and the young man who had followed him from Valletta.

Running, dodging around people on a sidewalk jammed with shoppers, Marten tried to keep his eye on his man. But there were too many people and he lost sight of him. He slowed and was about to give up when he saw him suddenly dart out of a crowd a half block ahead and then cut left onto a side street. Marten jostled around a pair of arguing shopkeepers, nearly knocked over a woman carrying a baby, then turned the corner just in time to see Salt and Pepper glance back, then cut left again, running onto a broader street filled with heavy traffic.

This was all old neighborhood, part of the Gothic Quarter, Barri Gòtic, with its thirteenth- to fifteenth-century buildings, outdoor cafés, street-level shops with apartments above. Lungs on fire, heart pounding, Marten ran on. Pulling up sharply to avoid a fast-moving motorcycle, he took the same turn Salt and Pepper had and ran on, his eyes searching the crowds on either side of the street. He was in full stride when he heard the sharp blare of a horn. A split second later a cry of horror went up from the people on the block in front of him. Then the horn stopped and the entire area went silent.

Marten rushed forward, moving through people seemingly frozen in place and looking toward something in front of them. Then he saw a large delivery truck stopped in the middle of the street, its front grillwork badly dented, the body of Salt and Pepper on the ground in front of it.

People stood around silent, staring. Marten moved in slowly and went up to Salt and Pepper. Kneeling down, he put a hand to his carotid artery trying to find a pulse. The truck driver, a male, thirty at most, stood by the open door to his cab. Half in shock, motionless.

Marten suddenly looked to the crowd around him. "Call an ambulance. Ambulance! Ambulance!" he said loudly, then twisted back, opened Salt and Pepper's sport coat and put a hand on his heart. Again he touched the carotid artery, held his hand there a few seconds, then slowly reached over, closed Salt and Pepper's sport coat, and stood up.

"Ambulance!" he said again, then moved away and off through the crowd. Around him he could see people on cell phones calling for help. Behind him the truck driver stood where he had been, frozen in place beside his truck.

Marten kept walking. All he needed was for the police to arrive and question him about the man hit by the truck. They would want to know his name. Ask if he was a doctor. And finding he wasn't, want to know why he'd gone to help as he had. Want to know what he had seen. What details he could fill in. He had no knowledge of Spanish law and how it applied to accidents but the last thing he wanted was to be interviewed by the police or the press or have his picture taken by the paparazzi or be a video snippet on local television news.

What he did want.

Was no connection to Salt and Pepper at all.

44

President of the United States John Henry Harris nodded a thanks to the counterman in the cafeteria car, then took his purchase, a sandwich and bottle of mineral water, to a small side table to eat. Other than the counterman there were six other people in the car, four men and two women, one older than the other. Of the men, two sat by a window drinking beer; another stood, paper coffee cup in hand, staring out at the passing countryside. The last sat at a table sharing a platter of small sandwiches with the two women. These three seemed harmless, a brother and sister and maybe an aunt, or husband and wife and his or her older sibling. It was the other three he wasn't so sure about.

Minutes before, they had left the city of Lleida after a stop in Zaragoza and were moving northeast with a stop at Valls before they were to arrive at the Barcelona-Sants station at a little past six in the evening. For the most part the trip had been uneventful with no one giving him as much as a second look, but at Lleida several armed men in uniform had boarded and shortly afterward four more had come on, dressed in civilian clothes but with the certain style and body movement that suggested they were some kind of plainclothes agents. It made him wonder if one or perhaps all of the other three men, the two sipping beer and the man standing looking out, weren't some kind of agents as well, Spanish or American. All three had come into the car after he had and were close enough to the far door to prevent him going out of it if they chose. The uniformed men or other plainclothes agents who had come on in Lleida could easily come in and block the door behind him. If he was right and they did, the game was over.

Harris quickly finished his sandwich and took another sip of water. Then, dutifully putting the paper plate the sandwich had come on in a trash receptacle, he walked past the man and women and left.

He walked the length of the next car and entered the one behind it, taking his seat in the second-class car next to the man in the leather jacket and black beret who had been his seating companion since Madrid. By now the man had turned toward the window, his beret pulled down covering most of his head, and was apparently sleeping. Harris took a deep breath and relaxed, then picked his folded copy of *El Pais* newspaper from the seatback in front of him and opened it.

It was now 4:44. The next stop was Valls at 5:03 and Harris wasn't sure what to do when they got there. He knew Hap Daniels would be more than determined to bring him home, he would be feverish. Not only had he become the first Secret Service agent in charge of a presidential detail ever to lose a POTUS, he would be embarrassed beyond measure and would take enormous flak from above to the point where there was every chance he would be fired. Personally he would feel he had monstrously let down a friend.

The Secret Service's first presumption would be that he had been a victim of foul play and would have acted accordingly. By now the CIA, FBI and NSA would be wholly involved. Madrid would have been scoured by Spanish intelligence and the Madrid state police. A larger search would have been expanded to include all of Europe and North Africa, with another team working out of the Rome field office covering the Middle East and into Russia and other former Soviet bloc countries. All of it done under blackout orders, or as they would call it, "under the cover of night." Yet by now they would have enough information to be reasonably certain of what had really happened, that he had gone out on his own. In result an angered Jake Lowe and National Security Adviser Jim Marshall would have made a convincing case that he had done it because something was gravely wrong, that he had suffered a mental breakdown of some kind. It was the only story they could make work, but it was a good one because, for the people responsible for protecting him, the whole thing would rise above the horror of the president being kidnapped to what Lowe and company would play as an achingly human story of the most powerful man in the world come apart.

Consequently everyone, from the group that had been in Evan Byrd's Madrid home the night before to the Secretary of Homeland Security to the Director of the Secret Service and on down would do everything in their power to make sure he was found and brought home and out of harm's way as quickly as possible, with only a few very select people having any knowledge at all of what was really going on.

"Home and out of harm's way" meant he would be delivered to Jake Lowe and company who would already have arranged for him to be placed in their care. Once that happened he knew the rest. He would immediately be spirited to a place remote enough and safe enough to isolate him and then kill him—a massive stroke or heart attack or something equally convincing.

The sound of the door opening at the far end of the car made Harris look up. Two of the armed, uniformed men who had boarded the train at Lleida entered and stood there surveying the passengers as the door closed behind them. Harris could see they were members of the CNP or Cuerpo Nacional de Policía, the Spanish federal police. Automatic weapons slung over their shoulders, they stood silently for a moment longer and then slowly started forward, the first CNP studying the passengers on the right side of the car; the second, the travelers to the left. Halfway down, the first CNP stopped and looked at a male passenger wearing a broad-brimmed hat, then asked to see his identification. The other CNP came over and watched as the man complied. The first CNP studied the man's ID, then handed it back, and the two continued on down the aisle.

Harris watched them come, then looked to his newspaper. There was little doubt they were looking for him, checking anyone who had even a remote resemblance to him or, in the case of the man with the hat, that they couldn't clearly identify.

They drew closer and he could feel his heart rate pick up, feel sweat bead up on his upper lip. He kept his head down, reading, hoping they would pass on by and go into the next car. Suddenly he saw a polished boot stop next to him.

"You," the CNP said in Spanish. "What is your name? Where do you live?"

His heart in his mouth, Harris looked up. The CNP was not looking at him but at the man in the beret dozing next to him. Slowly the man raised the beret and looked up. By now the second

CNP had joined the first. Harris felt like a lamb in the presence of two starving lions. All they had to do was turn their attention to him.

"What is your name? Where do you live?" the first CNP snapped again.

"Fernando Alejandro Ponce. I live at number sixty-two Carrer del Bruc in Barcelona," the beret said in Spanish. "I am an artist!" Suddenly he was getting indignant. "A painter! What do you know of art? What do you want with me anyway?"

"Identification," the first CNP said firmly. By now everyone in the car was looking their way.

The second CNP unslung his automatic rifle and slowly, angrily, Fernando Alejandro Ponce reached into his leather jacket and slid out some kind of identification card. He handed it to the first CNP.

Abruptly he looked to Harris. "Why don't you ask this man his name? And where he lives? Demand his identification? It's only fair! Go ahead, ask him!"

Jesus, God, Harris thought and held his breath, waiting for the CNP to take up the man's challenge and do as he demanded. The CNP looked at Fernando Alejandro's ID card, then handed it back.

"Well, are you going to ask him?" Angrily Fernando Alejandro waved his ID card at Harris.

"Go back to sleep, painter," the CNP said. Then, with a glance at Harris, he turned, and with his companion, continued on down the car. A moment later they went out the door at the far end.

Alejandro's eyes followed them all the way, then shot back to Harris. "*¡Bastardos! ¿Quién el infierno es él que busca de todos modos?*" he snarled. Bastards! Who the hell are they looking for anyway?

"*No tengo idea.*" No idea. Harris shrugged. "*No tengo idea en todos.*" No idea at all.

45

Twenty minutes after the accident in the Gothic Quarter Nicholas Marten quietly checked out of the Hotel Regente Majestic, apologizing to the sympathetic desk clerk still on duty and saying his newspaper had abruptly changed his assignment. Graciously she canceled his credit card deposit and tore up the receipt. Five minutes afterward he was clear of the hotel and back on the street carrying his small traveling bag, never letting Demi know what he had done. Clearly there was no way to know if Salt and Pepper had been called to the restaurant by the waiter or if he had tracked Marten to the Regente or if someone from the hotel had alerted him and he'd tailed him from there, but by checking out as he had he'd left no clear trail for anyone to follow.

Nonetheless they knew he was in Barcelona, and with Salt and Pepper dead it was only a matter of time before they sent someone else to take his place. Someone who would be able to recognize him but who he would not know. A stranger. The only advantage he had, if it was an advantage at all, was that now he knew who Salt and Pepper had been: *Klaus Melzer, 455 Ludwigstrasse, Munich, Germany,* a civil engineer.

Marten had known he was dead the minute he saw the savage dent in the truck's grillwork and the way his body was sprawled on the pavement in front of the vehicle. Feeling his carotid artery for a pulse had confirmed it. The rest, the pleading to the crowd to call an ambulance, the opening of his jacket to feel for a heartbeat, then the closing of his jacket and the second plea for an ambulance had all been show. He'd seen the slight bulge in the man's sport coat when he'd first bent over him. That was what he had wanted and what he taken as he left, Salt and Pepper's wallet. Inside he'd

found his German driver's license, credit cards and several business cards with his name and his firm's name: *Karlsruhe & Lahr,
Bauingenieure, Brunnstrasse 24, Munich.*

5:44 P.M.

Marten checked into the Rivoli Jardín Hotel. He was still in the
Gothic Quarter but several long blocks south of the Regente Majestic. Again, and with no other choice, he used his own name and
identification to register. Ten minutes later he was unpacked and
on his cell phone trying to get through to Peter Fadden in London.
Instead of reaching the *Washington Post* writer he got his voice mail
saying he was not available and to please leave word. Marten did,
asking Fadden to call him as soon as he could. Then he clicked off
and dialed the Hotel Regente Majestic asking for Demi's room.
The phone rang through but there was no answer. He clicked off
without leaving a message and with the gnawing feeling that maybe
it had been a mistake to let her go. She'd tried to get rid of him before and was angry all over again after the episode at the Four Cats,
and what had he done but put her in a cab and send her off?
It made no difference what she'd promised, all she had to do was
check out of the hotel and there was every chance he'd never see
her again. On top of that there was still that something about her,
her manner, the sense he'd had before that she was strangely unconnected and that everything she was about had to do with something else. Whether that had to do with her missing sister or if the
whole thing about her was made up and it was something else entirely it was impossible to tell. Whatever it was added to the dis-
comfort he felt about her now.

Marten put down the phone and picked up Klaus Melzer's—
Salt and Pepper's—driver's license. He turned it over in his hand,
then looked again at his business card. Never mind that Marten
had been handed off to him at the airport, why would a forty-
something German civil engineer be tailing him? It made no
sense.

Unless—

Marten clicked on his phone and dialed the Munich number
for Karlsruhe & Lahr listed on Melzer's business card. Maybe his

identification—driver's license, credit cards, business cards—was false, maybe there was no Klaus Melzer or Karlsruhe & Lahr at all. Ten seconds later the second half of his conjecture fell apart:

"Karlsruhe und Lahr, guter nachmittag." Karlsruhe and Lahr, good afternoon, a cheery female voice said.

Five seconds after that the first part went out the window too.

"Klaus Melzer, please," Marten said.

"I'm sorry, Mr. Melzer is out of the office until next week," the voice said in accented English. "Would you like to leave a message?"

"Do you know where he can be reached?"

"He's traveling, sir. May I have him return your call?"

"No, thank you. I'll get back to him."

Marten clicked off.

So there was a Klaus Melzer and there was a Karlsruhe & Lahr. That confirmation brought him back to his original thought—why had a middle-aged German civil engineer seemingly with a good job been following him? Why had the handoff from the young man to Melzer at the airport seemed so professional? Why had he run away when Marten was about to confront him? All he'd had to do was deny whatever Marten accused him of and that would have been that. There was nothing Marten could have done. But he hadn't and now he was dead.

"Dammit," Marten said in frustration then clicked on his phone and tried Demi once more.

He let the phone ring until the hotel operator came on.

"I'm sorry, Ms. Picard is not answering."

"Thanks," Marten said and was about to hang up when he had one more thought. "Has Reverend Beck checked in yet? He was coming in from Malta."

"Let me check, sir." There was a brief pause then the operator came back on. "No, sir. Not yet."

"Thank you."

Marten clicked off then took a determined breath and crossed the room to plug in his cell phone to recharge it. If Demi wasn't answering and Beck hadn't checked in, then where was she? Again he had the disturbing thought that she had already left, maybe to meet Beck, or even Merriman Foxx. If she had, maybe she was not in Barcelona at all but somewhere else. If so, this time she would have covered her tracks well, making sure there would be no trail he could follow.

46

5:58 P.M.

President John Henry Harris watched the countryside turn to suburb and then to city as Altaria train #01138 neared Barcelona. In the distance he could see the sunlight glint off the Mediterranean Sea. In five minutes they were due to arrive at Barcelona-Sants station. His plan was to transfer to the 6:25 Catalunya Express, which, barring difficulty, would get him into Gerona at 7:39. Once there, there would be no calling Rabbi David Aznar's house for directions because he knew his phones would be monitored by some piece of Hap Daniels's intelligence machinery and meant he would have to find Rabbi David's house on his own. But he had come this far without being discovered, and he had to trust his luck would hold and he could go the rest of the way without incident.

6:08 P.M.

The Altaria pulled into Barcelona-Sants station five minutes late. John Henry Harris stood with the other passengers as they collected their things.

He nodded to Fernando Alejandro Ponce, his leather-jacketed, beret-wearing artist seat-mate, then followed the others from the train. When he did his heart came up in his throat. Armed, uniformed police had blocked the exits and were checking the identification of everyone leaving the terminal. The lines felt like they were miles long. Harris's only thought was that Hap Daniels—under the directive of the Director of the Secret Service in Washington, under orders from the Secretary of Homeland Security, under orders from Vice President Hamilton Rogers and the rest of Jake Lowe's "pals"— had put his foot to the accelerator. It meant this sort of thing would be going on all over Spain, if not all of Europe.

6:12 P.M.

President Harris stood in the ticket line for the Catalunya Express which was scheduled to depart for Gerona in thirteen minutes. He had purposely not bought a transfer ticket to Gerona in Madrid when he'd paid his fare for Barcelona, simply because he didn't want to alert anyone who might have recognized him, or who might later be questioned, his ticket seller in particular, to his true destination. He wished now he had. The line to the ticket counter was twenty deep, and the police were walking up and down looking carefully at the people in line. And not just here, but at every ticket window.

6:19 P.M.

The line inched forward. People around him mumbled about what was going on. There was fear among them too, with memories of the horror that had gone on at Atocha Station on March 11, 2004, still achingly clear in their memories. Without doubt they were wary about the armed force around them. Many were half expecting a bomb to go off at any second.

6:22 P.M.

The line moved closer and Harris could see the ticket sellers in their cages checking the identification of every person buying a ticket, and CNP agents inside the ticket cages with them overseeing the process.

Slowly, easily, he stepped away from the line and walked toward the men's restroom. What he had to do was get out of the building and find some other way to Gerona. What that would be he didn't know, because he was certain every bus and train terminal would be under the same heavy surveillance.

Harris passed a news kiosk. Prominently displayed was *La Vanguardia,* apparently a major Barcelona newspaper. The front page had a photograph of himself leaving the presidential limousine, taken at some point the day before. The headline in Spanish read:

¡HARRIS HUYE AMENAZA DEL TERRORISTA EN MADRID!
—HARRIS FLEES TERRORIST THREAT IN MADRID!

Head down he kept on, passing shops, restaurants, and an ungodly number of uniformed police. Finally he reached the men's restroom and went inside, passing a policeman stationed just inside the door. Half a dozen men stood at urinals. Harris went immediately into a stall and closed the door. What to do next? This was a nightmare beyond nightmares. He wished to hell he would wake up from it and find it had all been just that, a gruesome dream. But it wasn't and he knew it. He had to find a way out of the building, even though he knew nothing of Barcelona let alone how to find some safe transportation to Gerona.

He sat down on the toilet and tried to think. For the moment, at least here, with the stall door closed, he was safe. But that would last only until someone else tried to use it or the policeman stationed at the door became suspicious and came to check on him. His first thought was to take a chance and call Rabbi David in Gerona and ask him to get in his car and drive there, then arrange for a place to meet and hide somewhere nearby until he arrived. But he knew from what was going on in the station that that was out of the question. If he had worried before that the Rabbi's phones would be fully monitored there was no doubt of it now. Seemingly every inch of everything everywhere was covered. His pursuers, even if they didn't realize it, were literally steps away from him.

It meant he had to slow things down and take them a step at a time, just as he had at the Ritz. The first move was to find a way out of the station. Once on the streets he could decide the next course of action. To do that he had to do what he had done in Madrid, use his knowledge of how public buildings were constructed and use the station's mechanical interior—the hidden corridors that contained the heating, air-conditioning, plumbing, and electrical systems—as a way out. The way a mouse or rat would find his way to freedom.

Harris stood up and flushed the toilet and was about to open the door when he saw a folded copy of *La Vanguardia* with his photograph on the cover lying on the floor near his feet. Immediately he saw it as a prop, something he could use to casually shield his face on the way through the station until he found an entrance to the maintenance corridors he was looking for. Additionally, he might learn something of the smoke-screen story the White House press corps had put out and see how "his friends," most especially the master manipulator Jake Lowe, had managed to sound the general alarm without telling the truth or upsetting the public any more than had already been done.

Quickly Harris picked up the paper, tucked it under his arm, then flushed the toilet once more, opened the stall door, and went out.

47

Nicholas Marten sat alone in the hotel lounge waiting for a cell phone call back from Peter Fadden who was now in Madrid, gone there to cover the story surrounding the abrupt evacuation of the president from the Hotel Ritz the night before. Fadden had been on with him momentarily, then had to click off to take another call, promising to call back right away.

His hair slicked back and dressed in fresh khakis, crew-neck sweater, and light sport coat, Marten looked appreciably different from the man who had checked into this same hotel and then checked out only a short while later. His situation was helped too by the fact that none of the hotel staff who had been on earlier were on duty now.

Demi, he'd learned to his great relief, had not checked out as he'd feared, moreover Reverend Beck had finally arrived and registered, though neither were in their rooms at present, or at least they weren't answering their phones if they were. Marten had checked the bar, coffee shop, and restaurant just to make certain they weren't there, and they weren't. Therefore he felt it safe to assume that unless they were in another guest room somewhere, they were not in the building.

His seat in the lounge gave him a view of the front door, the registration desk, and the elevators past it. Meaning that Demi or Beck or both would have to pass by him when they returned. He didn't like sitting there exposed as he was, but in his days as an LAPD detective he'd done enough surveillance to know the mechanics of it. Come and go once in a while, pretend you were waiting for someone who had yet to arrive. Ultimately, of course, he would have to leave, but not at the moment. And at the moment what he was doing was buying time waiting for Demi to return and for Peter Fadden to call. Time, on the other hand, was itself problematic. By now Foxx or whoever had set Karl Melzer on his trail would know Melzer was dead and would have scurried to get someone to take his place. After that there would be calls to every hotel in Barcelona looking for someone who had registered as Nicholas Marten—"I'm trying to find a friend" or "my cousin, his name is"—or something like that, Melzer's replacement would say. And even with as many hotels as there were in the city, it would probably take less than half an hour to find him. Then they would know where he was and the entire thing would begin again.

Marten was turning to get a better view of the front door when his cell phone chirped and he clicked on.

"This is Marten."

"It's Peter," Fadden's voice was as clear as if he were sitting beside him. "Sorry it took so long. The Secret Service took the president out of the hotel in the middle of the night to an undisclosed location. They're saying it was a credible terrorist kidnap threat and that the suspects are still loose and trying to get out of the country. They've got just about every Spaniard who can fit into a uniform trying to find them never mind what's going on with the Secret Service, CIA, and the FBI."

"I know, Peter, I saw the news."

"Whatever's going on I'm pretty much here alone. The White House press secretary shut down everything and sent the whole press corps back to Washington. Why, I don't know, except that's where all the official news will come from once something breaks. Of course they'll all turn right around and bring everybody back for the NATO meeting Monday in Warsaw. But that's not what you want to talk about. It's the Caroline Parsons thing. The clinic, that stuff."

"Yes."

"The clinic is legitimate. She was taken from her home to the Silver Springs Rehabilitation Center in Silver Springs, Maryland. She was there for six days until she was transferred to University Hospital. Dr. Stephenson was a consulting physician there and approved her admittance and then the transfer. No one on staff ever heard of or saw anyone who looked like Foxx."

Marten took a breath, then glanced around the room. Maybe a dozen people at most were gathered at surrounding tables. None were paying him the slightest attention. He turned back to the phone.

"Peter, I've got something else. Stephenson and Foxx belonged to a cult, a coven of witches—"

"Witches?"

"Yes."

"Oh for chrissake!"

"Peter, stop and listen," Marten demanded sotto voce. "I told you before how Foxx had a tiny balled cross tattooed on his thumb. Stephenson had one too. And maybe Beck as well."

Marten looked up as a young couple sat down at a small table next to him. He got up and walked toward the hotel's lobby, cell phone to his ear.

"That balled cross is the sign of Aldebaran," Marten said as he went, "the pale red star that forms the left eye in the constellation Taurus. It is also called the 'Eye of God.'"

"What the hell are you talking about?"

"Some kind of cult, Peter."

"And you think this 'cult' had something to do with Caroline Parsons's death and those of her husband and son?"

"Possibly. I don't know. But Foxx was increasingly upset when I questioned him. I told you he denied knowing Stephenson at all. Maybe your people found no record of him being at the clinic when

Caroline was there but she not only described what he looked like and what his hands looked like but the tattoo as well. Peter, he was at the clinic, believe me. Beck was with him in Malta. And now Beck is here in Barcelona and is expected to meet with him again soon. I'm trying to find out where and when. If I do maybe I'll find out why."

Marten had reached the lobby and was crossing it. A bellman pushing a luggage cart was coming toward him. He stopped and turned away.

"Peter, there's something else. Foxx, or someone, had me followed from Valletta to Barcelona. It was a professional job—one guy handed me off to another at Barcelona airport. I thought I lost him, but he showed up at a restaurant where I was having lunch. I found later he was German, a civil engineer working for a company in Munich."

"Why would a civil engineer be—?"

"That's what I said. But it's legitimate, I called his office and checked up on him."

"Where is he now?"

"Dead."

"What?"

The bellman passed and Marten turned back. As he did the elevator doors across the lobby opened. To his surprise he saw Demi walk out. With her was Reverend Beck and an older woman, Spanish or Italian maybe, and dressed in black.

"Peter, I've got to go. I'll check in with you when I can."

Instantly Marten clicked off then watched the threesome cross the lobby toward the front door. He held back as they went out, watching as Beck spoke with the doorman. A moment later a taxi pulled up, the three got in, and the taxi drove off.

Marten pushed through the door and went out. "Do you speak English?" he asked the doorman.

"Yes, sir."

"The three people who just left. I'm part of a group traveling with the Reverend. I was supposed to meet them somewhere but I lost my itinerary. Do you happen to know where they went?"

"To church, señor."

"Church?"

"The cathedral of Barcelona."

Marten smiled, "Of course, the cathedral. Thank you."

"You want to go there?"

"Yes, thank you."

"Well, you are in luck, as your friends were."

Marten was puzzled, "How do you mean?"

"Usually the cathedral is only open until seven. But this month until ten. It is a celebration, it was closed for a long time for restoration but has now just reopened." The doorman smiled, "So you want to go still?"

"Yes."

The doorman motioned for a taxi. A moment later it arrived. Marten gave him a ten-euro tip, then got in, and the cab pulled away.

48

7:40 P.M.

John Henry Harris stood in the doorway of a convenience store watching the woman work her section of the street. She was blond, with pale white skin that was almost porcelain. Twenty at most, she looked Scandinavian or German, maybe even Russian. Her nationality didn't matter; her profession did. With a revealing halter top and short, tight skirt, the way she walked up and down between cars every time traffic stopped, there was little doubt she was out there for hire and for the right price would probably do almost anything he or anyone else asked. And that was what John Harris needed now, someone to do what he asked—with no questions whatsoever.

He had no idea where he was except that it was a dozen or more blocks from the train station. A place he'd escaped from not as planned by using inner service corridors, because the few he found had either been locked or strongly guarded. What he had done instead was take an enormous chance and set fire to the rear of a newspaper kiosk that was close to an exit door; a diversion, as the military or police would call it. And it had worked. The attention of

Spanish security forces checking IDs at the nearest door had briefly been drawn to the flames and the near-panic from an already nervous public. Harris had calculated his timing and watched the guards rush from the door, and within seconds he was out on the street and gone.

"Señorita," he said as the light changed and traffic moved forward and his girl sashayed from the street and onto the curb. She looked at him and smiled, then came closer.

"*¿Habla español?*" Do you speak Spanish? he asked, hoping to hell she did. Not wanting to use English unless it was absolutely necessary.

"*Sí,*" she came a little closer.

He peered over the rims of his glasses. "*Quisiera un poco de su tiempo.*" I would like a little of your time.

"*Seguro.*" Sure, she grinned seductively and adjusted her halter top so that he could see more of her breasts.

"*No es lo que usted piensa.*" It's not what you think, he said quietly.

"*Lo que es, si paga el dinero, lo haré.*" Whatever it is, if it pays money, I will do it.

"Bueno," he said. "Bueno."

7:55 P.M.

Marten's taxi turned down one street and then another in slow traffic, moving back into the Gothic Quarter, where he had been earlier in the day. He was still up the air about Demi, still wary of what she was doing, still unsure if he could trust her. That she hadn't answered her phone the several times he'd tried to reach her and after he'd specifically told her he'd call didn't help. Nor did the fact that whatever Beck's mood had been in Malta he'd managed to calm down enough to ask her to follow him to Barcelona, and that now they seemed all buddy-buddy. It made him think that no matter what she'd confided to him about the witches and the sign of Aldebaran at the restaurant, she had done it simply to placate him, hoping it would be enough to make him go away and let her concentrate on staying in Beck's good graces so she wouldn't be left behind when he went to meet Merriman Foxx. It was a thought that made him wonder if that's where the three were going now, to meet Foxx at the cathedral. It also raised the question of who the woman in black was.

8:07 P.M.

Marten felt a presence and looked up. The taxi driver was watching him in the mirror. He'd glanced at him more than once before and now he was openly staring at him. Suddenly Marten had the feeling he'd stumbled into some kind of trap, that either the cab driver was Salt and Pepper's replacement or was a stringer like The Four Cats waiter, someone hired to look for him.

"What are you looking at?" he said.

"*No hablo English good,*" the man smiled.

"Me," Marten pointed to his face, "you recognize me? I am familiar to you?" If this man was trouble and taking him somewhere other than to the cathedral he wanted it to come out now, so he could do something about it.

"*Sí,*" the man said, suddenly understanding, "*Sí.*" Immediately his hand slid to the seat beside him and he picked up a copy of an evening newspaper. It was folded back and open to an interior page.

"You Samaritan. You Samaritan."

"What? What are you talking about?" Marten was thrown off.

The man pushed the paper over the seat. Marten took it and looked at it. What he saw was a large photo of himself bent over the sprawled body of his Salt and Pepper man, Klaus Melzer, with the truck that had hit him in the background.

"*Buen Samaritan a ningún extremo, hombre matado en calle,*" the caption read. Marten didn't understand the Spanish but he got the gist of it—he was good Samaritan for no reason, the man in the street was already dead.

"*Sí, Samaritan,*" Marten handed the paper back, swearing to himself as he did. Obviously someone in the crowd had taken a picture and sold it to the newspaper. They didn't have his name and there wasn't a story, so at least it wasn't about his having pilfered the dead man's wallet. Still, he didn't like it. It was bad enough he'd had to register at his hotel under his own name, but with his picture spread over the city like that it would make him all that much easier to find.

Abruptly the taxi sped up, traveled a half block, then turned down another street, moving deeper into the Gothic Quarter, which he now realized was not just a tourist area, but a sprawling ancient neighborhood where narrow streets emptied into other narrow streets and then into squares. It was a maze one could easily become lost in, something that might have happened to Klaus Melzer, a German, unfamiliar with the city, doing nothing more than trying to get away from a man pursuing him and running directly into the path of an oncoming truck. It was something that again made him wonder why Foxx, or whoever had hired the salt-and-pepper civil engineer, had picked him over a local and why Melzer had agreed to do it.

Just then the taxi slowed and stopped, its driver pointing toward a large square. Hotels and shops lined one side, while on the other stood a massive, ornate stone edifice with a complex series of lighted spires and bell towers that reached high into the evening sky.

"The cathedral, señor," the cab driver said. "Catedral de Barcelona."

49

8:20 P.M.

Marten crossed the square to join a group of English tourists as they walked up a series of stone steps and entered the cathedral.

The atmosphere inside the fifteenth-century building's vast and ornate interior was hushed, its muted lighting broken by the flickering of hundreds of votive candles resting on tables on either side of the nave.

Marten lingered as the group moved forward, his eyes scanning the room for Demi or Beck or the woman in black. Here and there people sat in silent prayer. Others walked respectfully around, gazing up at the architecture. At the far end of the nave was a high, elaborate altar. Above it towered Gothic arches that rose toward a ceiling he guessed was eighty feet high.

A raspy, echoing cough from someone near his sleeve brought him back to the purpose at hand and he moved forward, carefully, slowly. If Demi and her companions were there, he didn't see them. He kept walking. Still nothing. Suddenly, he wondered if Beck or Demi had said something to the hotel doorman as they left, and the man had purposely sent him on a wild goose chase and in reality they had gone somewhere else and not come here at all. It was enough to trigger a sense that he should go back to the hotel now and—suddenly he stopped. There they were, the three of them, standing on the far side of the nave, talking with a priest.

Marten crossed it cautiously, using tourists as screens, moving closer to where they were, praying they wouldn't suddenly turn and see him.

He was almost within hearing distance when the priest gestured off, and together the four moved in that direction. Marten followed.

A moment later he was in an inner hallway that ran alongside a large interior garden. Ahead he saw the priest lead the three around a corner and down still another hallway. Again, Marten followed.

Thirty paces and he was there, cautiously entering a chapel of some kind. As he did he saw the priest usher Demi, Beck and the woman in black through an ornate door near the rear. Seconds later the door closed behind them. Immediately Marten went to it and tried its wrought-iron handle. It didn't move. The door was locked.

Now what? Marten turned. An elderly priest stood not ten feet away looking at him.

"I was hoping to find a restroom," Marten said innocently.

"That door leads to the vestry," the priest replied in heavily accented English.

"The vestry?"

"Yes, señor."

"Is it always locked?"

"Except in the hour before and after services."

"I see."

"You will find a restroom that way," the old man gestured toward a hallway behind them.

"Thank you," Marten said, and with no choice, left.

8:45 P.M.

Five minutes later he'd walked through as much of the main church as he could trying to see where they might have gone. Other doors were either locked or opened onto corridors that led to still more corridors, but none seemed to take him in the direction of the chapel where they had been.

He retraced his steps and went out through the main entrance, then walked around the cathedral to the far side where he guessed the chapel was, looking for a doorway Demi and her friends might have come out. There was none. A hike around the rest of the massive building's exterior revealed only entrances that were darkened and closed and locked. That left only the main entrance, where he'd only moments before come out. That was where he went, blending in among the tourists and passersby on the square in front of the cathedral, to take a table at an outdoor café across from it where he had a clear view of the entryway. He ordered a bottle of mineral water and later a cup of coffee. An hour passed and they still hadn't come out. At ten the doors closed for the night. Frustrated, angry with himself for losing them, Marten got up and left.

50

RIVOLI JARDÍN HOTEL, 10:20 P.M.

Marten came off the noisy street jammed with pedestrians and bumper-to-bumper traffic and into the relative quiet of the hotel lobby. Immediately he crossed to the front desk to ask for calls or messages.

"Neither, señor," the clerk said politely.

"Did anyone come in asking for me?"

"No, señor."

"Thank you," Marten nodded then crossed to the elevator that would take him to his room on the fourth floor. A push of a button, the door opened, and he stepped into the empty car. Another push of a button, the door closed, and the elevator started up.

That he had no calls or messages and that no one had come looking for him was a distinct relief. It meant whoever had sent Salt and Pepper had yet to find a replacement who might have tracked him to the Rivoli Jardín. Demi, Peter Fadden, and Ian Graff at Fitzsimmons and Justice in Manchester had his cell phone number and would have gotten in touch with him that way. So for the moment, at least, he had a chance to breathe. No one knew where he was.

Demi.

His thoughts were suddenly on her and what she was doing or not doing. Obviously she was back in Beck's good graces or she wouldn't have gone off with him as she did. Where either of them was now and who the woman in black was, was anyone's guess. The fact was Demi remained a conundrum. It was true she had provided him with considerable information, especially as it related to the witches, the thumb tattoos, and the sign of Aldebaran, and that she had come to Barcelona hoping once again to meet with Merriman Foxx. On the other hand, and even though they were more or less after the same thing, she clearly wanted nothing to do with him. It made him think again of his impression of her when they had had lunch at the Four Cats; that as focused as she seemed, everything she was about seemed to have to do with something other than what was at hand. Whether that something was her missing sister, or if that story was even true, he had no way to know. What he did know was that a whole lot about her troubled him. It was as simple as that.

The elevator stopped at the fourth floor, the door opened and Marten stepped out into a deserted corridor. Twenty seconds later he reached the door to his room and swiped the coded electronic key through the lock. The tiny light turned from red to green and the lock clicked open. Bone weary, wanting only to shower and go to bed, he went in, turned on the hallway light, then closed the door behind him and locked it. To his left was the bathroom. Beyond it was the room itself. Dark with only the ambient glow from the street giving it any illumination at all. He walked just past the bathroom door and started to reach for the light switch to the room.

"Please don't turn the light on, Mr. Marten," a male voice sprang from the darkness of the room.

"Christ!" Marten felt ice run down his spine. Instantly he looked behind him. It would be impossible to get to the door, unlock it, then open it and get out before whoever was in the room had him. His heart pounding, he turned back, peering into the darkened room in front of him.

"Who the hell are you? What do you want?"

"I know you are alone. I watched you cross the street to the hotel from the window." The voice was calm and even quiet. This wasn't someone like the baggy-jacketed kid who had tailed him from Valletta to Barcelona or the German civil servant who had fled the instant he was challenged. And then, panicked, ran into the path of a truck.

"I said who the hell are you? What do you want?" Marten had no way to know if the man was alone or if there were others with him. Or if he was there to kill him or simply take him to Merriman Foxx.

Suddenly there was movement and he could see a lone male figure come toward him in the dark. In a swift move Marten undid his belt buckle and ripped the belt from his pants, wrapping it around his hand as a makeshift weapon.

"You won't need that, Mr. Marten."

Abruptly his "guest" stepped from the dark and into the spill of the hallway light. As he did, Marten's breath went out of him. The man who stood there was John Henry Harris, the president of the United States.

"I need your help," he said.

51

Nicholas Marten pulled the room curtains and then turned on a small lamp and turned to face the president, who had taken a chair and now sat facing him. If he had been startled before, he was all the more so now. The man he had met moments before was probably the most recognizable person in the world, but in an instant he looked entirely different, almost unrecognizable. His full head of hair was gone, showing a nearly bald pate, and he wore glasses. It made him seem older, even slimmer, or as he had thought, just "different."

"A toupee, Mr. Marten. They make them very well these days," the president said. "I've worn one for years. Only my personal barber knows about it. The glasses are clear, an addition picked up in a store in Madrid. A simple stage prop that helps with the overall appearance."

"I don't understand, sir. Any of it. Even how you found me or why you wanted to. You're supposed to be in—"

"An undisclosed location because of a terrorist threat, I know. Well, I am in an undisclosed location, at least for the moment." The president reached to a side table and picked up the copy of *La Vanguardia* he had taken from the rest room in the train station. A page was folded back and he handed it to Marten.

A quick glance told Marten everything. On it was the photograph of himself with the body of his Salt and Pepper man hit and killed by the truck. The same photograph the cabdriver had shown him earlier.

"I saw your picture, Mr. Marten. I hired a young woman to help me find you. I was alone and desperately in need of a place to go, and for the moment, at least, you have provided it. Serendipity or kismet, I think it's called."

Marten was still wholly puzzled. "I'm sorry, but I still don't understand."

"The young woman found where you were registered. It wasn't that far from where I was, so we walked here. I was let into your room by a generous desk clerk after I told him I was your uncle and had planned to meet you earlier but that my plane was late in arriving. He was skeptical but a few euros convinced him."

"That's not what I mean. You are the president of the United States. How could you be on your own like this, and even if you were why come to me when you could have called anyone?"

"That's just it, Mr. Marten, I couldn't have called anyone. And I mean anyone." The president fixed Marten with a look that told him how truly desperate his situation had been and still was. "I remembered you from our brief meeting at University Hospital in Washington. Caroline Parsons had just died and very nearly in your arms. You asked if you might have a moment alone with her. You remember?"

"Of course."

"I found out later that she had had a legal document drawn up giving you access to her private papers and those of her husband, Congressman Parsons."

"That's true."

"I assume it was because she thought her husband and son had been deliberately killed and hoped maybe you could find out what happened."

Marten was stunned. "How did you know that?"

"For the moment suffice it to say it's the primary reason I'm here and sought your help. Both Caroline and Mike Parsons were my very close friends. Obviously Caroline trusted you a great deal and you were equally devoted to her, or," John Henry Harris half smiled, "you wouldn't have kicked the president of the United States out of the hospital room." Harris's smile faded and he hesitated as if he weren't sure exactly what to say next, or how much to reveal, then Marten saw a look of deep resolve come over him, and he continued. "Mr. Marten, Mike Parsons and his son *were* murdered. So, I'm afraid, was Caroline."

Marten stared at him. "You know that for a fact?"

"Yes. No, I shouldn't say for a fact, but it was an admission by the people responsible for it."

"What people?"

"Mr. Marten, I want to trust you, I have to trust you because there is nowhere else for me to turn. And because of Caroline, I believe I can trust you." Again the president hesitated. Then Marten saw the resolve rise in him once more. "There was no terrorist threat. I left the hotel in Madrid on my own and under very difficult circumstances. You might say I escaped."

Marten didn't understand. "Escaped from what? From who?"

"Our country is at war, Mr. Marten. A war that is being secretly waged against me and our country by a group of people at the highest levels of government. They are made up of my personal advisers and people in my own cabinet. People that I have known and trusted for years. But people who, in reality and as a group, are probably the most dangerous and powerful in the country. To my knowledge this is the closest thing to a coup d'état America has ever experienced. As a result, my life is in grave danger, and so is the future of not just our country but many other countries. Moreover, the window in which I can attempt do something about it is extremely short. A little over three days at most. There is no longer anyone in the government that I can trust unconditionally. Nor do I have any friends or relatives this group won't have under close physical and electronic surveillance.

"That's why when I saw your photograph in the paper I knew I had to take the chance and find you. I had to have the confidence of someone and fortunately or unfortunately you are that person."

Marten was dumbfounded. Maybe in fiction the president of the United States came alone to your hotel room in the middle of the night and told you these things. Sat down and told you the country was being taken over from the inside and that you were the only person in the world he could trust to help him stop it. Maybe in fiction all that happened, yet this was not fiction, this was real. The president was there, not three feet away and visibly drained, looking at you with bloodshot eyes and relating these awful things and asking for your help.

"What do you want me to do?" Marten said finally in a voice that was little more than a whisper.

"At this moment I'm not exactly sure. Except—" John Henry Harris took a long, deep breath that was closer to a sigh of absolute exhaustion, "—that for an hour or two I would ask you to keep guard. It's been a damned long day. I need to think. But I need to sleep first."

"I understand."

Absently the president ran a hand over a stubble beard that was beginning to show. "This is still Friday, the seventh, isn't it?"

"Yes, sir."

"Good," the president smiled and Marten could see the fatigue begin to overtake him. As it did his eyes found Marten's. "Thank you," he said genuinely, "thank you very much."

SATURDAY

APRIL 8

52

"I don't know if it means anything, sir," Hap Daniels heard the voice of Secret Service intelligence specialist Sandra Rodriguez through his headset. "It's a pattern NSA analytical software picked up earlier this evening in Barcelona and was just evaluated."

"What pattern?" Daniels snapped. He'd been living on hope, black coffee, and adrenaline in the seemingly interminable hours since the president was first reported missing. Under emergency orders issued by the office of the vice president and overseen by George Kellner, CIA chief of station Madrid, the Secret Service had taken over a high level command post in a nondescript warehouse in Poblenou, an area of old factories and storehouses; a command post originally constructed by the CIA for their use in the event of a "terrorist issue" involving the U.S. embassy.

It was now approaching nineteen hours since the president had gone missing, and Daniels—encircled by the broad-shouldered bulldog Bill Strait, his deputy special agent in charge; the pale, expressionless Ted Langway, the Secret Service's assistant director in from Washington; CIA-Madrid Station Chief George Kellner, and a half-dozen other Secret Service presidential detail supervisors—sat in the darkened central control room of that converted CIA warehouse in the glow of dozens of computer screens manned by Secret Service and CIA technical analysts culling information from what was now a massive top-secret worldwide intelligence operation.

Standing in the background like a steel shadow and pacing back and forth as if his wife were about to give birth and was taking too long to do it, was the president's chief political adviser, Jake Lowe. BlackBerry in hand, wearing a headset connected to whatever line Hap Daniels was on at the time, Lowe had another line ready at voice command that would instantly connect him to a secure phone at the United States embassy a half dozen miles away, where National Security Adviser Dr. James Marshall and White House chief of staff Tom Curran had established what they called "a working war room." There they were connected by secure phone to the basement of the White House in Washington, where Vice President Hamilton Rogers, Secretary of State David Chaplin, Secretary of Defense Terrence Langdon, and Air Force General Chester Keaton, Chairman of the Joint Chiefs of Staff, had set up a war room of their own.

"We've got a record of twenty-seven phone calls placed between 20:00 hours and 20:40 hours this evening from six separate pay telephones all within a two-mile semicircle of the Barcelona-Sants station," Rodriguez said. "They were paid for with a phone card purchased at a tobacco shop on Carrer de Robrenyo."

Barcelona had been a watch point ever since a small fire had broken out at a newspaper kiosk inside the city's main railroad station early Friday evening. A fire, officials had quickly determined, that had been purposely set but with no apparent reason—theft, vandalism, or as a terrorist act—and that Spanish CNP officers on the scene were now calling a "diversionary tactic." But "diversionary" for what purpose? The only answer seemed to be that because the fire had erupted near an exit where the Spanish police were checking identifications someone inside the station—maybe the president, but more likely someone with a criminal record or on a terrorist watch list—had been trying to get past the police checkpoint. If so it may have worked because the officers at the door had, for a very brief time, left their post to investigate the fire and commotion inside.

"What's the connection to the POTUS?" Daniels pushed, weariness and frustration beginning to override his generally composed demeanor.

"That's why I said I don't know if it means anything, sir."

"If *what* means anything? What the hell are you talking about?"

"The pattern, sir. The calls were placed to local hotels. One after the other as if someone were trying to locate a hotel guest but didn't know in which hotel the person was staying."

"Get me the name of the tobacco shop where the card was purchased, the numbers and locations of the phones the calls were placed from, and the names and numbers of the hotels that were called."

"Yes, sir."

"Thank you," Daniels punched a number on the keyboard in front of him. "Find out if Spanish intelligence did an intercept of public telephones in Barcelona between 20:00 and 20:40 tonight. If so, see if they have a voice record of a series of calls made to area hotels in that time frame. I want to know if the calls were made by a man or a woman, what they were about, and what language the caller spoke in."

"Yes, sir."

"And do it fast."

"Yes, sir."

53

BARCELONA, RIVOLI JARDÍN HOTEL, 2:15 A.M.

Still party time. Horns, cars, motorcycles, unending traffic. People crowding the sidewalks. The sound of Brazilian and Argentine jazz filtering in through the double-glazed windows.

President Harris was asleep on the bed with Marten curled up on a small couch nearby when the chirp of Marten's cell phone woke them both.

"Who is it?" Harris was instantly awake and alert in the dark.

"I don't know."

The phone chirped again

"You better answer."

Marten picked the phone off a small table beside him and clicked on, "Hello."

"It's Demi," her voice was hushed and at the same time charged with immediacy. "You checked out. Where are you? I need to see you right away. I don't want to talk over the phone."

The president turned on a small bedside lamp just as Marten slid a hand over the telephone's receiver, "It's a woman. She wants to see me now. Four hours ago I would have killed for this call."

Harris smiled.

"It's not that," he took his hand away and spoke into the phone. "Are you still at the Regente Magestic ?"

"Yes."

"Hold on," again he covered the phone and looked to Harris. "This has to do with Caroline's death. The woman's name is Demi Picard. She's a French journalist traveling with congressional chaplain Rufus Beck. They're both here in Barcelona." Marten hesitated for the smallest moment. "I don't know if you're aware but the reverend is a close friend of Dr. Merriman Foxx."

"*The* Merriman Foxx?"

"Yes," Marten nodded, then spoke into the phone. "Give me your cell number, I'll call you back." Marten scribbled a number on a bedside table scratch pad, "Five minutes."

With that he clicked off and looked to the president, telling him what he had told Peter Fadden: that he had followed Foxx to his home in Malta and arranged to meet him by pretending to be a member of Congresswoman Baker's staff who needed some questions finalized before the subcommittee report was made final; that he met him in a restaurant and that Beck, another woman, and Demi Picard were with him; that he pressed him for information about his bio-weapons program and brought up the names of Caroline Parsons and her doctor, Lorraine Stephenson; and that he made up a story that Mike Parsons had left a memo questioning the veracity of his testimony. And then Foxx's angry reaction to everything.

"I found out early the next morning that both he and Reverend Beck had suddenly left Malta for places unknown. Ms. Picard was leaving too and wanted nothing to do with me when I questioned her about it. I found out where she was going and followed her here to Barcelona.

"You said you knew Caroline had been murdered, Mr. President. I wonder if you know Foxx was behind it, he and the same Dr. Stephenson he denied knowing. They inoculated her with some kind of bacteria that killed her. I'm all but certain it was one of his experiments, a piece of his bio-weapons program that was supposed to be dead but isn't. What Mike Parsons's committee was investigating when he and his son were killed. How Beck is involved I don't know, but he and Foxx are meeting somewhere here soon. Maybe even tomorrow. Demi knows more about it or she wouldn't be calling like this." Marten hesitated, trying to decide how to put the next part. He didn't have to, the president did it for him.

"You're thinking Dr. Foxx is part of the coup against me."

"Maybe, but there's no proof. All I know is that he was at the center of the subcommittee hearings denying his program was still in existence while at the same time he was still working his tricks on a live human being—Caroline Parsons."

"How is this Picard woman involved?"

"Supposedly she used Reverend Beck to get an introduction to Foxx. Her sister disappeared from Malta two years ago and she thought Foxx might open some doors that would help her to find out what happened, at least that's what she tells me."

"So she's incidental in all this."

"Maybe, maybe not. I don't know. But it's Foxx who's central here. He not only knows the *how* but the *why* about Caroline's death, and both of those answers may have a lot to do with the things you're up against."

The president looked away, trying to digest it all, "If you're right, it's the part of the package that's missing, the specifics of what they're planning to do. I know I should be surprised about Chaplain Beck, but nothing surprises me now."

He turned back and Marten could see the anguish in his eyes. "They are planning something horrendous, Mr. Marten. More terrible, I think, than either you or I could imagine. Part of it I know, the rest I don't. The whole thing came out of the blue. It's a major breakdown on my part. I should have known something was happening and seen through it; I didn't. As I said earlier, the timetable for me to do anything about it is incredibly short. If I'm caught, it's nonexistent."

Marten nodded toward the phone, "Maybe she can help. How much I can't guess, but it's more than we have right now."

Harris stared at him. "You said she wanted nothing to do with you. What makes you think you can trust her now?"

"That is a multimillion-dollar question."

"*Can you trust her,* Mr. Marten?"

"When I left my hotel in Malta I was tailed all the way to Barcelona by a young man. At the airport I was handed off to someone else. He was the dead man in the newspaper photo. He followed Demi and me to a restaurant where we went to talk. Afterward I tried to confront and question him. He ran away and I chased him. That was when he ran in front of the truck."

"You think it was Foxx who had you followed."

"Yes, to see who I might be reporting to."

"And you're suggesting this Picard woman had something to do with it?"

"That's what I don't know. She might be legitimate and a great help to us or she might bring the whole mountain down. For me it's one thing, for you, Mr. President, it's something else entirely. I guess what I'm saying—the call is yours to make."

Marten saw President Harris hesitate for the slightest moment and then make up his mind. "Ask her to come here now," he said, "but to tell no one where she is going. Give her the room number and tell her to come directly to it. Say nothing about me."

"You're certain?"

"Yes, I'm certain."

54

2:25 A.M.

Room lights out, Marten stood by the window watching for Demi. Below, the street remained a swirl of nightlife. Traffic at a crawl, the sidewalks filled with pedestrians, music floating from cars and open doorways. For Spain, for Barcelona, the night was still a pup.

Marten could hear the shower running in the bathroom, then heard it stop as the president turned off the water. A short while earlier an embarrassed John Henry Harris had asked to borrow Marten's toothbrush, and he'd given it to him without thought.

Then he'd asked to use his razor to shave, but Marten suggested he let his beard continue to grow as another level of cover and the president had agreed.

2:27 A.M.

Still no sign of Demi.

Marten looked back to the room. Not fifteen feet away, in the confines of the bathroom, the president of the United States was drying himself and dressing, preparing for what was to come next. The whole situation was impossible, even absurd, but it was happening nonetheless. The truth of it made Marten think of his brief conversation with the president just before he'd gone in to shower.

"You told me Dr. Foxx had been directly involved with Caroline's death, that he'd given her some kind of bacteria that had killed her," the president had said. "How did you know that?"

"Caroline had been injected with something by Dr. Stephenson after she broke down following the funeral of her husband and son. She woke up in a clinic where Foxx was, and he seemed to be overseeing her treatment. It was her sense and fear that either Stephenson had given her whatever poisoned her or Foxx had done it himself at the clinic."

"Sense and fear?"

"Yes."

"Sense and fear mean uncertainty. You were certain when you told me. Why?"

"Because of what Dr. Stephenson told me just before she died. She thought I was one of 'them,' whoever 'they' are, your 'friends' maybe, and that I was going to take her to 'the doctor,' as she put it. She meant Merriman Foxx."

"Just before she died?" the president had stared at him, incredulous. "You were there when she was murdered? When she was decapitated?"

For a long moment Marten said nothing. He was the only one in the world who knew the truth. Then he realized that now, at this point, there was no reason to hold it back, especially from the man who faced him. "She wasn't murdered, Mr. President. She committed suicide."

"Suicide?" The president was stunned.

"On the street near her home. It was night. I waited for her to come home and was trying to question her about what had happened to Caroline. She was frightened, I think more about being taken to 'the doctor' and what he might do to her than anything. She had a pistol. I thought she was going to shoot me. Instead she put it in her mouth and pulled the trigger.

"There was nothing I could do, and I didn't want to explain things to the police because then Foxx would find out about it. So I got out of there fast. The decapitation had to have been done shortly afterward. It meant someone had been watching her."

The president was clearly puzzled. "Why do something like that when she was already dead?"

"I asked myself that and came to the conclusion that a suicide by a physician of her prominence coming so soon after the death of one of her high-profile patients might raise eyebrows and have people start asking questions. Especially when it happened so soon after the deaths of that patient's congressman husband and their son. Murder is different. It's impersonal, it could happen to anyone. Besides there's no way to cover up a suicide done like that, Mr. President. It means whoever did it understood that and simply took her head."

"My God," the president breathed.

"That's what I said."

2:30 A.M.

Marten looked back to the street.

Still no sign of Demi.

55

"A woman made the Barcelona hotel calls, sir." Again the voice of Secret Service intelligence specialist Sandra Rodriguez came through Hap Daniels's headset. He was standing in front of a computer screen in the CIA warehouse clicking through an endless stream of reports from the mass of intelligence agencies trying and failing to locate the president.

"She sounded young and was speaking Spanish with a Danish accent. It took a while for Spanish intelligence to run the tapes and make some sense of it."

"What was she trying to find out?" Daniels pressed her.

"She was looking for a man, a hotel employee or guest, she didn't specify. All she had was a name, a Señor Nicholas Marten. Marten with an *e* not an *i*."

"Marten?" Hap Daniels said abruptly and looked up. Jake Lowe was staring at him from across the room, Daniels turned back. "Do we know if she located this Nicholas Marten?"

"Yes, sir. He's at the Rivoli Jardín Hotel. Barcelona, 080002."

"Thank you."

Jake Lowe had turned his back to the room and was talking by secure phone to National Security Adviser Jim Marshall in the war room at the U.S. embassy in Madrid.

"We may have something hot," Lowe said lowly and with urgency. "Spanish intel has located a Nicholas Marten at a hotel in Barcelona. Someone made a number of calls trying to find out where he was."

"Marten?" Marshall perked. "The same Marten connected to the Caroline Parsons circumstance?"

"Not certain."

"Do we know who was trying to find him?"

"A woman. We don't know who she is or why she was looking for him. Or even if it's *the* Nicholas Marten. But if it is, the president certainly would recognize him; he saw him in Parsons's hospital room then asked for more information on him later, and we delivered it."

"Mr. Lowe," Hap Daniels's voice came through a separate channel in his headset and he turned to see Daniels motioning to him, "you might want to look at this."

Immediately Lowe crossed the room to look at the computer screen Daniels, Station Chief Kellner, and Secret Service assistant director Ted Langway were staring at. On it was the newspaper photograph of Marten taken on the Barcelona street—the same photo the president had used to identify him.

"From yesterday's special late edition of the Barcelona *La Vanguardia*. That is Marten," Daniels said definitively.

"You sure?"

"Yes, I'm sure. I was with the president when we saw him at University Hospital."

"We have a confirm on Marten," Lowe said to Marshall through his headset, then looked to Daniels. "Locate him. But that's all. Just locate him and watch him. Don't let him know we're onto him."

Abruptly Daniels turned to Kellner. "You have assets in place in Barcelona?"

"Yes."

"Put them to work."

"Right."

"Hap," Lowe's eyes found Daniels's. "What's your gut tell you? Is the president with him?"

"I want to say yes, but there's no way to know until we get a confirm."

"I want us to do that ourselves."

Daniels's eyebrows furrowed in puzzlement. "I'm not sure I understand."

"We don't know his physical or psychological condition. What we do know is that he's ill and so whatever happens has to be done with extreme delicacy. When we go in it needs to be with people he will instantly recognize. Not strange faces, not CIA or Spanish intelligence," he glanced at Assistant Director Ted Langway, "not even you, Mr. Langway. I'd suggest you stay in Madrid." Lowe looked back to Daniels, "I don't want to make it any worse for him than it already is. If you want a direct order I can get it from the vice president."

"I won't need it, sir."

"Dr. Marshall will want to be there too."

"Dr. Marshall?"

"Yes."

Hap Daniels's eyes held Lowe's for the briefest second, "Yes, sir," he said and then turned and walked away, speaking into his headset as he went.

"I want a lead car, an armored van set up as an ambulance with two doctors and two EMT techs, and three security tail cars ready in Barcelona within the hour. Have a car pick up Dr. Marshall at the embassy and take him to the airport."

Again he looked to Station Chief Kellner. "Can you get Spanish intelligence to facilitate priority air clearance for a flight to Barcelona?"

"I think so."

"Hap," Lowe was looking directly at him. "How soon can we be in the air?"

"We get clearance, wheels up in twenty minutes."

"Good."

56

BARCELONA, RIVOLI JARDÍN HOTEL, 3:00 A.M.

Marten pulled back the curtain in the semidarkness in time to glimpse Demi Picard dodge through traffic and cross the street coming toward the hotel. She wore a light-colored trench coat with a large purse thrown over one shoulder and had a floppy hat pulled low over her forehead. If he hadn't been looking for her she would have been difficult to recognize, which was probably the idea.

Marten let the curtain go and stepped back from the window

just as President Harris came out of the bathroom and pulling on his clear-lensed eyeglasses.

"She's just crossed the street. She should be here in a few minutes," Marten said. "How do you want to play it?"

The president stopped and looked at him. He was still without his toupee and had put back on the same khaki pants, blue sport shirt, and brown jacket he had been wearing when Marten first saw him in the room several hours earlier.

"Mr. Marten," he said with an urgency Marten hadn't heard before. "I knew when I came to you I was taking a chance, but I had to find a place out of sight to rest, if even for a short time. Standing in the shower I had a chance to collect my thoughts. It's now three in the morning. Spanish federal police boarded the train I took from Madrid to Barcelona late this afternoon. Very luckily I got away without them recognizing me. The same as I managed to avoid them in the train station here. The hunt for me, secretive as it will be, will be massive. I know the procedures and agencies the Secret Service will use in trying to bring me in. That means there's every chance that by now they will have some idea where I've gone. It's possible they may even have intercepted the phone calls my female friend made in trying to find you. It won't be long before they put it all together and learn where I am. It means I need to get out of here right away, and the sooner the better."

"To go where?"

"If I told you and they found you, believe me when I say you would tell them."

"Then I can't let them find me, can I?"

The president studied him carefully. "Mr. Marten, you've helped a great deal already. If you try to do more you'll be getting in dangerously over your head."

"I'm already in over my head," Marten half smiled. "I'm probably going to get fired from my job too." The smile vanished, "If they come here looking for you they'll know who I am anyway. You asked for my help, Mr. President, and you still have it," Marten paused, then went on. "Besides, I've come this far because of what happened to Caroline Parsons and in a way so have you. If you're going, I am too."

"You're certain?"

"Yes, sir."

"Then I thank you most gratefully, Mr. Marten. But I also want you to understand something," the urgency in the president's voice was now compounded by a look of almost unbearable anguish, as if for the first time he realized the true enormity of his situation. "Out here, like this, I have nothing of the power of my office to draw upon. I have no authority at all. If they catch me and bring me back they will kill me. That makes me just some poor fellow on the run with the clock ticking down, and at the same time trying to stay alive and keep his country and I think an ungodly number of other countries afloat as well. To do that I have to find out what my 'friends' are planning to do and what they have the ability to do, and then find a way to stop it, whatever *it* is. Dr. Foxx seems to be a key figure here, maybe even its prime architect. Your friend, this Demi Picard, may be able to help us find him. She might even know where he is."

"You mean you want to take her with us."

"Mr. Marten, I've said time is very short. If she knows something about Dr. Foxx, I need to learn what it is. As I said before, I have probably lingered here too long as it is. So yes, dangerous and foolhardy as it might be if she is working for Foxx, I want to take her with us. That is if she'll go."

"I don't doubt that she'll go, because she wants very much to talk to me. But if she does, you'll run a great risk of having her realize who you are."

"I run the same risk here. If she can get us to Dr. Foxx or even near enough so we can find him ourselves, it's worth the chance," the president paused and his voice became nearly a whisper. "Mr. Marten, it means that much."

Abruptly there was a sharp knock at the door. A second knock followed. "It's Demi," she said from the hallway.

Marten looked at the president, "You're sure?"

"Yes."

Marten nodded, then opened the door. Demi came in quickly and he closed it. In almost the same instant he felt her hand on his arm. "Who is he?" She was staring at President Harris.

"I, uh—" Marten stammered. This was something they hadn't discussed at all. How to introduce the president to her.

"Bob," Harris took care of the situation himself, smiling and extending his hand. "Bob Rader, I'm an old friend of Nicholas. We bumped into each other unexpectedly."

She stared at him for a heartbeat longer, just enough to digest his presence, then looked back to Marten. "We have to talk. Alone. Now."

"Demi, Bob knows what's going on. Whatever you have to say you can say in front of him."

"No, it's something else."

"What?"

Her eyes flashed from one man to the other, "Four people came in off the street and into the hotel when I did. One was a hotel guest who rode up in the elevator with me. The other three, two men and a woman, went to the front desk. One of them carried a copy of *La Vanguardia*, the edition of the newspaper your photograph was in. The one taken with our friend in the yellow polo shirt from the restaurant, the dead man you were kneeling beside in the street."

"So?"

"I think they were police."

57

RIVOLI JARDÍN HOTEL, LOBBY, 3:07 A.M.

"¿Es este Señor Marten?"

Is this Mr. Marten? Barcelona police plainclothes detective Iuliana Ortega demanded, showing Marten's newspaper photo to a young, razor-thin night desk clerk. He looked at it and then to the two men behind her watching him, plainclothes detectives Alfonso Leon and Sanzo Tarrega.

Outside were ten more undercover officers. Two each in cars watching the building's two street-level public entrances, two more in a car parked at the rear of the building near a service/delivery entrance. The other four were on the rooftop of an apartment building across the street, two with night-vision binoculars, the others were sharpshooters armed with .50 caliber Barrett sniper rifles fitted with night-vision scopes. The first pair watched the street below, the second, the window of room 408.

In all there were thirteen card-carrying members of Guàrdia Urbana, the Barcelona police, yet none of them were what they pretended to be. The six in the stakeout cars were special agents from GEO, Grupo Especial de Operaciones, Spain's elite counter-terrorism corps; the others, those across the street on the roof and detectives Ortega, Leon and Tarrega were CIA-Madrid Station Chief Kellner's Barcelona "assets," CIA agents operating with the permission of the Barcelona police and Spanish intelligence.

"I asked you if this is Señor Marten." Detective Ortega pressed the clerk in Spanish once more, gesturing to Marten's newspaper photograph and trying to ignore the loud, pulsating Cuban jazz spilling from the hotel's Jamboree Club on the far side of the lobby.

"Sí," the young man nodded, his eyes darting nervously between Detective Ortega and the men behind her. "Sí."

"Another man is with him," she said definitively.

The clerk nodded again. Clearly he had no idea what this was about or what was going on.

Detective Tarrega moved in. "They are both in Señor Marten's room now?"

"Yes, I think," the clerk said nervously. "I can't swear to it, because I've been busy. But they would have to pass by the desk to leave, and I didn't see them. I've been here all night. The manager made me work a double shift. I didn't ask for the extra time, he just told me that was what I was doing."

"This other man. Who is he?" Detective Ortega pressed, "What is his name?"

"I don't know. He said he was Señor Marten's uncle. I let him into the room myself."

"What does he look like?"

"Like somebody's uncle," the clerk grinned sheepishly.

"Answer the question, please," Ortega demanded. "What does he look like?"

"Old—well not too old, but a little. Almost bald, with glasses."

"Bald?"   ·

"Almost, yes."

Detective Tarrega glanced at Detective Leon and nodded toward the elevator, then looked back to the clerk. "Please give us a key to Marten's room."

"I—it's against hotel pol—" the clerk started to argue, then quickly decided against it. Anxiously he picked up a blank electronic key, programmed it, and handed it to Tarrega.

Abruptly Tarrega looked at Iuliana Ortega, "Cover here, we're going up."

3:12 A.M.

The fourth-floor elevator door slid open and Tarrega and Leon stepped out. Seconds later they had taken up positions at either end of the hallway where they could clearly see the door to room 408.

They knew 408 was Marten's room. Not because they had asked the clerk but because they had hacked into the hotel's reservation system before they arrived and confirmed it. Confirmed too that Marten had made no calls from 408's telephone or ordered anything from room service. To them and to the agents outside, and for all intents, Nicholas Marten and his balding "guest" were still in the room.

58

U.S. ARMY CHINOOK HELICOPTER, TWENTY-ONE MINUTES OUT OF MADRID EN ROUTE TO BARCELONA, 3:16 A.M.

"Bald?" Hap Daniels took the radio call over the roar of the Chinook's engines. Immediately he looked to Jake Lowe and National Security Adviser James Marshall buckled into seats across from him.

"Assets are reporting a man was let into Marten's room claiming to be his uncle. He was bald. Or almost bald. Unless the POTUS shaved his head, we've got the wrong man."

"Maybe he did shave his head," Lowe glanced at Marshall, then looked back to Daniels. "Keep the assets where they are. Bald or not treat the situation as if he is the POTUS."

"When do we get there?" Marshall asked.

"Wheels down at Barcelona police headquarters at 03:40 hours. Another ten minutes to the hotel."

CHANTILLY, FRANCE, 3:25 A.M.

Victor was nestled in dark woods three-quarters of a mile from the Hippodrome de Chantilly alongside a turf practice track for the Chantilly racetrack's thoroughbreds called *Coeur de la Forêt*, the Heart of the Forest. It was still more than three and half hours before his targets would come by, yet even in the dark and damp of the woods Victor was comfortable and content.

They had flown him as promised first-class from Madrid to Paris. After that he'd done as instructed: taken a taxi from Roissy–Charles de Gaulle Airport to Gare du Nord Railway Station and from there a train to the town of Chantilly, where he checked into a room reserved for him at the Hotel Chantilly and where the M14 rifle and ammunition he would need—packed inside a locked golf bag with his name on the luggage tag and forwarded by rail from a hotel in Nice—were waiting. After that he'd taken a stroll in the woods, found the Coeur de la Forêt practice track and selected the spot where he was now and from where he would shoot when the jockeys worked out their thoroughbreds just after dawn.

3:27 A.M.

"Victor," Richard's soft and reassuring voice came through his headset.

"Yes, Richard."

"Are you in place?"

"Yes, Richard."

"Is everything alright? Are you warm enough? Do you have everything you need?"

"Yes, Richard."

"Any questions?"

"No, Richard."

"Then, good luck."

"Thank you, Richard. Everything will be fine."

"I know that, Victor. I know that very well."

Victor heard Richard click off, and he settled back into the leaves. He was at ease, even happy. The dark forest and night sounds around him, even the dewy dampness that had settled on everything, felt natural and inviting, as. if this was a part of the world—so far away and so very different from the desert scrub of Arizona where he had spent his entire life until they'd found him—where he truly belonged.

3:30 A.M.

A moth fluttered down and touched his face, and Victor reached up gently and brushed it away, careful not to harm it. He cared deeply for living things and had all his life, and all his life he had been chastised for it; too sensitive, too emotional, a crybaby, a mama's boy he'd been called, even by his own family. The names hurt deeply and suggested a weakness a male should not have, and as a teenager and later an adult he had tried to deliberately bury them. Fistfights and trouble in school; later, bar fights and assault-and-battery charges, now and again minor jail time. He didn't care—he was as tough and masculine as any situation called for, as tough and masculine as he needed to be. It was a pretense Richard had picked up on after their first few telephone conversations.

In doing so he had made Victor realize there was nothing wrong with how he felt and that those same emotions were shared by hundreds, thousands, even millions of other men. Certainly it was hurtful when people close to him criticized him for it, but it was nothing compared to the things others were doing in the world. Richard was talking about people who saw little value in life at all except as it furthered their own ends. Terrorists. Killers, whom the world paid lip-service to fighting but with few exceptions had little effect in stopping even with the use of massive armies.

It was then Richard had asked if he would be interested in joining an underground movement of freedom fighters dedicated to protecting the American homeland by defeating these people and their organizations around the world, and he had agreed immediately.

The man he had killed coming off the train in Washington,

Richard had told him several days beforehand, was a young base-ball player from Central America. But he was also a member of a terrorist organization setting up sleeper cells in the corridor be-tween Washington and New York and was leaving the country the next day to report to his handlers in Venezuela to arrange to bring more of their people and money into the U.S. The authorities knew about it but, because of their bureaucratic system with its layers of authority, had done nothing to stop him. It was necessary some-thing be done before he left the country, and Victor had.

It was the same in Madrid when Richard had insisted that he walk through Atocha Station and picture the horror the terrorists had done there. It was an act of terror that should have, and could have, been stopped long before it happened.

Following the president both in Berlin and Madrid had been a simple exercise. Richard wanted him to see firsthand how easy it was for anyone to get close enough to kill him despite the heavy se-curity. It was why he was here in Chantilly now, not just to test his shooting skills but also because the jockeys were part of a terrorist faction setting up in northern France. The idea was to take them down, little by little, one by one and by whatever means. This was war, and if no one else could fight it properly, people like Victor and Richard would.

So far Victor had played his part well. They valued his skills and dedication and told him so. To him that was most important of all.

3:35 A.M.

Victor put out a gloved hand and drew the M14 closer, letting it rest comfortably in the crook of his arm. He had only to rest and wait until the horsemen came by just before seven.

59

In a storm of flying dust and a deafening roar the U.S. Army Chinook helicopter touched down on the Guàrdia Urbana helipad. Instantly the engines shut down and the doors slid open. Seconds later Hap Daniels, his deputy Bill Strait, Jake Lowe, Dr. James Marshall, and four other Secret Service agents jumped out. Ducking beneath still churning rotors they went to three unmarked cars, their doors open, waiting on the edge of the tarmac. In an instant the men were inside, the doors slammed closed, and the cars screeched off.

Music and traffic filled the streets as if it were midday. Revelers came and went through the hotel's two main entrances as if the Rivoli Jardín were hosting a rolling citywide party, the center of which was the music pulsating from the Jamboree Club at the end of the lobby.

So far none of the six Spanish GEO special agents posted in the unmarked cars outside had reported seeing either the man identified as Nicholas Marten or his balding "uncle" leave the building. Nor had the assets on the roof of the building across the street seen any activity inside the drawn curtains of a darkened room 408. The only illumination coming from it at all seemed to emanate from a dim hallway or bathroom light that had been on since they arrived. Nothing had changed either for the CIA assets acting as Barcelona police detectives Tarrega and Leon stationed in the corridor outside room 408. The same was true for the female asset calling herself Iuliana Ortega on watch in the lobby. Bottom line, if their two "men of interest" had been in the room when they arrived, they were still there now.

The Jamboree Club was smoky and sweltering, packed wall to wall with mostly young and sweaty dancers. In the last hours the Cuban jazz had given way to Brazilian bossa nova and then to Argentine jazz.

"*Vino blanco otra vez, por favor.*" White wine again, please. "Bob," as President Harris had introduced himself to Demi, smiled at the young waitress and motioned for her to refill their drinks, then watched as she twisted away through the dancers toward the bar.

At 3:07 Demi had alerted them to the police downstairs. By 3:08 Marten had shoved his electronic notebook, tape recorder, toiletries, and other belongings into his traveling bag and thrown it over his shoulder. At 3:09 they were out the door and down the fire stairs at the end of the corridor. At 3:11 they entered the hotel lobby from a side hallway near the Jamboree Club and stopped.

"There," Demi said, pointing out Iuliana Ortega, the woman she had seen enter the hotel with the two men at the same time she had. She was sitting in an overstuffed lobby chair with a clear view of both the front entrance from the street and the elevators as if she were waiting for someone.

"Do you see the two men that were with her?" Bob asked.

"No."

The president looked at Marten. "They aren't police," he said quietly, then nodded toward the Jamboree Club. "It's as good a place as any."

At 3:13 they found a table and sat down. Quickly the waitress arrived and the president ordered white wine for the three of them. As the waitress left he took a napkin and made a note on it, then folded it and looked at Marten and Demi.

"By now they will have learned which room Mr. Marten is in and where they assume I am, since the clerk who let me in will have told them. The men will have gone up and be covering it, but they won't go in until the big guns arrive."

Marten leaned in, "There's a side entrance on the far side of the lobby, why don't we just go out that way?"

"There will be more outside," the president said quietly, "and watching all the entrances."

"How do you know all this?" Demi was looking at Bob carefully. Something was going on here and she didn't like it. "Who are you?"

"Bob," he said flatly.

Just then the waitress came back with their drinks. Marten paid her and she left. At the same time an exuberant voice came over the club's PA system announcing in Catalan: "Please welcome sizzling Basque singer-songwriter Fermín Murguruza!"

With that a spotlight came on and the handsome Murguruza bounded onstage singing. The audience went crazy. In seconds people were on their feet dancing as if everything else in their lives had been forgotten. It was a moment the president used to slip Marten the napkin he had written on. Marten pulled it into his lap and unfolded it. On it the president had scrawled:

The woman is CIA, probably the men too—Secret Service imminent!

Marten felt his pulse quicken and looked to the president. As he did, he heard Demi's breathless exclamation.

"Oh-mon-Dieu!" Oh-my-God! she said in French.

Marten glanced at her. She was staring wide-eyed at Bob.

Quickly Harris's eyes found hers. "So now you know. Don't say a word."

"I won't," she breathed. She stared a second longer in disbelief, then turned uncertainly to Marten. "What's happening here? I don't understand."

"Listen to me," the president leaned in trying to make himself heard over the din of Fermín Murguruza's music. "Any minute now the special agent in charge of my Secret Service detail will arrive. He and his men will have flown from Madrid. They have no idea what I'm doing or why, and frankly, at this point they don't care. Their job is to protect me at all costs. Above all they will not want known what's going on or that I am anywhere near here. Which is most likely the reason they haven't evacuated the building or locked it down. It would draw too much attention, and that's the last thing any of them want.

"They work very quickly and very efficiently. If they had arrived when we were still in the room by now we would have been hustled out the back way, thrown into waiting cars, and gone. No one would ever know I or they had even been here, let alone that something had happened.

"At the same time, those tactics give us a tiny window of opportunity because when they arrive, when my agent in charge comes through the door with his deputy and starts up to the room, the focus of every other agent will be on the plan to evacuate me. It's then, the moment he goes up, we go out. The three of us, right out the side entrance, onto the street, and into the crowd. I looked at both entrances carefully before I came in. Once outside we turn right and walk as a threesome down the block. At the end of it, maybe two hundred feet away, is a line of taxi cabs. Take the first one available and let me do the talking."

Marten leaned in, "You're basing all this on the certainty your special agent will come in through the front and not some other way."

"You're right, I'm not certain, I'm guessing. But that's because I know him well. Not only is he horrified the president vanished on his watch, he's worried as hell about my well-being and will want to get me out of here and into his custody as fast as he can. To do that he will take the shortest route to the object, and that is through the front door and up the elevators directly to the room."

"What if he doesn't? What if he goes in another way, crashes the room, and finds you gone. No one's seen you go out. It means you're still somewhere in the building. Attention or not, this place will be shut down before any of us can take another breath."

The president half smiled. "Let's just hope I know my man well enough to be right." Immediately he looked to Demi. "You were thrust into this because of Mr. Marten and what you might know about Dr. Foxx."

Demi started.

"Am I correct?" President Harris pushed her.

Marten calmed her, "I told you before, he knows, it's alright to talk in front of him."

"Yes, you are correct," Demi said.

"Then you understand that if Mr. Marten or I are caught whatever information you have come to Mr. Marten with will go for nothing because I won't be able to do anything about it and neither will he. That puts you directly on the spot."

"I don't understand," she said.

"Because of the newspaper photo they will know what Mr. Marten looks like, and quite obviously my people know what I look like, and if they were surprised by my lack of hair they won't be now that they've talked to the desk clerk. That brings us back to you because none of them know you," the president paused, looking her in the eye. Marten knew he was using the moment to judge her.

"What I'm doing, Ms. Picard, is putting your well-being and Mr. Marten's and mine fully into your hands. I'm asking for your help. Do you understand?"

"Yes."

"*Will* you help?"

Demi glanced at Marten, then looked back to the president, "What do you want me to do?"

3:45 A.M.

Demi got up from the table and went out into the lobby carrying her large purse. Left behind was the big floppy hat she had been wearing and her light-colored trench coat.

3:46 A.M.

Demi used a napkin to fan herself as she mingled with sweaty, high-spirited dancers getting air just outside the open doors to the Jamboree Club. Her real attention was on the main entrance.

Ten feet away Marten and President Harris stood watching just inside the club's doors. Marten had mussed up his hair, opened his shirt and had Demi's trench coat thrown cavalierly over one shoulder to hide his travel bag beneath it. The president, still wearing his clear glasses, had taken her big floppy hat and pulled it foppishly down over one ear, effectively, and for the most part, covering his baldness.

3:50 A.M.

Demi saw the four come through the front door and head directly for the elevators, one of them with a raincoat over his arm. The president's descriptions of Hap Daniels and Bill Strait had been perfect, as had been his prediction of their actions. The two men with them she recognized from her time in Washington: presidential adviser Jake Lowe and U.S. National Security Adviser, Dr. James Marshall. Abruptly she turned and walked back into the club.

"Now," she said.

3:51 A.M.

The threesome came out of the Jamboree Club walking arm in arm across the crowded lobby toward the side entrance. They were self-absorbed, laughing, half-dancing to the music as they moved through the crowd. They looked exactly as they wanted to look, a couple of half-drunken gay men and their party-loving straight girl out for the evening.

Five seconds and they were halfway to the door. Another three and they were almost to it.

"Not quiet yet," the president said, forcing a smile and stopping. "One more drink before we go." As quickly he turned them back. "Just outside," he said, "Secret Service agent who's been on my detail since the inauguration."

3:52 A.M.

The elevator slowed and stopped, the door opened and Hap Daniels, Bill Strait, Jake Lowe and James Marshall stepped out into the fourth floor hallway.

There was no need for Daniels to identify any of them to either Alfonso Leon or Sanzo Tarrega. They had known who they were and what they would be doing the moment the Chinook touched down at police headquarters. That Agent Strait carried a raincoat was no surprise either. It was to throw over the president's head just before they brought him out, making certain no accidental passerby or alert media person or any paparazzi lurking undetected would have the slightest chance for recognition, let alone a photograph.

3:53 A.M.

The three remaining Secret Service agents that had accompanied Daniels from Madrid made contact with the Spanish GEO operatives at the hotel's rear service/delivery entrance and then went inside to the service elevator.

At the same time the rolling stock Daniels had requested little more than an hour earlier from Madrid—a lead car, an armored van with two doctors and two EMT techs inside, and three security tail cars—pulled up and stopped beside the GEO car. Immediately their lights were turned off.

3:54 A.M.

The president, Nicholas Marten, and Demi stood in the crowd just outside the open doors to the Jamboree Club. Across the lobby they could see the slim desk clerk and CIA asset Ortega. The clerk was on the phone and busy. Ortega had moved from the chair where she had been sitting and now stood near the main entrance, watching it carefully.

"We're running out of time," the president said quietly. "We'll have to use the main entrance and hope the woman posted there is the only one and that the others are on strict assignment elsewhere. If we get past her, turn right outside and move into the crowd. If for some reason they get me, just keep going. If you try to help, somebody might get killed."

The president was about to start toward the door. "Wait," Marten said quickly and turned to Demi. "You speak French."

"Of course."

"You go first. When you get to the woman speak to her as if you were a French tourist separated from your group and looking for directions to the harbor. She might understand, she might not; it doesn't matter. We'll be right behind you. All we need is about five seconds of distraction to get past her. Once we're out, just thank her and leave. We'll meet you halfway down the block. Can you do that?"

"Yes."

"Good."

3:55 A.M.

Jake Lowe and Dr. Marshall stood pressed against the wall as Hap Daniels and Bill Strait moved to the door of room 408. The corridor behind them was covered by CIA assets Tarrega and Leon in the event they needed help or that a hotel guest tried to leave his or her room.

The three Secret Service agents who had taken the service elevator up from the rear entrance waited twenty feet down the hallway in a small L-shaped nook that housed the service elevator, the way the president would be taken down once they had him. The central elevator Hap and the others had taken up was locked and "temporarily out of service."

Electronic room card in hand, Hap Daniels looked at Bill Strait, who held the raincoat to be thrown over the president's head, then glanced at Jake Lowe and Dr. Marshall.

"Five seconds," he said quietly into the tiny microphone at his collar. He put up one finger, then two.

The four CIA assets on the roof of the building across the street tensed. The two watching the street shifted their binoculars to the window of room 408. The two sharpshooters with Barrett .50 caliber sniper rifles and night-vision scopes were already squared on it. If someone or some group was holding the president hostage he, she or they, would be dead in the next few seconds.

THE HOTEL LOBBY, SAME TIME

Marten and the president were steps behind Demi. Just beyond her they could see the female CIA asset standing just inside the hotel's main foyer. To their right they saw the desk clerk hang up the phone, then turn away and talk to someone.

THE FOURTH FLOOR CORRIDOR

Hap Daniels threw up fingers four, then five.

In one move he slid the electronic key into the latch. A half second later the red light on the lock turned green and he shoved the door open.

THE HOTEL FOYER

"Excusez-moi. Mes amis sont partis. Pouvez-vous me dire quelle manière c'est au port ? Là où mon hôtel est." Excuse me. My friends have left. Can you tell me which way it is to the harbor? Where my hotel is.

Demi had stepped in front of Iuliana Ortega, blocking her view of the hotel entrance. As she did, Marten and the president slipped past and vanished into crowded sidewalk outside.

"Trouvez un taxi, il est une longue promenade." Find a taxi, it's a long walk, Ortega said brusquely, then immediately stepped around her, trying to keep an eye on the door.

"Merci," Demi said, then turned and walked out.

"God dammit!" Hap Daniels yelled out loud.

Special Agent Bill Strait was right behind him. Jake Lowe and Dr. James Marshall rushed in from the hallway.

Room 408 was empty.

"Was he here?" Lowe pushed into the room with Marshall on his heels.

Daniels ignored him, instead spoke into his headset. "Lock down the building now! Nobody in or out. I want every last damn person checked. Along with every closet, toilet, hallway, every last inch, and that includes the goddamn air-conditioning ducts this time."

Suddenly Jake Lowe was in his face. "I asked you if he was here. Was the president here in this room?"

Daniels glared at him for a heartbeat, then calmed, "Don't know, sir," he said professionally, then abruptly turned back to his headset. "Alert Spanish Intel. Have their people already on post seal down a two-mile perimeter around the hotel. Ask them to authorize the detention of any Caucasian male inside it between forty and seventy who is either bald or partially bald. Also to authorize the apprehension and detention of Nicholas Marten. And keep the media as far away from this as possible."

Daniels looked to Marshall. "I think you better inform the chief of staff and the White House press secretary. They're both going to have a helluva lot of work and in a big hurry if this gets out."

"Was he here?" Jake Lowe asked again. This time quietly but very deliberately, his eyes stark with anger.

Hap Daniels looked at him, then tugged on an ear and glanced around the room. The bed was disheveled, as if someone had been sleeping in it. A chair was pulled back from a small writing desk.

Daniels turned and went down the hall and into the bathroom. A washcloth and several wet towels were on the sink. The bathtub was still wet, the shower head slowly dripping. For a moment Daniels did nothing, just stood there thinking. A second later he brushed past Marshall and Bill Strait, went back into the bedroom, and stared at the bed. He studied it for a moment and then went over and bent down and sniffed the sheets and then the rumpled pillow.

"What the hell are you doing?" Jake Lowe snapped. "Was he here or wasn't he? Or don't you know?"

Abruptly Daniels straightened up. "Aftershave."

"What?"

"Aftershave. On the pillow. The president has been using the same cheap stuff ever since I've known him."

"You mean he *was* here."

"Yes, sir, he was." Daniels looked at Bill Strait, "Get a tech team up here now, see what we can find out."

"Yes, sir." Strait turned and walked off down the hallway speaking into his own headset.

"Hap," Marshall leaned his six-foot, four-inch frame against the writing desk and crossed his arms in front of him. His manner was ice, "What do we do now?"

"Hope like hell we find him in the next twenty minutes. We don't, we can begin the whole process all over again."

61

4:03 A.M.

"La estación de tren Barcelona-Sants." Barcelona-Sants Train Station, the president said as he, Demi, and Marten climbed into the back seat of crisp yellow-and-black taxi number 6622.

"Sí." The driver put the taxi in gear and sped off just as the sound of sirens filled the air. The driver crossed a square, turned left and then slowed quickly to avoid hitting two Barcelona police cars crossing directly in front of him.

"The alarm is out," Marten said quietly. "They'll be watching the station."

"I know," the president said.

"Then—?"

"We'll see," the president sat back and pulled Demi's big floppy hat a little farther down over his forehead.

Demi looked at him, then turned to Marten. "Wherever you're going, I can't join you. It's what I had to talk to you about, why I came."

Suddenly two more police cars screamed past going in the direction of Marten's hotel. Just then they saw the line of stopped traffic.

"Mossos d'Esquadra. ¿En qué el infierno va?" Catalan state police. What the hell is going on? The cab driver looked at them in the mirror.

"¿Algo, quién sabe?" Something, who knows? The president shrugged, then quickly looked to Marten.

"Road block," he said sotto voce. "They'll be doing a vehicle search. There'll be more and then more after that. They build these things in concentric circles. Roadblocks funneled into checkpoints and then more outside them."

"Then we'll walk," Marten said

"Yes." Immediately the president looked to the driver. "Tire por favor encima." Please pull over.

"¿Aquí?" Here?

"Sí."

The driver shrugged and abruptly pulled to the curb. The three got out and the president paid the driver, giving him a large tip. "Usted nunca nos vio," he said, the big hat hiding his features. You never saw us.

"Nunca," the driver winked. Never.

Marten slammed the door and the cab drove off.

Uneasy pedestrians moved around them, increasingly concerned about what was going on.

"Terroristas." Terrorists. Some said out loud, "Terroristas," others whispered. "¿Basques, ETA?" someone asked. "No," several voices spat fearfully at once, "al Qaeda."

Drivers backed up for the roadblock were eerily quiet. Tension and dread anticipation filled the air. At another point in history they would have been impatiently yelling and honking their horns. Not now.

"Keep moving," the president said quickly, "stay in the crowd."

Marten nodded and took Demi by the arm, positioning her between himself and the president as they went. There was no doubt now the Secret Service knew the president had been in Marten's hotel room and that every stop had been pulled out to find them. All they could do was try and blend in to what was a long line of frightened people, people, they prayed, who would not recognize the man in the floppy hat shuffling along among them and then raise the alarm out of sheer surprise if nothing else.

Marten let three young men shove past them, then looked at Demi, "Before, in the taxi, you said you couldn't go with us. Why?"

Demi hesitated, then glanced at the president and looked back to Marten. "Reverend Beck is meeting Dr. Foxx *tomorrow*. In the early afternoon at the Benedictine Monastery at Montserrat in the mountains northeast of here. He asked me to go with him and I agreed. I have to go back to the hotel, we're leaving from there."

Marten and the president exchanged glances, then Marten turned back to Demi.

"He asked you to go, just like that?"

"Yes. For the same reason I came to Barcelona, to continue the photo shoot for the book."

"Did he say why he canceled your Balkan trip or why he left Malta the way he did?"

"All he said was that something came up unexpectedly and he had to meet someone here in the city. He didn't say anything more. Just apologized for leaving so abruptly."

Suddenly there was a convergence of sirens ahead. People surged past them as if something was happening. More followed in their wake. They moved with them, trying to stay hidden in the crowd. Demi glanced at the president, then looked back to Marten.

"I did what you recommended and told Beck you followed me to Barcelona, and that we met and talked. I expected him to show some anger or surprise. He didn't, instead he said something in passing to the effect that he wished you and Dr. Foxx had left things on a more congenial note in Malta. He didn't say why or even ask why you had followed me here or what we had talked about. It seemed to be of little interest to him, as if he had other things on his mind, but it gave me the sense that if you showed up in Montserrat while we were there he might find a way for you and Foxx to meet and talk things through. You could even say it was my idea, that way it wouldn't spoil my situation with him, especially when I ask his help in finding my sister."

Marten studied her. Even now, after what they'd just been through, it was hard to know if he could trust her; if she was lying, if the whole melodrama of Foxx and Beck so abruptly leaving Malta and then having her come to Barcelona afterward was all part of whatever they were involved with. And this seemingly offhand "peace offering" to Marten, this wish by Beck that he and Merriman Foxx had left things on a "more congenial note" seemed a very convenient way to get him to come to Montserrat on his own—to an isolated monastery where they could get him alone, then demand to know whom he worked for and was reporting to and afterward get rid of him altogether. If that were the case and Demi's late night call to rendezvous with him was their idea and not hers, he needed to learn as much as he could about what was going on before she went back to her hotel.

"Is the woman in black going with you to Montserrat?"

"Who?" Demi seemed wholly surprised.

"Earlier tonight you and Beck left the hotel and went to the cathedral. A woman in black was with you, an older woman."

"How did you know?"

"How I know isn't important. I'm interested in who she is and what she has to do with Beck."

"Her name is Luciana," Demi answered matter-of-factly and without hesitation. "She's an Italian friend of the reverend. She was with him at the hotel when I arrived."

"Is she the one he had to leave Malta to come here to meet?"

"I don't know, but it was she who arranged the trip to the monastery through a priest at the cathedral." Demi glanced at the people around her, then looked back to Marten and lowered her voice. "She belongs to the coven. She has the tattoo on her thumb. And yes, she's going with us."

Marten looked at the president. He could see he was puzzled. He knew there was information being passed but he had no idea what it was. Marten was about to say something, to try and explain but was cut off by the scream of a siren as another police car shot past them, its loudspeaker blaring, ordering drivers to pull to the side. Following in its wake were two large dark blue trucks marked Mossos d'Esquadra. A hundred yards ahead the vehicles stopped dead, the trucks' rear doors flew open, and at least two dozen heavily armed police jumped out.

"Dammit," the president blurted under his breath.

All around them people stared wide-eyed. "Terroristas." "Terroristas." "Al Qaeda." "Al Qaeda." The words came more quickly this time, more numerous and more fearful.

The president looked to Marten. "They're widening their net and turning up the heat. From here on out they'll have every street, every alley, shut down tight."

"Then we turn and go back," Marten said calmly.

"To where?"

"We're considerate fellows. The young lady was trying to get to her hotel and we thoughtfully escorted her."

Demi started. "You're going to my hotel?"

"At least you have a room, and I don't think they're going to let us in anywhere else. We'll have to fake our way past the people at the front desk."

"How are we going to get there?" Demi nodded toward the mass of snarled traffic. "If we take a cab we'll be stopped at the next roadblock. It's one thing if I'm alone. With you two we'll all be caught, and that will be that."

"She's right," the president said.

Marten hesitated, then looked back over his shoulder the way they had come. "We walk."

"What?" Demi blurted.

Marten looked back. "The same as here. We walk."

62

RIVOLI JARDÍN HOTEL, SAME TIME, 4:20 A.M.

Intense, heavily controlled chaos. Very nearly an exact repeat of what had taken place less than twenty-four hours earlier at the Hotel Ritz in Madrid.

Uniformed Barcelona police under the supervision of GEO agents and CIA assets Ortega, Leon, and Tarrega checked the identification of every person in the hotel. Guests were waked from sleep, their rooms searched, identifications checked. Hotel employees and patrons and musicians from the Jamboree Club were treated with the same polite ferocity. The police were following up on a tip that "known terrorists had checked into the hotel under false names"—two, it was rumored, had already been found and arrested. Even the affable Basque singer Fermín Murguruza was questioned and then released, all the while signing autographs for surrounding fans also being questioned. "Under the circumstances," Murguruza said proudly, "who would not try to help the authorities?"

Additionally, Hap Daniels's strict directive to check "every closet, toilet, hallway, every last inch, and that includes the goddamn air-conditioning ducts this time" was followed to the letter and then the entire procedure was repeated.

In room 408 a tech crew provided by Spanish intelligence and under the command of Special Agent Bill Strait inched over everything. One floor below, a meeting room had been turned into a Secret Service command post. A secure phone had been installed with a direct line to the U.S. embassy in Madrid and another to Washington and the working war room set up in the basement of the White House. Most obvious and pressing was the ongoing situation with the president, but increasingly worrisome was what to do about the upcoming NATO meeting Monday in Warsaw, where President Harris was to announce a new spirit of "political accord" and "solidarity against terrorism" despite the still-festering "difficulties" with Germany and France.

"Who's there with you?" Jake Lowe paced up and down, secure phone to his ear, on the line to Secretary of State David Chaplin at the White House while National Security Adviser James Marshall listened on the phone's extension just feet away. A weary, infuriated Hap Daniels stood partway across the room, one eye on Lowe and Marshall, the other on the small cadre of quickly-brought-in CIA techs working laptops and monitoring the Barcelona hunt for the president.

"*Terry Langdon and Chet Keaton. The vice president is on his way,*" Chaplin said.

"The president's ill, we're more certain than ever of that now. Moreover, he seems to have this American-Brit, Nicholas Marten, helping him. How and why and to what end we don't know." Lowe's clear-cut explanation was wholly for Hap Daniels's benefit.

"*Obviously he's very determined, and now he's got help,*" Chaplin said in the part of the conversation Daniels couldn't hear. "*As long as he remains on the loose he's dangerous as hell because he will find a way to expose us. That said, Terry's insistent about Monday. Everything's in place and he feels we can't let this situation hold us back. Worse comes to worst we'll announce he's got the stomach flu or something and the vice president will take his place in Warsaw. Meanwhile the media is starting to push for more information on what happened in Madrid and where the POTUS is now. The honeymoon hours are almost over; we're going to have to give them something."*

"Get the chief of staff and the press secretary on the line and we'll decide what to do now," Lowe snapped.

"David, can you hear me?" Marshall stepped in.

"Yes, Jim."

"Regarding Warsaw. Jake and I agree. We are going under the assumption all this will be put to bed and the president will be there as planned."

"Right."

"Terry, you there?"

"Yes, Jim," Secretary of Defense Langdon's voice came through strongly.

"I just explained to David, we all agree about Warsaw," Marshall glanced casually around the room, making certain Daniels or someone else wasn't being overcurious about his conversation, "we're going ahead as planned."

"Good."

"At this point no changes at all," Marshall turned to look at Jake Lowe.

"Right."

"More when we have something," Lowe said, and hung up. Marshall did the same. When he turned he saw Hap Daniels was watching him.

63

4:42 A.M.

The three were pushed back into the darkened doorway waiting for the police car to pass. When it did they lingered another twenty seconds to make sure a second car wasn't following behind it. Finally they stepped out and moved on. By now Marten, Demi, and President Harris had worked their way back to Ciutat Vella, the old city, with its ancient buildings and narrow streets. Streets that, except for the lone passerby or the startling wail of a stray cat underfoot or the bark of dog at the end of an alley as they passed, were finally quiet. That they had come this far unmolested was due to luck and because they had stayed in the shadows and followed their instincts. A turn here, another there. A stepping back in the dark and waiting for a person or vehicle to pass. The president, floppy hat pulled low, had stopped once to speak Spanish to an old man sitting alone on a curbstone, asking the way to Rambla de Catalunya, where Demi's hotel was. The old man had not even looked up, just simply pointed off and mumbled.

"Esa manera tres minutos y entonces da vuelta a la derecha." That way three minutes and then turn right.

"Gracias," the president said and they moved on.

Their constant fear was the stranger passing who by some quirk of circumstance might recognize the president and sound the alarm, or the police car still on patrol unexpectedly turning a corner, to have its officers suddenly stop and question them. Or that Spanish intelligence, the Secret Service or CIA assets were stationed on rooftops watching them through night-vision goggles and at any minute a helicopter would roar in from nowhere to hold them in the searing beam of its searchlight until unmarked cars arrived and special agents jumped out to take them away.

It was five, maybe ten minutes more before they would reach the relative safety of Demi's hotel. The plan was for Demi to go to her room and for them to follow shortly afterward. There in its quiet and relative safety they would have the chance to address the near-impossible task in front of them: find a way to get the president and Marten past the hundreds of police checkpoints and the thirty-odd miles to the monastery at Montserrat at or about the same time Demi arrived with Reverend Beck and the woman called Luciana for their rendezvous with Merriman Foxx.

It was a problem that brought Marten back to the question of Demi herself. She was a respected journalist and photographer using her profession, as she had said, to uncover the truth of her sister's disappearance from Malta two years earlier and trusting that Merriman Foxx might provide some answer to it. Whether the story of her sister was true or not everything seemed to center on the Aldebaran coven of witches and with it, the Machiavellian tale of ritual murder. That Foxx, Luciana, Cristina, the young woman who had been a guest at the dinner table in Malta, the late Dr. Lorraine Stephenson in Washington, and possibly Beck all wore the identifying tattoo of the coven intrigued him immensely. That Demi did not—Marten had scrutinized both her thumbs carefully without her knowing on more than one occasion—was equally interesting because she seemed to have gained access to them without trouble, most probably by convincing Beck to be one of the subjects of her book. That in itself raised another question—why Beck had let her; even to the point of inviting her to Barcelona after he'd so abruptly left Malta and providing a means for her transportation as well. Two things came immediately to mind; either the coven was wholly innocuous and, secretive as it might seem, had nothing to hide; or it wasn't, and Beck was leading her on for reasons of his own. If the second were true she could very well be walking into something exceedingly dangerous, maybe even deadly.

Whichever it was, whether she was using Beck or he was guiding her into something else, one thing remained unwavering: her determination to get Marten to the monastery at Montserrat and into the hands of Merriman Foxx.

The trouble was that in setting Marten up she had also set up the president. It was a bad situation, and both men knew it. They also knew they had no choice but to proceed. To them Foxx was the key to everything. What he knew they had to find out: the specifics of the plan against the Muslim states, when and where it was to begin, the names of those involved, and for Marten in particular, what he had done to Caroline Parsons. Moreover, the president not only wanted to know the details, he insisted they have it written down—a notepad, scratch paper, anything would do—dated and signed by Foxx. It was a document that once in hand would allow him to come out of the shadows without fear. By the time the Secret Service, a CIA team, or Spanish intelligence reached him he would have placed calls (and hopefully faxed copies) to the secretaries-general of NATO and the United Nations and to the editors-in-chief of the *Washington Post* and *New York Times*. Nothing would be kept back, none of it politically couched including the planned assassinations in Warsaw. It would be news that would explode across the world in seconds, and its ramifications would be enormous—economically, politically, and because of the horror of what it had promised, emotionally. But it had to be done, it was far too grave and far-reaching for anything but the truth.

So, trap or not, and hugely dangerous and immensely difficult as it might be, the attempt to reach the monastery at Montserrat had to be made.

That left only the next.

How to get there.

And what to do, when, and if, they did.

64

CHANTILLY, FRANCE, 6:44 A.M.

Victor stood in a thick jungle of trees three hundred feet back from the target area. The barrel of his M14 rifle rested in the V of a wooden makeshift monopod and was pointed through the gray mist of early morning toward the thoroughbred practice track called "Coeur de la Forêt." Even in the chill he was comfortable. This was what he did. And what they asked him to do. And what they fully expected he would do. Not could do, as if he were a low-level employee, but what he would fully execute as a marksman, as a professional.

"Victor." Richard's calm and soothing voice came over his headset.

"Yes, Richard."

"How are you feeling?"

"Fine."

"Not cold or damp."

"No, Richard. Just fine."

"The horses and jockeys are just leaving the training facility. In approximately thirty-five seconds they will be at the start of the practice track. Once there they will get their final instructions from the trainer. Ten to fifteen seconds after that the practice race will begin. It should take them about seventy seconds to reach where you are. Are you alright with that, Victor?"

"Yes, Richard."

"Afterward you know what to do."

"Yes, Richard."

"Thank you, Victor."

"No, Richard, thank you."

BARCELONA, 6:50 A.M.

Barefoot, pant legs rolled up, coffee cups in hand, and looking like early-rising tourists on holiday, Nicholas Marten and President of the United States John Henry Harris walked across the wet sand of low tide watching the first light of day break over the Mediterranean. Above and behind them was an outcropping of rocky cliffs that shielded the desolate stretch of beach where they were from the dirt road they had come in on. An X on a map would suggest they were about fifteen miles north of Barcelona somewhere between Costa Daurada to the south and Costa Brava to the north.

Isolated and away from the city proper, it gave them a brief respite, one carefully calculated to give the security forces time to fully execute their roadblocks and checkpoints, and then coming up empty to hopefully stand down or at least to ease their presence and let the city come back to some semblance of normal while they regrouped, re-worked their tactics and brought in more manpower. And it was just that window Marten and the president would use to make their move toward Montserrat. Both knew that once that second wave began, the scope and size of it would be unprecedented. John Henry Harris was not simply a missing person, he was a missing president of the United States and the determination of the Secret Service, CIA, FBI, NSA, Spanish intelligence and Spanish police forces to find him and bring him to what they assumed was safety would make his, and therefore Marten's, chance of escaping zero at best.

Marten glanced back. In the dim morning light he could see the protective cliffs above them and the small turnaround at the end of the road where the black Mercedes limousine that had brought them there was parked. Standing beside it watching them was its dark-suited middle-aged driver, the affable Miguel Balius, a Barcelonan raised in Australia who later returned to his native city. It was Balius's keen knowledge of Barcelona's streets and alleys that had helped them avoid the maze of police checkpoints and roadblocks and to the remote beach where they were now. That they had come this far was due to Balius's seemingly naïve creativity, Marten's original idea and Demi's smooth execution of it.

They had reached the Hotel Regente Majestic at 4:50 A.M. and gone immediately inside, Demi to the front desk and Marten and President Harris into the men's restroom just off the lobby, where they had cleaned up and waited. What Marten had suggested in the last moments before they reached the hotel was, if it worked, outrageous, but no more outrageous than the situation they were in—essentially trapped inside the city of Barcelona while Spanish security forces demanded identification from nearly everyone trying to leave it.

Marten's idea had come from the simple reality of their situation—they had to remain free of the massive net surrounding them and at the same time get to the mountain monastery at Montserrat, arriving sometime around noon. To that end he created a scenario that with luck and if played properly he thought just might work. Demi began it the moment they entered the hotel when she went directly to the front desk asking to see the concierge. The following is what she told Marten and the president she had said:

"My two cousins came in on an early-morning flight from New York for a family reunion. I went to meet them at the airport. It took a half hour to find them because the airline lost their luggage and they were off trying to locate it. They never did. It's still lost. On the way here we were caught up in whatever dreadful thing is going on in the city. It took an hour to get through one checkpoint. We had to show identification, everything."

"The authorities thought they had some terrorists trapped in a hotel not far from here," the concierge informed her. "They escaped. Or that's what we've been told, but they are still looking for them and that is the reason for all the chaos. I sincerely apologize for the inconvenience."

"It's not your fault, of course, and we all must do our part to stop these people. My problem, however, is not terrorists but my cousins. I don't like them to begin with. On top of that they are irritable and over-tired, neither can sleep, and one is crazier than the other. They want to spend the day sightseeing. I have other things to do. I'm also exhausted and want to sleep. I was thinking of a limousine, just have someone take them wherever they want to go, to see whatever they want to see and bring them back later this evening. Is that possible?"

"You want to do it now, at this time of day?"

"Yes, as soon as possible, and have whoever comes bring them something to eat, some bottled water and coffee. I don't want them waking me up to go to breakfast."

"I'm afraid it will be expensive."

"At this point, I don't care. Whatever it costs, charge it to my room."

"Very well, señorita, I will take care of it."

"One more thing. If the driver can find some way to avoid all of these tedious roadblocks and things . . . You understand, they'll just get more upset and want to come back early and then they'll take it out on me as if all this terrorist business was my fault."

"I will speak to the driver personally, señorita."

"Thank you, señor, thank you very much. I can't tell you how much this means to me."

At that point Demi started to turn away, then had one more thought.

"I'm sorry. I don't mean to keep imposing on you but other family members will be gathering in the hotel and the cousins coming for the reunion is a big surprise. I would hope your staff and the driver will be discreet. I wouldn't want someone accidentally talking about it and spoiling everything."

"As before, señorita," the concierge half-bowed, "I will take care of it."

"Thank you again, señor. Muchas gracias."

Ten minutes later Miguel Balius and his Mercedes limousine arrived. Breakfast, bottled water, and coffee were provided by the hotel's room service. Demi kissed cousins Jack (the president) and

Harold (Marten) good-bye—with a whispered demand from Marten as he kissed her cheek—"Not a word to Beck or anyone else about 'Cousin Jack.'"

"Of course not, silly," she'd smiled then reminded Cousin Jack to wear his big hat and be careful not to get too much sun, and then off they all went. She to bed. They to try and escape the enormous manhunt for them.

65

7:00 A.M.

It was still nearly fifty minutes to sunrise. Again Marten glanced back at the rocky cliffs, looking for any sign of forces moving in to entrap them, but he saw nothing. Immediately he looked to the sky, half expecting the sudden swoop of a helicopter or to hear the drone of a search plane. All he saw was the deserted beach; the only sound, the lap of the waves at their feet. A second more, and his attention went to President Harris.

"We need to get moving and soon," he said with urgency.

"Yes, I know," the president said, and they turned back across the sand toward Miguel Balius and the limousine in the distance. "I've been thinking about Merriman Foxx, Mr. Marten. What to do, if and when we get to Montserrat. How to get him alone without being caught ourselves and after that how to get him to tell us what we have to know.

"Yet as important as all that is, it is only part of what is going on. To my horror I suddenly realized that I am the only person on this side of the fence who knows anything about the rest their plan and if something happens to me those sons-of-bitches will be free to go ahead with it. And there's no question they will.

"I told you earlier, time is crucial but I didn't say why. Today is Saturday. On Monday I am scheduled to join the leaders of the NATO countries at a major conference in Warsaw."

"I know, sir, I read about it."

"What you don't know, what no one knows is what my so-called 'friends' have planned for that day. It's another part of the reason I crawled out through the air-conditioning ducts in Madrid. Why I came to you and why I'm here now. It's not just Foxx and whatever damned thing they have him preparing because whatever that is it will happen sometime *after* the NATO meeting," the president hesitated, his eyes probing Marten, as if he were still having trouble trusting anyone, Marten included.

"Please go on, Mr. President."

"Mr. Marten," the president made his decision, "the people conspiring against me are planning to assassinate the president of France and chancellor of Germany sometime during those NATO meetings. They want the current leaders removed so they can replace them with people in those countries sympathetic to their own ambitions. Exactly where and when or how the killings are to take place I don't know, but it will happen during the Warsaw meetings because they want it done on a world stage.

"They asked me—no, they demanded—that I issue a top-secret executive order authorizing those murders. I refused. In doing so I knew I had to escape or they would kill me. By law the vice president would then have become president and as a leading member of this conspiracy he would have no trouble whatsoever in giving it. The terrible irony is that in my absence the vice president will be in command anyway. The order will be given, Mr. Marten. Top secret, executed in the name of national security and authorized by the acting commander in chief."

"Jesus God," Marten breathed.

Anguish crossed the president's face. "I have no way to communicate that threat to anyone capable of taking action without being found out and having that line of communication immediately shut down. And with the people trying to find me knowing almost instantly exactly where I am.

"There is an annual meeting of the New World Institute, a global think tank of highly respected, high-profile business, academic, and former political leaders taking place this weekend at a resort called Aragon in the mountains just northwest of here. The meeting is closed to all but members and guests and like the World Economic Forum usually draws a large number of protest groups and with them an equally large gathering of media. As a result the security is heavy, supervised, I believe, by the Spanish Secret Service.

"I was to have been the surprise guest speaker at the sunrise service there tomorrow morning. A close friend, Rabbi David Aznar, lives in Gerona, an hour from here by train. He is presiding over the prayer service and was going to introduce me. I came to Barcelona hoping to use it as a jumping-off point to Gerona. Once there I'd planned to find my way to his home, tell him what was going on and hope that he could get me to Aragon and somehow past the security forces unseen so that I could still address the convention."

"And tell them what's happened."

"Yes. Politically and strategically dangerous maybe, but considering who they are, that they are meeting in seclusion and at a place relatively close by, and that there will be no media present—taken with the unbearable shortness of time before Warsaw and the fact that millions of lives are at stake—it would have been foolish of me not to attempt it. But then I realized the force looking for me was too great and that Rabbi David himself would undoubtedly be under physical surveillance with all of his electronic communications closely monitored. So the thought of reaching Aragon under his protection and addressing the assembly was no longer viable. At that point I knew I had to get off the streets before I was caught and taken somewhere and killed. That was when I saw the newspaper photograph and found you."

They were nearing the limousine now. Miguel Balius had opened the rear door and had towels over his arm for them to wipe the sand from their feet when they arrived.

Marten nodded toward Balius, "There's a good chance he will have had the radio or TV on, most likely listening to the news of what's been happening in the city. It's possible they may even have broadcast our descriptions, although that's doubtful because they don't want it to get out about you. Still, who knows what they've said or suggested? If he gets any sense that we're anything other than what he thinks we are he may want to do something about it."

"You mean alert the police."

"Yes."

They were almost to Balius, and he came toward them. "How

was the walk gentlemen?" he said in his Aussie-accented English, reaching to take their coffee cups. Behind him, through the open door to the rear passenger compartment, Marten could see the glow of the limousine's small-screen television. He'd been right—Balius had been watching it.

"Nice beach," Marten said offhandedly. "Anything new about what's going on in the city?"

"Only what we heard before, sir. The authorities are looking for terrorists they thought they had trapped in a hotel but who escaped. That's all they're saying. Very close-lipped about the whole thing."

"I guess they have to be these days," Marten glanced at the president. Just then his cell phone rang. He started to reach for it, then saw the president shake his head in a clear warning not to answer it.

The phone rang again.

"What if it's Demi?" Marten said carefully. "What if the family plans have changed and we are to meet somewhere else?"

The president took a breath. He didn't like it, but Marten was right; anything could have happened, and the last thing they could afford was to lose their lone connection to Merriman Foxx.

"Make it brief. Very."

Marten opened his phone and clicked on, "Demi," he said quickly as Balius handed the president a towel and he sat down on the limousine's rear seat to clean the sand from his feet.

"What the hell's going on in Barcelona?" It was Peter Fadden, keyed up and gruff as usual.

"The police are looking for terrorists." Marten said clearly so that the president and especially Miguel Balius could hear him. "Supposedly they had them trapped in a hotel but it didn't work out. They're checking everyone. The whole city feels like a war zone. You still in Madrid?"

"Yes. And whatever started here seems to have shifted there."

"What do you mean?"

"I've interviewed maybe twenty employees at the Ritz and none of them saw or knows anyone who saw the Secret Service make a move to take the president out of the hotel. Then yesterday morning the Secret Service was all over the place interviewing everyone about what they saw the night before. It was like something has happened to the president but nobody's talking. Then the entire press contingent that was supposed to follow him to Warsaw was flown back to Washington riding on the official story that he was taken to an undisclosed location in the middle of the night because of a reliable terrorist threat. Now the whole of Spanish intelligence seems zeroed in on Barcelona. Something big is going on. Is it really terrorists, or does somebody have the president and they're trying to keep it quiet?"

Marten glanced at the president. "You're asking the wrong guy."

"No, I'm asking a guy who's there and who might have some sense of it. I'm not thinking terrorists, Nick, I'm thinking Mike Parsons's committee. I'm thinking Merriman Foxx."

Suddenly President Harris was dragging his hand across his throat. Once, twice, three times. He meant for Marten to cut his conversation right away and get off the phone.

"Peter, let me get back to you," Marten said quickly, "soon as I can."

Marten clicked off and watched the president slide out of sight into the dark of the limousine's interior.

"Towel, sir," Miguel Balius held a fresh towel out to Marten.

"Cousin Harold can clean his feet in the car, Miguel. I would like to leave the area right away," the president said firmly.

"Now, sir?"

"Now."

"Yes, sir."

66

7:17 A.M.

Miguel Balius's foot touched the accelerator. For an instant the Mercedes' rear tires spun in the roadside gravel, then they caught and the limousine roared off, bouncing over what was little more than a dirt lane.

"Miguel?" President Harris said out loud, looking through the privacy glass that separated the driver's compartment from the passengers'. It was a test to see if he could hear their conversation without the passenger pushing the intercom button. Marten had done the same thing when they had driven from the Hotel Regente Majestic through the city's back roads to the beach. But he wanted to test it again to make sure.

"Miguel?" he said once more, but Balius didn't respond. Immediately he looked to Marten. "Your phone," he said.

"I understand," Marten said. "The Secret Service knows who I am and will have the number. They'll have a global satellite trace on it."

"Not just a trace. The NSA will have intercepted it and given the Secret Service the geographic coordinates in seconds. I know my men—they'll be scrambling like hell to get here as fast as they can. I appreciate why you took the call, and I let you. I shouldn't have. Just hope we got out of there in time."

"Mr. President," Marten leaned in, "that call was not from Demi."

"I gathered."

"It wasn't trivial. It came from a *Washington Post* investigative reporter. He knows about Caroline Parsons and her suspicion that she and her husband and son were murdered. He knows about Merriman Foxx and Dr. Stephenson. He's even found the clinic outside Washington where Caroline was treated by Foxx. The Silver Springs Rehabilitation Center in Silver Springs, Maryland.

"He's in Madrid, Mr. President. He's questioned the staff at your hotel there. He doesn't believe the official White House story that you were taken away in the middle of the night. He thinks you are the reason for the Spanish intelligence presence in Barcelona. That you may have been kidnapped and that Merriman Foxx had something to do with it."

"Who is this reporter?"

"His name is Peter Fadden."

"I know him. Not well, but I know him. He's a good man."

"I told him I'd call him back."

"You can't."

"If I don't he'll call me."

"We can't chance that, Mr. Marten. Turn the phone off and leave it off. We'll have to let Mr. Fadden assume what he wants.

We'll also have to trust that there has been no change in Ms. Picard's plans."

Now they were at the end of the beach road, and Balius swung the Mercedes left onto a narrow tarmac highway that led away from the shoreline and toward the distant hills. As the limousine straightened out, President Harris glanced at the small screen mounted in the rear of the front seat. The channel was tuned to CNN. A story about deadly rains in India played on the screen. The president watched a second longer, then touched the intercom button. "Miguel."

"Yes, sir."

"Friends were telling us about a place in the mountains near here, a monastery I believe," the president said easily, conversationally. "They said it was a place every tourist should visit."

Balius looked in the mirror and smiled proudly, "You mean Montserrat."

The president looked at Marten. "Was that the name, Cousin?"

"Yes, Montserrat."

"We would like to go there, Miguel."

"Yes, sir."

"Can we get there by noon? That would give us time to look around before we are due back in the city."

"I think we can, sir. Unless we run into more roadblocks."

"Why can't the police catch these people? There are hundreds of them, how hard can it be?" the president added an edge of crankiness and irritation to what before had been an easy, congenial manner. "People have other things to do besides wait in line at some checkpoint only to be passed through and ten minutes later stopped at another one."

"I agree, sir."

"We don't want to be late getting back to the city. You got around them before, Miguel. We're confident you can do it again."

"I appreciate that, sir. I'll do my best."

"We know you will, Miguel. We know you will."

67

"Mosca encima. Área coordinada abandonada. Repetición. Mosca encima. Área coordinada abandonada." Fly over. Coordinate area deserted. Repeat. Fly over. Coordinate area deserted.

Hap Daniels perked up at the sharp declaration of the lead Grupo Especial de Operaciones jet helicopter pilot. A heartbeat later came the voice of the pilot of a second GEO helicopter pilot.

"Confirme. Área coordinada abandonada." Confirm. Coordinate area deserted.

Hap Daniels was staring at a computer screen in front of him looking at an NSA satellite photograph of the Barcelona coast. He could see the city, the airport, the run of the Llobregat River from the mountains to the sea, the port of Barcelona, and to the north the Besós River and the coast beyond it reaching toward the Costa Brava. Daniels touched the keyboard in front of him and the picture enhanced once, then twice, then three times until the image zeroed in on 41° 24′.04″ N and 2° 6′.22″ E, the geographical coordinates the NSA had picked up from Nicholas Marten's cell phone signal. It was the coastline in an area north of the city and what looked like a stretch of deserted beach.

"Colonel, this is Tigre Uno," Daniels spoke calmly into his headset, talking to the commander in charge of the GEO air units and using the code name—Tigre Uno or Tiger One—given him by Spanish intelligence. "Please ask your lead pilot to pull up to fifteen hundred feet and survey the entire area. Please ask your second pilot to set down for an on-ground inspection."

"Roger, Tigre Uno."

"Thank you, Colonel."

Daniels took a breath and sat back. He was exhausted, exasperated, and still mad as hell, mostly at himself for letting all this happen. The reason didn't matter; the president should never have been able to slip away undetected. It was unforgivable.

Surrounded by computer screens, he rode in the command chair of the Secret Service's huge black SUV electronic communications unit that had been flown in from Madrid. In front of him, riding shotgun next to the driver, was his chief deputy, Bill Strait. Behind him, four Secret Service intelligence specialists manned computer screens monitoring surveillance traffic from a half dozen different security agencies and at the same time hoping, as they all were, that Marten would again use his cell phone.

Daniels glanced at the screen in front of him again and then looked around the vehicle's narrow confines to where Jake Lowe and Dr. James Marshall were buckled into fold-down jumpseats, staring in silence at nothing. They looked like deeply troubled warriors: fierce, strong, angry and uncertain.

Outside, the Barcelona cityscape flashed by. The only sound the scream of sirens of two Guàrdia Urbana police cars clearing the way in front of them. Directly behind followed the unmarked armored van with two Secret Service agents, two doctors, and two emergency medical technicians. Bringing up the rear were three unmarked Secret Service tail cars with four special agents in each.

Twelve miles away at a private airstrip just north of the city a private CIA jet ordered by White House chief of staff, Tom Curran, still working from the temporary "war room" at the U.S. embassy in Madrid, waited to fly the president to a still-undecided location Daniels thought would be in either central Switzerland or southern Germany.

"Vector 4-7-7," a young, curly-haired intelligence specialist said suddenly.

"What?" Hap Daniels responded.

"4-7-7. We've got another call."

Immediately Daniels switched frequencies. At the same time electronic triangulation began on the signal. Instantly a new set of geographical coordinates popped up, superimposed over a map of northeast Barcelona on the screen in front of him.

"You're sure it's Marten's cell?"

"Yes, sir."

Jake Lowe and Dr. Marshall reacted intensely, each directly tuning his own headset to the audio feed.

Again Daniels enhanced the picture on his screen, this time ze-roing in on the green foothills north and just east of the Besós River. A half-second later he put a hand to the earpiece of his headset as if he was trying to hear more clearly. "What the hell are they saying?"

"Not they. Just one voice, sir. It's the incoming call."

"Incoming from where?"

"Manchester, England."

"Where in Manchester?" Dr. Marshall snapped.

"Quiet!" Daniels was looking at no one, just trying to under-stand what was being said.

What they heard was a lone male voice speaking softly but de-liberately:

"*Alabamese. Albiflorum. Arborescens. Atlanticum. Austrinum. Calendulaceum. Camtschaticum. Canandense. Canescens.*"

"What the hell is he talking about?" Jake Lowe's voice stabbed through a half dozen earpieces.

"*Cumberlandense. Flammeum.*"

By now everyone was looking at each other. Lowe was right. What the hell was he saying?

"*Mucronulatum. Nudiflorum. Roseum.*"

"Azaleas!" Bill Strait barked suddenly. "Somebody's reading off the names of azaleas."

"*Schlippenbachii!*"

Suddenly there was silence as Marten's cell phone went dead.

"Did we pick up the coordinates?" Hap Daniels demanded from the techs behind him. Just then a crosshair of coordinates came up on his screen superimposed over an enhanced satellite picture of the piedmont and marked off in a five-square-mile grid.

"He's in the area inside the grid, sir," the disembodied voice of an NSA navigator came back from three thousand miles away.

"We have better than that, sir," the curly-haired intel specialist behind Daniels smiled, then touched his mouse. Abruptly all the screens shifted to a different view of the same image. Immediately he enhanced it five, and then tenfold, and they saw what looked like an apple orchard with a dirt road cutting through it. He en-hanced it once more, and they saw a wisp of a vehicle's dust trail lift from the road itself.

"Got 'em!" he said.

68

Golf bag over one shoulder, suitcase in hand, Victor boarded first-class car number 22388 of the Chantilly to Paris train and found a window seat near the front.

Ten minutes earlier he had checked out of his hotel and taken a taxi to the station. By then most of the frantic activity had died down. The police cars, the emergency response team, and the ambulances had long disappeared around a bend in the road, going, he was told, to a place he knew well—the "Coeur de la Forêt."

"Leave the weapon and walk away," Richard had told him over the headset. And he had, the same way he had left the smiliar M14 rifle in the rented Washington, D.C., office four days earlier when he'd shot and killed the Colombian national wearing the New York Yankees jacket as the man emerged from Union Station.

The train lurched and began to move forward. As it did, Victor saw a police car pull into the station parking lot and four heavily armed policemen emerge from it. For a moment he tensed, worried the stationmaster had been alerted and the train would be stopped, its passengers questioned about the incident that had taken place little more than ninety minutes earlier when two jockeys had been shot and killed on the Chantilly racecourse practice track by someone hiding in the woods. Someone who was an excellent marksman and who had taken both men down with a single shot from a hundred yards away as they'd raced past on thoroughbreds running neck and neck, the bullet passing through the skull of one rider and then a hundredth of a second later through that of the other. Someone who, as the riderless horses ran on, left the murder weapon behind and simply walked away in the gray morning mist of the Coeur de la Forêt.

7:52 A.M.

The train picked up speed and in a blink the Chantilly-Gouvieux station was out of sight. Victor sat back and relaxed. Richard had told him there was nothing to worry about, to take his time, have coffee, even breakfast, and not make a show of leaving; and he'd been right. At every step, Richard had been right.

He looked out the window and watched the French country-side pass by. Here, as in Coeur de la Forêt, the deciduous trees were beginning to leaf out. Bright green and filled with the hope of a glorious summer. He felt happy, even mischievous and, most particularly alive.

Like a boy who had just turned fourteen and was gobbling up the world around him.

69

RURAL FOOTHILLS NORTHEAST OF BARCELONA, 7:55 A.M.

A terrible thudding roar followed by a huge shadow passing directly overhead made the young driver of the farm truck suddenly slow and look up through its cracked windshield. For an instant he saw nothing but fruit trees and sky; then a Mossos d'Esquadra jet helicopter came straight toward him over the treetops. In a blink it was gone. Five seconds later another police helicopter followed, this one flying lower than the first and blinding them in a storm of whirling dust.

"¿Qué el infierno?" What the hell? he cried out and looked wide-eyed at the two young farmworkers squeezed into the seat beside him.

In the next instant two Mossos d'Esquadra cars screamed down the dirt road directly in front of him. Two more raced in from the rear.

"¡Cristo!" he yelled. Immediately his right foot slammed the brake pedal and the truck slid to a stop in the whirlwind of dust kicked up by the police cars and the helicopters hovering just overhead, one two hundred feet higher than the other.

Seconds later the three men were facedown in the dirt, uniformed police everywhere, submachine guns at their heads. The doors to the truck thrown wide open.

Slowly the driver dared to look up. When he did he saw men in dark suits and sunglasses emerge from unmarked cars that had come in from the grove on either side and start toward them. Then something else caught his eye. A huge, polished black SUV appeared through the shade of the orchard trees and slowly approached.

"¿Dios mío, cuál es?" My God, what is it? The young worker next to him breathed.

"¡Cállate!" Shut up! A barrel-chested policeman shoved the barrel of his submachine hard against the side of his head.

Hap Daniels was the first from the SUV. Then came Bill Strait. Then Jake Lowe and then James Marshall. Daniels glanced at them and then started for the truck.

The whirling dust and the thudding roar from the police helicopters overhead made it almost impossible to see, let alone hear or think. Daniels said something into his headset, and almost immediately the helicopters moved up and away to hover five or six hundred feet higher. The dust settled and the sound diminished.

Lowe and Marshall watched Daniels reach the truck, look inside the cab, then walk around it. Seconds later he motioned to one of the Mossos d'Esquadra officers to climb into the vehicle's open staked flatbed. A second policeman followed. Immediately two of Hap Daniels's dark-suited, sunglass-wearing Secret Service agents joined them.

"It's right there, sir," Daniels heard the voice of the curly-haired intel specialist from inside the SUV come through his headset.

"Where?"

"Somewhere near their feet."

"Here!" One of the agents said sharply.

Lowe and Marshall rushed forward. The special agents helped Daniels into the truck and then showed him.

Nicholas Marten's cell phone lay in a large cardboard box filled with irrigation equipment, hose connectors, and sprinkler heads. No apparent effort had been made to conceal it. It was right on top, as if someone had walked by, seen the box, and dropped it in.

Hap Daniels stared at it for a long moment, then slowly turned and looked off. This time there was no need curse out loud. His expression said everything.

The game was still on.

70

8:07 A.M.

Miguel Balius pressed down on the accelerator, and the Mercedes picked up speed. They were headed away from the coast and toward the mountains. Earlier he had avoided a checkpoint for vehicles leaving Barcelona simply by heading back toward it. Several miles later he'd taken a side road near Palau de Plegamans, then turned north onto a country highway. Shortly afterward Cousin Harold had asked how to use the limousine's phone, saying he wanted to place a call abroad. Miguel had explained and Cousin Harold had picked up the phone and punched in a number. Quite obviously he'd reached his party because he chatted for a few brief moments, then hung up and turned to talk with Cousin Jack. Several minutes later he'd made his one and only stop—at the edge of a dusty apple grove, where Cousin Harold relieved himself behind a parked farm truck. As quickly they were off again.

Whoever his passengers were they were clearly middle-class Americans, hardly the terrorists the government troops were searching for, or at least the dark-skinned Islamic stereotypes he and most of the world had come to expect when the word "terrorist" was mentioned. His customers were jet-lagged and tired and simply wanted to spend the day away from the city and seeing the sights, with Montserrat as their current destination. If they didn't relish going through the traffic backups and tedious procedures of road-blocks and checkpoints, neither did he. Besides, there was nothing illegal in what he was doing. It was his job to do what his clients asked, not wait in lines of traffic.

Miguel glanced in the mirror at his passengers and saw them watching the small television screen. They came to see the countryside and were watching TV. What the hell, he said to himself, it's their business.

And it was their business.

Wholly.

The attention of both men was locked on the small screen, where a female CNN reporter was doing a live stand-up in front of the White House, where it was still early morning. There had been no further reports on the circumstances of the president's hasty middle-of-the-night retreat from the Hotel Ritz in Madrid, she said. Nor was there information on the location where he had been taken, nor anything definitive about the nature of the terrorist threat or the terrorists themselves. But the people thought to be directly responsible had been traced to Barcelona, where they narrowly escaped a police raid and were now the subject of a massive manhunt that covered most of Spain and led all the way to the French border.

The piece ended and CNN went to a commercial. At the same time the president picked up the TV's remote and pressed the mute button and the television went silent.

"The Warsaw assassinations," he said to Marten quietly. "On a normal day I would have immediate access to the French and German leaders and could warn them personally. I no longer have that luxury. Still. Somehow. The president of France and the chancellor of Germany must be told of the danger at Warsaw, and I don't know how to do it."

"You're certain it will be Warsaw?" Marten asked.

"Yes, I'm certain. They want to make a public show of it to

instantly gain world sympathy for the people of Germany and France. It will help smooth the call for rapid elections in both countries and work to quell any political infighting that might keep their people from being elected."

"Then we need to find a way to alert them in a way that's not tied directly to you."

"Yes."

"What about the media? What if it came from *The New York Times, The Washington Post, The L.A. Times,* CNN or any other major news organization?"

"Who's going to tell them? Me? It's impossible for me to use any electronic communications device, period. Neither can you. You took Peter Fadden's call. They will have recorded your voice. They will be listening as much for yours as mine. At one point I even thought about entrusting Ms. Picard but decided against it for any number of reasons, primarily because no one would believe her, and if she tried to explain and the tabloids got ahold of it there would be a massive story that the president had run away from the Secret Service and gone crazy. It's the last thing we need."

"What about Fadden himself?" Marten said.

"I considered that. He has the credibility to call the press secretaries of both people and be put through. He could tell them he has classified information that comes from the very highest sources and then alert them to what is to happen in Warsaw. If he did it that way they would take the warning very, very seriously and make certain it was passed on to their Secret Service people. The trouble is there's no way to reach him, even if we found a way to have a third party do it."

"Because he called me."

The president nodded somberly. "Every electronic transmission he makes or receives will be intercepted and his every move watched. I'm sure the Secret Service is all over him right now. I just hope for his sake that he stays in Madrid and doesn't press the issue of what he knows about Merriman Foxx or suspects about me. If he gets aggressive it could get him arrested, maybe even killed. So we're back to square one, Cousin. What in the damn hell to do now. We have this information that has to get out but there's no way to do it."

Marten was about to say something when something caught his eye. He looked toward the front of the car. Miguel Balius was watching them intently in the mirror. Whatever he was doing, Marten didn't like it. Immediately he pressed the intercom button, "What is it, Miguel?"

Miguel started in surprise. "Nothing, sir."

"Something must have interested you."

"It's just that your cousin, sir, well he seems vaguely familiar." Miguel was embarrassed to have been caught but told the truth anyway. He looked to the president, "I know I've seen you somewhere before."

The president smiled easily, "I don't know where that would have been. This is my first time in Barcelona."

"My memory's quite decent, sir, I'm sure I'll think of it." Miguel watched him a moment longer, then looked back to the road.

Marten glanced at the president, "Remember what Cousin Demi told them about us."

"That we're a little crazy."

Marten nodded. "Now's the time to show it. Tell him before he figures it out."

The president was suddenly apprehensive, "Tell him *what*?"

Marten didn't reply. Instead he looked to Miguel and pressed the intercom. "You know why he looks familiar, Miguel?"

"Still working on it, sir."

"Well stop trying. He's the president of the United States."

President Harris felt his heart come up in his throat. Then he saw Marten grin broadly. Miguel Balius stared at them in the mirror and then a smile crept over his face as well.

"Of course he is, sir."

"You don't believe me, do you?" Marten kept on. "Well my cousin *is* the president of the United States. He's trying to have a day or two of peace and quiet away from the pressures of the job. That's why we wanted to avoid the roadblocks. It could be very dangerous if someone found out he was riding around without the Secret Service protecting him."

"That right, sir?" Miguel was looking at the president.

The president was caught; all he could do was go along. "I'm afraid you've guessed our secret. It's why we want to take back roads, farm roads, anything to stay off the beaten path."

Miguel's smile grew broader. They were playing with him and he knew it, "I understand your situation completely, sir. Later I can tell my grandkids I chauffeured you all over, took you to the beach, then helped you get the sand off your feet and drove you straight to Montserrat, all the while avoiding a thousand police roadblocks set up to nab terrorists."

Abruptly Marten tensed. "You have grandchildren, Miguel?"

"Not yet, sir. My daughter's expecting."

Marten relaxed. "Congratulations on becoming a grandfather. But you understand you're not to tell anyone else about this, not your daughter, not even your wife."

Miguel Balius raised a ceremonious hand from the steering wheel. "On my word, sir, not a soul. 'Discreet' is the company motto."

Marten smiled, "All in a day's work."

"Yes, sir. All in a day's work."

Marten sat back and looked at the president. Harris's expression said everything. Miguel was one thing. The problem of Warsaw and how to warn the leaders of France and Germany about what lay ahead was something else entirely. Something that, for the moment at least, there was nothing at all they could do to correct.

71

THE HOTEL GRAND PALACE, BARCELONA, 8:40 A.M.

Jake Lowe and James Marshall entered a four-room suite reserved by White House Chief of Staff Tom Curran, still working out of the U.S. embassy in Madrid. Secret Service tech specialists had taken over one of the three bedrooms and were working quickly to set up a communications center that would include secure phones to the Madrid embassy and to the working war room at the White House. Neither man had slept in over twenty-four hours, and both were grubby and exhausted and sported stubble beards. Moreover, it had been some time since they'd had the luxury of an extended private conversation. Lowe led them into a small drawing room and closed the door.

"This nightmare gets longer by the minute," he said. "It's inconceivable that he can stay a step ahead of everything."

Marshall took off his suit jacket and draped it over the side of a chair, then flipped on a television set and found CNN. He watched for a moment and then crossed to where a light breakfast was spread out and poured himself a cup of coffee.

"Coffee?"

"No," Lowe ran a hand through his hair and walked over to look down at the street. A moment later he turned back, clearly troubled. "He's determined to break us. You know that."

"Yes, but he won't succeed."

"We had that same confidence in him before, remember?" Lowe said, his fatigue and anger coming through. "That's how he got to be president. And how he got out of the Ritz and why he is still out there on the loose."

"Let's examine it," Marshall said coldly, then with one eye on the television eased into a straight-backed chair. "First off, it still remains all but impossible for him to communicate with anyone electronically without us knowing about it and in turn knowing where he is. It's all that much harder for him now that we know the geographic area where he is. Add to that the size of the force hunting them. He and Marten may be needles in a haystack, but straw by straw the hay is being taken away. It's only a matter of time, hours at most, before the floor is bare and the needles are right there in front of us.

"Next, the vice president is on his way to Madrid for a secret conference with the Spanish president on the situation with the POTUS."

"I know," Lowe snapped at something he was well aware of. "Should have wheels down there within the hour. What the hell's that got to do with it?"

"Everything. What our esteemed president has unwittingly done is give us an extraordinary opportunity to put the vice president front and center in the global war against terrorism. He's terrific at this stuff, almost as good as Harris himself. This is your territory Jake, and you should smell it! Why keep his arrival a secret? He's as concerned about the war on terror as the president and in the president's absence he's stepping on Spanish soil to say so. Let's get him up here this afternoon, send him through the streets of Barcelona, jacket off, sleeves rolled up. Have him talk to some civilians, get him a few sound bites with Spanish police working the checkpoints. Let him tell the world how proud he is to be here representing America in the president's place. Have him state how seriously President Harris takes these security threats and how determined he is not to let them interfere with his appearance in Warsaw or the speech he will give to the NATO leaders gathered there, a speech he is personally working on while he remains in seclusion. What we have, Jake, is a one-in-a-million chance to show the world public that the vice president is a bona fide take-charge guy." Marshall smiled thinly, "just hours before tragic circumstances make him king of the hill."

"You're forgetting Peter Fadden," Lowe came back across the room. "He knows about Caroline Parsons, he suspects something about Mike Parsons's death, he knows the Merriman Foxx connection, and he's not buying the official line about what happened to the president. He keeps pushing, the next thing we've got *The Washington Post* right on top of us."

"I didn't forget Peter Fadden, Jake. As soon as we have a secure phone I'll make a call to Washington and make sure he stops pushing. As for the president. Maybe we should hope Hap, the CIA, and Spanish intel don't find him at all."

"What do you mean?"

"I mean we would do well to trust that the Reverend Beck has sprinkled enough crumbs for Nicholas Marten to be well on his way to Montserrat in hopes of confronting Dr. Foxx. As we know from the hotel business last night, from the Fadden call this morning, and the little trick with the cell phone in the farm truck, he's doing everything he can to elude us. The only reason for that is because the president is with him. Both have a reason to confront Foxx and if they reach him before Hap finds them." The slightest smile crossed Marshall's face, "Marten will vanish and we'll have the body of a president we can fly to the 'undisclosed location' where he 'already is' and where he unfortunately suffered a sudden heart attack or something else Dr. Foxx will deem more appropriate. The whole thing would be much simpler and cleaner that way anyhow, don't you think?"

Lowe looked to the television. A CNN story about a plane crash in Peru was followed by live coverage from Barcelona and the massive ongoing search for the fugitive terrorists in which twenty-seven people had already been arrested and more arrests were expected.

Lowe clicked off the TV and turned to Marshall. Sweat glistened on his forehead. His normally ruddy complexion was pale. Deep weariness was taking hold.

"I'm tired, Jim. Tired of thinking. Tired of this whole damn thing. Make your call to Washington and then grab an hour's sleep. It's what I'm going to do. We need it, both of us."

72

9:00 A.M.

Miguel Balius glanced in the mirror at his two passengers on the far side of the privacy glass, then looked back at the curving country highway in front of him. This was the second rural road he had taken in the last forty minutes, both to avoid roadblocks. The first had come on a major highway leading into the hills toward Tarrasa when he'd seen vehicles in front of him suddenly slowing and then being directed into a single lane by heavily armed police. His solution had been simply to take the next exit and work his way through a network of suburban streets to the town of Ullastrell and then follow a secondary road south to a highway that swung them north again toward Montserrat. It was on that road, at Abrera, where he'd run into the second roadblock. Here he had reversed course and taken a side road that skirted the town of Olesa de Montserrat and put him onto the curving highway where they were now, headed northwest into the mountains toward Montserrat, a long way around but better than being caught at a roadblock and having the authorities discover that his passengers were the president of the United States and his cousin.

Miguel laughed to himself. He had been told when he'd started that he should expect them to be a little "loco." And they were. But he'd driven people a lot crazier than these two—rocks stars, movie stars, national soccer heroes, tennis icons, men with other men's wives, women with other women's husbands, men with other men, women with other women, people about whom he couldn't tell who was either, in sex or relationship—and so this was nothing. He just grinned and went along with it. To him, as the "cousin" called Harold had said, it was "all in a day's work" and if the balding man with glasses and a light growth of beard did somehow look familiar he certainly didn't look like the president of the United States. But if he wanted to act as if he were—the most powerful man in the world taking a day or two off from the pressures of office and asking to avoid roadblocks along the way—it was fine by him.

Did the thought cross his mind once again that these two might be the terrorists the authorities were looking for? Of course, especially when they kept insisting he avoid roadblocks and checkpoints. But on closer examination he felt as he had before, that they hardly resembled the kind of people the world over had come to expect a terrorist to look like. Moreover, what terrorists rented a limousine, went barefoot drinking coffee at the beach, and then drove around seeing the sights and pretending to be the president of the United States and his cousin while the authorities were everywhere looking for them?

Again he glanced at his passengers. The one called Cousin Harold had taken a pad of limousine stationery and was writing something on it. Done, he handed it to the one called Cousin Jack when he wasn't playing president of the United States. Miguel grinned once more and looked back to the road. What were they doing now, playing tic-tac-toe?

"It's the sign of Aldebaran." Marten indicated the diagram of a balled cross he'd drawn on the limousine stationery and handed to President Harris. "The pale red star that forms the left eye in the constellation Taurus," he went on, repeating what Demi had told him the day before in Els Quatre Gats, in Barcelona. "In the early history of astrology it was considered to emanate a powerful and fortunate influence. It is also called—"

"The Eye of God," the president said.

"How do—?" Marten was astounded.

"I know?" President Harris smiled gently, "I was a Rhodes scholar, Mr. Marten. I studied at Oxford. My major was European history, my secondary study was theology. The sign of Aldebaran figured in each, if not prominently, but it was certainly there if it was pointed out and one had the kind of demanding, detail-oriented professors I did. The sign of Aldebaran is thought to have been used as an identifying mark by a secretive cult of sorcerers that may have held strong political influence in Europe during and after the Renaissance, and perhaps even in following centuries. It's not known for certain, because the movement, if indeed there was one, left behind no documents or written history, at least that we know of. All that remains is rumor and supposition."

"Let me add another piece of rumor and supposition from the Renaissance era. The Machiavelli Covenant. Do you know of it?"

"No."

"Allegedly Machiavelli wrote an addendum to his famous *The Prince*," again Marten repeated what Demi had told him. "In it he created the concept of a secret society made powerful by its members' documented participation in a yearly, very elaborate ritual killing. The idea was that deliberate and verified complicity in murder bound them together in blood and gave them license to operate very aggressively, even ruthlessly as a group knowing they could all hang if what they had done was found out. It would have made for a pretty intimidating bunch, especially if those involved were members of an already powerful and influential group."

The president's eyes narrowed. "What does that or the sign of Aldebaran have to do with—?"

"You said a secretive cult of sorcerers," Marten cut him off. "Were they sorcerers or witches?"

"It depends where and in what era you're referring to."

"What if I said here and now, Mr. President."

"I don't understand."

"Merriman Foxx has the sign of Aldebaran tattooed on his left thumb. Reverend Beck may have one as well. It's not possible to tell without close examination because he has a skin pigmentation disorder. Caroline Parsons's doctor, Lorraine Stephenson, had the same tattoo. So, according to Demi, did her missing sister. These people are members of a secretive coven of witches that takes as its identifying symbol the mark of Aldebaran." Marten glanced past the security glass. Miguel's eyes were on the road. If he could hear them now—if he could have been listening-in all along—he gave no indication of it. Marten looked back to the president.

"You said strong political influence, Mr. President? What if this is more than just something between your 'friends' and Merriman Foxx? What if it involves the witches too? What if the Machiavelli Covenant was not some rumored codicil to *The Prince* but real? Something a particular group took as its bible and put into practice? What if your secretive cult of sorcerers actually did exist? What if it still does? And not just in Europe but in Washington?"

President Harris took a deep breath and Marten could see the awful pressure of what was happening beginning to take its toll, both as a man and as president. "If there is truly an answer to that, perhaps Dr. Foxx will be able to provide it." The president looked at Marten for a moment longer then turned toward the window to stare at the passing countryside. If anything, he seemed even more troubled and introspective than before.

"We are going to Montserrat, Mr. Marten, hopefully to find Dr. Foxx and confront him," he said, still staring off. "Never mind what he did as a scientist, the experiments he performed, the weapons he developed—he was also a professional soldier most of his life." Now the president turned from the window to look at Marten directly. "He may be in his late fifties, but from what I've read about him he's fit and strong. And tough. The damnable project we have to know about he's probably been working on for years, developing it to the point where it's now ready for use. Why do we think he will tell us anything about it? There is no reason to believe he will say anything at all. Why should he? If I were him and in the same situation I certainly wouldn't." A look of despair came over him. "I wonder, Mr. Marten, if after everything, we are not prepared for the adversary we may be lucky enough to face. If he will just laugh at our questions and in the end we will have nothing."

"I think, Mr. President," Marten said quietly and with strength, "it will depend on where and under what circumstances the questions are put to him."

73

"Muchas gracias," Peter Fadden nodded appreciatively to the front desk clerk. Then, scrawling his name on the credit card receipt, he picked up his bag and headed for the front door, already late for his eleven o'clock flight to Barcelona.

Outside, the hotel doorman signaled for a taxi. It pulled up and stopped, then immediately drove off without a fare. Fadden and the doorman exchanged surprised glances; then the doorman signaled for the next cab in line. Like the first cab, it pulled up and stopped. Only this time the driver did not drive off. Instead he got out and looked at the doorman for a directive.

"Aeropuerto de Barajas," Fadden said before the doorman could answer. Then he tipped him, pulled the rear passenger door open, tossed his bag onto the seat, and climbed in after it. Seconds later the taxi pulled away.

BARCELONA POLICE HEADQUARTERS, SAME TIME

Hap Daniels and Special Agent Bill Strait were like the rest of the Secret Service contingent who had flown up from Madrid, physically and mentally drained and feeling grubby as hell from the more than twenty-four hours of intense, nonstop insanity. While rooms had been reserved for them at the Hotel Colón across from the cathedral of Barcelona, temporary sleeping quarters had been set up here in a basement-level meeting room next to the central command headquarters, where a group of thirty-six Barcelona police, Spanish intel, CIA, and U.S. Secret Service agents labored over a communications system jammed with information coming in from checkpoints and search teams. A group overseen by Hap himself.

"Twenty minutes," he said to the command team, flashing ten fingers two times. "Twenty minutes is all I need."

Immediately he motioned for Bill Strait and went into the sleeping area, where a half dozen other Secret Service agents napped on hastily-set-up cots and where he planned to lie down and close his eyes for those precious twenty minutes.

Strait came in and Hap closed the door, then walked his deputy to a far corner and away from the others.

"What's going on is not foul play," he said in a sotto voice. "It's not the work of terrorists or some foreign government or agents. This is 'Crop Duster,' the POTUS, trying to get away."

"I don't understand your point, Hap," Strait said in the same low voice, "we've been going on that premise since Madrid. He's ill."

"If he's ill I'm a three-legged donkey. He shinnied out of the Ritz's air-conditioning ducts. Took off a hairpiece we never knew he had and made it from Madrid to Barcelona without being seen. He found Marten without anybody knowing, and he got out of the damn hotel and out of the city right under our noses. This is not somebody who's ill. It's somebody who's determined as hell not to be caught and is being damned smart about it."

"People do all kinds of things when they're screwed up, Hap. Even presidents."

"We don't know he's screwed up. All we know is what we've been told by Lowe and Dr. Marshall. And unless there's something they're not telling us, they're just guessing. Either that or it's what they want us to believe."

"*Want* us to believe?"

"Yes."

Strait stared at him. "You're tired, tell me that in a half-hour when you wake up."

"I'm telling you right now."

"Okay, then what the hell is going on?"

Just then an agent on the cot nearest them coughed and rolled over in his sleep. Daniels glanced around the room, then led Strait through an adjoining door and into a vacant men's restroom.

"I don't know what's going on," he said the moment they were alone. "But I think back to that late meeting at Evan Byrd's house in Madrid. The people who were there, the vice president and almost the entire cabinet, Crop Duster wasn't expecting them to be there, and he wasn't the same when he came out of the talks with them. The whole ride back to the hotel he was quiet and distant, never said a word. A few hours later he's gone, lighting his way with matches he picked up at Byrd's house. Not long afterward he ends up with this Nicholas Marten who he asked me to check up on before any of this began."

Daniels took off his jacket and loosened his tie, "I'm going to lie down and close my eyes for twenty minutes. Maybe when I wake up, I hope things will be clearer. In the meantime I want you to go outside, go someplace you won't be overheard, use your cell phone, and call Emilio Vasquez at Spanish Intel in Madrid. Ask him to very quietly put an electronic intercept on Evan Byrd's phones. He might not like it, but tell him it's a personal favor to me. If he has trouble doing it, tell him I'll call him myself when I get up."

"You think Evan Byrd has something to do with this?"

"I don't know. I don't even have a thought about what *this* is. I just want to see who he's in touch with and what they have to say to each other."

74

MADRID, 9:30 A.M.

Peter Fadden watched the city pass in a blur, barely aware of the taxi's blaring radio playing American rock 'n' roll oldies, his psyche a churning jumble of conflict, exhilaration, and dread. He had called Nicholas Marten because he was certain he was onto something that involved the president, what had happened to Caroline and Mike Parsons and their son, and the congressional hearings surrounding the testimony of Merriman Foxx. And because the center of a huge and intense manhunt for what Spanish authorities were calling "fugitive terrorists" was concentrated right where Marten was, Barcelona.

He had talked to Marten just after seven, little more than two hours earlier, a conversation Marten had abruptly ended by telling him he would get back to him as soon as he could. So far that hadn't happened, and three attempts to reach him had achieved nothing more than a connection to his voice mail. So where was he? What the hell had happened?

If Fadden was right and the authorities were looking for a person or persons other than terrorists, as far as he'd been able to tell none of the other media people had yet picked up on it. That meant if he could break it he just might have an exclusive on an incident of major political, even historic, proportions.

The question was how to handle it. He had been around far too long not to know that if he called his editor at *The Washington Post,* no matter how confidential their conversation, whatever he said would be reported to the executive editor. Because of it, there was every chance someone in the Washington press corps would learn about it, and soon the flood gates would open and he would be trampled in a stampede of others rushing to the scene; and that was something he wasn't about to let happen.

9:35 A.M.

Fadden watched the familiar landscape. They were on Calle de Alcalá and about to pass Madrid's famous bull ring, the Plaza de Toros. Moments later they would be crossing Avenida de la Paz. Fadden knew the way to the airport well. In five years as a *Washington Post* foreign correspondent in London, two in Rome, two in Paris, and one in Istanbul, he had been to Madrid countless times. By his calculation and with the flow of traffic, he should reach the terminal in less than twenty minutes, giving him just enough breathing room to make his Iberia flight to Barcelona.

9:37 A.M.

They passed Avenida de la Paz, and Fadden took a moment to close his eyes. He'd been up into the early morning talking to everyday staff at the Ritz—busboys, maids, kitchen, cleaning, and maintenance people, night managers, hotel security. Afterward he'd worked in his hotel room until nearly four making notes. At six thirty he was up showering and making his airline reservations and then calling Nick Marten. A little over two hours' sleep—no wonder he was tired.

Suddenly he felt the taxi slow. He opened his eyes as the driver made a right turn onto a side street and continued down it.

"Where are you going?" he snapped. "This isn't the way to the airport."

"I am sorry, señor," the driver said in broken English. "There is nothing I can do about it."

"About what?"

The driver glanced in the rearview mirror. "Them."

Fadden turned around. A black car was right behind them. Two men wearing dark glasses were in the front seat.

"Who the hell are they?"

"I'm sorry, señor. I have to stop."

"Stop? Why?"

"I'm sorry."

Immediately the driver pulled to the curb, the oldies American rock still blasting from the radio. An instant later he threw open the door, then got out and took off on the dead run, never looking back.

"Jesus God!" Fadden blurted, fear and realization stabbing through him. His hand went to the handle and he shoved the door open. His feet hit the curb just as the black car slid to a stop behind. He didn't even look, just took off running. Seconds later he reached a cross street and ran into it without looking. A blast of horn was followed by a shriek of tires. Fadden went up on his toes, pirouetted like a running back, and dodged around a blue Toyota van that nearly hit him. Then he was on the far sidewalk and charging into a small plaza. He darted left and then right around a fountain. Then took the gravel path on the far side of it. A brief glance over his shoulder and he could see them coming. They wore jeans and sweatshirts and had military haircuts. They looked and felt American.

"Christ!" he breathed, and kept on.

Just ahead he saw a shrub-lined pathway leading from the plaza and onto the street beyond. Lungs on fire, he took it. Ahead he saw a stopped city bus letting off passengers. There was no reason to look back. They would still be coming. The bus was still thirty feet away and he was running with everything he had. He fully expected a blow from behind or a flying tackle that would take his legs out from under him. Twenty feet more, then ten. The bus door was starting to close.

"Wait!" he yelled, "wait!" The door opened again just as he reached it. In a heartbeat he was onboard, the door closed and the bus pulled away.

75

MANCHESTER, ENGLAND. THE BANFIELD COUNTRY ESTATE, HALIFAX ROAD. 9:43 A.M.

A heavy mist hung across the rolling deep green fields. Rain clouds drifted above the distant hills. From the hilltop where Ian Graff stood he could see the river and if he turned, the Banfields' newly constructed great house—all twelve thousand square feet of the glass, steel and stone of it. None of which suited English history or the rolling rural setting where it sat. But it was the landscape Fitzsimmons and Justice had been paid to design not the house. It was the landscape, this damp Saturday morning, he had come to once again, plans rolled up and tucked under his arm, to survey one last time before presenting them—no thanks at all to Nicholas Marten—to Robert Fitzsimmons who would again submit them to the young, newly very wealthy, newly married, very testy, Mr. and Mrs. Banfield.

Graff twisted his jacket collar up against the mist and was just turning his Wellington-booted feet back toward the main house when he saw the dark blue Rover sedan parked at the bottom of the hill and two men in raincoats coming up the muddy path toward him.

"Mr. Ian Graff," the first man, stocky and black-haired with a touch of gray at the temples, called out. It wasn't a question as much as the voice of authority. They knew who he was.

"Yes."

The second man was tall and his hair was all gray. He reached into his raincoat pocket as he drew closer and took out a small leather case. He flipped it open and held it up, "John Harrison, Security Service, this is Special Agent Russell. One hour and twenty minutes ago you placed a call from your office to the cell phone of a Nicholas Marten."

"Yes. Why? Is he in some sort of trouble?"

"Why did you make the call?"

"I am his supervisor at the architectural landscape firm of Fitzsimmons and Justice."

"Please answer the question," Agent Russell moved closer.

"I called him because he asked me to. If you look around you will see the acreage that we are about to begin landscaping. Among the many plantings are to be azaleas. He was working on the plan and asked me to go down the azalea list because he had forgotten the name of a specific type he wished to use. I retrieved the list and called him and recited the names."

"Then what?"

"The connection went dead. I tried calling him back but I had no luck."

"You said he asked you to call him," Agent Russell spoke again. "Are you saying he called you and asked you to call him back?"

"In a manner of speaking, yes. He called my house thinking it was Saturday and I would be at home. My housekeeper took the call and then relayed the message to me at my office."

"Your housekeeper."

"Yes, sir. Although I'm not sure why he called the house. He knew I would be at the office, we are far behind on a critical project. This one," Graff gestured at house and the land around them.

Agent Harrison stared at Graff for a moment longer, then glanced at the surrounding countryside. "Nice piece of dirt. Don't like the house though, style doesn't fit."

"I agree with you, sir."

"Thank you for your time, Mr. Graff."

With that Security Service agents Harrison and Russell turned and started back through the mud for their car.

"Is he in trouble?" Graff called after them. "Is Mr. Marten in trouble with the government?"

There was no reply.

76

Peter Fadden had ridden the city bus for two stops, gotten off, then walked a half block where he turned down a side street and entered a small café sprinkled with a few midmorning customers. Immediately he went to the men's restroom. Several moments later he came out, glanced down the hallway into the kitchen and established that there was a rear entrance and way out if he needed it. Satisfied, he went back into the main room and took a seat at a table where he could see the door and ordered a cup of coffee.

He had his wallet, his passport, his BlackBerry, and, for the moment at least, his life and his freedom. The rest—his suitcase and his briefcase containing his laptop—he'd left in the taxi, things the men who'd come after him would now have in their possession. It was the laptop that concerned him most. The hard drive contained all of his notes: his interviews with hotel staff people at the Madrid Ritz, his collection of material about Merriman Foxx, Dr. Lorraine Stephenson, the Washington, D.C., clinic where Caroline Parsons had been taken before she was admitted to University Hospital, and his suspicions about the manhunt in Barcelona and the possible fate of the president.

The problem now was what to do about all of it.

At this point he desperately wanted to get in touch with his editor at *The Washington Post* but he knew that was problematical at best. The only way the men who had come after him could have known who he was was because they had been tapped into the frequency of Marten's cell phone. It meant they had heard their conversation, probably even recorded it. Worse, it meant they had the number of his BlackBerry, which was no doubt how they found him at his hotel and probably the reason the first taxi had driven away without picking him up—because the second had a driver who worked for them and would do as he was told. It was the reason he had taken the side street as he had and then pulled the taxi to the curb and run away.

Now that they had his BlackBerry frequency they would be monitoring it, so he couldn't use it without giving his position away. Moreover, because he had said what he had about the president and Mike Parsons's committee and Merriman Foxx, he could be all but certain the phone numbers and e-mail addresses of anyone listed in his BlackBerry Rolodex—nearly everyone he knew in Washington and in *Post* bureaus around the world—would be under surveillance as well. Who was doing all this, he had no idea, but it had to be at a very high level if they were monitoring Marten's cell phone and then, so soon afterward, sending the crew cuts after him. The business of the taxi cabs meant they hadn't been sent to have a simple conversation with him. That they could have done at the hotel.

Topping off everything was the element of time. Whatever was happening was happening fast. If the president was in trouble, he was in trouble right now. It meant Fadden had to find someone out of the loop. Someone who had a prestigious voice that would be listened to and whom he could trust unconditionally needed to be told about it as quickly as possible.

10:22 A.M.

Fadden entered a small tobacco shop four doors down from the café. He glanced around, then went up to the only other person in there, the shop's heavyset proprietor sitting behind the counter smoking a cigar.

"Do you speak English?"

"Poco." A little. The man said.

"I would like to buy a phone card."

"Sí," the man said, "sí," and stood up.

WORLD HEALTH ORGANIZATION, GENEVA, SWITZERLAND. 10:27 A.M.

Dr. Matunde Ngotho, executive director of the WHO/OMS Human Genetics Program, had just left a Saturday-morning investigative conference and was entering his office on Avenue Appia when his cell phone rang.

"Matunde here," he said, clicking on.

"Matunde, it's Peter Fadden."

"Peter!" the research doctor smiled broadly at the voice of his old and dear friend. "Where are you? In Geneva I hope. Yes?"

Matunde waited for a response. He got none.

"Peter?" he said. "Peter, are you there?"

Peter Fadden stood frozen in place, staring wide-eyed at the tall crew-cut man standing just behind him at the street corner public telephone. For some reason he felt cold though the temperature outside was nearly eighty degrees. Now the crew cut reached in and lifted the receiver from his hand and hung it up on the phone's cradle. Vaguely Fadden remembered reaching his old college roommate in Geneva. Remembered hearing his voice and at the same time feeling a sharp pain near his right kidney, as if a needle had suddenly been inserted and then withdrawn. He saw an umbrella in the crew cut's hand. He wondered why. It wasn't raining. In fact there wasn't a cloud in the sky.

77

10:30 A.M.

Nicholas Marten stared vacantly out the window as Miguel Balius maneuvered the limousine over a narrow bridge spanning a muddy river. A full minute passed and then two, then Marten's focus abruptly sharpened as if he had just completed a thought process. With a glance at President Harris, he touched the intercom button.

"Miguel?"

"Yes, sir."

"You must have been to Montserrat before."

"Many times."

"What's it like?"

"Like? Like a small city built into a mountainside half a mile straight up from the valley floor. A feat of incredible engineering."

The president sat forward, suddenly aware that Marten was gathering information and in the process working on a plan for what they might do when they got there.

"There are many buildings, some centuries old; the basilica, a museum, a hotel that has a restaurant, there's a library, a refectory, too many to list." Miguel bubbled with the enthusiasm of a tour guide, alternately looking at Marten in the mirror and watching the road in front of him as he drove. "You can drive to it or reach it by cable car from the valley floor. A funicular railway takes you higher into the cliffs if you want. All around are pathways that go off in every direction. Some have ancient chapels along the way, but most are long abandoned and nothing but ruins. The saying goes there are 'a thousand and one paths that crisscross the mountain.' You won't be disappointed. But be warned, it will be crowded. It always is. Montserrat has become as much a tourist stop as a religious retreat."

"There's a chance we might meet some friends there," Marten dug deeper. "You said there's a restaurant. If we wanted to have lunch, is it just a sandwich shop or is there more to it?"

"No, not a sandwich shop. A regular restaurant. Tables and chairs, everything."

"Do you know if they serve soft drinks? Colas, mineral water, things like that? I ask because one of the gentlemen has a personal medical situation and has certain needs because of it."

"Sure, colas, mineral water, coffee, wine, beer, anything you want."

The president listened carefully. Marten was asking very specific questions, as if he knew precisely what he wanted.

"Is there a restroom, you know, a toilet, nearby? I wouldn't want to suggest something that wouldn't be appropriate for his condition."

This part Harris understood. Marten was trying find a public place where Merriman Foxx might meet him and then a place not far off where they could get him alone.

"I think, yes," Miguel kept his eyes on the road. "It's in the back, near the door where they bring in the supplies."

Marten perked. "A door that leads outside?"

"Yes, sir."

"This door, is it near any of the thousand and one pathways you mentioned? Say if we wanted to take a walk after lunch."

"Right you are, sir," Miguel beamed, his Australian accent and his years there creeping through, clearly enjoying the part of helpful host. "One way goes down to the loading dock, the other up the hill and into the mountain trails. In fact one of the old ruined chapels is right up the trail from it."

"You paint a wonderful picture, Miguel."

"It's my job, sir. Besides, Montserrat is wonderful. At least for the first fifty visits or so."

Marten smiled, then clicked off the intercom and looked to the president. "Before, I suggested the way to get answers from Foxx depended on where and under what circumstances the questions were put to him. If we play it right and we're lucky we can get him up that path to the chapel alone. After that it might have to get physical."

"Go on."

"We get to Montserrat and let Demi find us. When she does I'll arrange to meet Foxx and suggest the restaurant. If he agrees, the two of us will come in and find a table near the back. Meantime you're already there, at a table near the door to the rear pathway. You've got your big hat on, you're drinking something and have your head down, maybe reading a newspaper. He doesn't even look at you. Or if he does he has no idea who you are. Hopefully no one else does either.

"Foxx and I sit down, look at the menu, talk about nothing for a few minutes. Then I tell him I'm not comfortable having a serious exchange in public and suggest we go for a walk alone outside. The door's there, probably with an exit sign. I ask the waiter where it goes. He tells me. I ask Foxx if it's okay with him. Even if he's got people with him he'll agree because he wants to know what I know. We get up and go out the door. Thirty seconds later you follow. By then we should be up the path and nearing the chapel."

"You think he'll go. Just like that."

"I told you, he wants to know about me and will have no reason to suspect anything. Montserrat is his call not mine. If he's nervous I'll tell him he can frisk me, I have nothing to hide."

The president studied Marten carefully. "Alright, so everything works and you're alone on the path with him and near the chapel."

"We see you coming up the trail behind us. I suggest we go inside, have our talk in there in case more people come."

"What if he doesn't want to go? I told you before, he's been a professional soldier most of his life. He's tough and wary—he's not going to do something he doesn't want to."

"This time he will."

"How do you know?"

"He won't have a choice."

Again the president studied him, was ready to ask what he meant and then decided not to push it. "Then what?"

"You used to work on a farm, didn't you?"

The president nodded.

"Ever try to hold down a reluctant pig or calf while the vet gave it a shot?"

"Yes."

"Were you able to do it?"

"Yes."

"Well, it'll be sort of the same thing here. And it's going to take two of us, the vet and the handler. I'm afraid you're going to have to get your hands a little bit dirty."

"I have no trouble with the manual-labor part, not in this situation," the president cocked his head. "I just don't get what you mean to do. We have no access to drugs or hypodermic syringes. Even if we did there's no time to—"

"The restaurant, Cousin. Everything we will need will either be on the table or on the menu."

78

10:37 A.M.

They were twenty minutes out of Barcelona, heading north and west on the A2 *autopista*. The van was white. Its driver, a large man named Raphael. Painted on its doors in a black scroll were the words of its origin and destination: *Monasterio Benedictino Montserrat*.

Reverend Beck and Luciana rode in the seats directly in back of Raphael. Demi was behind them, alone in the third row of seats, her camera gear and equipment bag beside her. She was looking off, trying not to think of Nicholas Marten and the president and what she had done. Or rather of what she'd decided she had no choice but to do.

Ever since Marten's confrontation with Dr. Foxx in Malta it had been clear that both Foxx and Reverend Beck had been upset. In turn she had been afraid it would spoil, even end, her relationship with Beck. And she thought it had when he'd so unexpectedly left the island the next morning, but then the concierge had called with the reverend's apology and his invitation to Barcelona.

Shortly after she had arrived at his suite at the Regente Majestic and been introduced to Luciana, where he'd surprised her by saying he understood that her interest in him was due not to his religious vocation but to his association with Aldebaran coven, which he guessed was the real subject of her book, and not the purported photo essay on "clerics who minister to prominent politicians." Moreover, he'd told her the reason she had tagged along on his European trip was because she knew he was coming to the coven's yearly gathering.

But instead of demanding she leave immediately he surprised her once more, telling her he had discussed her with the coven's elders and they had agreed to open up their proceedings, even allowing her to take photographs. In truth, there was nothing at all evil about the coven and at this point in history they felt there was no reason to keep their rituals secret.

Still, they required a quid pro quo: Nicholas Marten.

"As you have suspected," Beck told her, "Dr. Foxx is a member of the coven. He is currently at the monastery at Montserrat preparing for the coven's assembly. His falling out with Marten in Malta over his congressional testimony in Washington is a situation he is still upset about. He would like to clear the air before any more time passes and before any of it finds its way into the press."

If Marten would come to Montserrat, Beck would arrange a private meeting between the two, something he was certain Marten would agree to: "Otherwise he wouldn't have followed you to Barcelona and then taken you to lunch at The Four Cats. Undoubtedly he thinks you might bring him and Dr. Foxx together."

If Demi was startled by Beck's knowledge of her meeting with Marten, she didn't show it. As for his revelation that she knew about the Aldebaran coven and his involvement with it, he seemed content with the idea that her interest was merely professional, a writer and photographer's search for a story. Moreover, all he had asked was what Marten himself had asked, that she tell him where Dr. Foxx would be and when.

What she had not known at the time, nor had she told anyone since, was that a second person would be accompanying Marten to Montserrat: the president of the United States.

79

BARCELONA POLICE HEADQUARTERS,
SPECIAL COMMUNICATIONS ROOM. 10:45 A.M.

Hap Daniels had just come in from his twenty-minute catnap. He was pulling on his headset and looking around for Bill Strait, anxious to know if he'd reached Spanish Intel in Madrid and arranged the electronic tap on Evan Byrd's phones, when a familiar voice crackled through his earpiece.

"Hap, it's Roley." It was Roland Sandoval, the Secret Service special agent in charge of Vice President Hamilton Rogers's protective detail. Daniels knew Rogers had secretly arrived in Madrid a short while ago and gone directly to the U.S. embassy to join White House Chief of Staff Tom Curran for a scheduled private meeting with the president of Spain to discuss the disappearance of President Harris.

"Yes, Roley."

"We've just cleared the vice president for a wheels down at Barcelona at thirteen-hundred. After that he has an hour tour of the area."

"Tour of the area? Why? Why the hell now?"

"That's direct from the chief of staff. Acting White House wants to show the country's concern for the terrorist situation even while the POTUS is 'out of touch.' Afterward he'll come back to Madrid and spend the night at Evan Byrd's home before his meeting with the Spanish prime minister tomorrow."

Daniels bit his tongue in outrage and for the longest moment said nothing. Finally he answered with a simple. "Okay, Roley, we'll coordinate this end. Thanks for the heads-up."

There was distinct click as Agent White signed off. "What the hell?" Daniels swore under his breath. The VPOTUS. Tour of the area. That meant media coverage. Sound bites and photo ops. Then as quickly Rogers would be on his way back to Madrid and to Byrd's residence. Something was going on, but he had no idea what it was.

Again he looked for Bill Strait. If Vice President Rogers was spending the night at Evan Byrd's, they had to get an electronic eavesdrop on his phones.

"Hap," Bill Strait's voice came over his headset.

"Where are you?"

"In the cafeteria. Got time for a cup of good Spanish coffee?"

"Damn right I do," Hap clicked off and was starting to remove his headset when another voice came on.

"Agent Daniels?" The voice was male and had a British accent.

"Yes."

"This is Special Agent Harrison, MI5 in Manchester, England. We've just interviewed a Mr. Ian Graff, Nicholas Marten's employment supervisor in Manchester. He says Marten contacted him via his housekeeper earlier this morning and asked him to call his cell phone with a listing of types of azaleas."

"What do you mean 'via his housekeeper'?"

"He called his home and had the housekeeper call Mr. Graff at work. Though Graff seems to think Marten would have known he was at work all the while and called there directly."

"How in hell did Marten contact him? We would have picked up his cell phone location in seconds. What was it, a pay phone?"

"No, sir, he's getting sloppy. He used the mobile phone of a Barcelona limousine service, Limousines Barcelona. The car is currently out for day hire to two gentlemen. They were picked up at the Hotel Regente Majestic just before seven this morning."

"Do we know where the car is right now?"

"No, sir. But we have its description, license number, and mobile phone number."

"You didn't tell the limo company why you called?"

"No, sir. We were just gathering information. Done via a phone company billing and records check."

"Thank you, MI5. Good work. We appreciate it very much."

"Our pleasure, sir. Anything else, let us know."

Daniels took down the limousine's numbers, then clicked off. This was the break he'd been hoping for. The question was what to do about it. Give it to anyone else—his own people, the CIA, Spanish Intel, or the Barcelona police—and Jake Lowe and Dr. Marshall would know about it in seconds. Give it to no one, and before long somebody at MI5 would be wondering why no action had been taken on their information and start making noise about it. What he had to do was think. Hard to do surrounded by a roomful of police and special agents working computers and dissecting information. He decided the best thing was to join Bill Strait in the cafeteria for a cup of good Spanish coffee.

80

10:55 A.M.

Miguel Balius's concentration was on the road in front of him. The small village they were passing through led to familiar hilly countryside beyond. Soon afterward they would begin the long winding climb into the mountains toward Montserrat.

"Miguel," Cousin Harold's voice came over the intercom. "Do you have a map of Barcelona and the surrounding area?"

"Yes, sir. It's in the seat pocket in front of you."

He glanced in the mirror to make sure Cousin Harold found it, then looked back to the road. Excluding accidents or more roadblocks, it should take them no more than forty minutes to reach the monastery, unless they changed their mind and wanted to go somewhere else, and that had been the reason for the map.

"Here, here, here, and here," Marten had the map spread out on the seat between them and was using a pen to draw vertical and then crossing horizontal lines on it, making a grid that went outward from Barcelona itself and into the countryside. It was the kind of framework he was certain the Secret Service and Spanish forces would be using to find them and close them off. By now the immense expansion and regrouping of the units that had concerned them earlier would be fully under way. The number of troops looking for them would be at least double the original force, if not more, and they all would be working the grid, scouring each area foot by foot, then securing it and moving on. This time there could be no backtracking as they had done in the city the night before and was the reason Marten had taken the chance and used the limo's mobile phone to call Ian Graff in Manchester.

Marten looked to the president. "By now the NSA will have traced the call Ian Graff made back to my cell phone and some agency, the police or British Intelligence, will have tracked him down in Manchester, listened to his story, then traced the call I made to his home to the mobile phone here in the car. My hope then was that we would already have been at the monastery and Miguel would have been long on his way. When the authorities caught up with him all he'd have had to say was that we asked him to drop us off at some village or other along the way and he had. He could name any of the half-dozen we passed through. No one would ever know he wasn't telling the truth. After all he said 'discreet' was the company policy."

"Well, so far, nothing's happened. So maybe your Mr. Graff was harder to find than you think," the president said. "Maybe luck is finally on our side."

"We're not at the monastery yet, either. If they call Miguel, they'll probably use his cell. We wouldn't know who placed the call—it could be his wife—until we were surrounded and it was too late."

"So far he hasn't picked up his phone," the president said.

"Maybe they don't want to tell him. Just broadcast the license number and description of the car. It might take a little longer but they'd still get us."

"What are you suggesting?"

"We either have him drop us off and soon, then try to get to Montserrat on our own or—"

"Or what?"

"Tell Miguel some of what's happening and ask for his help. Both are dangerous. The only thing we have going for us is Miguel himself and the company policy. It's the old joke; our chances of getting out of this are between slim and none and slim just left town."

President Harris glanced out at the rugged countryside, then pressed the intercom. "Miguel," he said evenly.

"Yes, sir."

"How much longer before we get to the monastery?"

"Without roadblocks or other problems, a half hour or so."

"How far by miles?"

"The route we're going twenty or so, sir. Mostly uphill."

"Thank you."

The president clicked off the intercom and took a breath, then looked to Marten. He was as drawn and grave and intense as Marten had ever seen him. "Miguel seems decent and honest. He knows the land, the roads, and the people. He knows intricacies of the language I do not. Under the circumstances he seems far more an asset than a liability."

81

BARCELONA, 11:05 A.M.

Armed with the MI5 information about Marten's limousine number and a fake business card he kept for a variety of "necessary circumstances," Hap Daniels stepped from a taxi, paid the driver and waited until the cab pulled away. Then he turned and started toward the garagelike structure that housed Limousines Barcelona.

Minutes earlier he'd been in the cafeteria at Barcelona Police Headquarters where Bill Strait had confirmed he'd talked to Emilio Vasquez at Spanish Intel in Madrid and asked him in Hap's name to very quietly put electronic surveillance on all of Evan Byrd's telephone communications.

"It has to do with the effort at hand," Vasquez had said without emotion, a statement more than a question.

"Yes."

"Considering the situation, if Tigre Uno asks, then it will be done."

"N-O," Strait said.

"N-O, of course." N-O. Not Officially. There would be no official tapping of Evan Byrd's phones. It was to be done covertly with anyone involved fully aware and prepared to deny it had ever been done.

Immediately afterward Hap finished his coffee and left, telling Strait he needed a walk to think things over. If they needed him they had his BlackBerry, his emergency pager, everything. He walked for three deliberate blocks before turning a corner and hailing a taxi. Asking the driver to take him to a cross street address that was in a short walking distance of Limousines Barcelona, he suddenly began to understand what the POTUS, "Crop Duster," must be feeling and had felt when he'd crawled through the air ducts at the Hotel Ritz; that he had no idea who he could trust. And for Hap that meant Bill Strait, even the entire Secret Service detail. Maybe they were wholly innocent but there was no way for him to be absolutely certain.

What he did know was that he didn't trust Chief of Staff Tom Curran; didn't trust "Crop Duster's" chief political adviser Jake Lowe; didn't trust National Security Adviser Dr. James Marshall; and he didn't like the overtly opportunistic feel of the vice president suddenly flying into Barcelona for a twenty-minute photo and sound bite op and then retreating to Madrid and Evan Byrd's home. It immediately put the VPOTUS alongside the others on his "do not trust" list.

Now, thinking about it, he remembered who else was at the late-night meeting at Byrd's residence: Secretary of State David Chaplin, Secretary of Defense Terrence Langdon, and the Chairman of the Joint Chiefs of Staff, United States Air Force General Chester Keaton.

"Christ," he said under his breath. What if they were all in this together?

But in *what?* And what had they asked or demanded of the

president that had put him so into a corner that he had no other choice but to run?

Romeo J. Brown
Private Investigator
Long Island City, NY

Limousines Barcelona's day manager, smartly dressed, forty-year-old Beto Nahmans, turned the business card over in his hand then looked to Hap Daniels sitting in one of two stylish chrome and black leather chairs across from his desk.

"I understand you have the mobile number and license plate number of one of our cars," Nahmans said in crisp English.

Daniels nodded. "I've been retained by a security firm investigating insurance fraud. We believe one of the people we are following is a passenger in that limousine. It's my job to find him and give him the chance to voluntarily return to the U.S. for prosecution before we ask that he be taken into custody."

"And what might this person's name be?"

"Marten. Nicholas Marten. Marten with an *e*."

Nahmans swiveled in his chair, punched a series of numbers into a keyboard, and then looked at the computer screen in front of him.

"I'm sorry, sir. We have no record of a Nicholas Marten as a passenger in the vehicle you are referring to. Or any other for that matter."

"No?"

"No, sir."

Daniels's manner hardened. "That's not an answer I like."

"It's what we have," Nahmans smiled faintly. "I'm afraid it's all I can tell you."

Hap Daniels sighed and looked at the floor, then tugged at an ear and looked back. "What if I were to have Spanish Intelligence ask for that information?"

"The answer would be the same. I apologize."

"Suppose they presented an official document requiring you to submit a list of each and all of your clients for the past two years. Their names. Where they were picked up, who was with them, how long they were gone, and what address they were returned to."

"I don't think that would be legal," uncertainty flashed through Beto Nahmans' eyes and Daniels took full advantage of it.

"Would you like to find out?"

Three minutes later Daniels walked out of Limousines Barcelona. Day manager Nahmans had given him three names. A *Cousin Jack*. A *Cousin Harold*. And *Demi Picard*, a woman who had ordered the limousine a little before seven that morning, charging it to her room at the Hotel Regente Majestic.

82

11:15 A.M.

Miguel Balius stood wide-eyed and in shadow next to a broken-down table in the corner of what had once been some kind of stone millhouse. Above him most of the roof was open to the sky, while outside, a roaring stream passed just feet from what at one time must have been a supporting wall.

"It's alright, Miguel. Take a deep breath. Relax. No bad men here." Cousin Jack leaned against the far corner of the same table talking easily. He no longer wore the glasses he had sported from the beginning when Miguel first picked them up at the Hotel Regente Majestic. He also had a full head of hair, or rather a perfectly fitting hairpiece Miguel had not seen before. That was until "Cousin Jack" had stepped from the rear seat of the limousine moments earlier suddenly transformed into the man the entire world recognized as the president of the United States.

"Discreet, Miguel, discreet," Cousin Harold, Nicholas Marten, urged gently from behind.

"Discreet, yes, sir," Miguel breathed, his entire being glued to the man in front of him. At the cousins' request he had driven off the main road and taken a dirt road through the woods to the edge of a stream and the remains of this stone building where he'd parked the Mercedes. The cousins, it seemed, had wanted to wade in a "Spanish stream" as they'd earlier waded in the Mediterranean. At the time the request seemed no more odd than any of their other behavior. Then Cousin Jack had emerged from the car, his hairpiece on and without his glasses, and said:

"Miguel, my name is John Henry Harris, and I *am* the president of the United States. This is Nicholas Marten. We need your help."

Miguel Balius said simply, humbly, and instantaneously. "What can I do for you, sir?"

BARCELONA, HOTEL REGENTE MAJESTIC. 11:20 A.M.

Romeo J. Brown
Private Investigator
Long Island City, NY

The concierge studied Hap Daniels's business card. "Insurance fraud?"

"In the U.S., yes, sir."

The concierge pressed his fingertips together, "Ms. Picard is a guest here. She ordered the limousine this morning for people she said were her cousins. They had just flown in from New York, were jet-lagged and could not sleep, and wanted to see the sights of Barcelona."

"One man was older and nearly bald. The other tall and in his early thirties."

"Yes."

"Where is Ms. Picard now?"

"I believe she left the hotel some time ago," the concierge shifted positions behind the front desk.

"Do you know where she went?"

"I have told you all I know, señor."

Daniels stared at him; it was the same "privacy of clients" treatment he'd received at the limousine company. Only here he could hardly threaten a visit by Spanish Intelligence. The hotel, he guessed, probably had three hundred rooms. The argument over a threat to have Spanish Intelligence, or tax or local civil authorities demand an accounting of who had stayed there and why over even a short period would, at the very best, be time consuming, and time was something he had precious little of.

"Muchas gracias," he said finally, and started for the door, then turned back, "I wonder if you could tell me the time?"

The man looked at him.

"The time of day?" Daniels tapped his watch. "It stopped." Hap leaned in earnestly, resting his hand on the counter in front of him, the corner of a hundred-euro bill sticking out from under it.

"This Ms. Picard," Hap said quietly. "What does she look like?"

The concierge smiled and looked at his own watch, then leaned in and lowered his voice. "Very attractive. French, a professional photographer. Short dark hair. Navy blazer, tan slacks. Cameras over one shoulder and small equipment bag over the other. She left with a middle-aged African-American male and an older European woman in a white van with the lettering of the monastery at Montserrat."

"I'm sorry, I didn't get the time," Hap said loudly enough to be heard by people passing by.

"Eleven twenty-three, señor," the concierge matched his own watch to Hap's and at the same time palmed the hundred-euro bill.

"Eleven twenty-three," Hap smiled. "Gracias."

"Eleven twenty-four now, señor."

"Gracias," Hap said again. "Muchas gracias."

"Photographer? Montserrat?" Hap said to himself as he came through the Regente Majestic's front door. A half-beat later his cell phone rang. He picked it from his belt and clicked on. "Daniels."

"Where the damn hell are you?" It was Jake Lowe and he left no chance for reply. "We need you at the hotel right away!"

"What is it?"

"Now, Hap! Right now!"

83

Jake Lowe, National Security Adviser Marshall, and Hap Daniels stood alone in the special communications room of the four-room suite Lowe and Marshall had taken as their Barcelona crisis headquarters. The door was closed and they were gathered in front of a video monitor waiting for a secure feed to come through from the White House communications center in Washington.

"Go ahead," Lowe said into a headset connected to a secure phone on the table beside him. There was a short pause; then static showed up on the screen followed immediately by the beginning of a thirty-second video clip. A clip that upon their approval would be sent to FOX News for immediate distribution to major television and cable networks worldwide. The video was complete with a time and date stamp that began at 2:23 P.M. yesterday, Friday, April 7. It showed President Harris, alive and well at the "undisclosed location" he had been taken to following the terrorist threat in Madrid. He was seen in a rustic conference room with National Security Adviser Marshall, Secretary of Defense Terrence Langdon and Secretary of State David Chaplin. They were all in shirtsleeves, notepads and bottled water in front of them, diligently going over what was reported to be notes and text for the speech the president would give to NATO leaders Monday in Warsaw.

It wasn't old recycled video from another place and time; it was all new, and in a setting Hap had never seen before.

"How the hell did you do that?" he said as the screen went blank at the finish and he looked at Marshall. "You're here. Langdon's in Brussels, Chaplin's in London," his eyes went to Lowe, "and Crop Duster's someplace . . . else."

"I asked for your opinion," Lowe said coldly. "Is the video credible from a Secret Service point of view? From the point of view of any global security professional who might see it?"

"Somebody breaks it down technically, I don't know. But from where I stand, yeah, it works," Hap said evenly. "There's just enough, and so far no one should have a reason to scrutinize it closer or believe it's anything but what it's supposed to be."

"So far?" Marshall said quietly. "What do you mean by 'so far'?"

"If the POTUS suddenly shows up somewhere on his own, then what? How do we explain that?"

Lowe stared at him in icy silence, and Daniels could feel his rage, his pent-up anger at the whole thing. Abruptly Lowe turned away and spoke into his headset. "Release the video," he said, "release it now."

84

11:55 A.M.

Demi put out a hand to steady herself as the white Monasterio Benedictino Montserrat van made a sharp turn up the long, winding mountain road leading to the monastery. High above her and in the distance she could see the structure itself. It looked like a medieval fortress in miniature, a tiny city built into the cliffs.

Now she shifted her gaze and looked back inside the van. Raphael, the driver, was intent on the road and a large tour bus directly in front of them. Behind him, Beck and Luciana were silent, intent on something they were reading.

Demi looked at Luciana more closely. She was dressed in black and had a large black purse on the seat beside her. It was essentially the same thing she'd worn yesterday when Demi first met her. It made her wonder if it was a uniform of sorts, a classic costume for a classic witch, if there was such a thing.

Demi had told Marten and the president she had no idea who Luciana was. It was a lie. Luciana had been the center of her attention for years and was the wellspring of everything. For the last two decades she had been the *sacerdotessa,* the high priestess of the secret Aldebaran *boschetto,* the coven. As such she had mastered the intricate skills of her craft, most specifically those of ritual and psychic influence, and meant she had authority over all of the coven's followers and that included Reverend Beck and Merriman Foxx.

A widow with piercing green eyes and striking black hair and still remarkably handsome at sixty-six, Luciana owned Pensione Madonnella, a small hotel on the Italian island of Ischia in the Bay of Naples where she had been born. Further research—in the form of a hired private investigator—had established that she left the island two or three times a year for ten days or so at a time to visit small towns and villages in north and central Italy where she would meet with others of the coven, men and women alike, who carried the tattoo of Aldebaran on their left thumb. Immediately afterward she returned to Ischia to oversee her business.

Then, and always at this same time of year, she came to the monastery at Montserrat, where she would check into the Hotel Abat Cisneros and spend the greater part of a week. What she did there or even if it involved the *boschetto,* Demi had not been able to discover. But whatever it was, it apparently involved Reverend Beck and probably had for some time, because for the last dozen years he had taken his vacation and gone to Europe during the same period. Yet it had not been until yesterday when Demi came to Beck's suite at the Regente Majestic and found the *sacerdotessa* seated on a couch and having coffee with him that she put Beck's excursions to Europe together with Luciana's sojourns to Montserrat. In retrospect it was a moment and revelation she might well have been prepared for, but she wasn't and finding Luciana there, introduced by Beck as his "good friend," nearly took her breath away.

12:00 NOON

A sharp jolt as the van bounced over a hole in the road brought Demi back from her muse. To one side steep sandstone cliffs rose straight up almost within arm's reach. On the other, across the Llobregat River and the valley below, lesser hills faded into the distance. Again she looked at the driver and then to Beck and Luciana, still silent, still intent on their reading.

Patience, she told herself, *patience and calm. You are almost there. After all these years, after everything. Soon we will be at the monastery. After that—pray it all works—we will meet Dr. Foxx and then be taken to wherever the ritual takes place. There, finally, to witness the rites of the coven.*

Suddenly time compressed and with it came a kaleidoscope of memories. Like her supposed innocence concerning Luciana. The story she had told Marten of the search for her missing sister had been a lie. There was no sister. She was searching for her mother. And she had been missing not for two years but eighteen, vanished when Demi was eight. Nor had she gone missing from Malta but from Paris, where her parents had moved from their native Italy soon after they were married, her father changing their name from the Italian Piacenti to the French Picard.

Her mother had been fifteen when Demi was born and twenty-three when she disappeared while on her way to a neighborhood market she had visited countless times. A police investigation turned up but one single fact: her mother had never reached the market. A check of hospitals and the city morgue turned up nothing. A week passed. And then two, and then three, with no sign of her whatsoever. People wandered off all the time, the police said, and for a myriad of reasons. Sometimes they came back; more often they didn't. Not because anything had happened to them but because they didn't want to. And that was how it was left. An open police report and she and her father, nothing else.

A second blow came barely four months later when her father was killed in an industrial accident at the automobile factory where he worked. Suddenly an orphan, and following a provision in her father's will, Demi was sent to live with a distant aunt who taught French and Italian at an exclusive boarding school outside of London. There the two shared a small apartment on campus, and because her aunt was on the faculty, she was enrolled in the school. Her aunt, it turned out, was distant in more ways than one, which made the chief benefits of her new life a good education and that she would learn English. The rest of growing up was left solely to her.

She'd been living with her aunt for several months when a trunk arrived from Paris. In it were some of her mother's personal things:

clothes; a photograph taken only days before she disappeared, her brown eyes intense, yet calm and very peaceful; some books—mostly in Italian; and a number of abstract sketches her mother had drawn as a hobby. Aside from her mother's photograph and a few of her clothes, the rest was of very little interest to a girl approaching her ninth birthday; a girl still heartbroken and confused, feeling abandoned and terribly alone; a girl too, who was convinced her mother was still alive and who watched the mail every day hoping for the letter from her that never came; a girl who carried her mother's picture everywhere and who searched the face of every female stranger she saw—hoping, praying, certain, that one day she would see that familiar face, one that would suddenly smile in recognition and throw her arms around her, promising never to let her go again.

The passage of time did little to ease Demi's pain or sense of loss. And although her aunt strongly tried to dissuade her, the idea that her mother was alive grew stronger with every beat of her heart. But as the days and years passed and nothing came of it, all she could do was immerse herself in her schoolwork and watch in abject loneliness as she saw her classmates' mothers and fathers come to pick them up to take them home. For weekends, holidays, vacation trips, and summer breaks.

Then, on the morning of her seventeenth birthday, a letter arrived from an attorney in Paris. Inside was a small envelope and with it a brief note telling her that by codicil to his last will and testament it was her late father's wish that "this be held to be delivered to you on the occasion of your seventeenth birthday."

Puzzled, she opened the envelope to find a note written in her father's hand and dated shortly before his death.

My darling Demi—

I am writing this and then putting it away for you to read later when you might better understand. I know you loved your mother terribly and must miss her enormously still. It would be unnatural for you not to wonder what happened to her, most probably for years to come, if not for the rest of your life. But for your sake and the sake of your children and theirs, accept it that your mother loved you as much as any mother can love her child and leave it at that. Do not, I underscore, do not, under any circumstances, attempt to learn her fate. Some things are far too dangerous to

know, let alone try to understand. Please take this warning deeply
to heart as an everlasting plea for your own safety and welfare.
                              I love you so much and always will,
                                                            Dad

The note stunned her. Immediately she called the lawyer in
Paris who had sent the letter, wanting to know more. That was all
there was, he told her, adding that he had no idea what the note
contained, only that the firm was simply executing a provision in
her father's will. Afterward she'd hung up and gone scurrying to the
only place she thought she might find more, the trunk. But there
had been nothing other than what she'd seen a hundred times; the
clothes, books in Italian, and her mother's artistic drawings. This
time—and maybe because she had found nothing else and because
they were in her mother's hand and therefore very personal—she
concentrated on the drawings. There were thirty-four in all and in a
variety of sizes, some of which were small, the size of greeting
cards. It was one of these that caught her attention; a simple sketch
of a *balled cross*. In the lower right hand corner beneath it, written
in small letters and in her mother's hand, was one word—*Boschetto*.

Boschetto

The sketch and the word beneath it combined with what her father had written, sent a gnawing chill through her. Immediately she
went to her purse and took out her mother's photograph. For the
thousandth time Demi studied her face. This time her eyes seemed
far more intense, as if she were deliberately staring right at her.
Again Demi read her father's note. Again she looked at the drawing.
Again she stared at the word. Once more the chill came.

The photograph, the note, the sketch, the word.

It was then she realized that a huge part of herself was missing
and had been for all these years. It was a deep, almost overwhelming
sense that she would never be whole until she learned if her mother
was alive or dead, and the truth of what had really happened. In that
moment too she wondered if somehow all of this, coming now when

she was nearly of age, had been sent to her by her mother as a way of trying to communicate with her, to give her clues to her fate.

The moment was a turning point in her life, one in which she swore to her mother that she would do whatever it took and for however long it took—and at whatever cost—to find out what had happened. It was a pact that was intensely personal and for the two of them only. One she vowed never to share with another human being. And to this moment never had.

"You have been very quiet, Demi. Is anything wrong?"

The immediacy of Reverend Beck's voice startled her, and she looked up to see him looking at her over the seat-back. Now Luciana turned to look at her too, her green eyes suddenly stark and penetrating.

"I'm quite well, thank you," Demi smiled.

"Good," Luciana said without expression, "we still have far to go."

85

12:10 P.M.

Miguel Balius parked the limousine behind a row of trees between the tiny Montserrat-Aeri railway stop and the small cable car terminal where the green-and-yellow gondolas began the trip that took them straight up over rocky cliffs to an upper terminal nearly two thousand feet above. Then, at Marten's request, he locked his traveling bag with its electronic notebook, tape recorder, and personal effects in the trunk, and walked his newfound "cousins"—President Harris once again without his toupee and wearing glasses and the big floppy hat he had borrowed from Demi the night before—to the path leading to the lower terminal. There, in the shadow of a large tree, he stopped and watched them go down, walking separately toward the terminal as if they were strangers and had just come from the railway station.

Marten bought his ticket first, round trip from the lower terminal to the top and then back down again. A moment later the president did the same and then followed Marten out to the platform to wait with a handful of tourists for the car above to come down. It arrived in minutes. Its doors opened and a dozen passengers got out. Then those waiting entered, a uniformed worker closed the door, and the green-and-yellow car began its ascent. The entire time there had not been so much as a glance or a word between them. It hadn't been necessary, they already knew what was next; it had been worked through at the crumbling stone building by the stream in the minutes after Miguel had most willingly, respectfully, and enthusiastically "been brought into the family."

"The restaurant is called Abat Cisneros and is part of the Hotel Abat Cisneros. The service door to outside is down a corridor and directly past the restrooms. Once through it there is a pathway directly outside," Miguel said definitively, then picked up a sharp piece of rock to draw a rough diagram of the monastery complex on the old building's dirt floor, carefully scratching in the details of what he was talking about.

"This way leads down to the area where they bring in the supplies; the other way goes up and around a sharp turn hidden by trees. About thirty yards farther are the ruins of the chapel I was telling you about," He drew an X on the floor to mark the ruins. "It's overgrown and hard to see even from the path. But it's there and if you can get Foxx to it, it will serve your purposes quite well."

"Good," Marten said, then looked to the president. "Assuming Demi was telling the truth, she, Beck, and Luciana should be at the monastery with Foxx when we get there. We can expect their first step will be to try and find me and deliver me to Foxx. That is unless Demi's told them about you. If she did, they'll be looking for you as well, and that changes things altogether."

"It doesn't change anything." President Harris was resolute. "If Foxx is there we have to find out what he knows. If he's alerted my 'friends,' we'll deal with that when it happens. There is no other choice."

"Alright," Marten accepted the president's tenacity, "but at least we can make it a little more difficult for them. We go to the cable car terminal separately. Buy our tickets singly. Tourists who don't know each other. From what Miguel says the gondola is small, people are crowded together. If for some reason you're recognized and a fuss is made I'm still free to get to Foxx on my own, while you're left to your," Marten let go a half-grin, "'political wiles' to get out of it. If nothing happens and we reach the upper terminal, we still go off individually." Immediately he looked to Miguel, "Once I get to the monastery, where would the most logical place be for someone to find me?"

"The plaza in front of the basilica."

"Okay," Marten turned back to the president. "Most likely it's Beck who will do it. If Demi did tell them about you and he's looking for both of us he'll be disappointed and wonder if she told him the truth or if you simply chose not to come. In either case he will be confronting me alone.

"He might mention Demi, he might not, but he'll break the ice with small talk, then bring up Foxx, say that he's there and suggest the two of us meet to talk over the discord still lingering from what happened in Malta. Just what that will entail and where we don't know, but the certainty is they'll be trying to run the show, which is something we don't want. My response should be that if the good doctor wants to talk to me it should be in a public place. I'll suggest the restaurant. For lunch, a drink, whatever. In the meantime—"

"I will have gone directly there, made certain where the men's restroom is and the exit door to the outside beyond it that Miguel described," now it was the president's turn to smile. They had been together for less than a day and already they were finishing each other's thoughts and sentences. "With luck I will have found the pathway and the ruined chapel, then come back and taken a table near the door and, head down, a beverage in hand, be reading a newspaper or tour guide when you and Dr. Foxx enter."

"You will also have purchased the appropriate items from the menu."

"Of course."

"You're a good student, Cousin," Marten said, then looked to Miguel. "Once we're done with Foxx we're going to have to get out and fast, before he's found. The cable car is too slow and confining, and besides, we might have to wait for it. What we need is for you to be waiting at the monastery to drive us out. The trouble is the limo. At some point, if they haven't already, the police will have its description.

Right now it's pretty well hidden, but bringing it out in the open and up the long road to the monastery is too risky."

"I will get us another vehicle, Cousin Harold."

"How?"

Miguel smiled, "As I said, I have been to the monastery many times. I have friends who work there, I also have relatives who live nearby. Whatever it is, I will have something waiting." Again he picked up the rock and squatted down next to his sketch of the monastery's layout. "This is where you will come out," he said, scratching a large X into the dirt, "this is where I will be," he scratched a second X, then looked up. "Any questions?"

"No. Thank you, cousin," the president said genuinely.

"You're welcome, sir," he said. At that moment a great and magnificent grin burst across Miguel's face like a dazzling ray of sunshine. In that moment he knew he had just become a liftetime member of their exclusive and very tiny, "cousins' club."

Marten glanced across the gondola as it climbed rapidly toward the upper terminal. Demi's floppy hat tilted to one side, President Harris stood alone on the far side of the car, gazing out the window. A somewhat eccentric everyday tourist riding up with a half dozen other everyday tourists, most all of whom had their faces pressed to the glass as he did, watching the terminal below quickly become little more than a dot in the distance.

86

12:20 P.M.

Demi felt the rise of her pulse as the Monasterio Benedictino Montserrat van reached the top of the long mountain road and made a sharp turn into the monastery's restricted parking area. Through the windows she could now see up close the grouping of sand-colored stone buildings she had glimpsed from far below. No longer in miniature, it still looked like an isolated fortress-city, untouchable against the half-mile-high limestone cliffs and encompassing among other things its famed basilica, a museum, restaurant, hotel, and private apartments.

Abruptly the van's passenger door slid open. A young priest stood outside in the bright sun.

"Welcome to Montserrat," he said in English.

Moments later he was leading them across a plaza filled with tourists and then up a series of steps toward the basilica. Beck carried a small overnight bag; the witch, Luciana, her large black purse; Demi, a small equipment bag with photographic supplies and a smaller bag inside it holding personal toiletries, and two professional cameras thrown over one shoulder; one, a 35mm Nikon, the other, a Canon digital.

The priest led them under a stone arch and into the basilica's inner courtyard, which was packed with more tourists. A clock high on the basilica's tower read 12:25. They were precisely on time. Immediately Demi thought of Cousin Jack and Cousin Harold. She wondered where they were—if they were still with the limousine driver and on their way here, or—she felt her stomach clench in a knot. What if they'd been stopped at one of the roadblocks? What then? What would she do? What would Beck?

"This way, please," the priest led them down a long porticoed corridor and past a series of arched stone panels inset with heraldic symbols and what appeared to be religious inscriptions written in Latin. Then she saw it, and her heart caught in her throat. Encased in one of the last panels was the stone sculpture of an early Christian Crusader. Chain mail covering his head and neck, he rested an arm on a triangular shield. Carved into the shield was the balled cross of the Aldebaran. This was the first time she had seen it anywhere outside of books or drawings or the tattoos on the left thumbs of members of the coven. She wondered how long the piece had been there and who else over the years or even centuries had seen it and recognized the sign and knew its meaning.

"Through here," the priest turned them down another corridor, this one narrower than the first and lined with row after row of flickering votive candles. Where before there had been numbers of tourists, now there were few. With every step they were getting farther and farther from the center of activity.

Demi heard her cameras click together as they touched. At the same time she felt an icy chill touch the nape of her neck and then creep across her shoulders. With it came the sound of her father's voice whispering the warning he had written to her so many years earlier—*Do not, under any circumstances try to learn her (your mother's) fate.*

Fearfully she looked back. Except for the rows of flickering candles the walkway behind them was empty.

Five more steps and the priest stopped at a heavy wooden door cut into a stone archway. Immediately he turned to a wooden panel set into the stonework next to the door and slid it back. Inside was an electronic keypad. He punched in four numbers, pressed the pound key, then slid the panel closed and turned an iron knob on the door. It opened easily, and he gestured for them to enter. They did and he left, closing the door behind him.

Compared to the noonday brightness outside, the place seemed inordinately dark. Slowly their eyes became accustomed to it. They were in an office of some kind with a number of ornate high-backed wooden chairs lining one wall and a massive bookcase against the wall opposite. An enormous wooden desk and large leather chair behind it sat near a closed door at the far end. The ceiling was high and arched, while the walls themselves appeared to be of the same aged stone as the monastery's complex of buildings. The floor was the same, worn shiny in places by the foot traffic of people and time.

"Wait here please, Demi," Beck said quietly, and then led Luciana toward the door at the end of the room. Reaching it, he knocked, and then they entered and Beck closed the door behind them.

87

12:35 P.M.

Demi waited alone in the dim light and silence; the door they had entered through, closed behind her; the one at the far end where Reverend Beck and Luciana had gone out, shut too. Whether they had left to find Dr. Foxx or to do something else entirely she didn't know.

Once more she looked around the darkened chamber. The high-arched ceiling, the high wooden chairs against either wall, the great wooden desk at the end, the stone walls, the worn stone floor. There was history here. Much of it old. All of it Christian. She wondered if her mother had come here so many years earlier. Wondered if she had once stood where Demi did now. In this room, in this dim light.

Waiting.

For what?

For whom?

12:40 P.M.

Again she heard her father's warning. With it came something else, the memory of a person she had long tried to keep from thinking about: a bald, armless octogenarian scholar she had met six years earlier at the beginning of her professional career when she worked for the Associated Press in Rome.

A photo assignment had taken her north into Umbria and Tuscany. A free day in Florence had given her the opportunity to explore used-book stores—the same as she did everywhere she traveled in Italy—searching for material on Italian witchcraft and looking for anything that might reveal a *boschetto* or coven, past or present, that took as its marker the sign of Aldebaran. It was a search that until that day had turned up nothing. Then, in a tiny bookshop near the Ponte Vecchio, she came upon a slim, tattered fifty-year-old book on Florentine witchcraft. Skimming it, she stopped abruptly at its fourth chapter. Its yellowed title page all but took her breath away. The chapter's title was *"Aradia"* and beneath the printed word was an unmistakable illustration—the *balled cross of Aldebaran*. Heart pounding, she bought the book immediately and took it back to her hotel room. The chapter, like the book itself, was slight, but in reading it she learned of an ancient and secretive *boschetto* of Italian female witches, the *strega* she had told Nicholas Marten about. Called *Aradia* after a fourteenth-century Wise Woman who brought back La Vecchia Religione, the Old Religion, the *boschetto* revived a number of ancient Traditions—an unwritten body of laws, rites and doctrines—and put them into practice in northern and central Italy during the fifteenth and sixteenth centuries. There the chapter ended. The significance of the sign of Aldebaran was never mentioned, nor was word *Aradia* used again anywhere in the book.

Desperate to know more, Demi went to bookstores and museums and visited occult societies and scholars in the Tuscan cities of Siena and Arezzo. From there she went to Bologna and then Milan and finally back to Rome. In all she found nothing more than a brief note that in 1866 an American writer and historian traveling in Italy had learned that a manuscript containing the name Aradia and describing "the ancient secrets of Italian witchcraft" existed somewhere in Tuscany. He searched for months trying to find it but without success. He did, however, come upon an Italian witch named Raffaella who allegedly had seen it and told him of its contents. His conclusion was that the secrets of *Aradia,* or at least Raffaella's interpretation of it, were little more than a mixture of sorcery, medieval heresy, and political radicalism. His analysis ended there, with no mention whatsoever of the sign of Aldebaran.

After that Demi found nothing. Even among the most committed academics further knowledge of the *Aradia* coven that used the sign of Aldebaran seemed non-existent. Internet searches turned up nothing. Museum queries and phone interviews with practicing witches and witchcraft historians around the world ended the same way.

Then, nearly a year later, and now working for Agence France Press, she learned of a reclusive scholar named Giacomo Gela. A bald, emaciated octogenarian and former soldier who had lost both arms in the Second World War, Gela lived in a tiny room in a small village near Pisa and had made the study of Italian witchcraft his life's work. Contacting him, she heard the pause in his voice when she mentioned *Aradia.* When she asked if she might visit and told him of the reason behind her request, he agreed to see her immediately.

In Gela she found a man of immense intellect who not only knew about the enigmatic *Aradia* but about a more secretive order hidden within it. Called *Aradia Minor,* it was referred to in writing simply as the letter *A* followed by the letter *M* but written in a combination of Hebrew and Greek alphabets as "א μ" which made it look more like a vague and innocuous symbol that would be of little more than passing interest to almost anyone. Even to Gela, the true origin of *Aradia Minor* remained a mystery. What he did know was that for most of the latter half of the sixteenth century it had been centered on the Italian island of Ischia in the Bay of Naples, the birthplace and home, Demi would later discover, of Luciana. In the early seventeenth century, and probably in the interests of security, *Aradia Minor* was decentralized and moved back to the mainland, its *boschetti* scattered clandestinely throughout countryside, largely in the region between Rome and Florence.

Aradia Minor's caution was not without reason, for among its Traditions were annual rites that celebrated ancient and often brutal pagan ceremonies that involved blood oaths, sacrifices of living creatures, and human torture, and were performed before several hundred members of a powerful order called the Unknowns. What the purpose of these ceremonies was or whom this group of *unknowns* was remained a mystery. What was acknowledged was that the celebration of these rites began in the late 1530s; that they were held at various temples secreted throughout Europe; and that they were performed annually and for years at a time throughout the centuries, only to go suddenly and inexplicably dormant, sometimes for decades or more, before beginning once again.

Chillingly, Giacomo Gela believed this was one of *Aradia Minor's* active periods; its identifying marker, the sign of Aldebaran; its singular Traditions still practiced. Where it was centered, or why it existed, or for what reason, remained as unclear now as it had in the past, yet he was certain there had to be a strong rationale behind it, one that was highly focused and required not just great secrecy but considerable funding because too many people were involved and the pageant was too regular, too guarded, and too extreme for the expense not be substantial.

It was then Gela's eyes had narrowed and his voice had become shrill with warning, "Do not take anything you have learned here further than the walls of this room."

The expense was not *Aradia Minor's* alone, he told her; history was littered with the corpses of those who had tried to know more. To make certain she fully understood, he bared a secret few people still living knew—that while it was true he had lost his arms in the Second World War, the butchering had not come in battle; instead it had happened when he had inadvertently come upon one of *Aradia Minor's* ceremonies in an alpine forest deep in the Italian Dolomites where he was on patrol. That he was alive today was only because those who cut off his arms purposely failed to finish him off.

"To kill me would have been easy. Instead they bound my wounds and carried me from the woods and left me by the roadside. The reason, I now know, was to leave behind a hideous living reminder, a warning for anyone else who might try to find out what happened and attempt to uncover the secrets of *Aradia Minor*."

Abruptly his eyes had locked on hers and his voice had suddenly raged with fury: "How many hours of how many days of how many years have I sworn at God, damning him, wishing they had finished me. The life I have lived like this, and for as long as I have, has been far crueler than death could ever be."

The way Gela spoke, the sound of his voice, the rage in his eyes, the way he sat there armless and cross-legged in his tiny room, was horrifying. In combination with her father's letter it might well have been enough then for her to abandon her journey altogether. But she hadn't; instead she had deliberately pushed it to the back of her memory, locked it away, and kept it there.

Until now. Waiting here, alone, in this room, in this corner of the monastery, he suddenly broke free of her memory. She saw his face in front of her. Again heard his sharp warning. *Do not take anything you have learned here further than the walls of this room.*

A sound near the back of the room made the vision fade and Demi looked up. The door had just been opened and Reverend Beck and Luciana were coming toward her. A third person she couldn't see clearly was with them. Then as they neared, she did.

"Welcome, Demi, I'm pleased you could join us," he said warmly. His face, his shock of white hair, his hands with their extraordinarily long fingers, unmistakable.

Merriman Foxx.

88

The green-and-yellow cable car reached the upper terminal and stopped. A moment later an attendant opened the doors and the passengers began to file out. Marten glanced at the president, then followed an Italian couple out of the car and up the walkway toward the monastery.

Forty seconds later he reached the top of the walkway and stopped. The monastery complex was directly across from him. The buildings he could see all seemed to be constructed of the same beige-colored sand or limestone. The edifice closest to him and on the far side of a paved roadway was seven stories high. One nearby was eight. Another near it was ten and had a huge kind of bell-tower on top. And these were only a part of the whole. The main attraction, the basilica, was across a wide plaza and up a broad stone staircase, both of which were filled with tourists.

12:50 P.M.

Marten walked leisurely across the plaza, making it relatively easy for Beck to find him. As he went, a man passed him from behind and kept on walking. President Harris.

12:52 P.M.

Marten kept walking. Ahead of him he saw the president veer left, pass a tour group, then disappear beyond them, following Miguel's directions, going toward the Hotel Abat Cisneros and the restaurant that was part of it.

Marten slowed his pace and looked around, playing the first-time visitor trying to get his bearings and decide where to go next. He wondered whether Demi had lied to them. That neither she nor Beck nor Luciana nor Merriman Foxx, for that matter, was any-where near here. That she had sent them miles out of the way while she and the others met Foxx somewhere else entirely, maybe even in Barcelona itself.

"Mr. Marten," the deep, velvety voice of Reverend Rufus Beck suddenly called out. Marten looked up to see the congressional chaplain alone, walking toward him across the plaza from the direc-tion of the basilica.

"Mr. Marten," Beck said again as he reached him. "How nice to see you. Ms. Picard told me you might be coming."

"She did?" Marten tried to sound surprised.

"Yes," Beck smiled warmly. "I was just coming from services; perhaps you would care to join us for a cup of coffee."

"By 'us' you mean you and Ms. Picard."

"There will be two others, Mr. Marten. A good friend of mine from Italy, a woman named Luciana, and a friend of yours, Dr. Foxx."

"Foxx?"

Again Beck smiled. "He asked me to find you. He wanted to re-solve any 'misgivings' you might have had following your conversa-tion in Malta. The restaurant in the hotel here has a small, private room where you and he can speak openly."

"Restaurant?"

"Yes, unless you'd prefer to meet somewhere else."

Marten grinned at the irony. Here they were trying to get Foxx to the restaurant, and now he was inviting him to the same place. The private room might be a problem, but with Beck and Demi and Lu-ciana right there it would be all the easier to tell Foxx he preferred to talk to him alone and suggest they take a walk outside.

"The restaurant's fine, Reverend," he said graciously. "I'd be more than happy to hear what Dr. Foxx has to say about my 'mis-givings.'"

89

"Welcome to Montserrat, Mr. Marten," Merriman Foxx stood as they came in. Demi and the witch, Luciana, sat opposite Foxx at a round linen-covered table, coffee steaming from cups before them, a small plate of shortbread cookies or polvorónes in the center of the table. There was a chair for Beck, and a waiter brought another for Marten. The room was as Beck had said, both small and private.

"You know Ms. Picard," Foxx nodded congenially across at Demi. "And this is Signora Luciana Lorenzini, a dear friend of some years' standing."

Marten nodded at Demi, then looked to Luciana, "It's a pleasure, signora."

The restaurant was indeed part of the Hotel Abat Cisneros and was, as Miguel had described it, just down from the basilica and built against the towering mountainside. The singularity of the private setting meant that the president would not know where Marten was until he and Foxx left and Marten tried to steer him toward the door that led to the pathway outside. If the president got nervous and came looking for him, he might walk right into the room itself, something, which besides exposing him physically, would put them at a severe disadvantage in trying to get Foxx alone.

Marten glanced at the doctor, trying to read him as he sat down. The physician-scientist-murderer was dressed in a close-fitting tweed jacket with dark slacks and matching mock turtleneck sweater. The Albert Einstein mass of unkempt white hair was like a trademark. Marten had only to look at his hands to again hear Caroline's voice, suffering and filled with fear—*The way he touched my face and my legs with his long, hideous fingers; and that horrid thumb with its tiny balled cross.*

Marten realized now there was something else to Foxx's appearance. His physical stature. He was bigger and stronger than he'd first seemed when they'd met at the Café Tripoli in Malta and he was dressed in the bulky fisherman's sweater. From the way he'd stood and greeted him when he and Beck had come in, Marten could see an agility too, an athletic ability, the thing Marten had sensed earlier when he'd thought about Foxx's selection of Malta as a place to live, simply because of the mountains of steps to be climbed simply to get around. As if staying in top physical condition was something instinctive to him, a habit from his military days in the South African Defense Force. It meant, as the president had warned, that he would be difficult to subdue. Marten would have one chance at him, and it would have to be fast and decisive and a total surprise. What happened afterward wouldn't be much easier, and the president would have to be right there to help.

"How was your trip, Mr. Marten?" Foxx asked congenially as the waiter set a cup and saucer in front of Beck and filled the cup with coffee and then the same for Marten.

"From Barcelona or from Malta?"

"Either," Foxx smiled.

"Both were fine, thank you," Marten glanced at Demi, who avoided his look by picking up the plate of polvorónes and offering them to Luciana. Marten watched her for a brief moment longer, trying to get some sense of whose side she was really on, then turned back to Foxx.

"Reverend Beck invited me to join you because of what happened in Malta. He was concerned that I might have had some misgivings about our conversation there and suggested you might like to clear them up."

"'Clear them up,' that is a good way to put it, Mr. Marten," Foxx smiled lightly. "I would be happy to do so and will; my only difficulty is that there is someone who should be here but who is not."

"What do you mean?"

"You came to Montserrat with someone else did you not? John Henry Harris, the president of the United States." Foxx smiled again. He was relaxed and matter-of-fact, a simple comment about a guest who was not there.

"The president of the United States?" Marten grinned broadly. "That's hardly the company I keep."

"Until lately, Mr. Marten."

"You know more than I do."

Marten picked up his coffee and sipped at it. As he did, he shot a glance at Demi. It was grave and accusatory, as if she was the one who had told them about the president. This time she did not look away; instead, she gave a faint shake of her head. It meant how they knew was not her doing. She'd told them nothing.

"Might I suggest you locate your companion and ask him to join us, Mr. Marten." Foxx lifted his coffee cup and held it in both hands, his long fingers wrapped around it, "I think you will both be quite interested in what I have to show you. Perhaps even a great deal more than interested."

For a moment Marten didn't respond. Clearly they knew the president was there, or at least were assuming he was. Denying it would only prolong the situation, dangerously if Foxx had alerted the president's "friends" and the Secret Service or the CIA were on the way. So the question was what to do about it. The original plan had been for the president to remain in the background until Marten could get Foxx alone outside, but with the doctor's sudden and surprise demand for his presence, all that had changed. Even the idea of Marten getting Foxx alone was all but gone. That left them with no plan at all and the president wholly at Foxx's mercy, which was something Marten couldn't let happen.

"I'm not so sure I know where he is. Or even if he's still here. It might take some time to find him if I can find him at all."

"At the risk of sounding presumptuous, Mr. Marten, I think it's safe to assume that the reason the president came to Montserrat was to see me." Once again Foxx smiled pleasantly. "So I rather doubt he would leave before we met. Nor do I think he would be pleased if you denied him the opportunity."

Marten studied Foxx for a heartbeat, then took a sip of coffee, set the cup down, and stood.

"I'll see what I can do."

"Thank you, Mr. Marten. Neither you nor the president will be disappointed, I promise."

90

Marten left the restaurant and crossed the plaza, going back the way he had come in. Other than Beck and the women, Foxx seemed to be have been alone, and maybe he was. After all, this was Montserrat, not Malta, where he had a home and was seemingly headquartered. On the other hand, all Marten had to do was remember Salt and Pepper to appreciate the long reach that the South African had.

Demi remained the puzzle she'd been all along. The shake of her head across the table in her silent refusal to accept blame for Foxx's knowledge of the president's being there hadn't helped. Clearly it had been intended to make him believe her, but there were still too many things unanswered, among them how Beck had found him so quickly. Clearly the reverand hadn't been as indifferent to his arrival in Barcelona as Demi had said. Moreover, they had known he was coming to Montserrat and when, and that was something only Demi could have told them. To that extent she had set him up.

Foxx's sudden and deliberate inclusion of the president, however, changed everything and dramatically, elevated the stakes of the game. It made Marten even more curious about what Demi was doing. Unless she was working with Beck and therefore in Foxx's camp, which still seemed probable, what else could be so compelling that she was willing to give up the president of the United States to get it, especially now, under the circumstances, most of which she knew well?

On the other hand, if she was doing something else and her head shake meant she was telling the truth, it would mean Foxx's knowledge of the president's whereabouts had come from somewhere else—Miguel or the president's "friends." Thinking that way he had to assume it was the latter because Miguel had proven himself a man far too honest, humble, and forthright for such things, and because by now the president's "friends" would be fully aware he had been in Marten's hotel room in Barcelona the night before and would assume that since neither had been caught he was still with him. Therefore if Marten was going to Montserrat, the president would be too. It was something they should have considered beforehand and been prepared for, but they hadn't and so they had literally walked right into the "Foxx's lair."

Still, they had one thing going for them, if it could be called that—the president had yet to reveal himself. It meant they still had the chance to get out and away before the Secret Service or CIA showed up and the trap was snapped shut once and for all.

1:18 P.M.

Marten left the plaza and turned right, walking past the multistoried building he'd seen as he'd come up from the cable car terminal. At the far end he turned right again, passed under a high archway, and then worked his way back toward the restaurant in a group of tourists, all the while looking to see if he was being followed; as far as he could tell, he was not.

At this point he'd made a complete circle and again approached the Hotel Abat Cisneros and the restaurant, where Cousin Jack should now be ensconced, waiting somewhere near the hallway leading to the men's restroom and the door to the pathway outside. Here Marten had to make absolutely certain he wasn't being tailed. Purposely, he walked past the restaurant's main doorway and entered the Hotel Abat Cisneros itself. Inside, he crossed the lobby, took note of the interior entrance to the restaurant, then walked into a small bar across from it. He waited for the bartender, then ordered a bottle of beer, took it to a table where he could watch the door, and sat down. His plan was to wait three minutes, and if no one suspicious came in, get up and leave, entering the restaurant directly from the hotel itself.

1:23 P.M.

Marten took a sip of beer and casually looked around. The only people there were the ones he had seen as he entered, the bartender

and six customers; two each at separate tables and two at the bar itself, where a television was tuned to CNN International and an
athletic-looking male reporter was speaking from behind the an-
chor desk.

"In a video just released by the Department of Homeland Security," he said, "we are about to have a look at President Harris at the
undisclosed location he was taken to by the Secret Service after the
terrorist threat in Madrid. With him are National Security Adviser
James Marshall, Secretary of Defense Terrence Langdon and Secretary of State David Chaplin."

Abruptly the picture cut to the video. It had a running time and
date stamp that began at 2:23 P.M. (yesterday), Friday, April 7 and
showed President Harris in a rustic room during a working session
with his advisers.

"The president wants it known," the reporter said in a voice-
over, "that he is safe and well and fully intends to meet with European leaders as scheduled at the NATO meeting Monday in
Warsaw."

Abruptly the clip ended and the reporter tied it up with a simple "We'll have more on this later." There was a fade out and a commercial popped on.

"My God," Marten breathed, "they've got everything covered."

Another sip of beer and he looked away from the television and
toward the door. So far no one else had come in since he'd entered. Forty seconds passed, then fifty. If someone was following
him, they would have been there by now. Marten put down his
glass and started to get up. As he did another television story
caught his attention. This time the location was Chantilly, France.
Two jockeys had been shot and killed early that morning while
working out racehorses at a practice track that ran through a
nearby forest. The killer had evidently been lying in wait in the
woods and fired from the cover of the trees, then afterward simply
walked away, leaving the murder weapon, a United States military-
issue M14 rifle, behind, as if to both taunt and intrigue investigators. What added considerably to the mystery was that both
jockeys had been killed with the same bullet, the shot passing
through the head of the first man and then penetrating the skull of
the second. It was a shot investigators deemed either accidental—
there had been only one intended victim—or eerily intentional, as

if the killer was deliberately demonstrating his skill. In either case the French police had never seen anything like it. Nor, in all his long-ago days as a Los Angeles Police Department homicide detective, had Marten.

Cousin Jack saw Marten come in but didn't acknowledge him. Seemingly unmindful of the noisy group of children and parents crowding a large table nearby, he was sitting as planned, alone at a small table near the back of the restaurant's main dining area and at the end of a short hallway leading to the restroom area and the door to outside beyond it. Still wearing his glasses and Demi's big floppy hat, an unopened bottle of sparkling Vichy Catalan mineral water at his sleeve, he was apparently engrossed in a glossy Montserrat guidebook.

Marten stopped for a moment as he entered, then glancing around, casually crossed to where the president was and took a seat at the table next to him. "Foxx knows you're here," he said quietly. "He's in a private room down the hall. He wants you to join us. How he found out I'm not sure, but I don't think Demi told him and I seriously doubt Miguel did either. That leaves—"

"Only one reasonable answer, and we both know what it is," the president raised his head and looked at Marten, his expression stone-cold, "If there was ever any doubt my 'friends' were in league with Dr. Foxx, that uncertainty has been erased."

"If you want more," Marten said, "CNN just played a video clip that supposedly came from the Department of Homeland Security. It showed you in a rustic cabin someplace, clean shaven and with your hairpiece on. With you were the secretary of state, the national security adviser, and the secretary of defense. The report said the video was made yesterday afternoon and that you would still be in Warsaw Monday as planned. As an extra punch the video had a date/time stamp on it confirming it."

President Harris's eyes narrowed in anger. Deliberately he turned back as if to study his guidebook. "The men's restroom is just down the hallway behind us," he said without looking up. "The door to the outside is immediately past it. Once through it there is a service pathway that comes up from the plaza. Twenty feet in the other direction another path leads off along the cliff face, then turns and disappears from sight under an umbrella of trees. Thirty, forty yards after that are the ruins of an ancient chapel, all as Miguel said. Inside the chapel is what is left of two small chambers. Either will suffice for our chat with Dr. Foxx."

"You still want to go ahead with this?" Marten was incredulous.

"Yes," the president didn't look up.

"Cousin," Marten suddenly leaned in, speaking urgently and in a sotto voice, "I don't think you fully appreciate what's going on here. Foxx thought you were coming but he couldn't be sure until I showed up. Now they know, and I'm sure your 'rescuers' have been alerted. For all we know they could be somewhere here now waiting for you to reveal yourself. When you do they'll take you out of here and into their version of 'protective custody' fast. Cousin, we have to leave and leave now. Go out the back way, call Miguel on his cell phone, then wait somewhere out of sight until he comes. And after that, to quote you, 'God help us.'"

The president closed the guidebook and looked at Marten deliberately, his eyes filled with resolve, "This is Saturday afternoon in Spain; the NATO conference is Monday morning in Warsaw. Our clock is fast ticking down and with it the information we must have from Foxx. My 'rescuers' could arrive in minutes or in hours. If it's minutes we're out of business anyway; if it's the latter, we still have time to do something."

"You're taking a hell of a gamble, Cousin, you know that."

"It's only a gamble when you have a choice." Abruptly Harris stood, "Let's not keep the good doctor waiting any longer than we already have."

91

Merriman Foxx was alone and making notes in a pocket organizer when Marten and President Harris entered the private dining room. Demi, Beck, and Luciana were gone, and the table itself had been cleared.

"Ah, gentlemen," Foxx smiled and stood up, as he had when Marten first arrived. "I am Dr. Foxx, Mr. President, it is a great pleasure to meet you, sir." He waved a hand at the empty table, "I'm afraid the others decided to go off and explore on their own. And while we might sit here and chat among ourselves, I think our time could be more interestingly spent if I showed you my laboratory."

"You have a laboratory here?" Marten was surprised.

"Also an office and small apartment," again came Foxx's congenial smile. "All most kindly provided by the Order. It gives me a pleasant respite from all the attention and the undue and unfair questions that have long been put to me about the Tenth Medical, as well as a quiet place to work."

"I'm always curious about another man's workplace, Doctor," the president said with no emotion whatsoever.

"So am I, Mr. President. This way, please," Foxx smiled once again and ushered them toward the door. Marten shot Harris a warning glance but got no response.

Merriman Foxx led them past the crowded plaza in front of the basilica and then down a narrow stone walkway lined on one side with rows of red and white votive candles.

Marten looked back over his shoulder as they went but saw no one. It was curious that Foxx was alone—no companions, no body-guard, not even Beck for that matter. But then, except for Demi and Beck and the young woman Cristina, he had been alone when Marten met him at the Café Tripoli in Malta. And according to Beck, Foxx had left there by himself, leaving the reverend to escort the women back to their hotel. So in essence Foxx had been alone in Malta and was alone now. Maybe it was simply his choice or style. Or confidence. Or arrogance. Or all of them put together. After all he was *the* Dr. Merriman Foxx, the man who had controlled the Tenth Medical Brigade and all its covert operations and "innovations" for more than two decades. The same Merriman Foxx who had very recently sat alone through a U.S. congressional inquiry into the workings and disbanding of that brigade. The same Merriman Foxx who had personally supervised the heinous murder of Caroline Parsons and was now a key player in far more grandiose plans for genocide.

Marten was certain Foxx had become who he was out of conceit and sheer will and that by now the idea of bodyguards or henchmen would be an affront to his own force of character. That was unless they were somewhere there unseen and watching, and had been all along.

"This way, please," Foxx turned them down a side walkway and ten seconds later down another. They all looked the same, stone passageways lined by high narrow stone walls that in turn led into others and then into others, one virtually indistinguishable from the next.

The farther they went into this maze the more concerned Marten became. Just finding their way back out and to the area where Miguel would be waiting with the car could become hugely difficult, especially if they were in a hurry. Moreover, Foxx's easy smile and genial manner made it easy to forget that beneath it all was a shrewd, cruel, and ingenious murderer who not only had killed Caroline Parsons but was deeply involved with the president's "friends" and whatever monstrous "plot" they were masterminding. So who knew where he was leading them, or who or even what might be waiting when they got there?

In addition, Montserrat itself was an impossible setting. Religious site and tourist destination or not, it was in reality, what he had feared, a small, isolated city set into a high, desolate cliff face miles from anywhere. A place a man could vanish from in a heartbeat and never be found.

Marten was certain that President Harris was as aware of their situation as he was. At the same time he knew the president had far more on his mind than his own safety and that his primary objective was finding a suitable place to get Foxx alone and question him. Which was clearly why he had chosen to let the doctor show the way, especially in the absence of Beck or a bodyguard or anyone else who might interfere. It was why too, despite his fears, Marten knew he had no other choice but to go along and follow the president's lead.

"We're here, gentlemen," Foxx stopped at a heavy wooden door inset in a stone archway.

"A little privacy away from the throngs," he said with a smile then slid open a wood panel in the stonework next to the door. Inside it was an electronic keypad. Quickly he punched in a code and pressed the pound key, then slid the panel closed and turned an iron knob on the door. The door opened and Foxx ushered them into a large dimly lit room. The ceiling was high and arched. Several tall wooden chairs lined one wall, while a massive bookcase covered the other. The only other furniture was a large wooden desk with a lone chair behind it at the room's far end. Behind it to the right, an ornate carved wooden door was set into an arched nave.

"This was a church council room for many years," Foxx said quietly as he led them down the room toward the nave, "I merely inherited it."

They reached the nave and Foxx opened the door, then guided them into another room, carefully closing the door behind them.

This room was much larger than the first and far different. Twenty feet wide and probably thirty long, it was illuminated by a series of eerily luminous grow-lamps suspended over two dozen bubble-topped rectangular tables.

"This is my work now, gentlemen, and I wanted you to see it firsthand." Foxx indicated the tables. "No bacteria, no spores, no deadly molecules, nothing to be grown into the implements of war.

"What I did before as head of the Tenth Medical Brigade was done to serve my country in a time of mounting national crisis. From the 1960s onward we were confronted by developing guerrilla movements. There were insurgencies in the former colonies of Mozambique and Angola, military training camps in Tanzania and Zambia, most of it funded and supported by Cuba and the Soviet Union. The counterinsurgency programs we used were developed by the French in Algeria and by the British in Malaysia and Kenya, but they weren't working well enough for the major war we knew was to come. We needed to develop new and innovative weapons, and those included chemical and biological because that same kind of weaponry was being developed for use against us."

"What are these?" President Harris asked abruptly, indicating the rows of bubble-topped tables, as if Foxx's ongoing monologue was just so much idle chatter.

"What I wished to show you, sir. Plant life. Food and energy for tomorrow. Genetically developed seedlings that can be grown to maturity in weeks almost anywhere on earth at a fraction of the cost of such things now. Fruits and vegetables far richer in nutritional value than anything currently available. Variations on corn, soybean, alfalfa, sunflower, strawberry, blueberry, and cranberry. Then there are the grass and forage species for erosion control, pasture, and wildlife. All of which can be grown quickly and easily on a massive scale in almost any kind of soil and require minimal irrigation. Certain varieties of corn, soybean, and peanuts can be grown in the same manner and as quickly and cheaply processed into low-cost, production-level, clean-burning fuel that does not warm the atmosphere. We are also working with a concept known as 'cellulosic ethanol,' a process that makes fuel from farm waste—corn stalks, straw, and even wood." So far Foxx's attention had been focused primarily on the president, now he turned to Marten.

"In Malta you accused me of experimentation on human beings. And you were correct, I did. But only on the terminally ill and with their permission in an attempt to save their lives and in turn save our own people.

"But those programs are all long past. Wholly disbanded, their documentation destroyed. Many of the people who participated in them are now dead. In the twenty-odd years since, in the face of one unwarranted charge and indictment after another brought by people who either don't understand or had political agendas all their own, I have worked alone, either in Malta or here at Montserrat, my vocation dedicated not to war but to the future well-being of the planet and the creatures on it."

"Alone?" Marten asked as if he were referring to Foxx's scientific studies, but really to see how he would react. If indeed there were others they weren't aware of, out of sight and waiting for a signal from Foxx.

Instantly Foxx picked up on the reference. "You mean do I have security people here protecting me?"

President Harris quickly covered for Marten, "I believe he was referring to other scientists."

"Of course," Foxx said politely. "Now and again they come and consult with me. Most work part-time when they can. All voluntarily. We communicate almost exclusively over the Internet." Foxx glanced warily at Marten then looked back at the president. "As for the work itself. If you still doubt me, you are welcome to see the many other experiments that are here and in various stages of development. There are notes, journals, scientific records on everything. All of which you are free to examine. But I must ask you to say nothing of what you observe. None of this can be made known until processes are completed and legally documented and the patents are secured. When they are, the rights to them will be turned over to the United Nations. The profits, as you might imagine, will be staggering."

"You seem to have become quite benevolent, Doctor," President Harris said. "Yes, I would like to see more. The experiments. Your notes, your journals, everything."

"Of course."

92

Foxx led them toward another door, this one made of some kind of burnished steel. Reaching it, he stopped, then slipped a security card from his jacket pocket and swiped it through an electronic pad on the wall next to it. Immediately the door slid back to reveal a long, low, jagged sandstone tunnel seemingly cut into the core of the mountain itself and lighted by bare lightbulbs mounted every twenty feet or so on an exposed wire crudely attached to the tunnel's ceiling.

"This is one of a network of mining tunnels cut through these mountains nearly a century ago. Most are long abandoned. Few people even know they exist. We were fortunate enough to make use of this one," Foxx said as he bent low to lead them down a rough wooden walkway raised over a damp floor and next to jagged stone walls oozing here and there with trickles of groundwater. "Once most of this area was part of what is now the Mediterranean Sea. At the time a large river ran from the higher elevations out to the gulf, creating large subterranean caves. Now, centuries later, the caves are far above sea level. They are dry, the air fresh and the temperatures particularly consistent over time. Those things combined with the size of the chambers and their relative isolation create a situation very nearly perfect for my research."

If Marten had been concerned earlier, he was doubly so now. Never mind being lost in the maze of the monastery's walkways outside, this was a place hidden away from everyone and everything, and they were entering it with a horrific criminal. Whether Foxx was alone or not, Marten was convinced they were walking into some kind of trap and that it was more than foolhardy to take even another step with him. Again, he shot the president a warning glance.

As before Harris ignored him, instead turning his attention to the tunnel itself; its uneven jackhammered walls, its earthen floor, its low, jackhammered ceiling.

Whether the president liked it or not Marten knew he had to intervene and quickly. "Mr. President," he said sharply, "I think we've gone far—"

"We're here, gentlemen," Foxx suddenly turned a corner in the shaft and they were face to face with another of the burnished steel doors. Again Foxx swiped his security card through an electronic reader on the wall next to it. As before, the door slid back, to reveal a cavernous chamber twice the size of the one they had been in moments earlier.

Foxx went in first. As he did, Marten took the president by the arm to pull him back.

"We're fine, Cousin," Harris said quietly, and followed Foxx inside. Marten swore under his breath and followed. A half second later the door slid closed behind them.

Marten and the president looked out on a sea of bubble-top tables in a compartment that must have been a hundred feet long, at least sixty wide, and twenty high. At the far end were a number of steel cages,. Both large and small.

"Yes," Foxx acknowledged, "I was doing some experimental work with animals. But there are none here now."

"Do the people who run the monastery know about these chambers?" Marten asked.

Foxx smiled, "As I said previously, the Order has kindly provided for my needs."

Marten saw the president look around, the same as he had in the tunnel. The rough-hewn limestone walls, the ceiling, the floor. Abruptly he turned his attention to a large stainless-steel bench with heavy wooden uprights at one end and a large mechanical drum at the other. In between a second piece of stainless steel was mounted above a dual track that ran the full length of the surface. "What is this, Doctor?" he asked.

"A production table."

"It looks like some sort of medieval torture machine."

"Torture machine? Well, perhaps for plants," Foxx smiled his easy, accommodating smile. "Seeds are spread out across the stainless-steel surface, then covered with a special plastic sheeting.

The drum heats up and is run back and forth over the sheeting, cooking the seeds to the degree that they are ready for instant planting in a special soil similar to that found in the grow-benches in the other room. It's an incubator of sorts. Like everything else here, efficient, innovative, and harmless."

Harris glanced at Marten, then looked back to Foxx. "Actually, I preferred the idea of it being a torture table. Something a man might be fastened to in order to have him confess his sins or treacheries."

"I'm not sure I understand," Foxx said.

In an instant Marten understood why the president had ignored his earlier warnings and why he had been looking around both in the tunnel and in here. He was searching for security cameras, microphones, other surveillance apparatus. He, of all people, should know what to look for. The Secret Service would have shown him almost everything in its arsenal, an asset that, combined with his own grit and knowledge of building construction, had been the primary reason he had been able to escape from the hotel in Madrid. Marten had been concerned that they were far too alone and isolated, that Foxx had them trapped. President Harris saw just the opposite. It was the doctor, not they, who was alone. While they couldn't be certain they were not under some kind of surveillance, the president was taking the same hard gamble he had by coming to meet Foxx in the first place.

"We would like you to talk to us, doctor," he said quietly. "To tell us about your plan for the Muslim states."

"I'm sorry," Foxx acted as if he didn't understand.

"Your plan. The program you and my good Washington friends have drawn up to devastate the Middle East."

"You disappoint me, Mr. President," Foxx smiled again. "As I have just shown you, the last twenty years of my work have been for nothing but prosperity, health, and goodwill toward the inhabitants of this planet."

The president suddenly responded in anger, "That's not going to cut it, doctor."

"What did you give to Caroline Parsons?" Marten said suddenly.

"You asked me something like that before, I have no idea who or what you are—"

"The Silver Springs Rehabilitation Center in Silver Springs, Maryland. Dr. Lorraine Stephenson helped you."

"I've never heard of the place. Or, as I also told you in Malta, of a Dr. Stephenson."

"Hold up your left hand," Marten snapped.

"What?"

"Hold up your left hand. Thumb pointed out. I want the president to see the tattoo on it. The sign of Aldebaran."

Foxx suddenly bristled, and Marten could see the rage come up in him, as it had at the Café Tripoli in Malta. "That's quite enough, gentlemen. We're finished here. I'll show you out."

Abruptly he turned and started for the door. As he did, he slid a small electronic device from his jacket pocket and started to speak into it.

93

2:13 P.M.

In a heartbeat Marten was behind him, his forearm pulled hard across his windpipe cutting of his air supply. Foxx cried out in surprise, then struggled wildly, trying to rip free and dropping whatever the device was he'd pulled from his jacket. But Marten only strengthened his grip. Foxx's chest heaved as he fought for air. Abruptly Marten shifted his pressure to the carotid arteries on either side of Foxx's neck, this time shutting off the blood flow to the South African's brain. Foxx thrashed and kicked. But it was no good. One second. Two. Three. Then he went limp in Marten's arms.

Marten looked to the president. "Hurry!"

The president pulled the belt from his trousers, stepped around Marten, and tugged Foxx's arms tight behind him. Then, as if he were back in his California youth and hog-tying a steer, he crossed Foxx's hands over each other and wrapped the belt around them. Seconds later he and Marten hefted the South African onto the stainless-steel table, sliding his bound arms down over the top of one of the upturned table legs as they did.

2:16 P.M.

Groaning, coughing, his chest heaving as his lungs fought to draw in air, thirty seconds later Foxx regained consciousness. Another minute and the fog began to clear from his brain and he looked into the faces of Cousin Jack and Cousin Harold. Then his eyes swung to Marten and his presence sharpened.

"That was a police hold," he rasped. "You were a policeman once. Maybe still are."

The president glanced at Marten, but Marten didn't acknowledge. He looked back to Foxx. "I want to know what you have planned for the Muslim states."

For a long moment Foxx was expressionless; then slowly he smiled. A great, broad, chilling grin full of arrogance, even defiance. It was the look of a learned madman, one fully capable of executing a plan of mass murder and thoroughly enjoying it. "Only goodwill, gentlemen."

"I'll try once again. I want to know what you and your friends in Washington have planned for the Muslim states, for the Middle East."

Foxx's eyes darted between the president and Marten.

"One last chance, doctor," the president said.

Foxx looked at the president. "Mr. Marten seems to have put some rather peculiar ideas in your head."

The president took a breath and looked to Marten. "I think we should proceed, Cousin." Abruptly he slid a half-liter bottle of Vichy Catalan mineral water he'd purchased at the restaurant Abat Cisneros. He handed it to Marten.

Marten took it, then stared at Foxx. "Sparkling water. 'Con gas' as they say here. Maybe a little primitive for someone like you, doctor. An old border cop showed it to me. He used it to get drug traffickers and people smugglers to talk. They usually did."

Foxx's eyes went to the bottle. If he knew what was about to happen, he didn't show it.

"One final time, Dr. Foxx," President Harris said carefully. He wanted no misunderstandings. "What do you have planned for the Muslim states?"

"Peace on earth," Foxx smiled once more. "Goodwill toward men."

Marten looked to Harris, "You have a napkin from the restaurant?"

"Yes."

"The barnyard animals we talked about, held down for a shot from the vet. They don't like it; the doctor won't either. Take the napkin and stuff it in his mouth, then grab his head and hold him hard."

The next came fast and ugly. President Harris pulled a white cloth table napkin from his pocket and shoved it toward Foxx's open mouth. Foxx snapped it closed, twisting his head to the side. Marten hesitated for a split second, then closed his fist and drove it like a hammer into Foxx's stomach. Foxx cried out, and the president stuffed the napkin into the wide-open gorge of his mouth.

At the same time Marten twisted the top from the Vichy Catalan bottle, put his thumb over the top, and shook it hard. The bubbles inside collided violently, compressing into what was very nearly a handheld bomb. Foxx tried to twist away again. But the president had his head in a vicelike grip. Marten shook the bottle again, shoved it under Foxx's right nostril, and released his thumb.

An explosion of compressed air and mineral water shot up Foxx's nose. He groaned, the pain in his sinuses, in the front of his brain, excruciating. He kicked and flailed wildly, trying to pull away, to spit the napkin from his mouth.

The harder he fought the harder Marten followed. Shaking the bottle, again and then again, blasting the carbonated water up one nostril and then the other. Foxx was strong, as Harris had promised and Marten had seen in the restaurant. Jerking back, he got a knee up and slammed it into the president's face. Harris cried out and started to fall back, then recovered, holding on as Foxx wrenched one way and then the other, trying over and over to spit out the napkin so he could breathe and at the same time avoid Marten's onslaught.

"That's enough," the president said.

Marten ignored him. Kept on. Thumb over top of bottle. Shake of bottle. Bottle up against Foxx's nose. Pull back thumb. Release cannonade of carbonated water.

"I said that's enough! I want answers, not a dead man!"

Suddenly Foxx's eyes twisted up under their lids, and his flailing all but ceased.

"Stop! Stop it!" President Harris let go of Foxx and grabbed Marten, pulling him away. "Enough! Dammit! Enough!"

Marten stumbled back to stare at him wide-eyed. The prize fighter shoved into his corner, chest heaving, eyes locked on his beaten and pummeled quarry, confused, wondering why the fight had been stopped.

Abruptly Harris moved in, blocking Marten's view of Foxx and getting right in his face. "You're letting what he did to Caroline Parsons run away with you. I don't blame you, but right now your own private feelings are something none of us can afford."

Marten didn't react.

The president stayed in his face, nose to nose. "You're killing him. Do you understand me? If you haven't already."

Slowly Marten regained his composure. "Sorry," he said finally. "I'm sorry."

The president stayed where he was for a moment longer, then turned to Foxx. His head was at an angle. His eyes still turned up under their lids. Mucous and spent mineral water ran from his nose and onto the table. He snorted, trying to get air and at the same time get rid of whatever liquid still remained in his nasal passages.

Immediately Harris bent over him and pulled the napkin from his mouth. There was a resounding gasp as Foxx's lungs filled with air.

"Can you hear me, doctor?" the president said.

There was no reply.

"Doctor Foxx, can you hear me?"

For a long moment nothing happened, and then came a vague nod of the head. The president eased him over, and Foxx's eyes came down from under their lids to stare at Harris.

"Do you recognize me?"

Foxx nodded almost imperceptibly.

"Can you breathe?"

Again the nod. Stronger this time. So was his breathing.

"I want to know what you are planning for the Middle East. When it is to happen, exactly where, and who else is involved. If you won't tell me we will repeat the procedure."

Foxx didn't respond, just lay there staring at the president. Then ever so slowly, his eyes went to Marten and held there.

"What are you planning for the Middle East?" the president repeated. "When is it to happen? Exactly where? Who else is involved?"

Foxx lay silent and motionless, staring at Marten. Then his eyes came back to Harris and his lips moved. "Alright," he breathed, "I will tell you."

The president and Marten exchanged hugely emotional glances. Finally. After everything. They were going to have an answer.

"Tell me all of it, every detail," the president demanded. "What are you planning for the Middle East?"

"Death," Foxx said with no emotion whatsoever.

Then, with a sharp glance at Marten, he bit down hard, grinding his teeth together.

"Grab him!" Marten yelled, moving toward Foxx. "Grab him! Open his mouth!"

Marten shoved a stunned President Harris aside, then took hold of Foxx's jaws and tried to pry them open. It was too late. Whatever it was worked extremely fast. Merriman Foxx was already dead.

94

2:25 P.M.

Hap Daniels flung a rented dark maroon Audi around a tour bus and accelerated up the steep road leading to the Benedictine monastery at Montserrat. When he got there it would be needle-in-the-haystack time, fighting through a mass of tourists looking for a balding, toupee-less John Henry Harris and Nicholas Marten, whom he had seen in person only once and then very briefly.

At the same time he would be trying to find an attractive young French photographer called Demi Picard who, as the concierge at the Regente Majestic had said, had short dark hair, wore a navy blazer and tan slacks, and was most likely in the company of a middle-aged African-American male and an older European woman. Add to that the fact that he was following a raft of information he thought was correct but had no way of knowing for certain and going to a place he'd never been. Never mind that he was traveling on little more than coffee, adrenaline, and twenty minutes' sleep.

He passed another tour bus, then several cars, then squealed around a sharp turn. As he did he glanced up at the cliffs above him and got a momentary glimpse of the monastery and the mountainside into which it was built. How many more turns there were in the road or how much longer it would take to get there he had no way to know.

He had come this far because of the story he'd told his deputy, Bill Strait: that Assistant Secret Service Director Ted Langway, still in Madrid and working out of the U.S. embassy there, "has been on my ass all morning asking for a detailed briefing. [Which was true.] He just called again [which wasn't], so I don't have any damn choice but to talk to him. I'm going to check into the hotel, deal with him, then take a shower and a real nap, a couple of hours anyway. Call my cell if you need me."

With that he'd put Strait officially in charge, made certain things were coordinated between his Secret Service detail and the vice president's for the vice president's 13:00 arrival at Barcelona Airport, then gone to the Hotel Colon, where the Secret Service had reserved a number of rooms. Once in his room, he'd taken a quick shower, changed his clothes, then armed himself and left by a side door. Fifteen minutes later he drove the maroon Audi rental fast out of Barcelona, headed for the monastery at Montserrat. By then it was seven minutes past one in the afternoon. Seven minutes since the vice president of the United States, Hamilton Rogers, had touched down on Barcelona soil.

2:28 P.M.

"Suicide pill. Poison capsule buried in his right rear upper molar," Marten turned from Merriman Foxx's body to look at the president. "All he had to do was give it one good crunch to activate it, and he did. I worried he might do something like this earlier but I never thought he would have it as a permanent implant."

"If there was ever any doubt of how committed these people are, there's none now," the president said grimly. "It's what it must have been like in the Nazi camp in World War Two. Hitler, Goebbels, Himmler, and the rest hammering ahead with their genocidal crusade, all the while they have Dr. Mengele doing his horrible experiments at the extermination camps. Who knows what would have happened if he ever began to use them on a massive scale?"

"The difference now is that our Dr. Mengele is dead."

"His plan isn't dead. Neither is theirs," Harris snapped. "And we didn't learn a damn thing about it. Nothing." Abruptly he looked off, to just stand there detached and silent. Clearly he was thinking about what to do next.

Marten watched him. He'd been too rough on Foxx and he knew it. The president was right. It had all been emotion. About Caroline, about everything she had meant to him for so much of his life, every piece of it compounded by his rage over her murder. On the other hand it was clear the South African had long been prepared to take his own life if he had to. He was a professional in the field of human pain and might well have been aware of his own physical threshold, of how much he could stand without breaking, and that had been both the reason and the motivation for the implant; it was not the fear of death but the fear of giving up information that would harm the cause. It made the president's remark about the commitment of these people all the more terrifying. These weren't a handful of zealots; they were part of a highly organized, well-funded, hugely dangerous movement.

"Mr. President," Marten said abruptly. "I think we can safely assume that at some point Foxx confirmed your presence here to your Washington friends," he walked over and picked up the BlackBerry-like device Foxx had taken from his pocket and then dropped when Marten grabbed him. "I would bet he was trying to contact them when I got him. They don't hear from him and soon, they're coming fast and right here. It's what I said earlier, we need to call Miguel and get the hell out. Go back to the tourist area and hide somewhere until he comes."

"I don't believe they would leave their entire operation to one man to execute," the president said calmly, as if Marten had never made his plea. "Not something on the scale they're working on. I don't think Foxx would permit it either."

Immediately he turned and walked past the bubble tables toward the cages at the far end of the room. "If this place served as his main headquarters, there's every chance his records are stored somewhere here, probably all digitalized and on computer files. We find those and we might have some kind of answer."

"Damn it, Cousin," Marten was getting angry. "You're doing it again. Whether you want to believe it or not, your 'rescuers' are coming. And when they get here, one way or another, they'll kill you."

"Mr. Marten, Cousin," President Harris spoke quietly and without emotion. "I appreciate what you are trying to do and what you've done already. But there may well be something here of immeasurable importance, and I can't chance not finding it. If you want to leave, I understand. It's quite alright."

"If I want to leave?" Marten's impatience boiled over. "I'm trying to protect the life of the president of the United States. That's you, if you haven't forgotten."

"Understand something, Cousin. This president has no intention of leaving until he has done anything and everything he can to find an answer to what these people have planned."

Marten stared at him. Yes, they might find something that would reveal Foxx's plan somewhere in this cavernous underground but it was far more likely they wouldn't. Just finding a starting place could take hours, even days, and they didn't have minutes. On the other hand, he knew they at least had to try.

Marten took a breath. "Whatever files Foxx might have in this place," he said with resignation, "he wouldn't have left them lying around in his outer office."

"True," Harris smiled inwardly. Marten, he was extremely relieved to know, was back in the fold. "And there were only experiments and work tables in the first lab and in this one."

"So there have to be areas here we haven't seen." Marten put Foxx's electronic device in his pocket, then went to Foxx's body, turned it over, and slid the security card Foxx had used to get them into the chambers from his jacket pocket. He held it up to Harris, "I doubt he had the chance to shut everything down."

95

Hap Daniels eased the rental Audi into the monastery's parking area, one jammed with cars and tour buses. In front and above him he could see the stone edifices that comprised the mini-city itself. He continued on, slowly, intensely, the thing most immediate on his mind was a place to park the car.

Under other circumstances he would have gone directly to security, identified himself, and requested their help. Parking would have been an afterthought. It wasn't now. He could tell no one who he was or why he was there. At the same time he needed to find a place to leave the Audi where it wouldn't be towed and where he had immediate access to it if he had to bring the president to it on the run. In result all he could do was drive up and down through the parking area until he either found an open space or someone pulling out, the same as anyone else.

He made a turn and was starting down the same row he had just passed when his cell phone rang. Immediately he clicked on, "Daniels."

"*It's Bill, Hap,*" the voice of Bill Strait crackled through the tiny speaker.

"What is it?"

"*Crop Duster's been located.*"

"What?" Daniels's heart jumped in his throat.

"*He's been placed at a monastery called Montserrat in the mountains outside Barcelona. Two CIA recovery teams are on the way now by helo to bring him in. Wheels down at the monastery at 15:15.*"

"Bill," Hap pressed him, "who gave you this information? Where did it come from?"

"*Chief of Staff in Madrid.*"

"How the hell did he find out?"

"I don't know."

"Who ordered in the CIA?"

"Specifically?"

"Yes."

"I don't know either. It all came from the embassy in Madrid."

"It should have been run through us first."

"I know, but it wasn't."

"Two teams isn't much."

"More are on the way from Madrid."

"Any word on Crop Duster's condition?"

"None."

Suddenly Daniels saw a green Toyota start to back out of a parking space a half dozen spaces in front of him. He touched the accelerator and the Audi shot ahead. Then he stopped short, blocking the road behind him, waiting for the Toyota to fully clear the space.

"Hap, we've got our own helo on the way. We need you here now. Wheels up for Montserrat at 15:20."

"Ten-four, Bill, thanks," Hap clicked off. "CIA?" he said out loud. And only two teams? Just what CIA were they? Regular ops or some special branch under the wing of the Secretary of Defense and the others? How far and wide did this thing go? And where did Bill Strait fit in it? Whose side was he on? And how was he going to tell Bill he couldn't make the helo to Montserrat because he was already there?

Just then the Toyota cleared the parking space and drove off. Daniels hit the Audi's accelerator and started to swing into the vacated spot. In the same instant a motorcycle with a sidecar cut in front of him, its rider claiming the space. Hap slammed on the brakes. "Hey! That's my space!" he yelled out the open window.

"First come, first served," the rider said brusquely, and climbed off the machine.

"I was here first!"

The rider ignored him and instead hurriedly took off his helmet and locked it in the motorcycle's storage compartment.

"Get that thing the hell out of there!" Hap shoved the car door open and stepped out.

The rider walked off and in seconds disappeared into the crowd leading to the plaza in front of the basilica.

Hap glared after him, his patience and very nearly his sanity all but gone. "I'll get you, you bastard," he breathed. "One day I'll find you and get you good!"

96

2:50 P.M.

It was all colors and images, as if floating through a dream.

Demi remembered only pieces of it.

"We have things to do," the Reverend Beck had said barely seconds after Nicholas Marten left the private room at the restaurant Abat Cisneros to find the president. In no time Demi had collected her cameras and small equipment bag and followed Beck and Luciana out the door. Seconds later they were crossing the plaza in front of the basilica and walking toward the funicular railway that climbed into the mountains above the monastery to the ancient hermitage of Saint Joan.

It was there as they entered the funicular's green car she began to feel a kind of euphoria she had never before experienced. At almost the same time the colors started to come and the reality around her—Reverend Beck, Luciana, the monastery, the funicular itself and the tourists crowding inside it—began to fade. Something in the coffee maybe. It was a fleeting thought that dissolved into a soothing, near-psychedelic mist of translucent crimson and then turquoise and then sienna. A slow, gentle swirling midnight blue tinged with yellow followed.

Hand in hand was the vague memory of walking past the ruins of an ancient church and seeing a small silver-colored SUV parked at the side of a narrow mountain road. A handsome young driver stood by as Reverend Beck helped her into the backseat. After that came the sense of the SUV moving off and then accelerating over the uneven road. Beck seemed to be in the seat beside her, with Luciana riding in front beside the young driver.

Soon they were traveling across a long rocky plateau and then the SUV forded a rushing mountain stream and climbed through an area of conifers; and then they were dropping down into a small valley filled with spring grasses and where a thin layer of fog was beginning to settle. Not long afterward they passed under a high stone arch and then shortly came upon the ruins of still another ancient church, this one near the base of a towering rock formation. It was here they stopped and got out and Beck led them up a steep winding path.

Moments later they passed beneath a towering rock formation and walked across a natural stone bridge with chasms on either side that fell away sharply hundreds of feet below. The far side was in deep shadow, and as they reached it she saw the entrance to a large cave with several monks in dark hooded robes standing watch on either side of it.

"La iglesia dentro de la montaña," Beck said as they entered. "The church within the mountain."

Inside, the cavern rose to an enormous height and was lighted by the flickering glow of what seemed a thousand votive candles. Here, more of the robed and hooded monks kept watch. Then they entered a second chamber. Like the first it was aglow with candle-light. Only here stalactites and stalagmites hung from the ceiling and rose up from the floor in spectacular combinations.

They were partway across this second chamber when she saw the church. It was a place that, in the state of euphoria she still experienced, seemed to be the sanctuary she had been expecting. Entering, she saw a series of stone arches rising far above the nave to form the ceiling, while beneath it two wooden galleries, one on either side and mounted on massive timbers, sat a dozen feet above huge hand-hewn paving stones that made up the floor. Directly ahead, at the nave's far end, was an ornate gilded altar.

Demi turned to look at Beck, as if to question him about it, when she saw a young woman in a white ankle-length dress coming toward them. She had striking brown eyes and a luxurious mane of black hair that fell to her waist. Quite possibly, she was the most beautiful creature Demi had ever seen.

"Demi," the woman smiled broadly as she neared, "I'm so pleased you came."

Demi stopped short. Who was this woman who seemed to know her? Suddenly she seemed strikingly familiar. But how did she know her? And from where or when? Then she realized: Cristina. The young woman who had been with them at the Café Tripoli in Malta.

"You must be tired from your journey," Cristina said warmly. "Please let me take you to your room so that you can rest."

"I—" Demi hesitated.

"Go with her, Demi," Reverend Beck smiled reassuringly, "you wanted to know about the coven of Aldebaran. This is a part of it. Tonight you will see more. And tomorrow, more than that. Everything you wanted to know, you will find out. Everything."

Demi studied him—his smile, his manner of being—as he stood there. At almost the same moment the feeling of euphoria faded, as if whatever drug she had ingested earlier had abruptly worn off. Suddenly she remembered her cameras and the equipment bag she had had with her earlier. "My things," she said to Beck.

"You mean these," Luciana came up from behind. One of the hooded monks accompanied her and carried Demi's cameras and equipment bag. Bowing gently, he handed them to her.

"Thank you," she said, still shaken by the uncomfortable memory of her drugged journey there.

"Please," Cristina took her by the arm and together they crossed the nave toward an area Demi had not yet seen. As they went Demi looked down at the large paving stones beneath their feet. Most had been polished to a high sheen by the trample of feet over time. Similarly, most all had names carved into them; family names, she thought. The curious thing was they were not Spanish but Italian.

"They are family tombs," Cristina said quietly. "Beneath this floor are the earthly remains of the honored dead, interred over the centuries."

"Honored dead?"

"Yes."

Again Demi heard her father's warning and in the next instant saw the tortured face of the armless octogenarian scholar Giacomo Gela. At the same time a voice deep inside her whispered that she had opened one door too many, that this was a place to which she should never have come. Abruptly she looked back, as if for a way out.

Luciana was gone and Beck was alone in the center of the room watching her and at the same time talking on a cell phone. Behind him, at the far end of the nave where the church ended and the caves began, four of the hooded monks stood guard. She realized then that they—and those outside by the stone bridge and no doubt others she had yet to see—were the keepers of this place and that in all probability no one ever entered or left without their consent.

"Are you alright, Demi?" Cristina asked gently.

"Yes," she said, "I'm quite alright. Why wouldn't I be?"

97

2:55 P.M.

Marten and the president stared at the horror. Neither man able to speak, barely able to breathe. They had entered Merriman Foxx's most interior laboratory. Come there almost as if the madman had deliberately planned it. Were he still alive he might well have had the audacity to show it to them himself. That he was dead mattered little. One way or another, it seemed, he had simply wanted them to see it. Or rather, *experience* it.

They'd found their way here because there had been nowhere else for them to go. The security card Marten had taken from Foxx's jacket pocket only allowed them to go forward, not back the way they had come. They could enter a room, cave, shaft, or chamber through the sliding burnished steel doors that marked each, but they could not leave by that same door. The security system would not allow it. The only way out was through a similar door at each room's farthest end. A door that, one after another, led only deeper into the core of the mountain and into more of his laboratories.

The first three had been little more than medium-sized, well-lit rooms, either natural caves or carved from the stone itself. Connected by the same dripping tunnels and boardwalks they had passed over at the beginning, each had contained the complex machinery of an advanced biochemist's lab. From the layman's point of view the equipment appeared to be apparatuses for continued agriculture study and application. Among them were machines that tested and analyzed water for various contaminants: viruses, bacteria, salts, metals, or things radioactive.

Each chamber was checked carefully and then they moved on. In none had they found so much as a computer, file cabinet, or other kind of information-storage device, primitive or otherwise. What they did find were computer screens with keyboards and mouses that suggested they were all wired into a master unit located elsewhere.

"If I wasn't claustrophobic before I'm getting there now," Marten said as they left the last chamber, then were immediately forced into what was nearly a twenty-foot-long crawl space beneath a huge slab of rock.

"Don't think about it," the president said as they reached the end, then stood upright and started down a rickety boardwalk over a particularly damp section of dimly lit shaft.

The tunnel here went downward at a steep angle and then turned sharply at a right angle and went down farther still. By Marten's guess each section was at least five hundred feet long, which made the combined total the longest distance between chambers by far. Finally they saw another burnished door at the end of it. Reaching it, Marten swiped the card and they entered a narrow entryway that led to a darkened room beyond. This time he picked up a small piece of wood that had broken off from the boardwalk and slipped it between the door and the wall frame, leaving the smallest opening as the door slid closed behind them. Not much, but something they could pry open if they wanted to, or had to. He hadn't done it before because if they'd chosen to go back it would only have been into the previous shaft or chamber, where the door was already locked. It would have been a retreat to nothing. He'd done it this time because of a sudden and unnerving sense of dread, a feeling that the space they were about to enter was nothing like anything they had seen before, and going back into the tunnel where they'd been would be far better than staying where they were.

They crossed the dimly lit antechamber to stop halfway across at a translucent curtain made of heavy plastic. A slit down the middle ran from top to bottom, permitting entry. Whatever was on the far side was in darkness.

"Light switch anywhere?" the president asked.

"Not that I can see." Marten stepped to the curtain, carefully put a hand through the slit in the middle, then spread it and stepped through.

Immediately a sensor activated and the room was bathed in light.

"Oh God!" Marten exhaled in horror as he saw what was before him.

Row upon row of human bodies or parts of them lined the sides of two central aisles that reached nearly the length of a football field to the end of what was a huge limestone cavern. All were encased in large aquatic holding tanks filled with some kind of preservative liquid. Tanks that for another purpose might have held tropical fish or live lobsters.

Numb with shock and disbelief, they walked forward in silence, Merriman Foxx's last and seminal work before them. The bodies and body parts floated as if entombed in their own dreams. Men, women, children, of every race and age imaginable. Each tank had a handwritten card marked with what was apparently a specimen number followed by an entry and removal date. Dates and specimen numbers of previous inhabitants were neatly crossed out above. A closer look revealed that the subjects were kept in the solution for approximately three months before being replaced. The records were in descending order and revealed that the earliest experiments had begun seventeen years earlier. What the three-month waiting period was for they had no answer other than to assume it involved some part of Foxx's research. Whatever that research was, the questions it raised were enormous. How had these people been selected? How had they come to be there? Where and how had they died? Where and how long had they been kept alive beforehand, and what had been done to them during that time? Finally, what had happened to their bodies—in all those years there would have been hundreds if not thousands of them—afterward?

And then there were the corpses themselves. Tragic, hideous, floating. Their eyes, the ones that still had eyes, stared blankly out through the brine at nothing. The expression of each nearly the same, extreme pain—and with it a desperate pleading for help, pity, intervention, anything at all to stop it.

Curiously, in none was there a look of anger or a seething for revenge. That wasn't part of it. Clearly, they had no idea they were victims of human action or carried a suspicion that anything unnatural had been done to them.

Halfway down Marten stopped and looked at the president, "You know what these people represent?"

"The general populace."

"Yes. And I think they had no idea. No thought at all that they were guinea pigs. They had become ill, that's all they knew."

"That's my sense too," President Harris said. Almost immediately the chilling thought struck, "What if that is the plan? The thing Foxx was working on and finally developed to production level. Disease. Bacteria. A virus. Some kind of massive, fast-moving, deadly force that seems wholly natural and is uncontrollable except by the people doing it."

"A man-made pandemic."

"One that has no appearance of being a weapon," the president looked to the floating corpse in front of him. A woman, twenty-five at most, her eyes pleading for help like the others. Abruptly he turned back to Marten, "The world is already being set up for it. One way or another it's in the media almost every day. Right now all it's doing is alarming the public. With the main beneficiaries being higher stock prices for drug companies and giving more power to those already in power, both declaring they are doing everything they can to prevent it from happening. Yet all the while the real thing is being planned."

The president stepped away from Marten to walk along the tanks, deliberately looking in at the victims, as if to fix in his mind forever the awfulness of what he saw. Finally he looked back, his eyes stark with fury.

"God bless these people here and all the ones that have gone before them. And God *damn* Merriman Foxx. And God *damn* all of them who are involved in this. And may God help all of us if what Foxx learned and developed has already been put in motion."

"We need tissue samples," Marten said urgently—his own anger and certainty that Caroline Parsons was dead because of these experiments—muted by what had to be done. "We have to find his files. His notes, charts, everything and anything we can get our hands on. We have to know what this is."

From somewhere came a distinctive *hiss*. Both men looked up at once. Along the edge of the ceiling, running the length of the chamber, were heretofore unseen gas jets. The *hiss* increased as more jets opened.

"Gas!" Marten said sharply. "Poison or explosive, don't know which. I'll bet controlled by a timer the minute the lights went on. Take a deep breath and hold it! We're getting the hell out of here!"

"Tissue samples! Foxx's files! His notes!" The president was going nowhere without them.

"My call this time, Cousin," Marten abruptly clamped his hand over the president's mouth and nose and wrestled him hard toward the plastic curtain at the end of the room. "We're leaving. Right now!"

98

SAME TIME. 3:11 P.M.

Hap Daniels watched a lone commercial helicopter come in over the mountaintop. It circled once then dropped down toward the monastery's helipad. Hap knew what none of the curious onlookers could know: the emergency services/VIP helipad had just become a landing site for a covert CIA operation ordered to find the president of the United States and take him out of there.

After the confrontation with the motorcycle rider it had taken Hap almost twenty minutes to find a questionably legal parking space close to the helipad. If, as he suspected, the ops were coming by command of the group the president was running from, they would already know where within the huge complex he was. How many there would be he didn't know, but in all likelihood they would have at least four ground agents plus the pilot and probably a copilot. Then there would be the second helo, circling somewhere out of sight, a backup team waiting in the event they were needed. Whether any of them knew the truth behind their assignment, who had ordered it and why, or that they were making an end run around the Secret Service made little difference, they would all be highly trained operatives whose obligation was to protect and maintain the continuation of government and whose sole assignment would be to rescue the president and get him out of there safely, fast and unseen, with as little attention as possible. After that they would take him to the CIA jet the chief of staff had waiting at the private airfield outside Barcelona and from there to a location even the Secret Service hadn't been alerted to. What would happen after that he didn't want to think about.

What it all did was give Hap one simple directive, prevent them from getting the president onto the helicopter. Somehow he had to take custody of him before they got him anywhere near the aircraft. It would be a hugely difficult and dangerous undertaking even if they were legitimate CIA because the safety of the president would come before anything, and anyone, himself included, who tried to interfere ran a very good chance of being shot dead on the spot.

If they were not legitimate CIA, or if they were part of some special covert branch of it, or even some special operations military force working at the order of the vice president and the others, his task would not be just difficult, it would be about as suicidal as you could get.

Whoever they were, his plan had to be simple, and it was: watch them land, follow them to their destination, then wait and watch. It was when they brought the president out and neared the helicopter, his work would begin. With the Audi positioned nearby, his move would have to be ultrafast and utterly decisive. Under other circumstances a specific protocol would be in place. He would call a trusted CIA supervisor and say he needed the name of the POC (point of contact) on this operation. Getting it, he would call out the man's name, flash his Secret Service credentials and say he was the special agent in charge and was taking custody of the POTUS himself.

But this was not "other circumstances." He was the last man

between the president and his life or death. He would have only one move and that would come in the final seconds, when he stepped from the crowd, held up his Secret Service credentials and yelled who he was, telling the Ops forcefully there was just-received information of an imminent threat to their operation and that he was relieving them of their mission. Then he would take the POTUS into custody and head for the Audi. All the while hoping to hell the president would read the play as fast as it happened, trust him, and order the ops aside. Surprise, timing, execution, and sheer luck would be everything. The margin for error was zero.

The sudden chirp of his cell phone broke his train of thought. He picked it off his belt and looked at the originating number. It was Bill Strait. It meant the Secret Service helo in Barcelona was readying for a wheels-up to Montserrat, and Strait was wondering where the hell he was.

Suddenly it occurred to him that Strait had told him the CIA helo would have wheels down at Monsterrat at 15:15, while the Secret Service helo wouldn't be ready for wheels-up in Barcelona for the trip to Montserrat until 15:20. He hadn't thought about it at the time but why that long a delay? Did someone want to make certain the CIA got to the monastery before the Secret Service did? If so, who had arranged it? Someone at the embassy in Madrid or Bill Strait?

"Roger, Bill," Hap said as he clicked on.

"Where the hell are you?"

"Why did it take us so long to get the helo ready?"

"They were out at Barcelona Airport refueling. They'd just touched down when I alerted them. Why?"

"You alerted them, not the chief of staff?"

"Yes, me. Hap, for chrissake we're ready to go. Where are you?"

"Go without me."

"What?"

"I'm tied up on something else. I'll check in later. Go without me. That's an order."

With that Hap clicked off. "Damn it," he breathed. Was the refueling just bad timing or something else? Could he trust his deputy or couldn't he?

A thundering, thudding roar was followed by a storm of flying dust and debris as the helicopter touched down on the helipad exactly on schedule. Immediately the pilot cut the engines, the doors opened and four men in dark glasses and wearing suit coats climbed out. They ducked the still-churning rotor blades and moved off fast toward the steps leading to the basilica.

"Here we go," Hap Daniels said to himself, "here we go."

99

3:22 P.M.

The ops moved quickly through the crowd in front of the basilica, then, like a wave, turned down a walkway and disappeared from sight.

Hap dodged around a group of schoolchildren walking in line toward the basilica, trying to keep up. A moment later he was on the walkway the ops had taken. Tourists were everywhere. He swore under his breath and kept moving, his eyes searching the walkway ahead, afraid he had lingered too far behind. Ten paces more and saw them turn down another walkway. He pushed around two chattering women and followed, his eyes on the apparent leader. He was thirty at most and very fit with dark, short-cropped hair and a particularly broad nose that looked as if it had been broken more than once. Just then they reached a convergence of walkways and Broad Nose stopped to get his bearings. In seconds he'd made a decision and led the ops down another walkway, one with red and white votive candles lining its far wall.

Hap stayed back as much as he dared, following as they took another turn and then another, then disappeared around a corner. Eight seconds later he rounded the same corner and pulled up. They had stopped at a heavy wooden door set into a stone archway. Broad Nose slid open a wood panel next to it, revealing an electronic keypad. Hap saw him punch in four numbers, then slide the

panel closed and turn the iron knob on the door. It opened and they
entered quickly, shutting the door behind them.

Where they were going inside, or how long it would take them to
find the president, Hap couldn't know. He wished to hell he had
Bill Strait and the rest of his Secret Service team there; wished too
that he could have contacted one of the CIA supervisors so he
could know just who these ops were. Even then he would have
been unsure if he could trust either of them. It was a situation he
hated but there it was. Suddenly it occurred to him that the ops
might bring the president out another exit, one somewhere else in
the complex. It made him think that his best plan would be to go
back and position himself near the helipad, make his move as they
rushed the president toward the helicopter.

He was turning, starting to head back, when he saw a familiar
figure suddenly step from the shadows on the far side of the walkway and go up to the door. He stopped abruptly and watched the
man slide the panel open and punch four numbers into the keypad
as if he knew the code perfectly. Immediately afterward he slid the
panel closed and reached for the doorknob.

"What the hell?" Hap breathed. The man was the motorcycle
rider. Clearly he wasn't an op or anything like it, more like a messenger sent to pick something up. If the ops did bring the president out
this way and at the same time his motorcycle man went in, anything
could happen, and the president would be directly in harm's way.

Hap moved just as the man pushed the door open. A heartbeat
later he shoved a 9mm Sig Sauer automatic pistol behind the man's
ear.

"Freeze, right there!"

A gasp went out of him and he stopped right where he was. In
a split second Hap pulled him from the doorway and shoved him
back into the shadows where he'd been hiding.

"Who the hell are you?" Miguel Balius stared him in the eye.

100

"It's not who I am," Hap breathed, "it's who you are, where the hell you were going."

"I'm supposed to meet my cousins," Miguel said carefully, all too aware that this was the man whose parking space he had stolen.

"Cousins?"

"Take it easy. It was only a parking space."

"What's in there?" Hap nodded toward the door to Foxx's office.

"I don't know."

"You're going inside to meet your cousins but you don't know what's there."

"I've never been here before."

"No?"

"No," Miguel held his ground.

Hap glanced back at the open door. So far nothing had happened, at least from what he could tell from there. He looked back to Miguel. "I've never been here before either. Let's find out what's there together."

They came through the door slowly and into dim light. Miguel first as a shield, with Hap's Sig Sauer tight against his ear. There was one large room with tall chairs along one wall, a massive bookcase against the other, and a large wooden desk at the end of it. Just beyond it, and to the right, a closed ornate wooden door was set into an arched nave. That was all, no ops, no sign of them, only silence.

"Where does that door go?"

"I told you before, I don't know."

"Suppose we find out," Hap started him down the room toward the door.

"Who are you?" Miguel asked carefully as they went. Clearly the issue was not about the parking space, that had been a coincidence. This man was a professional, an American. But who was he working for? Foxx? The four men he had seen enter? Or was he one of the pursuers the "cousins" were avoiding? Or was he doing something else entirely?

Hap didn't answer, instead he pulled his eyes from the door they were approaching to glance behind them. It was an instant Miguel might have used to throw him to the floor and run. But he hadn't come here to run away, even under this circumstance. He was here for his "cousins." He'd been waiting at the bottom of the hill for more than three hours without a word from them and anxiety had roiled in his gut. He was certain the reason he hadn't heard was because they were in trouble. It was why he had abandoned the limousine and borrowed the motorcycle from an uncle who lived in the nearby town of El Borràs, then raced it up to the monastery as he had and into the parking space ahead of this American. Why he had gone to the restaurant and learned from the headwaiter that the men he described as his "cousins" had met with Merriman Foxx in the private dining room and that afterward the three had left together, going in the direction of the office Foxx was known to keep there. He was in that office now because of his "cousins." Whoever this man here was, gun or no gun, he would be damned if he was going to let him harm either of them.

"Hold it," Hap suddenly stopped them where they were and listened. There was nothing, not a sound. Something was wrong. Four special ops guys had come in. The only exit other than the front was that far door, and they had to have gone through it. If they had the president and were coming back out that same way, at least one of them should have been posted at it.

It was then Hap realized he'd made an awful mistake. The ops did have another way out and were taking it. "Christ!" he said, twisting away from Miguel, starting for the front door. In that same second a dull reverberation shook the entire building as if it were an earthquake. Hap and Miguel were knocked to the floor. An avalanche of books thundered from the massive bookcase. Choking dust and debris rained down from the ceiling.

Hap was up in an instant, unsure what had happened, trying to regain control, his 9mm Sig Sauer swinging toward Miguel.

"No! No! Don't!" Miguel yelled, throwing his hands in the air.

Just then the door at the far end of the room wrenched open and the ops came through it on the run. Broad Nose first, a second op with buzz-cut red hair and jacketless was right behind him. Both had machine pistols in their hands. On their heels came the last two ops. They had a man by the arms between them, his feet dragging on the floor. Red Hair's missing jacket was thrown over his head to keep him from being recognized.

"Special Agent Daniels, United States Secret Service!" Hap yelled, his Secret Service ID held high in his left hand, the 9mm Sig Sauer lowered to his right side. "You're relieved of mission. I'm taking the president into custody."

"No can do," Broad Nose said with no emotion at all.

"Repeat. You are relieved of the mission," Hap showed the Sig Sauer. "Don't make it hard."

"Won't." Broad Nose and Red Hair swung their machine pistols at the same time. Hap twisted away, hitting the floor as a barrage of gunfire chewed up the wall where he had been. The other ops rushed for the door. Miguel lunged for his jacket-covered "Cousin" as they went past.

Surprised by Miguel's sudden move, the ops twisted away. As they did the jacket came off and their charge was clearly seen, his body limp, his head slumped over. It wasn't the president. It was Merriman Foxx.

Now Broad Nose was at the door. "Get him out!" he shouted at the ops, then squeezed off a burst at Miguel as he dove behind the wooden desk. At the same time Red Hair swung his machine pistol at Hap. It was too late, Hap was firing from the floor.

BOOM! BOOM! BOOM!

Hap could see his slugs explode Red Hair's right arm. The gunman screamed, and Broad Nose dragged him through the front door, squeezing off a burst at Hap as he did. The others followed in a rush, throwing the jacket awkwardly back over Foxx's head, dragging him with them. As they went out Broad Nose stepped back into the doorway and sprayed the room with a final burst, making sure the men inside weren't coming after them.

101

Hap was on the floor but didn't know why. He had a vague memory of the motorcycle man bending over him, checking his carotid artery and shoving a handkerchief or some kind of material up under his shirt, pressing it tight against his left shoulder. Then he'd turned abruptly and left. After that things started to fade and he nearly blacked out, or maybe he had blacked out. What brought him back was the sound of emergency sirens outside and the ringing of his cell phone, which he could see clearly lying on the floor nearby alongside the Sig Sauer automatic. Slowly he moved to touch the Steyr TMP machine pistol dropped down from a sling over his shoulder that had been there all along but that he'd never had the chance to use. It was then the motorcycle man came back.

"Come on," he said, "your left shoulder, you took a bullet, maybe two. The police and fire brigade are coming. Get your feet under you."

Hap stared at him. "Who the hell are you?"

"My name is Miguel Balius. Get your damn feet under you!"

Miguel grabbed Hap's good arm and pulled him up, propping him against the wall while he scooped up his cell phone and the Sig Sauer. Then he had Hap's good arm again and was taking him fast toward the door.

Fresh air hit them and they were outside, the motorcycle right there. Miguel helped him into the sidecar, then jumped onto the seat, started the engine, and they were off and flying down the walkway as fire brigade and police units rushed toward them. A wall of uniformed men and women going door to door checking for people who might have been injured in the earthquake or whatever it had been that had so violently shaken the buildings.

Miguel reached the end of the walkway and turned the motorcycle down another. At almost the same moment a heavy, pulsating roar came from the far side of the basilica. A half second later the ops helicopter lifted up over the top of the building, hovered overhead for the briefest moment, and then flew off to the north.

102

BARCELONA, HOTEL GRAND PALACE, 4:10 P.M.

Jake Lowe and Dr. James Marshall were alone in the special communications room set up in their suite. Suit jacket off, sleeves rolled up, tie loosened, Lowe paced up and down, a secure phone to his ear. Marshall, all six-foot-four of him, sat at a work desk in the room's center, two laptops in front of him, yellow scratch pad at his sleeve, a headset plugged into Lowe's secure line.

"Gentlemen," Lowe said into the phone, then abruptly paused, as if to make certain what he said next would be absolutely clear.

"This is where we stand," he said finally. "The ops have come and gone from the monastery. Dr. Foxx was found dead in one of his 'clean' labs. His remains were evacuated after a brief battle with the Secret Service. The ops did not identify themselves, nor did they identify Dr. Foxx. They left the monastery by civilian helicopter without further incident.

"There was no sign of the president. I repeat, there was no sign of the president. Earlier communication with Dr. Foxx confirmed his presence and that of Nicholas Marten at the monastery.

"Dr. Foxx's body was found in an innermost 'clean' laboratory and strongly suggests he was confronted by a hostile situation. Since neither the president nor Marten was found at the scene and because any doors they might have used for escape were electronically locked behind them, we must presume that they took the only route available, and that was the tunnel to the rear of the lab where Dr. Foxx was found.

"Very shortly after the ops arrived there was an explosion in that tunnel. Most reliably, gentlemen, the result of mechanisms Foxx put in place during construction."

Gentlemen.

Plugged into the same secure transmission and scattered across Europe and in the United States were the others: Vice President Hamilton Rogers with President John Henry Harris's chief of staff, Tom Curran, in the U.S. embassy in Madrid; Secretary of State David Chaplin, at the U.S. Embassy, London; Secretary of Defense Terrence Langdon at NATO headquarters in Brussels; Chairman of the Joint Chiefs of Staff, United States Air Force General Chester Keaton, at his home office in rural Virginia.

"*Are we to believe the president is dead?*" Terrence Langdon asked from Brussels.

"Terry, it's Jim," Marshall cut in, "I don't think we can assume anything. But based on the info received from Foxx earlier and from what the ops observed, it's all but certain he and Marten were in that tunnel when the explosion occurred. If that is the case there is very little chance—let me qualify that—there is 'no chance' either could have survived."

"*We know Foxx set up a line of succession in the event anything happened to him. It was how he ran the top-secret programs in the Tenth Medical Brigade. But let me ask a very direct question. In truth, can we proceed without him?*"

"Affirmative," Marshall said. "No question. It's simply a matter of alerting his chain of command."

"*Do we know details of what happened to him? Was the president there and involved?*"

"We don't know. But whatever happened, we couldn't have had his body found there and then have an investigation take place."

"*People will have seen him at the monastery.*"

"He was there off and on all the time. He had his office, his clean labs that he openly showed people. Officially he will have departed right after he left the restaurant. It won't be a problem."

"*The Secret Service,*" General Keaton said from Virginia, "*the agents who were there will make a report if they haven't already. Then what?*"

Lowe glanced at Marshall, then spoke into the phone, "There were two men, Chet. Only one identified himself as Secret Service.

It was the president's SAIC, Hap Daniels. Who the other man was we don't know. How either of them got there we don't know either. But Daniels was shot and hasn't been heard from since. When and if he reports in, the orders are to have him brought directly to us for debriefing. Once that happens he will be informed that the ops he encountered were South African Special Forces commandos working under orders to secretly repatriate Dr. Foxx to South Africa for new hearings regarding himself and the Tenth Medical. The circumstances under which he was discovered made it politically expedient that he be found dead at his home in Malta. The South African government fully apologizes for any mix-up that might have caused Agent Daniels his injury."

"*I don't like it.*"

"None of us like it. But there it is. Besides, he has no idea who the ops were and he certainly didn't find the president. And if he says he went there based on information from our embassy in Madrid it will be pointed out that all concerned mistakenly thought the information had come from the CIA and not the South Africans."

"*If there was an explosion in the tunnel someone is going to go in to check it out,*" Vice President Rogers raised another concern. "*What happens when they find the president's body?*"

"They won't," Lowe said with cold confidence. "That tunnel leads to Foxx's Number Six lab, the ugly one. As Foxx described it, it was designed to automatically destruct if the proper codes weren't keyed in upon entry, at the same time any access to it would be sealed off. If that happened, and according to the Ops report from the scene we have to presume that it did, right now that tunnel is blocked by a two-hundred-thousand-pound slab of rock crushed down against the door to the last of Foxx's monastery-side labs. The other end is sealed off by a thousand cubic yards of interior landslide. Foxx was a perfectionist. What's there will look like a natural earth-fall inside an old mining tunnel. There would be no reason to believe anyone would be in there. It's one of a whole chain of tunnels the authorities know have been sealed off for decades."

"Gentlemen," Marshall cut in, "unless the president was in the lab itself, which he might well have been, the only other place he could be is in the tunnel itself. If he's there he has no way out. For all intents it will become his tomb. If it has not already. How we go about officially discovering what happened and how we recover the body we will contend with later. Right now and most thankfully he and his ideas are no longer an issue. We need to move on, and quickly."

"*Agreed,*" Secretary of State Chaplin said from London.

"*Jim—*" Langdon jumped in from Brussels.

"Still here, Terry," Marshall said.

"*We're damn short on time. The final go ahead for Warsaw has to be given and soon.*"

"I concur."

"*Vote.*" Langdon said.

His demand was followed by an immediate and unanimous chorus of "Agreed."

"*Nays?*"

From Madrid, London, Brussels. From rural Virginia. From the men in the room at the Hotel Grand Palace in Barcelona came only silence.

"Then the vice president will sign the Warsaw order forthwith," Lowe said. "Correct, Ham? No backing out from you."

"*I'm a hundred-percenter, Jake, you know that. You all know that. Always have been. No backing out here,*" Vice President Hamilton Rogers said from Madrid. "*Chet, you will confirm the Warsaw operation when it is operational.*"

"*Yes sir. You bet,*" Air Force General Chester Keaton's powerful voice stabbed across three thousand miles of ocean.

"Good," Lowe said, "then we're done and on to the next. See you in Warsaw, gentlemen. Thank you and good luck."

With that Lowe hung up and looked to Marshall. "I want to feel relieved. Somehow I don't."

"You're thinking about the president."

"We don't know for sure, do we? What if somehow he's still down there and alive?"

"Then he's got a hell of a lot of digging to do," Marshall took off his headset, then got up and crossed to a side table to pour drinks. Malt scotch, neat. Double shot for each. Done, he handed a glass to Lowe.

"It's less than forty-eight hours to Warsaw. The vice president believes he's in charge, the others accept it. Even if somehow the president did manage to pull off an Easter surprise it would be all but impossible for him to do it in that time. Even if he did, the only way out would be over, under, or through that monster two-hundred-thousand-pound slab of rock and into Foxx's monastery chambers. He does that, shows up Christlike, we get him the hell out of there in one damn hurry. Soon after that he's dead from a heart attack and the vice president officially becomes president. Unnerving, yes, a little. But either way it's still all ours."

Lowe stared at him, "Do we have ops waiting if he does show?"

"In Foxx's office?"

"Or anywhere else."

"Jake, it can't happen."

"Do-we-have-ops-waiting?" Lowe articulated deliberately.

"You're serious."

"I'm damn serious. I want ops in Foxx's monastery chambers and anywhere else he might show up Easterlike. Inside, outside, upside down. There's a whole series of mining tunnels back there. What if he did escape the explosion and is alive and in one of them trying to find a hole to climb out through? What if he finds it? What then?"

"That could take a lot of bodies."

"Mr. National Security Adviser, we are at war, if you haven't noticed."

Marshall studied Lowe for a long moment, then touched his glass to his. "You want it done, it is."

Lowe didn't move, just stood there, glass in hand.

"Have a little faith in your own organization, man," Marshall said. "Have a little faith."

Lowe drained his glass in one swallow and set it down. "The last time I had that kind of faith it was in a son of a bitch named John Henry Harris. Twenty-two years of faith, Jim. Everything was right with him until it went wrong. So until we either have him or confirm he's dead, I don't know a goddamn thing," Lowe's eyes came up and found Marshall's and held there. "Not a thing."

103

Matches.

The matches the president still carried from the diversionary fire he'd started in the Barcelona train station to escape the Spanish police. By Marten's count there were eleven left. Seven had already been used to get them this far in the pitch black of the tunnel, wherever "this far" was and whatever tunnel this was. He could hear the president breathing and knew he was resting somewhere close by. "You okay?" he asked in the darkness.

"Yes. You?" the president's voice came back.

"So far."

They had left Foxx's hideous lab at 3:09, escaping the rush of gas pouring from the jets built into the room and going back up the tunnel the way they'd come in. The trouble was the door at the far end was locked and there was no other entrance. It meant they had no place to go except the hideous lab from which they'd just escaped. That left only the tunnel they were in and gave them nothing to do but wait until the gas escaped Foxx's chamber and the shaft filled with it. It was in that moment of terrible realization they felt the slightest waft of fresh air. They followed it twenty feet or so and found a slender opening in the tunnel wall just wide enough for a man to slip through. On the far side was a narrow sandstone passage that dropped swiftly away and then quickly became little more than a crawl space. Marten lit one more match and they could see it continue on for another thirty feet before it turned and disappeared from sight. Where it went or if it simply ended there was no way to know. But it was filled with fresh air and they didn't dare go back to the main tunnel, so they took it. Marten first, wriggling through with his feet and elbows, the president right behind doing the same.

At the end of the thirty feet the shaft turned sharply and they had to inch around it. They continued that way in pitch black for another hundred feet and then the narrowness and tight press of the passage suddenly gave way to a larger chamber and they were able to stand upright. Another match and they could see they were in what appeared to be an old mining tunnel with a rusted narrow-gauge ore-car track running down its center. Apparently they had entered somewhere midtunnel so to know which direction to go was nothing more than a guess, which they did, turning right and moving off in the dark, using the rails as a guide. By Marten's watch it was then 3:24.

Seven minutes later, at 3:31, the tunnel veered left and they followed it. At 3:37 exactly a thundering explosion rocked the entire mountain. The tunnel ceiling fifty feet behind them collapsed and in seconds the entire shaft filled with a rolling cloud of choking dust.

Immediately they dropped to the floor, hugging it, fearful even to breathe. Then, hands clamped over noses, coughing and spitting and still following the ore-car rails, they crawled off in the only direction they could go.

By 3:50 most of the dust had settled and they got to their feet and moved on, one following the other, the one behind holding the belt of the man in front so as not to get separated in the inky darkness, ready to pull him back in the event the ground suddenly disappeared beneath his feet.

At 4:32 they heard the sound of dripping water and stopped. Another match showed the tunnel continuing on around a bend and at the same time revealed a small pool of collected groundwater where the tunnel wall touched the floor. Water to drink and to wash the dust from the face and eyes.

"You first, Cousin," the president coughed.

Marten grinned, "Sure, get the peasant to test for poison before the king tries it."

Marten saw the president smile just as the match went out. The moment was fleeting but in the awful black that followed it was a moment of humor shared. Not much but something.

Afterward they drank and washed out the dust and then sat down to rest.

104

Hap Daniels sat on the edge of the bed watching the young doctor finish bandaging his shoulder. They were in the cramped upstairs bedroom of a small house near the Llobregat River and on the outskirts of El Borràs, a town in a valley north and east of Montserrat, that belonged to Pau Savall, Miguel's uncle. A stonemason and housepainter, it was Pau who had lent Miguel the motorcycle and behind whose home the Limousines Barcelona Mercedes was now hidden.

A final layer of bandage and the doctor was done. Standing, he looked at Hap through rimless glasses.

"Usted es muy afortunado," he said quietly. "Ambas son heridas suaves del tejido fino. Descanse esta noche; usted puede ir mañana."

"He says you are very lucky," Miguel said from where he stood at the foot of the bed. "You have taken two wounds. Both are in the soft tissue. The bullets went all the way through. You will be quite sore and stiff but alright. He wants you to rest for tonight, tomorrow you may go."

"You have much luck, mi amigo," the doctor said in a halting mixture of English and Spanish. "God only knows the reason for it. That is why you have un amigo like this," he nodded toward Miguel, "he is God's helper. Now, if you will permit me, my children await me at supper." With that he said something in Spanish to Miguel and the two started across the room.

Hap saw them stop briefly at the door and the doctor hand Miguel something, and then they both left.

Hap took a breath and ran a hand over his bandaged shoulder, remembering the painful ride down from the monastery in the cramped sidecar of Miguel's motorcycle. It had seemed to take a lifetime but in truth had been little more than twenty minutes. Twenty minutes after that the doctor had come.

By that time he'd had a couple of solid hits of local brandy, learned who Miguel was, who the men he had called his "cousins" were, and that the reason Miguel had helped him was because he had identified himself as a Secret Service agent and risked his life to save the man he thought was the president. He learned too that Miguel was the limousine driver who had brought the president and Marten to Montserrat from Barcelona and how he had come to have the keypad combination that allowed him to enter Foxx's office.

Miguel had gone to the monastery's restaurant to find his "cousins." The headwaiter had seen them leave with Merriman Foxx and gave him directions to Foxx's office. He'd been almost to the door when the ops had come and he'd quickly stepped back into the nearby shadows. When Broad Nose used the keypad, he'd watched carefully. The numbers were 4-4-4-2. Remembering numbers came easily to him, the result of too many days playing the national lottery, of too much money spent, of too many numbers remembered out of sheer hope.

It was then Hap had learned it was Foxx who had been the slumped white-haired figure the ops had carried out. He'd known him only by reputation and because of the secret subcommittee hearings on terrorism. He'd never seen him or even seen a photograph of him until that moment when Miguel charged the ops thinking they had the president, and the jacket came off, exposing him.

Why the president had enough interest in Foxx to risk coming all the way to Montserrat he had no idea until Miguel confirmed some of what he already suspected; that the president's Washington "friends" had planned an action the president refused to take part in—a mass genocide against the Muslim states—and that Merriman Foxx was the prime engineer of it. The president had no details of the plan and that was the reason he and Marten had gone to the monastary: to force Foxx to reveal the plan's particulars in an effort to stop it. Whether they had been successful or not, there was no way to know.

5:35 P.M.

Miguel came back into the room carrying a glass of water and a small envelope. "Take these," he handed Hap the water and slid two white pills from the envelope. "For pain. The doctor gave them to me. There are more in here." He set the envelope on the bedside table.

"After the ops left and before I blacked out, you went through that door in Foxx's office," Hap took a drink of water but ignored the pills. "I would guess to look for the president. You didn't find him or we wouldn't be here like this. Was there any sign he had actually been there?"

"Please take the medication."

"Had the president been there?" Hap pressed him forcefully. "And if he had, where the hell did he go that the ops didn't find him?"

"My uncle is downstairs with his wife," Miguel said quietly. "Only they and the doctor know you are here. They will check on you before they go to bed. They can be trusted. Anything you want or need they will provide." Miguel started for the door.

"You're leaving?"

"I will see you when I get back."

"You have my BlackBerry."

"Yes," Miguel took it from his jacket pocket, then came back and handed it to Hap.

"What about the guns? There were two of them."

Miguel opened his jacket, slid Hap's Sig Sauer automatic from his waistband, and set it on the table next to him.

"Where's the other one, the machine pistol?"

"I need it."

"For what?"

Miguel smiled gently. "I think you are a good man who must rest."

"I said, for what?" Hap pressed him.

"Age nineteen to twenty-four, Fourth Battalion, Royal Australian Army, Special Operations Command. I know how to use it."

Hap stared at him. "I didn't ask for your résumé, I asked why you need the machine pistol!"

"Good night, sir," Miguel turned for the door.

"You don't know if the president was even there, do you?" Hap barked after him. "You're guessing!"

Miguel turned back. "He was there, sir." He took a step, lifted something from a dresser top, then walked over and set it on Hap's lap. It was Demi's big floppy hat.

"He was wearing it when I left him, part of his disguise. I found it in one of the laboratories beyond the office we were in. The door and part of the wall leading from the laboratories to whatever was beyond them was crushed. Blocked by a huge wall of stone. Probably the result of the earthquake or whatever it was that knocked us to the floor. In a day or two people with heavy digging equipment might be able to break through it to the other side. Even then there would be no guarantee of what they might find.

"Somewhere on the far side of that mass of stone, inside the mountain and those surrounding it, caves connected by old mining tunnels run for miles. If he is alive he will be in one of those caves or tunnels. A storm is coming but for a time there will be moonlight and there are ways in from the top. That's where I'm going. To me your president and Nicholas Marten are family. It's my duty and choice to find them, whether they are alive or dead."

"Your limousine, it's parked out back under some trees."

"What about it?"

"You bring people up into the mountains a lot?"

"Yes, I bring people to the mountains quite often." Miguel was impatient, time was everything, this questioning wasting it.

"Keep an emergency kit in the trunk?"

"Yes."

"A large one?"

"Señor Hap, I am trying to get to your president. Please excuse me," again Miguel started for the door.

"The kit. It has those small, folding survival blankets, the kind that have a reflective side? You know, Mylar, like the firefighters use?"

Miguel angrily swung back. "Why these questions?"

"Answer me."

"Yes, we have them. It's a company regulation. One for each passenger and the driver. We keep ten."

"What about food? Emergency rations?"

"Some health bars, that's all."

"Good, bring the whole damn kit." Abruptly Hap stood up. Then immediately put out a hand to steady himself.

"What are you doing?"

Hap grabbed the 9mm Sig Sauer, stuck in it his belt and put the pain pills in his pocket. "I'll be damned if you're going alone."

105

PARIS, HOTEL BEST WESTERN AURORE, 5:45 P.M.

"Good evening, Victor."

"Hello, Richard. I've been waiting all afternoon for your call."

"There was a delay, I'm sorry."

"I saw the story on TV about the shooting at the Chantilly race course. They talked about the two dead jockeys. But there wasn't much more."

"You haven't been approached by the police, have you?"

"No."

"Good."

Victor was in his underwear, lying on the bed, the television on in the background. He'd come that morning by train from Chantilly and taken a cab from the train station, Gare du Nord, to the hotel where he was now, opposite another railroad station, Gare de Lyon. There he'd had a room-service breakfast, then showered and slept until two. After that he'd waited, as instructed, for Richard to call. As he had in Madrid, he'd grown more anxious as the hours passed, worrying that Richard would not call, maybe not ever. If the night went by without hearing from him he didn't know what he would do. He honestly didn't. In fact the idea of killing himself had crossed his mind more than once. It was certainly an answer. Something he could do. And very possibly would do if Richard had not called by—he set the time—eight the next morning. But then Richard had called and it was alright and he felt warm and wanted and respected again.

"Again I apologize for the delay, Victor. It took some time for the final arrangements to be made."

"It's alright, Richard, I understand. Some things get complicated, don't they?"

"Yes, they do, Victor. Now here are your instructions. Train number 243 leaves Gare du Nord for Berlin at 8:46 tonight. There is a first-class ticket being held in your name at the customer service window. You can be on the train, Victor, can't you?"

"Yes."

"Good. You will arrive in Berlin at 8:19 tomorrow morning. At 12:52 in the afternoon, train number 41 will leave Berlin for Warsaw and arrive at 6:25 in the evening. A very nice room has been reserved for you at the Hotel Victoria Warsaw. I will call you there before midnight. Is that satisfactory, Victor?"

"Yes, of course, Richard. I always do as you ask. That's why you depend on me, isn't it?"

"Yes, Victor, you know it is. Have a safe trip, I will call you tomorrow."

"Thank you, Richard. And good night."

"Good night, Victor. And thank you too."

106

LA IGLESIA DENTRO DE LA MONTAÑA,
THE CHURCH WITHIN THE MOUNTAIN, 5:55 P.M.

Demi's room was like that of a convent, sparse and very small. A simple dressing table was near the door, a hand mirror and washbasin resting on it. To the right was a commode with a fold-down top. A view of the sky through the tiny window near the ceiling told her it was still daylight. The single bed was hard and had no sheets, only a pillow and two blankets. On it she had set her two cameras and small equipment bag in which she had packed a small plastic bag containing her toiletries and another that held her camera accessories—extra memory cards and battery charger for the Canon digital and two dozen rolls of color film for the 35mm Nikon. What was not there, and what she was certain she had brought with her when she left the Hotel Regente Majestic in Barcelona that morning and had checked again when she arrived at Montserrat, was her cell phone. Somewhere along the way it had vanished, thereby severing any private communication she might have with the outside world.

Or so whoever took it undoubtedly thought.

Taking the phone was an action that earlier would have served as a harsh reminder of the warnings of her father and Giacomo Gela and raised an anxiety level that could easily have run away with her because of the monks, the extreme isolation of the church, and the fact that she had been drugged for her hallucinatory journey to it.

Instead, discovery of the missing phone strengthened her resolve and sharpened her senses, prompting her to remember that she was very nearly to the end of a desperately long and almost impossible journey. One that she had dedicated her life to and one she had so privately vowed to her mother she would complete whatever the cost. Fear or the threat of violence would not cripple her. Not here, not now.

Moreover, she'd not been wholly reckless or her plans without forethought. Beneath the man-tailored shirt she wore under her blazer and just above her waist was a specially tailored belt that for all intents resembled some kind of delicate undergarment but was, in fact, a lightweight nylon carrier for a smart phone; a combination phone/camera with broadband access and special software that made it possible to use it in wireless conjunction with the her Canon digital to instantly upload photographic images to her Web site in Paris. She had done it successfully across Europe and in the U.S., and most recently in Malta and Barcelona. Her main concern here had been connectivity, not just because of the isolated mountain location but because she was inside the church itself. But that worry had disappeared the moment she'd seen Beck talking on his cell phone in the church nave. It answered her question about connectivity and meant whatever she photographed could be transferred to Paris in a millisecond.

As a test, she took a photograph of her room, sent it to her Web site, then took out the smart phone and dialed her number. It took a moment to connect. When it did, she brought up what she had just photographed: the photo of the room she now stood in. The system worked perfectly.

She was about to take a second photo as a system confirmation when there was a sharp knock at the door.

"Yes," she said, startled.

"It's Cristina."

"Just a moment," quickly she slid the phone back into its holder under her shirt, then went to the door and opened it.

"Are you rested?" Cristina smiled gently.

"Yes, thank you. Please come in."

Cristina still had on the long white dress she had been wearing when Demi arrived. She carried a similar dress over her arm, the only difference was the color, not white but deep scarlet. She handed it to Demi.

"This is for you, to wear tonight."

"Tonight?"

"Yes."

"What is to happen tonight?"

"The beginning of forever."

"I don't understand."

"You will. . . ." Cristina stared at her in silence and then turned for the door, "I will return for you in an hour."

"Before you go—"

"Yes?" Cristina turned back.

"May I take your picture?"

"Now?"

"Yes."

"Alright."

Demi went to the bed and picked both cameras from it. Three minutes later she had a complete record of Cristina, in her white dress and with the background of Demi's room. Half of it shot with the Nikon on 35mm film, the other half with the Canon digital, the images recorded on its memory card and at the same time trans-mitted to her Web site in Paris.

"Is that all?" Cristina smiled her warm gentle smile.

"Yes. Okay."

There was a pause, and once more Cristina stared at Demi, her look deep and penetrating, as if she were studying her for some very personal reason. Then abruptly her gaze shifted. "See you in an hour," she said easily, and then was gone.

Demi closed the door after her and then stood motionless against it, a ghostly chill creeping through her. Only once in her life had she seen the look that had been in Cristina's eyes those few seconds before.

Only once.

And that had been in the lone photograph taken of her mother just days before she disappeared; her eyes, like Cristina's brown and intense but at the same time calm and very peaceful. Cristina was twenty-three. The same age her mother had been when she vanished.

107

6:18 P.M.

Marten and the president moved forward in the pitch black of the tunnel as if they were blind, following the old ore-car rails by the touch of their feet, the same way they had for nearly an hour and a half.

They walked close together, single file, the one behind still gripping the belt of the man in front of him. Four times they had stumbled over something and nearly fallen. The man behind doing his job by tugging on the front man's belt, keeping them both on their feet. Once they'd both fallen together. That time Marten had been in back, and the president, thinking he saw a gaping hole before them, suddenly twisted away, sending Marten crashing down on top of him and forcing out a loud grunt as he fell hard over one of the ore-car rails. After that they began shifting off more often so the front man didn't bear the brunt of the unknown for too long and begin to think he was seeing things when he wasn't or fear that the man behind would suddenly stumble and knock them both to the ground instead of concentrating on where he was going.

Once again they shifted, this time with Marten taking the lead. In the past hour the president had said little or nothing and Marten began to worry that he had been hurt in the fall.

"You okay?" he asked.

"Fine. You?"

"So far."

"Good, let's keep going."

And that was as far as the conversation went. It was then Marten realized the president was not hurt but thinking, and probably had been for a long time.

Another five minutes and they switched places. Another six and they switched again. Their dialogue the same each time. Okay? Yes. Good. Keep going.

"Today is still Saturday," the president said suddenly, his voice hoarse from the dust and dryness. "Other than the day my wife died, this has been the longest of my life."

Marten didn't know how to reply and so said nothing. A full thirty seconds passed and then the president spoke again.

"I think it is safe to say that by now my 'friends' or their representatives will have found Foxx's body and realized the explosion was a fail-safe aspect built into Foxx's master plan to keep anyone from discovering what was practiced in that lab.

"If they knew I was with him—which we have already assumed—by not finding me they will presume I am somewhere in the shaft, either dead or hopelessly trapped inside it. It means that soon, if not already, the vice president will take charge and authorize the Warsaw killings.

"Once those murders take place the next part of their plan will be put into action. French and German elections will be called for very quickly. Their people, the people they want in power, however they have arranged it—and they have arranged it, because they told me so and I believe them—will be elected, thereby guaranteeing full support from both countries in the United Nations. After that it is only a matter of time, maybe even days, before the genocide against the Muslim states begins.

"On the beach this morning I told you about the annual gathering of members of the New World Institute that is taking place right now at the Aragon resort in the mountains not far from here. I also told you the original plan was for me to be the surprise guest speaker there at Sunday's—tomorrow's—sunrise service, and that that was my destination when I left Madrid. My full intention was to address them as scheduled and tell them the truth about what has happened and warn them about what is yet to happen. I still have that intention, Mr. Marten."

Marten said nothing, just kept walking, his right foot touching the edge of the right-hand rail, leading the way, keeping them on track.

"Achieving that goal is not impossible, Mr. Marten. I've flown over these mountains before. I know where the resort is and in relation to Montserrat. I used to fly crop dusters in California. I know what things look like from the air. Unless we got completely turned around when we entered these tunnels, and I don't think we did, we've been pretty much going in a straight line away from the monastery and toward the resort."

"How far might the resort be, the way the crow flies?" Marten asked.

"Fifteen, eighteen miles. Twenty at most."

"How far do you think we've come in here?"

"Four, maybe five."

"Mr. President, Cousin," Marten suddenly stopped and turned to face him. "Good intentions aside, we have no map, no way to know where these tunnels lead. They could curve without us being aware of it and suddenly we're going in a whole different direction. Or maybe we're not going in the direction you think we are and are on some spur line going north, south, east, or west. Even if we are on track there is no way to know if there are rockfalls ahead blocking the shaft in any number of places. And even if it does run straight and clear we have no idea how much farther it goes. It could end in a half mile or twenty. And the resort could still be another forty miles overland after that. And that's assuming there's a way out at the end. If these tunnels are as old as they seem, with the rails as rusted as they are, they will have long ago been sealed off to keep the public out."

"What are you trying to tell me?"

"What neither of us want to hear, let alone think. That hopeful as you are to address those people, the reality is we may never get out of here. All along I've been trying to find an air current that would suggest an opening. A crack, a crevice, anything we could try to break open or squeeze through to the outside. We've passed several but none large enough or with air current strong enough to make me think it was worth using up what energy we still have.

"If we reach the far end of this shaft without finding something more promising, we will have to come back and look for a side tunnel we might have missed in the dark, if there are any. After that if we still haven't found something, I don't know. I'm sorry to rip up your hopes, Mr. President, but at this stage there's not a damn thing you can do about those people you want to address or the killings at Warsaw or the genocide itself. Right now the only lives that matter are ours, and if we don't find a way out there's a very real chance we'll die in here. With water I give us maybe ten days, two weeks at best."

"Light a match," the president said abruptly.

"What?"

"I said light a match."

"Mr. President, Cousin—we're going to need every match we have left."

"Light it."

"Yes, sir," Marten reached down and fished the matchbox from his pocket, then took out a match and struck it.

The flame lit the president's face like a torch. His eyes were frozen on Marten's.

"It is not yet seven o'clock Saturday night. Sunrise tomorrow is a long way off. There is still time to get to Aragon and address the gathering there. Still time to stop the murders at Warsaw. Still time to stop the genocide in the Middle East. This president will not die in here, Cousin. He cannot and he will not. Far too much is at stake."

In the flickering light Marten saw a man racked with exhaustion; clothes torn, face and hands ripped and bloodied and scraped raw, every pore, every strand of hair, from beard to head, coated with dust and dirt and grime. A man who might well have been beaten but who wasn't.

If he wasn't, neither was Marten. "You will not die here, Mr. President," he said, his own voice as hoarse as the president's. "Somehow we will find a way out. Somehow you *will* address those people."

The president's eyes held on Marten's, "I won't let you get by with just that."

"What do you mean?"

"I want your promise. Your word."

The flame on the match dwindled to nothing. What seconds before had been a staggeringly noble idea, an impossible dream, or just a plain crazy hope Marten had bought into, the president had suddenly turned into a deeply personal pact. Raising the level of the game so that the task before them became more than a commitment of mind and body, it became one of the soul.

"You are a stubborn bastard," Marten whispered.

"Give me your word."

Marten hesitated and the match burned out and once more the dark invaded everything.

"You have it," he whispered finally, "you have my word."

108

EL BORRÀS, 6:55 P.M

Hap Daniels gritted his teeth as the motorcycle bounced down a narrow dirt path and Miguel followed two other motorcycles toward the Llobregat River. Of the three machines only Miguel's had a sidecar. The others were straightforward Hondas. The first was ridden by Miguel's nephew, Amado. The other carried José and Hector, two of Amado's friends. None was older than eighteen, but they had lived in El Borràs all their lives and knew the mountainous territory, with its air shafts, natural chimneys, and entryways to the caves and old tunnels, and the tunnels themselves, inside out. Hap hadn't liked the idea of the others coming along, but Miguel had assured him each young man was completely trustworthy and would say nothing of what they were doing or whom they were looking for even if they were stopped.

"Believe me," Miguel told him, "even if we are lucky enough to reach the president, they won't recognize him—you might not either. To the boys he will be a missing American friend who was exploring the caves and got trapped inside the mountain when the big rockslide or earthquake or whatever it was hit."

The three machines slowed, then stopped as they reached the river. The Llobregat here was probably fifty yards wide, muddy and fast-flowing from the runoff of winter rains. Miguel looked at Hap in the sidecar.

"There's a gravel buildup beneath the water. It looks deep but isn't. Still, anything could happen."

"Cross it," Hap said without expression.

Miguel signaled Amado, and the first two motorcycles started across, Amado first, then Hector driving the second machine. Partway across Hector nearly lost it in the rush of water. Then he gained control, gunned the engine, and made it across, stopping to wait with Amado. A half second later Miguel twisted the throttle, the motorcycle inched forward and entered the water and started across. The rush of swift water threatened to sweep them away but Hap's weight in the side car steadied it and with a bounce and roar of the engine they crossed to the others. Again Miguel signaled Amado, and the young man led off, taking them up a steep gravel trail.

Rough as it was on Hap, the motorcycle had been the thing to use. They were going up into the foothills and then to mountain trails beyond. A car was useless and walking would take far too long. Moreover, Hap hardly had the stamina to walk very far anyway.

7:10 P.M.

The sun dipped over the mountain ridges just above them, putting the dirt trail they climbed into full shadow. Hap was leaning forward, trying to find some way to ease the pain in his wounded shoulder as the motorcycle bounced mercilessly over the rough terrain, when his BlackBerry sounded. He took it from his jacket and looked at the source of the call. When he saw it was Bill Strait, he clicked off, then turned off the ringer. In that instant he thought of the encrypted text message Strait had sent him at 4:10 P.M.

Hap. Trying for hours to reach you. Where the hell are you? Chief of Staff reports at 4:08 P.M. from Madrid that "Crop Duster" was not, repeat NOT, at the monastery at Montserrat. CIA Ops took brief hostile fire from unknowns at monastery office of a Dr. Merriman Foxx. Our mission to Montserrat aborted mid-flight. Returned to base at Barcelona. CNP (Spanish police) and Spanish Intel investigating hostile fire. WHERE THE HELL ARE YOU? ARE YOU OKAY?

Hap glanced at Miguel as he guided the motorcycle up a narrow rain-rutted trail in the increasing darkness. Until a few hours ago he had never seen this man in his life. Now he was trusting him and three young Spaniards with his life and that of the president, if he was still alive. It was something he should have been able to call Bill Strait for; order him to fly a full contingent of Secret Service, CIA, Spanish Intel, and Spanish police out here on the double to scour the hills and mountaintops looking for any passageway that would give them access to the areas below where Miguel believed the president and Nicholas Marten might be, and at the same time demand a demolition crew be sent to blast through the rock from inside Foxx's office complex.

There was, and always had been, an iron bond between Secret Service agents, trust beyond measure. That was until now, until all this had happened, and where he, like the president, had no idea how far this thing went or who in God's name he could trust. So as much as he wanted to, as much as he should have been able to do so under any circumstances, Bill Strait wasn't contacted, his message not replied to.

"Damn," Hap swore bitterly to himself. How he hated mistrust, especially when it was his own and he didn't know who or what to believe.

"Hap," Miguel said suddenly.

"What is it?"

"There," Miguel pointed at the sunlit crest of the mountains four or five miles in the distance.

At first Hap saw nothing, then he did. Four helicopters were coming in over the top of the ridge and then dropping down into the shadow on this side of the mountain.

"Who are they?"

"Not sure. Probably CNP, the federal police. Maybe Mossos d'Esquadra. Maybe both."

"Coming this way?"

"Hard to tell."

"Miguel!" Amado shouted and was pointing behind them.

Both men turned to see five more helicopters. They were still in the distance but coming toward them fast at just above ground level.

Hap looked to Miguel, "Get us out of sight! Amado, the other guys too!"

109

7:17 P.M.

Miguel signaled Amado and the others to follow, then gunned the engine and the motorcycle literally flew up the face of the steep rocky embankment. The machine roared and bucked and spit, kicking out loose stones for what seemed an eternity and then they reached the top and the terrain leveled off. Miguel drove another twenty yards, then saw the sharp, cavelike overhang of an enormous sandstone formation and pulled in. Seconds later the others joined them.

"Cut your engines," Miguel said in Spanish.

They did, holding their breath and looking back, waiting in silence. All they saw was the darkening rocky terrain of the high sprawling mesa where they were. For a full minute nothing happened, and they thought maybe the helicopters had flown off in another direction. Then suddenly and with a thundering, ground shaking roar they appeared. All five of them. Coming over the ridgeline toward them. In seconds they passed overhead, not twenty feet above the overhang where they were hidden.

The first four were Spanish CNP, the fifth, Hap knew only too well. The big U.S. Army Chinook they'd flown in from Madrid to Barcelona. It meant the Secret Service was here and that the detail would be under the command of Bill Strait.

Immediately he dug out his BlackBerry and switched it on hoping Strait had left a second text message that would give him information he did not have. The text was there: What he saw was not what he was hoping for but not wholly unexpected either.

> Hap, tried to reach you again! We've been advised by U.S. Madrid that 'Crop Duster' may have been at the monastery after all and is possibly trapped inside old mining tunnels by landslide. CNP units, CIA and USSS on route now.
> More.
> Informed it was you who exchanged hostile fire with ops at Montserrat and that you may have been hit. Where the hell are you? Please confirm location and condition.
> More.
> Ops were not CIA. U.S. Madrid was misinformed. Ops were S.A. Special Forces commandos under covert orders to repatriate Dr. Foxx to South Africa.
> S.A. government has apologized to State Department and to U.S. Madrid.
> More.
> A lot of this doesn't make sense. As you know USSS info on 'Crop Duster's' probable presence at Montserrat and CIA ops mission to retrieve him came from White House Chief of Staff at U.S. Embassy Madrid. How could COS and CIA station chief confuse CIA ops with S.A. Special Forces unit? Also how could original 'Crop Duster' mission have become one to repatriate the S.A. doctor and then to finding 'Crop Duster' at same site? Was he in the tunnels all the time then got caught in the landslide and nobody knew it? Is this something at executive level we don't know about? Maybe some kind of meeting between 'Crop Duster' and the S.A. doctor? Have attempted to make contact with USSS assistant director Langway reported still in Madrid. So far unsuccessful.
> More.

If you are able, you are directed to contact Jake Lowe or National Security Adviser Marshall immediately for debriefing. Maybe they'll tell you what's up.

This is a direct order from VPOTUS. Please acknowledge.

More.

Very concerned personally. Where the hell are you? Have you taken fire? Do you need help? Dammit, Hap, please acknowledge or have someone do it for you!

Bill Strait's confusion about the info from COS U.S. Madrid was wholly understandable. That was if any of it was true, which was highly unlikely. The ops he'd exchanged fire with at the monastery were sure as hell not South African commandos; they were as American as Kansas. They knew the president was there and it was he they had come to get. The Foxx thing had to have been a sidebar, part of something else.

As for Bill Strait, it was impossible to tell if he was caught in the middle and just trying to do his job or if he was on their side and involved with it. Did he want to find Hap as badly as he did because he was a Secret Service brother he genuinely cared about or because Hap was trouble and they wanted to make sure he was out of the picture?

Hap grimaced at the thought, then put the BlackBerry away and looked to others grouped under the overhang and now bathed in a harsh shaft of golden light as the setting sun found an opening between distant mountain peaks.

"Ask Amado how far it is to the first chimney or tunnel opening," he said to Miguel, "and if we can get there on foot without being seen."

Miguel turned to his nephew and spoke Spanish, then turned back. "It's only one air shaft of many, and we have to start somewhere. They chose this one because they think that this is about how far they might have come inside the tunnel since the landslide."

"Where is it?"

"About a half mile. We can go the minute the sun sets."

Hap stared at Miguel, then motioned him closer. "If the president and Marten are in there," he said, trying not to have Amado and his friends overhear, especially if they understood English, "we have to find them and get them out before the Spanish police do."

"I know."

"What you don't know is that there are CIA and U.S. Secret Service agents with them. Most, if not all, both Spanish and American, think they are on our side. That their mission is to rescue the president and bring him to safety."

"You mean they might try to kill us."

"No, I mean they *will* kill anyone who gets in the way. We're talking about the president of the United States. You saw those helicopters. There will be more, a lot more. We're up against an army of people who think they're doing the right thing."

"One man, a thousand. To me that is my family in there. It is the same with you. Yes?"

Hap took a breath. "Yes," he said finally. Standing up against covert ops was one thing, but having to exchange fire with a legion of innocently involved Spanish police, CIA, and his own Secret Service agents, some of whom might be covert themselves, was something else. Still, they had no choice. "What about the boys?" he said.

"I will take care of the boys."

"You have the first-aid kit from the limo?"

"Yes."

"Take out the survival blankets. You take three and give me four."

"Alright," Miguel nodded, then watched Hap a half second longer. "How is your shoulder?"

"It hurts like hell."

"The pain pills."

"This is no time or place to be drugged up."

"Any more bleeding?"

"Not that I know. Your doctor did a good job."

"Can you walk?"

"Yes, I can walk, dammit!"

"Then let's go," Miguel stood abruptly and went to the motorcycle. He snapped open its storage compartment and took seven of the small folded, Mylar-coated survival blankets from the first-aid kit and a half dozen health bars. Next came a water-filled camel-pack, two large flashlights, and the Steyr machine pistol. He gave four of the survival blankets and half the health bars to Hap, handed him a flashlight and stuck the other in his belt, then slipped the camel pack over his shoulders and slung the machine pistol across his chest. As he did, the shaft of sunlight abruptly dimmed to the deep purple of twilight as the sun passed behind the mountain peaks. Immediately he signaled to the others. A half beat later the five started off across the rock and scrub mesa.

110

7:32 P.M.

Twice Marten and the president had picked their way over and through enormous piles of dirt and rock, the result of underground landslides. It would have been difficult under any circumstances, but in the pitch black it had been impossible to know how far the slide reached and if what they were doing was nothing more than removing stones from a mountain, all the while eating up precious time. Still, they'd done it, then broken through and kept on.

Somehow we will find a way out. Somehow you will address those people.

Marten's emotional promise to the president had concentrated their efforts on a search for an air current that would lead them to a passage large enough to squeeze through, break through, or climb out of. To do that they needed an open flame that would burn far longer than a match, and to that end Marten dedicated his cotton undershirt, rolled up tight, with one end torn loose and hanging down to serve as a wick. It took two of the precious few matches left to get it going. When it did it burned long enough to get them several hundred yards farther down the tunnel, where they stumbled on a pile of long-abandoned tools. Most were rusted through or rotted away, but among them they found three they could use.

One was a sledgehammer with its handle still secured to its head. The other two were picks, or rather a pick and a pick handle that held angled down served as a kind of torch and replaced Marten's undershirt, which had burned to little more than a rag and had to be abandoned. The pick handle's light was merely a glow compared to the burning shirt but in the unbearable darkness it enabled them to illuminate the tunnel a good fifteen feet in front of them.

By now they no longer walked single file but side by side in the center of the rails with Marten carrying the pick and sledgehammer, President Harris the torch. Both were hungry and nearing exhaustion but those were words never mentioned. Instead their focus was on the torch, with each man silent, waiting, praying, for the flare up that would indicate an air current.

"I have no proof," the president said suddenly. "None at all."

"Of what?"

"Of anything," he looked to Marten, his expression grave. It became all the more so as he put his thoughts into words. "As you know, the original plan was for me to take the information we got from Foxx and call the secretaries general of the United Nations and NATO and the editors-in-chief of the *Washington Post* and *New York Times* and tell them all the truth. Instead we find ourselves trying to find a way out of these godforsaken tunnels so that I can address the congregation at Aragon. But why? To tell them what? That there is a massive conspiracy under way and that Dr. Foxx had full knowledge of its particulars?

"What good is that? Foxx is dead, the details for the genocide dead with him. His secret lab and everything in it we can assume is wholly destroyed because he planned it that way. We can say what we saw, but it's not there. My 'friends' will say I am 'ill,' that I have suffered a breakdown. That fleeing from my hotel room in Madrid in the manner I did and then running away and hiding are confirmation of it.

"You can stand up for me but it will do no good. President or not, it simply becomes my word against all of theirs. If I accuse them of planning the Warsaw assassinations they will smile compassionately as if that is proof of my illness and then simply postpone them. If I accuse them of plotting genocide against the Muslim States, I become even crazier, a ranting fool." In the dim flickering light, Marten saw the president's eyes fixed on his, and they were filled with utter despair. "I have no proof, Mr. Marten, of anything."

"No, you don't," Marten said forcefully, "but you can't forget the bodies, the body parts, the faces of those people floating in the tanks."

"Forget them? Their images are branded into me as if they were molten steel. But without some kind of proof . . . they never existed."

"But they did exist."

The president looked back to the torch and walked on in silence, his shoulders hunched forward, almost as if he had given up. For the first time Marten realized that while it was personal courage and sheer determination that had brought him this far, the president was not the kind of man who was most comfortable alone and in his own company. He wanted others around him. He wanted the give-and-take of it, even to the point of disagreement. Perhaps to help him clarify his own thoughts or get another perspective on things, or to find some level of inspiration he had either lost or never had.

"Mr. President," Marten said firmly, "you must address the convention at Aragon. Speak of the Warsaw assassinations. Tell them what has happened. Tell them how and where and when and by whom the idea and then the ultimatum was presented to you. Do that and what you said will be correct. Your 'friends' will have no choice but to call off the killings, at least for now. If they don't they will prove you were right. In the meantime antennas will go up everywhere. You are still the president of the United States. The public will listen. The media will listen. You can order an investigation into everything Foxx was involved with, the same way you can order an investigation of your 'friends.' Yes, you will be putting yourself on the spot, but no more than you already have. Just the act of making it all public, whatever the reaction, will slow, maybe even stop, what they are planning to do.

"No, you don't have the evidence you would like, but it's *something*. You don't always need the deed to be done to kill its intent. If nothing else, you will have saved the lives of the president of France and the chancellor of Germany."

The president looked over as they walked. In the faint light of the torch Marten could see the extreme weariness in him. The burden that was his, the toll it had taken, was taking still. He wished there were some way to ease it. He wished to hell that they could just sit down for a steak and a beer or a dozen beers and talk about baseball or the weather and forget everything else.

"Would you like to stop and rest for a few minutes?" he asked quietly.

For the briefest moment there was no response. Then, almost as if he had shifted into some other gear, the president's eyes sharpened, his shoulders came back, and he stood upright once again.

"No, Mr. Marten, we'll keep going."

111

7:40 P.M.

Bill Strait watched the darkening landscape below as they circled the area one last time and then came in across the flat of a rocky mesa. Seconds later the big Chinook helicopter touched down in a storm of flying dust and dry vegetation and the pilot cut the engines. Strait glanced across at Jake Lowe and National Security Adviser James Marshall, then unbuckled his harness and was the first out the door as the crewman pulled it open. Lowe, Marshall, and then seventeen Secret Service agents followed. Lowe and Marshall were dressed in hastily put together wardrobes of khaki pants, hiking shoes, and ski parkas. The agents, like Bill Strait, were armed, and wore jeans, windbreakers, and hiking boots. All carried night-vision goggles.

"This way," Strait said, then ducked under the still-churning rotors and walked rapidly toward a Spanish CNP helicopter that had touched down on a rocky shelf fifty yards away and where CNP captain Belinda Diaz waited with her twenty-man team.

Strait, in the absence of Hap Daniels, had become the SAIC, the special agent in charge of the entire mission. The situation— as the USSS, the CIA, and the CNP understood—was that the president was assumed to be somewhere in the tunnels, trapped there after what was officially being called "an earth movement." Although he was thought to be in the company of a man named Nicholas Marten it was necessarily assumed there could be others and that the president was now, and had been all along, a victim of foul play and therefore in grave danger. The mission, therefore, was a "live rescue" and was to be treated that way until they knew otherwise.

In all, nine helicopters had come in to land at exterior coordinates of a circular ten-mile perimeter. Aside from the Chinook, the other eight helos were CNP. Five carried twenty-man squads of heavily armed CNP mountain-trained police. The remaining three had eighteen-man CIA teams. All nine carried a two-man sound unit, audio experts equipped with hi-tech listening devices. In addition three more eighteen-man CIA teams were on route from Madrid and one hundred Secret Service agents were coming in from the USSS controlling field office in Paris to land at Costa Brava Airport in Gerona to then be ferried to the site here by CNP helicopters. ETA here for the CIA/Madrid teams was 8:20 P.M. For the USSS/Paris, 9:30 P.M.

7:44 P.M.

Captain Diaz glanced at Lowe and Marshall, then looked to Bill Strait. "We are here," she said in English, her right index finger touching a terrain map open on the ground as a radio clipped to her belt crackled in Spanish with the give-and-take of CNP communication between other units. Diaz was probably thirty-five, attractive, confident and very fit, and, like all the CNP, heavily armed and dressed in a camouflage jumpsuit.

"We are looking at a large mountainous area covering approximately one hundred square miles." Diaz put the terrain map aside and opened another. It was a copy of a 1922 ore company map showing the location of its shafts. Diaz pointed to it.

"These lines represent the tunnels in use at the time the mine was closed. As you can see, the main shafts run here, here, here, and here. The largest tunnel coming from the direction of the monastery would be this one," she indicated a line drawn in red, "and the one a person or group coming from there most likely would follow if they were trying to get out. That is, as far as we can tell. These tunnels, these shafts, are very old, not used for more than eighty years. Sections of many will have collapsed. It means the map is helpful but not reliable."

"Suppose they did take this tunnel," Strait said. "Two of them or twenty," Strait indicated the main shaft, "and using the 3:37 time of the earth movement as a starting time, how far would they be along it by now?"

"It would depend on the state of the president's health. If they have to carry him. Or stop to give him medical attention. Or if they have lights. As you might imagine, the shafts are dark as a tomb. Also if they chose this tunnel and not one of the several dozen others down there."

"Might they have gone another way?"

"We are not with them. They could have done anything for any reason. This main tunnel could have been blocked and so they took some other. We have come to this location because it is the most direct and therefore the most likely route out if it has not been blocked by cave-ins. We are on the outermost edge of it and will make our way toward the monastery while other teams will work from there toward us while others still will explore the side tunnels. We—" Diaz stopped suddenly to listen to a radio communication directed at her.

"Sí, sí," she said finally into the tiny microphone on her lapel. "Gracias." Again she glanced at Lowe and Marshall, then turned to Bill Strait.

"Drilling equipment is being flown in now. Soon they will begin to bore into the tunnels from above and then send down night-vision cameras equipped with listening devices."

"Good," Strait said, then turned back to the map, "assume they are in this tunnel. How close are we to an exterior entryway, a chimney where we can get in?"

"Very difficult to answer. The chimneys are not mapped. We have to find them and have asked help from the Agentes Rurales, the mountain and forest patrol, who know the area. But even if we find chimneys or access points there is no way to know how big they are. If someone can get down and into the shaft or if they

THE MACHIAVELLI COVENANT • 377

would have to be cut or drilled or blasted. Something else," Captain Diaz shifted her gaze to take in Marshall and Jake Lowe, "something you must understand, gentlemen. It is quite possible that those inside, if in fact they are down there, are dead, your president included."

"That's why we're here, Captain," Lowe said quietly. "One way or the other, we're going to bring him out."

112

PARIS, GARE DU NORD, 8:10 P.M.

"Thank you," Victor smiled and pocketed his first-class ticket, then turned from the passenger services window and walked back toward the platform area. Train 243 for Berlin was to leave at 8:46 but would not arrive in the station until 8:34. That gave him a little more than thirty minutes to kill. The last ten would be spent on the train making sure he had his assigned seat and that his suitcase was stored. Taking one's seat early was important because even with a reservation people often sat where they wanted. If one's assigned seat was already taken trying to get it back usually involved some level of confrontation that was often in a foreign language. He had seen more than one of these become heated, and an argument over a seat that might bring a trainman or the police was the last thing he needed; especially the police, who might ask to see his passport and want to know where he was going and where he had been. But at the moment there was no train and therefore no seat, which meant he still had nearly twenty minutes to either sit and wait or wander around the station, neither of which he liked because it left him at the mercy of the public. The major story of the day, at least in the Paris tabloids, seemed to be the single-shot murder of the two jockeys early that morning in Chantilly. And newspapers at kiosks throughout the station had it as their lead.

L'OMS A TUÉ LES JOCKEYS?
DEUX AVEC UN PROJECTILE!
MUERTRE DANS LES BOIS DE CHANTILLY!

(Who killed the jockeys?
Two with one shot!
Murder in the Chantilly woods!)

Chantilly was twenty minutes by train from Paris, and Gare du Nord, where he was now, was the same station he had arrived in when he'd come from Chantilly. How did he know that someone there, someone he might simply pass by, hadn't seen him in both places; a railroad worker maybe or a commuter he had shared the morning train with who was returning home and might suddenly remember him?

Victor kept his head down as he walked. When he had killed the man in the New York Yankees jacket in Washington, Richard had been right there to meet him and get him out of there, driving him straight to the airport and putting him on a plane before the story was even reported. Here it was different, here he was alone and at the mercy of the faces in the crowd and he didn't like it. All he wanted was for the train to come so that he could board it and claim his seat and at least get that much out of sight.

He carried his bag into a small restaurant across from the tracks. There was room at the counter and he sat down. "Coffee," he said to the counterman, "black, please."

"Café noir?"

Victor nodded. "Café noir."

113

Demi walked alongside the line of sixty monks, photographing them as they left the candlelit caverns and entered the church, walking single file, heads bowed, chanting as they went. She used the Canon digital first and then switched to the 35mm Nikon, then back to the Canon, the smart phone concealed beneath the long scarlet dress Cristina had brought her, secretly transmitting the Canon's images to her Web site in Paris.

The monks' collective song echoed off the temple's stone surfaces like a delicate prayer, its single melodic line rising and then slowly falling only to rise once more. At first Demi thought the chant, like the family names on the great stones above the burial vaults on the church floor, was in Italian but it wasn't. Nor was it Spanish, instead it was sung in a language she had never before heard.

The monks circled the church once and then again and then left, passing through a high portal to an ancient stone amphitheater outside. There the verse was repeated twice more and then twice again as they formed a semi-circle in the light of three bonfires that burned in a triangle on the outside edges of a massive circular stone. A stone that was the amphitheatre's centerpiece and had carved at its midpoint the balled cross of Aldebaran.

Demi moved guardedly to a place across from the bonfires, near the amphitheater's seating area where there were easily two hundred spectators—men, women, children—the very old to infants held in their mother's arms. All were dressed in the same long scarlet gown Demi wore.

Beyond the bonfires she could see the valley she had passed through on the way there and where the thin ground fog of earlier in the day had now grown heavy, rising up like sea mist and begin-

ning to swirl in around them. Above everything rose the high
mountain peaks, which served to isolate the church and over which
a full moon slowly ascended above darkening clouds.

Suddenly the monks' chant stopped and for a long moment
there was silence. Then a powerful male voice rose from the dark
behind them. Deep and melodic, it sounded as if it were some kind
of pagan calling, a brief prayer to the spirits spoken in the same language as the monks.

Immediately the spectators responded as if a chorus, repeating
in unison whatever had been said.

The voice came as before, carrying out from the darkness. Then
a hooded, black-robed figure stepped into the light of the bonfires
and moved to the center of the stone circle. Instantly the figure
raised its arms and threw back its head. Demi felt the breath go out
of her. It was Reverend Beck, the first time she'd seen him since
they'd arrived. Immediately she stepped away from the congregation and into the shadows. Cameras up, she began photographing
deliberately: Beck, the congregation, the monks, using one camera
and then the other as she had before.

Head thrown back, arms held high above his head, Beck thundered a command to the heavens as if he were reaching to the
moon and beyond to call spirits forth from the night. Immediately
he turned to the darkness between the bonfires. Again he raised his
arms and spoke the same command he had just thrown toward the
sky. For a long moment nothing happened and then a vision in
white slowly appeared from the dark, moving past the bonfires into
the circle.

Cristina.

Beck turned toward the congregation and spoke again, his right
arm extended, making a sweep of the stone's great circle. The congregation responded. Repeating what he had said and then adding
words that Demi could describe only as sounding like the names of
distant stars. There were four in all, spoken quickly and in staccato
as if they were calling forth Gods.

Cameras firing, Demi inched closer.

Now Beck stepped out of the firelight. In his place, so quickly
it almost seemed like a magical trick, Luciana appeared. Her robe
was bright gold and in her hand she carried a long, ruby wand. Her

rich black hair was pulled back in a tight bun. Equally dark eye makeup was accentuated by theatrical streaks that ran dagger-like from the corners of her eyes to the hollows of her ears, while hideously long nails, eleven inches easily, were fixed to the tips of her fingers.

In a move as graceful as a ballerina's, she stepped behind Cristina and drew a circle in the air above her head with the wand. Then, with the same suppleness, she stepped away to pass the wand around the great circle of stone. Done, she looked to the congregation. Her bearing and manner that of the high priestess, the *sacerdotessa*, she was. Abruptly she called out a phrase filled with power and certainty, as if she had just cast a spell. Then she stepped forward to the circle's edge, her eyes moving fiercely across the congregation and called out the certainty once more.

And then again.

And then again.

114

8:47 P.M.

"Listen!" Marten said and stopped, the axe-handle torch burned short and was now little more than a flicker in the pitch black of the tunnel.

"What is it?" The president stopped too.

"Don't know. Sounded like it came from behind us."

They listened intently, but there was nothing.

"Maybe I'm crazy—" Marten said at the silence, then: "There. Hear it?"

From somewhere behind them came a distant high-pitched screeching. It went on for maybe twenty seconds, stopped, then started again.

"Drilling," the president said quickly, "through stone. I've cut enough wells to know the sound."

"Your 'rescuers' have arrived. They know we're here."

"No, they *think* we're here. But they're still behind us. A mile, more if we're lucky," instantly the president's eyes found Marten's. "Once they cut into the tunnel they'll drop in listening equipment, maybe night-vision cameras. Sound carries through these shafts almost as sharply as it would under water."

"How many do you think there are?"

"Up there, coming after us?"

"Yes."

"Too many. From here on not a word above a whisper. And whatever that word is, make it damn short."

Marten stared at him for the briefest moment, then turned the torch forward and they moved on.

8:50 P.M.

The expanse of rock they were crossing was black as midnight. Miguel stopped and swung his flashlight behind him, lighting the way for a lagging Hap Daniels to catch up.

"Careful with that damn light, you can see it for miles," Hap rasped as he came forward. By now he was cradling his left arm in a sling fashioned from his necktie to help ease the strain on his shoulder.

Behind them a full moon struggled through thickening clouds descending over the distant mountaintops. Rain was coming and they knew it. When it would arrive, how heavy it would be, and how much time they had before it reached them were unanswerable questions.

"You sure you want to keep on?" Miguel was watching Hap as he moved close. It was obvious he was struggling and in pain.

"Yes, dammit."

"You want to rest for a minute? Take the pain pills?"

"Where the hell are the guys?"

"Here!" Amado's voice popped from the dark a dozen yards in front of them. Instantly Miguel swung his flashlight toward a rocky precipice twenty feet away.

"Jesus God!" Hap grabbed Miguel's arm with his good hand, "turn that thing out!"

8:52 P.M.

Hap and Miguel peered into a fissure in the rocks below. Ten feet down Hector and José huddled around a large fracture in the stone, their flashlights illuminating the way for Amado as he climbed down into it. A second later he disappeared from sight. Immediately José followed.

"How far does it go?" Miguel said just loud enough to be heard.

"Maybe thirty feet more," Amado answered from below.

"To what?"

"Another break in the rock."

"When you reach it use the stones. See what you get."

Miguel took a breath and looked at Hap. Then they waited.

Three full minutes passed. Finally they heard it.

CLACK, CLACK. CLACK, CLACK. CLACK, CLACK.

Amado was hitting two stones together in the shaft below, making a sound that would carry a great distance through the rock openings and hopefully into the hard surface of the tunnel underneath.

CLACK, CLACK. CLACK, CLACK. CLACK, CLACK.

Amado tapped the stones again.

All five held a collective breath listening for a return signal.

Finally they heard Amado's voice, "Nothing."

"Again!" Miguel demanded.

"No! No more!" Hap said sharply. "That's the end of it!"

"Why?" Miguel stared at him in surprise, "How else are we going to find them in an endless tunnel?"

"Miguel, the Spanish police, the Secret Service, the CIA. They will have brought in all kinds of listening and night-vision devices. If the president and Marten can hear those rocks, they will too. They find us, we will vanish. All of us, the boys, you, me. Then the president is dead."

"So what do we do?"

"Find a way into the tunnel and walk it."

"Walk it?"

"Flashlights. Mark where we came in, mark our trail along the way so we can get back. Amado and his friends know their way inside these tunnels. That's why we're here, yes?"

Miguel nodded.

"My men don't know those shafts, and I'm betting the Spanish police don't either."

Miguel's face twisted up in anguish. "We're five against all that. It's not possible."

"Yes it is. We just have to do it better and faster and very, very quietly."

"Hap, you are in no shape to climb down in there. Stay here, I'll go with the boys."

"Can't."

"Why?"

"I don't know the exact satellite positions. But at some point soon they will be directly overhead. When they are they will provide thermal images of the heat radiated by bodies on the ground. The authorities know who their men are, where they are, and how many."

"You mean they will be able to see us."

"They'll see whoever's out here that isn't one of theirs."

"Then I think you better go down into the shafts."

"Right."

115

9:03 P.M.

Jake Lowe and Dr. James Marshall stood just outside the Chinook helicopter looking toward a rocky flat where Bill Strait's Secret Service team and Captain Diaz's CNP unit had set up work lights and were cutting their way down through the soft sandstone with power saws.

Behind them, inside the Chinook, a medical team—two doctors, two nurses and two emergency medical technicians—made preparations to receive an injured president. Thirty yards away Bill Strait, Captain Diaz and a seven-man team of Secret Service, CIA, and CNP tech specialists worked to set up a command post from which they could coordinate the activity of the teams in the field.

Lowe glanced behind them to make sure they were alone, then looked at Marshall. "The Spanish police could be a real problem if the president is alive and says something," he said quietly.

"We can't very well send them home."

"No, we can't."

"Jake," Marshall stepped closer and lowered his voice, "the police believe what everyone else believes, that the president is either dead, the captive of Marten or a terrorist bunch, or simply stumbling along mentally ill. If they bring him out alive anything he says will be taken as the ramblings of a man who has undergone major psychological trauma. In minutes he'll be here and in the Chinook and then we're gone."

"It's still too damn iffy. Too much can still go wrong," Lowe looked off, clearly troubled, then abruptly turned back to Marshall. "I'm just about ready to put the brakes on Warsaw. Call it off. I mean it."

"Can't do that, Jake, and you know it," Marshall said coolly. "The vice president has given the go-ahead. Things are moving forward and everyone knows it. We pull it back now we show major weakness, not only with our people but with our friends in France and Germany. So relax, we're the ones in control. As I said before, have a little faith."

Suddenly there was a scurry of activity at the command post. Bill Strait was standing up, talking animatedly into his headset. The others had stopped to watch him, Captain Diaz included. Lowe and Marshall started toward them on the run.

"Repeat that please," Bill Strait said, his hand to his headset trying to hear clearly while still monitoring the tense communication between his own teams using other broadcast channels. "Good! Damn good!"

"What is it?" Lowe said quickly as he and Marshall came up. "Your tech guys hear something? Pick up sounds? Is it him? The POTUS?"

"Not yet, sir. A CNP team has broken into the main tunnel this side of an underground landslide near the monastery. CIA unit is going in now."

"Agent Strait," Captain Diaz pulled off her headset. "Our team

at this end," she nodded toward the lighted work area in the distance, "has just cut through. Six men are on the floor." Abruptly she
looked to Marshall and Lowe.

"The old maps gave us a tunnel length of approximately twelve
miles. That length is now proving correct, which means the maps
are reasonably accurate. A team somewhere near the halfway point
has located a chimney and is working down it. Another team is
working through a fissure toward one of the side tunnels. Drilling
units seven and four have reached soft stone three miles apart.
How long it will take them to get into the main shaft we can't know.
For the teams that are already inside and those to come afterward
everything depends on what they find there. If it's open all the way
or if rock falls or landslides block the way."

Lowe looked to Bill Strait. "How many men do we have in the
tunnels now?"

"About sixty. Another thirty or so when the other teams crack
through. That many more when the rest of Captain Diaz's team and
our ops hit the tunnel floor over there. The CIA ops from Madrid
are on the ground now and have been assigned coordinates along
the top of the main shaft. Agentes Rurales teams who know the
area are assisting them to find other ways in. Satellite coverage
for digital visual photographic and thermal imaging won't happen
for another ninety minutes until the satellite is overhead. With the
night and this weather we're not going to get much if anything from
the visual imaging, it's the thermal imaging, the heat signature coming from bodies on the ground or exiting the shafts, we will be looking to recognize."

Lowe was openly upset and raising his voice. "So basically this
whole operation is at the mercy of a few drilling machines and several hundred men with microphones, night goggles, and picks and
shovels."

"I'm afraid we're in a hot pursuit situation here, sir. You run
with what you have, lots of bodies and old-world technology."

"Where the hell are those hundred more Secret Service people
coming from Paris?"

Strait looked from Lowe to Marshall. "On Spanish soil now.
Wheels down here at new ETA 9:40. Gentlemen, every team here
is professional, CNP, CIA, USSS. If the president is down there he
will be found."

"I'm sure he will. And thank you," Marshall said, then took Lowe by the arm, and they walked off toward the Chinook.

"You're pushing it, Jake," he said firmly. "Take it easy, huh? Just take it easy."

116

THE AMPHITHEATER OF LA IGLESIA DENTRO DE LA MONTAÑA,
THE CHURCH WITHIN THE MOUNTAIN, 9:20 P.M.

Demi stood at the edge of the crowd, as unobtrusively as possible photographing the ceremony taking place in the Aldebaran circle where the sixty monks knelt at its outer edge, heads bowed, chanting in the same undecipherable language as before. Behind them the three bonfires still roared, their embers drifting up into an eerie night sky; the full moon all but lost in the clouds of an approaching storm that announced its ferocity with a spectacular lightning show over the distant valley.

Her white dress flowing around her, Cristina sat like a goddess on a simple wooden throne in the circle's center as, one by one, scarlet-gowned children came to her from the darkness beyond the bonfires; each waiting his or her turn and then slowly and reverently walking into the firelight to approach her. Each child carried something live; a dog or cat or, in the case of several of the older children, an owl, leashed and tethered to a leather arm gauntlet like a falcon, for blessing.

And bless them Cristina did, smiling compassionately and lovingly to each, then saying something unheard and kissing them on one check and then the other, and afterward passing her hand over the creature they had brought, reciting some kind of short prayer as she did. Her words, barely audible, spoken in the same language used by the monks and by Beck and Luciana. Afterward the child moved off, drifting into the darkness beyond the bonfires and the next took its place. All around the adults watched, silent and spellbound, while below, at the edge of the firelight, Luciana and the

Reverend Beck stood witness, as if divine shepherds overseeing their flock.

Demi was utterly perplexed. She wondered how the sign of Aldebaran on her mother's drawing, the Aldebaran thumb tattoos Merriman Foxx, the late Dr. Lorraine Stephenson, Cristina, Luciana, and probably Reverend Beck wore, fit with all this. Especially this simple touching children's ceremony that blessed dogs and cats and owls. What spirits had Beck been calling forth from the night? What role did Cristina play? What was the significance of any of it?

Maybe it was, as Beck had said, that the coven and its rituals were harmless and there was nothing that couldn't be shown to the world. If so why had she been drugged for her journey here? What had Foxx wanted with Nicholas Marten that involved any of this? What of her mother's disappearance? Her father's warning? Or that given her by the armless Giacomo Gela? And what had he witnessed so many years ago that caused his captors to so heinously mutilate him? Moreover what was the connection of the sign of Aldebaran to the centuries-old cult of *Aradia Minor* and its Traditions; blood oaths, sacrifices of living creatures, human torture? Where was its several-hundred-member audience, the powerful order called the *Unknowns*?

Had Gela been wrong or even crazy, a bitter armless octogenarian living alone for decades who had fabricated a secret, ancient culture upon which to blame his own condition? Demi saw no sign of any of it. Just families and children and animals. What was here to be feared?

117

9:35 P.M.

Hector and José were already on the tunnel floor, their flashlights pointed upward. Fifty feet above them Amado worked in a tight, sharply sloping chimney helping Miguel ease Hap down, his arm, by necessity, taken from its makeshift sling. The constant throbbing in his wounded shoulder eased somewhat by a pain pill reluctantly taken.

9:40 P.M.

The three were still twenty feet above the tunnel floor when they felt the earth begin to shake. Seconds later they heard it. One, two, three, four, and then five. The thundering chop of helicopters coming in and passing overhead at a low level.

Miguel looked at Hap. "More police? CIA?"

"Secret Service," Hap said coldly. "Flown in from Paris."

"How do you know?"

"Because it's my damn job to know!" Hap flared. It was the last thing they needed, more bodies working against them, agents thinking they were helping when they were doing just the opposite. "I would have called them in myself." He looked at Amado below him, "How much further?"

"Not much," Miguel said, then grinned. "The drop is still enough to kill you."

"Next time bring a ladder."

9:43 P.M.

"Laser!" Marten said in a hoarse whisper, pulling the president back against the tunnel wall in the inky black.

"Where?"

"Ahead."

"I didn't see it."

"It went on, then off. Either a mistake or they were hoping to get lucky. The last thing they want to do is give themselves away."

"Listen."

Once again came the sound of a drill cutting through stone.

"It's closer," the president's voice was little more than a whisper.

"A second rig?"

Abruptly the sound came again. This one closer than the other.

"And a third."

"They're in front of us with lasers," Marten said. "How far away or how many, we don't know. They're closing in behind us. And then there was that sound before. Like rocks slapped together. What the hell that was, I don't know either."

Suddenly the president raised what was left of the torch. Little more than a glowing ember. He lifted it high and close to Marten's face so that he could see him clearly. "You gave me your word that we would get out of here and that I would address the convention at Aragon. Damn it to hell, we are not going to let them take us now. I'm holding you to your promise."

"Mr. President, take that damn stick out of my face," Marten glared at him.

President Harris stared, then lowered the glowing pick handle. "I'm sorry."

Suddenly there was another flash of laser through the tunnel. Then a second, held longer this time. They could hear the distant echo of footsteps, men moving quickly along the tunnel toward them. From behind came another screech of drill. It held for ten seconds, then its pitch suddenly rose. Immediately the whine diminished.

"They've broken through," the president said.

"Give me that," Marten said quickly, and grabbed the glowing torch, then started back the way they had come.

"What are you doing?"

"Looking for help, Cousin. Looking for help."

9:45 P.M.

Marten ran along the track as fast as he dared in the dark, the glowing pick handle held near the tunnel floor, the president on his heels. Then the president caught up.

"Fifty, a hundred yards back, the torch flared." Marten kept moving, his voice barely a whisper. "Just a little. Not enough to think about at the time but there was an air current of some sort. Maybe a crack in the wall big enough we can squeeze into until those laser guys pass, then we go back the way they came, the way we were headed. If they got in, there's a way out."

Behind them a shot of laser light bounced off the tunnel walls. Now they could hear the echo of voices in front of them. Marten ran on another twenty yards, then slowed. "Somewhere here," he stopped and ran the glowing stick along the tunnel floor and then up the walls.

Nothing.

Another shot of laser bounced off the tunnel ceiling behind them. From the darkness in front came the steady drum of running feet.

"Come on," the president breathed.

"Nothing. Maybe I was wrong."

Marten started to move on when suddenly the torch flared up.

"There! You found it!" the president said.

Marten twisted back and pushed the brand toward the wall. The flame rose higher. Then they saw it. A small, three foot square opening in the tunnel wall just where it met the floor and all but obscured by the wooden ties of the ore-car tracks.

Marten moved closer. The flame rose higher still.

Another blast of laser came from behind them. This time it held longer, lighting up the entire shaft a half mile back. The sound of men running toward them from the other direction became more distinct.

"Get in," Marten commanded. The president dropped to all fours and squeezed into the cutout. A heartbeat later Marten followed. Like that they were gone. The tunnel where they had been, black as coal. As if they were never there.

118

Marten and the president pushed farther back into the cutout. One shoved breathlessly up against the other. Two full-size men crammed like rag dolls into an impossibly tiny space.

They could hear the rush of feet approaching in the tunnel

outside. The sound got louder, then louder still. Then the men were just outside the opening only inches away. In another instant they were past it. There had easily been twenty, maybe more. Within the next minute they would come full on the force coming toward them from the opposite direction. They would confer for precious brief seconds, then each head back the way they had come. Checking and double-checking the route they had so swiftly passed through.

"Move! Now!" the president whispered, and started to shove out toward the tunnel.

"No." Marten pulled him back. "If there are more still coming we'll walk right into them."

"What do we do?"

"Wait."

"We don't have time. They'll turn back in a second when they run into the other squad. We have to take the chance and go now."

"Alright." Marten started to move, then suddenly stopped as the glow on the near-dead brand flared again. "Hold it," he moved the glowing pick handle to the side of the cutout. The glow became brighter. He blew on it and got a flame, then raised the torch and looked around.

"This place has been made with a different kind of tool than was used to dig the main tunnel. And it wasn't done eighty years ago either."

The president perked and followed the torch as Marten moved it around. "It's an air-transfer duct."

"Why? And from where to here?"

"Hand me the torch."

Marten did. The president turned up on an elbow and crawled farther back into the cutout.

"What do you see?"

"There's a steel vent, maybe two by three. It drops straight down into what looks like another shaft underneath."

"Can we fit through the vent?" Marten asked.

There was sudden noise in the tunnel outside. They heard the oncoming rush of feet, the snap of orders being given. The search team was coming back fast.

"We don't have a choice."

9:55 P.M.

The wind was rising, the heavy clouds beginning to spit rain, as an increasingly anxious Jake Lowe turned up the collar of his parka and pushed past Spanish police hastily erecting a protective tent over the command post. He reached the control area and moved in to look over the shoulders of Bill Strait and Captain Diaz.

For the last minutes he had been standing back, watching the communications teams monitor exchanges between the CIA, Secret Service, and CNP units in the tunnels and their counterparts scattered over the rock formations above. More than once he'd looked over at Jim Marshall, huddled to the side, chatting and drinking coffee with the presidential medical team waiting for the word that would put them into action. But that word had not come. Nothing seemed to be happening. A sudden shared laugh by Marshall and the medical crew pushed him over and sent him moving toward Strait and Diaz.

Was he the only one who was concerned about what would happen if the president suddenly turned up alive and well and talking and refusing to be taken to the CIA jet? Not only would Warsaw and their entire plan for the Middle East be dead in the water, they—all of them, from the vice president on down—ran the very real risk of being arrested and tried for attempting to overthrow the government. The penalty if convicted was death.

"What the hell's going on down there?" he suddenly asked Bill Strait. But it wasn't a question as much as it was a demand, even an accusation.

For a moment Strait ignored him. Finally he turned. "Five teams are inside the main shaft," he said patiently. "Three more are searching side tunnels. The rest are on standby for relief duty. The team working this end just met up with the unit that broke in midpoint the other way. All they found was a lot of dark tunnel. They've called for lights and are retracing now."

"What about the satellite? Where is it?"

"Another forty minutes until it's overhead, sir," Strait glanced at Marshall as if he wished he'd take Lowe aside and away. "The satellite, the thermal imaging, is not an end-all. It will not show us what's going on underground."

"When *are* we going to know what's going on underground?" Lowe pushed him hard.

"I can't tell you that, sir. There's a lot of area down there."

"In the next ten minutes or the next ten hours?"

"We are in the tunnels, sir. The Secret Service, the CIA, the CNP."

"I know who the hell is down there."

"Maybe you would like to go down yourself, sir."

Lowe flared at the insubordination. "Maybe you'd like to find yourself shoveling shit in Oklahoma."

Suddenly Marshall stepped in and turned Lowe away. "Jake, everybody's a little strung out here. There's enough tension as it is. I told you before to relax, do it. It would be good for everyone."

Strait's hand suddenly went to his headset, "What? Where? How many?"

Diaz looked at him. So did the medical team. Lowe and Marshall turned back fast.

"Go over the entire area again. We're sending in the standby teams. Lights are on the way, yes."

"What the hell is it?" Lowe was right in his face.

"They found fragments of what looks like a recently burned undershirt. Like somebody was using it as a torch. There are what appear to be rather unclear footprints of two men. They lead back through the tunnel."

"Two?"

"Yes, sir, two."

119

10:05 P.M.

The tunnel was little more than the height of a man standing and about twice that wide and was dimly lit by battery-powered emergency lights mounted high on the tunnel walls every hundred feet or so. Wood timbers bolstered the walls and ceiling that had, between large pieces of natural stone, been sprayed with a thin cement coating, probably to keep the dust down. The steel track down the center was a single, shiny monorail that led, like the tunnel itself, into the murky distance in either direction.

"We wanted to know how Foxx got the bodies in and out of his lab," the president said quietly, "here it is."

Marten took a moment to get his bearings then looked down the shaft to his left, "As far as I can tell, that way leads back toward Foxx's lab." He looked right. "That has to be the direction where they came from. The bodies loaded on a monorail sled or something."

"Then that's the way we go," the president was already moving in that direction. "This tunnel was dug directly beneath the other so it couldn't be read by satellites or surveillance aircraft. Everyone knew of the old tunnels, so no one would suspect they were being used as cover for something else. This is all Foxx's design. I'll bet copied from the secret underground weapons factories that armed Germany for World War Two."

"It's well-engineered alright," Marten was looking up. "It wasn't just chance we found that vent, there are a lot more at this end at least, probably one every two hundred feet. We missed them because they're well-hidden but soon enough those guys will find them too."

"Something else," the president kept moving. "Gas jets mounted near the emergency lights. Bigger than the ones in the lab, much bigger. Maybe five or six inches. Why this whole place didn't go up with the first blast I don't know."

"You make it sound like we're walking on the inside of a bomb."

"We are."

120

10:12 P.M.

The monks' chant echoed powerfully across the amphitheater. The moon had disappeared, replaced by steady rain and a show of lightning against the mountains that was accentuated every now and then by enormous claps of thunder. But the storm and its elements were incidental to what Demi saw before her, that held her frozen where she was.

A great live ox stood tethered by chains in the center of the Aldebaran circle. The chanting monks had formed a ring just outside it and were slowly moving counterclockwise around it as one by one the children came from the dark beyond the still fiercely burning bonfires to reverently place bouquets of flowers at the animal's feet. When the children were done, their elders came. More than a hundred of them, one by one in prayerful silence, to lay still more bouquets before the ox.

What astonished and held Demi's unwavering attention was that the animal stood in the center of a roaring fire. Yet it was seemingly at peace, unafraid, and either unfeeling of the intense heat and flame or unaware of what was happening to it.

"It is neither a trick nor magic," a voice behind her said gently. Demi whirled to see Luciana behind her. "The beast is on a spiritual journey. It feels no pain, only joy." Luciana smiled assuredly. "Go on, walk closer, go near. Photograph it. That's why you have come, isn't it?"

"Yes."

"Then do it. Record it for all time. Especially its eyes. Record the peace, the joy all creatures feel when they take the journey. Do it and you will see."

Luciana swept an arm toward the spectacle, and Demi went. Gathering her cameras, she stepped through the ring of monks and moved toward the burning beast. As she did, an elderly woman moved in to lay spring flowers at the animal's feet and to say a brief prayer in the same language the monks were chanting.

Demi used the digital camera first, the one that would instantly transmit the images to her Web site in Paris. She took a wide shot first, then zoomed closer for another. Finally she moved in full on the beast's head. She felt the tremendous intensity of the fire, saw the heat waves through the lens. Again she heard Luciana's words:

Record it for all time. Especially its eyes. Record the peace, the joy all creatures feel when they take the journey. Do it and you will see.

Luciana was right. What Demi saw in the eyes of the ox, what the camera recorded, was a look of exceeding peace and, if indeed animals did experience it, joy.

Suddenly the flames roared up and the ox disappeared from her view. She stepped back quickly. An instant later the animal's enormous body collapsed into the fire, sending a massive shower of sparks skyward into the night. At that moment the chanting stopped and everything went silent. All around her people had bowed their heads.

The beast's great journey had begun.

121

10:24 P.M.

Marten and President Harris were half running, half walking, purposely staying on the monorail's wooden ties, trying desperately to leave no footprints, no sign they had been there, nothing to follow. That the president had a good thirty years on Marten made little difference. Both men were sweating and exhausted, running on little more than fumes. Their mental and physical state made all the worse by the certainty that it was only a matter of time, minutes, even seconds, before their pursuers found one or more of the vents that would lead them down to the shaft where they were now.

The best they could do was trust they would reach the end of the tunnel before that happened, and when they did they'd have enough time to find a way out through whatever entryway Foxx had used to bring his victims to the holding tanks. Yet hopeful as that idea was, it brought up something else. What if that area, whatever it was, was still active? What if there were guards? Or others of Foxx's crew? It was a thought that chilled but at this point could make no difference. They had only one way to go and that was straight ahead.

National Security Adviser Marshall was tucked in the back of the Chinook making notes on his laptop when the helicopter's door slid open and Jake Lowe came in soaking wet from the rain. Up front the helicopter crew dozed in the cockpit. Halfway down, the medical team played cards. All the while Bill Strait's ongoing communication with the search teams working underground crackled incessantly over the speaker system.

Lowe walked directly to Marshall, "I need to talk to you," he said. "Alone."

Thirty seconds later they stepped out of the Chinook's warmth and light and into the dark and rain. Lowe slid the door closed behind them. Marshall flipped up the hood of his parka.

"Treason," Lowe said fearfully, and jabbed a finger in the direction of the mountains lit by intermittent flashes of lightning. "He gets out of those tunnels alive. He talks and people start to believe him. The same thing Hap said not long after all this started—what happens when he shows up? And where the hell is Hap anyway?" Lowe kept on. "Was he really shot? Is he dead? Or is he out there somewhere knowing what the hell's going on and doing something about it?"

Marshall studied him. What he saw was a mentally fatigued, increasingly upset Lowe finally beginning to lose it.

"Let's walk," Marshall said, and started off in the rain, heading them across a rocky flat and away from the Chinook's light spill. "Jake, you're tired," he said after a time. *Paranoid* was the word he wanted to use but didn't.

"We're all tired," Lowe shot back. "What the hell's the difference? The thing is we have to call Warsaw off. Right now. Before it gets to where it can't be called off. We do that and he comes out of those tunnels talking, accusing us, warning the French and Germans about it. Then nothing happens. It makes him a loony, gone over the edge, the way we've played it all along. But if the killings take place, we're all waiting for the hangman. And it won't be just for treason either. There are other things they can come after us with, especially when they find out about Foxx and what he was doing. The kind of things that came out of the Nuremberg trials. War crimes: performing medical experiments without the subjects' consent. Conspiracy to commit war crimes. Crimes against humanity."

They walked farther into the storm. "I thought we talked about that, Jake," Marshall's tone was even, wholly without emotion, "calling it off. We can't do it. Too many things are already in motion."

The rain came down harder. Lightning danced across the nearby peaks. Lowe was unwavering.

"You don't understand any of what I'm saying, do you? He's still the goddam president. He comes out of those tunnels alive and talking and the assassinations take place? For chrissakes listen to me! The vice president has to withdraw his order. Now, tonight! We don't, we lose everything!"

They were a hundred yards from the Chinook. The same distance to their left was the glow of the command post.

"You really think he's coming out alive and we can't handle it."

"That's right, I think he's coming out alive and we can't handle it. We're not prepared to handle it, this is a situation no one ever considered."

Just then a huge lightning flash lit up the countryside for miles around. For an instant everything was as bright as midday. They could see the rugged terrain, the Chinook, the hastily put-up tent housing the command post, the steep canyons that fell sharply away from the path they were on. Then the dark came again and with it a deafening clap of thunder.

Marshall took Lowe by the arm. "Watch your step, this is a narrow trail, you don't want to go over the side."

Lowe took Marshall's hand away. "Damn it, you're still not listening!"

"I am listening, Jake, and I believe you're right," Marshall was calm and thoughtful. "We were never prepared for anything like this, none of us. Maybe the risk is too great. We can't chance blowing the whole thing, not this far into it." Another lightning flash and Marshall's eyes found Lowe's. "Okay, Jake. Let's make the call. Tell them what we think. Have the vice president withdraw the order. Put it on hold."

"That's good," Lowe said with immense relief. "Damn, damn good."

122

"No! No!" José suddenly pulled back in the narrow chimney and re-fused to go farther.

"What the hell's wrong?" Hap looked sharply to Miguel.

They were probably four hundred feet underground in an awk-wardly twisting limestone channel that dropped sharply downward into a claustrophobic darkness that, even with the illumination of their flashlights, had become increasingly disquieting. Moreover, this was a second chimney down, one far beneath the first one they had descended through, and all of them, the boys included, were becoming more and more on edge.

"Tell him it's okay, we understand," Hap was pale, his shoulder throbbing, already into a second pain pill. "Tell him we all feel the same way. But we have to keep going."

Miguel started to speak to José in Spanish. He'd barely started when the youngster shook his head again. "No!" he spat. "No más!" No more!

Nearly forty minutes earlier they had reached the section of tunnel where the boys thought Miguel's friends might be, if they were there at all. Amado and Hector, getting to it first and the others soon afterward. They'd hardly gone a hundred yards when they heard the rush of men coming toward them in the dark. Miguel started to turn them back when Hector took him by the arm.

"No, this way," he said quickly and led them dangerously for-ward toward the oncoming men to another break in the rock, a fis-sure that even with lights would be almost impossible to find unless one knew the tunnel very well. It was steep and narrow and led farther down in an abrupt, twisting sweep deeper into the earth. They had climbed down it for a full thirty seconds when they heard the rescuers pass by its hidden opening and stopped. And it was there they remained, all but trapped as still more forces joined the others above. Finally Amado had looked to his uncle.

"These are more than just 'friends' who are lost."

"Yes," Miguel glanced at Hap and then back to his nephew. "One of them is an official of the United States government."

"And these men, these police forces hunting him, want to do him harm."

"They think they are helping him but they are not. When they find him they will bring him to people who will harm him, but they don't know that."

"Who is this man?" Hector asked.

Hap had trusted them so far and right now he needed all the help and trust he could get. "The president," he said definitively.

"Of the United States?" Amado blurted in broken English.

"Yes."

The boys laughed as if it were a joke and then they saw the expressions on the faces of the men.

"It is true?" Amado asked.

"Yes, it's true," Hap said. "We have to get him out and away from here without anyone knowing."

Miguel translated the last into Spanish then added, "The man who is with him is good, the president's friend. It is up to us to find them and get them away from the police and to safety. Do you understand?"

"Sí," each boy said. "Sí."

It was then Hap glanced at his watch and looked to Miguel. "Before, the boys said they thought they knew about how far the president might have come since the landslide. That was two and half hours ago. They know the tunnel. Where do they think he and Marten might be now, assuming they're still alive and moving at about the same speed?"

Miguel looked at the boys and translated.

The boys looked at each other, had a brief discussion, then Amado looked to his uncle. "Cerca," he said. "Cerca."

"Near," Miguel translated. "Near."

It was then they heard the movement and voices of the men in the tunnel above. They had come back and were much closer, their voices echoing clearly down to where they were. Miguel was afraid they would be discovered, and Hector moved them farther down, inching them along through a chimney that turned and twisted like the coils of a snake. Less than five minutes later José had stopped them with his sudden "No!" Refusing to go any farther.

"What is it?" Miguel asked him in Spanish.

"*Los muertos*"—the dead—he said, as if only seconds before he had realized where he was and where this chimney led, and it rocked him to his soul. "*Los muertos,*" he repeated, clearly terrified. "*Los muertos.*"

Hap looked to Miguel. "What is he talking about?"

A brief exchange in Spanish followed. Miguel to José, who remained silent, then to Amado, whom he finally got the truth out of.

"Down there," Miguel gestured farther down the chimney, "is another tunnel. It has a single track. Traveling along it he has seen a 'streetcar' filled with the dead."

"What?" Hap was incredulous.

"More than once."

"What is he talking about?"

Miguel and Amado had an exchange in Spanish. Then Miguel translated.

"A few months ago José and Hector were exploring and found another tunnel, the one he is talking about that is below us now. It's much smaller and newer and sprayed with a cement coating. A single steel track runs down the center of it. There was a hole at the top of tunnel. It is how they saw into the shaft and where they were looking when the streetcar-kind-of machine came along. Dead bodies were stacked on it like firewood. They got scared and climbed out and told no one what they saw. Two months later they dared each other to come back. They climbed down and waited and then saw it again. This time bodies were being taken in the other direction. José became certain that if he ever went down there again he would become one of them. He believes it is Hell."

For a moment Hap stared unbelieving, trying to digest it. Then he asked a simple question. "Is there a way, besides this chimney, to get from that tunnel up there," he pointed to where they had been, "down to the tunnel where the bodies were?"

Once again Miguel turned to the boys and translated. For a moment no one said anything; finally Hector spoke, scratching two lines in the stone with a piece of rock as he did. Miguel translated what he said.

"The shaft below runs level. The shaft above starts high then slopes lower. Where we are it is maybe sixty feet between them. Much further down it is less than twenty and there are cutouts all along it, he thinks for air, so yes it is possible to get from one to the other."

Hap listened carefully to Miguel's translation. As he did he heard more noise from above. Suddenly the hair stood up on his neck.

"There are a lot people still up there," he said with urgency. "Dead or alive, if the president was in that tunnel they would have found him by now and we would have either heard their reaction or they simply would have gone."

Suddenly Miguel realized what he was saying. "You think my cousins are in the lower shaft!"

"Maybe, and maybe close by. Let José stay here if he wants, the rest of us are going down to find out."

123

10:44 P.M.

"We've got direct overhead satellite coverage now, sir," a young Secret Service tech specialist was looking over his computer screen at Bill Strait. "Very clear thermal picture of our movements aboveground, sir. So far there is nothing else."

"Bill," Strait looked up as Jim Marshall suddenly came into the command post, pulling the hood back from his parka. He was soaked through and pale as death.

"What is it?" Strait said.

"Jake and I were out on a trail in the dark. We were talking. He was still upset. He lost his footing and slipped. I tried to grab him but it was too late. I heard him land. He fell a long way. My God, he's got to be dead!"

"Oh good Lord!"

"Bill, you've got to get some people down there fast. Alive or dead we have to get him out. We can't have people asking what he was doing up here. The accident will have to have happened somewhere else, probably the location where we're supposed to have the president. He was out walking alone after a meeting and slipped and fell."

"I understand, sir. I'll take care of it."

"I want to inform the vice president right away. I'll want a secure phone," he glanced around at the closeness of the others, "and privacy."

"Yes, sir. Of course, sir."

124

10:49 P.M.

The monorail track followed a long bend in the tunnel. Marten turned to look back as they started around it. It was their last straight view of the tunnel behind. If their pursuers had found the shaft, so far there was no sign of them.

"How much farther can this thing go?" he said as he caught up to the president.

"It doesn't," President Harris was staring straight ahead. Fifty yards in front of them the tunnel ended abruptly at a massive steel door.

"Now what?" Marten said.

"Don't know."

They covered the distance to the door quickly and in silence. The monorail track passed through it at ground level, a cutout precisely machined to accommodate it. The door itself was fitted to geared, machined rails on either side, making it obvious that the door opened by rising straight up.

"It's got to weigh five tons," the president said. "There's no way we're going to open it by hand."

"There," Marten said and indicated a small red light mounted in the door itself just above eye level. "It's an infrared sensor, like the remote on a TV. Foxx must have designed—" Suddenly he pulled Foxx's BlackBerry-like device from his jacket, then stepped in front of the sensor and pressed what appeared to be the POWER key. A light came on. He looked at the panel. Among its array of buttons was one marked SEND. He pointed it at the sensor and pressed it. Nothing happened.

10:54 P.M.

"There's got to be an entry code of some kind," Marten said, working one combination of the number/letter keys and then another. Finally he tried devising patterns using a grouping of nine keys with raised symbol-like figures that were mounted on the gadget's lower half. Still nothing happened.

"We have to go back down the tunnel," the president said. "It's not going to work!"

"To where?"

"Foxx was a military man. He wouldn't have built something like this without giving himself a way out if things went wrong. Somewhere along the way he would have created an emergency exit, probably more than one."

"We saw nothing."

"Then we missed it, Mr. Marten. We simply missed it."

10:57 P.M.

The president and Marten rounded the long turn in the tunnel going back the way they had come. Each man studying the ceiling and the side of shaft closest to him, looking for an area in the cemented tunnel wall that might have been cut out and then replaced.

Then Marten saw it. Maybe a half mile down in the dark of the tunnel. The briefest flash as an emergency light glinted off steel.

"They're coming!" he said quickly.

Both men froze, staring down the shaft in front of them. A split second later they heard the distant sound of men running toward them.

"The vents!" the president said suddenly. "The way we came down. They'll get us back up into the other tunnel!"

10:58 P.M.

They reached the bend in the tunnel and cleared it on the run, trying to get out of the line of sight and at the same time looking for the air vents above where the tunnel wall met the ceiling.

"I don't see them," Marten cried out.

"They've got to be here. We've seen them the whole way alo—" The president's words were cut off by a loud splintering crack in the tunnel roof just ahead. A split second later there was a sharp cry and the body of a young man crashed through it to land on the tunnel floor not twenty feet in front of them.

"What the hell!" Marten yelled.

10:59 P.M.

Hector was picking himself up as they reached him.

"Don't think he's a cop," Marten said quickly and glanced down the tunnel behind them.

"He's not American either!" The president looked up at the shattered dark hole in the tunnel ceiling where Hector had fallen through. "If he came down, there's a way up!"

"Cousins!" Miguel's joyous face suddenly appeared in the hole.

"Miguel!" The president was incredulous.

"Miguel," Marten jumped on it, "there are fifty guys right behind us!"

"Tell Hector to boost them up," a second voice barked from the darkness, then Hap Daniels moved into view. He wasn't looking at Marten or the president, he was staring at Miguel. "Now! Dammit! Fast!"

11:00 P.M.

The president came up first, then Marten, then Hector.

11:01 P.M.

They could hear the men coming.

"They'll see the hole," Miguel spat.

"They know we're here somewhere," the president said. "We had to burn Marten's undershirt for light. They'll have found it."

"Where?" Hap said.

"In the upper tunnel."

Abruptly Hap handed the president his flashlight. "You and Marten, get up the chimney and fast. It's steep and full of tight spots but you can make it. We're right behind you."

The president hesitated.

"Now!" Hap commanded, and president and Marten started up.

Immediately Hap looked to Miguel." We're going to have to give them the boys."

"What?"

"Amado and Hector. They were exploring the tunnels. Their flashlight went dead. It was pitch black. They got scared and decided to burn Amado's undershirt to see their way. It finally went out. They got lost again. Flashlight lost somewhere too. They wandered around, found this tunnel, then the hole here. Broke it open and were about to start up. If those guys are looking for two men. There they are."

Miguel hesitated. This was crazy. Amado was his nephew. He couldn't do it.

"Miguel, tell them now! And tell them to delay whoever gets them for as long as they can. Cry. Beg. Scream with relief. Be afraid their mothers will kill them if they find out. Anything. We've got to have time to get the president away from here."

125

Demi crossed the church floor in the darkness. Cameras over her shoulder, she used a lone candle to light her way as she moved from ancient paving stone to ancient paving stone, looking at the family names carved into them. Stones, Cristina had told her, that marked family tombs and held the earthly remains of the honored dead.

Outside, the storm was abating; the thunder and lightning were fading in the distance, the rain had become little more than a drizzle. Inside, the church was silent; the families, the monks, Cristina, Luciana, and Reverend Beck long gone to their quarters. Demi had done the same, gone to change back into her street clothes and bide her time, waiting until she felt it was safe to leave her room and make her way undisturbed to the church nave.

CORNACCHI, GUARNIERI, BENICHI.

She read the names on the tombs and moved on.

RIZZO, CONTI, VALLONE.

She moved farther across the floor.

MAZZETTI, GHINI.

"The name you are looking for is Ferrara," a voice came from the darkness.

Demi started and lifted her candle to peer into the darkness. "Who's there?"

For a moment she saw nothing and then Luciana stepped into the light offered by the candle. A hooded monk was with her. Luciana no longer wore the gold dress of earlier, instead she was dressed in a black robe similar to those of the monks. Her false, hideously long nails were gone, but her dark eye makeup with the searing dramatic streaks that ran daggerlike from the corners of her eyes to the hollows of her ears remained. The effect of it all, the black robe, the makeup, her sudden presence here in the dark of the church in the company of a lone monk was, at best, unnerving.

"Come," she waved a hand, "the tomb is over here."

Ferrara

"Move your candle closer, so you can see the name clearly."

Demi did.

"Say it. Say the name," Luciana insisted.

"Ferrara," Demi said.

"Your mother's name. Your family name."

"How do you know?" Demi said, startled by the revelation.

"It is why you are here. Why you befriended Reverend Beck and then Dr. Foxx. You wanted to know the secrets of Aldebaran. Why you met with the unfortunate Giacomo Gela, who then told you of Aradia Minor."

Demi moved the candle closer to Luciana and the monk. "I want to know what happened to my mother," she should have been afraid, she wasn't. This was about the fate of her mother and nothing else.

Luciana smiled, "Show her."

The monk took the candle from Demi, then knelt beside the marking stone and removed it. Beneath was an ancient bronze chest. Twenty-seven dates were engraved on its lid. The earliest was 1637, the last was exactly eighteen years ago. The year her mother vanished.

"Your mother's name was Teresa," Luciana said.

"Yes."

"Remove the closure," Luciana said quietly.

The monk turned back the cover of the chest, then held the candle close. Demi could see rows of silver urns. Each one set into a special bronze square, each with a date engraved on it.

"The ashes of the honored dead. Like the great ox tonight. Like Cristina tomorrow."

"Cristina?" Demi was jolted.

"Tonight the children honored her as they honored the ox. She is joyous. As is her family. As are the children and the others."

"What are you telling me?" Slowly Demi's defiance began to fade. In its place came fear.

"The ritual was to honor those about to begin the great journey."

"These were honored?" Demi looked back to the urns.

"Yes."

"My mother?"

"Yes."

"These other urns are all women of my family?" Demi didn't understand.

"Count them."

Demi did, and then looked up. "There are twenty-eight. But only twenty-seven dates are engraved on the cover."

"Look at the date on the last urn."

"Why?"

"Look at it."

Demi did as Luciana commanded. When she did puzzlement crossed her face.

"Tomorrow."

"It is a date not yet engraved on the chest because as yet the urn holds no ashes," Luciana smiled slowly, her eyes filling with an immense darkness. "There is one woman in your family not yet counted."

"Who?"

"You."

126

11:30 P.M.

National Security Adviser James Marshall sat at a small folding table in the back of the command post tent. He was alone, isolated for privacy as he had asked, his headset connected to a secure phone.

On the same secure line were Vice President Hamilton Rogers; President John Henry Harris's chief of staff, Tom Curran; Secretary of State David Chaplin; Secretary of Defense Terrence Langdon; and the Chairman of the Joint Chiefs of Staff, Air Force General Chester Keaton, now aboard a CIA jet enroute to Madrid.

"They caught two local boys supposedly lost in the tunnels. Still no sign of the president or Marten. The boys are being brought here for interrogation now. Nobody's really sure of what's going on." Marshall turned casually and looked around, making certain none of Bill Strait or Captain Diaz's communications team had wandered close by, then turned back and lowered his voice.

"We must assume what we have all along, that both men are either sealed in the tunnel outside Foxx's dirty lab, were in it when it exploded and are dead, or will be brought to me immediately if somehow they're found alive, then sedated and flown directly to a waiting CIA plane. If we do otherwise, we'll start thinking like Jake Lowe, and that's no good. There can be no weak links. None.

"I remind you there is a long and powerful history here, one we have long embraced and sworn allegiance to. This is not the first time its resolve has been tested. It will not be the last. Our charge from the beginning has been to ensure the success of the operation at hand. Nothing has changed. Are we clear on that, gentlemen?"

"*Absolutely clear, Jim,*" Vice President Rogers said quietly. "*Anyone disagree, say so now.*"

A unified silence followed.

"*Good,*" the vice president said. "*Chet, you have an exact on Warsaw?*"

"*Fail-safe at 15:30 tomorrow.*" General Keaton had the same quiet, confident tone as the vice president.

"*Good. Thank you, Dr. Marshall. You've handled it very well. Until tomorrow, gentlemen, good luck and Godspeed.*"

127

11:42 P.M.

The president, Marten, Hap, and Miguel huddled inside a dark turn of chimney thirty feet below where it met the upper tunnel.

Three times before they had stopped in the dark, breaths held, hearts pounding. The first had been when several of the rescuers had climbed into the chimney from below after Amado and Hector had been caught. They'd heard them talking as they came, arguing whether the boys were alone as they'd said and that there was no else. They must have concluded they'd told the truth because they'd climbed only a few minutes longer before turning back. The second had been to rest and give the president and Marten water from Miguel's camel pack and two health bars each from the limousine's emergency kit. The third had been when they'd heard someone coming down from above. Hap had instantly pushed the president and Marten back behind them, and then he and Miguel had waited with guns in hand as whoever it was continued down. Then a flashlight beam appeared around a turn in the rock. Sig Sauer up, Hap had been about to identify himself when José appeared. He'd been listening for them and scrambled down to meet them when he heard them come.

"These are the Americans I told you about," Miguel said when they were face to face. José had stared for the briefest moment, then looked past them down the chimney and asked for Amado and Hector.

"They are helping," Miguel told him in Spanish.

"Helping where?"

"They are with the police."

"The police?"

"Yes," said Miguel in Spanish. "Now it's your turn; please lead us back up."

Ten minutes later they neared the top and Hap stopped them again, asking Miguel to send José the rest of the way to see if the upper tunnel was clear and if it was safe to go the hundred yards down it to the chimney they had initially come down through and that they would use to climb out.

That had been three minutes earlier. So far he hadn't come back.

Until they stopped here conversation between them had been brief utterings, mostly commands or warnings. All of it spoken in voices barely above a whisper.

As they waited, Miguel realized something had to be addressed and soon—Hap's fear that the president had been, and might still be, afraid to trust him. It was a subject he appointed himself to resolve.

Immediately he slid back and huddled close to the president.

"Cousin," he said, "Hap appreciates that under the circumstances you had no way to know who you could trust, himself included. It was the same for him as he started to learn things. It was very difficult because he wasn't even sure he could trust his own brothers in the Secret Service. He even got shot because of it."

"Shot?"

"Two bullets in the shoulder at Foxx's monastery office when he went there looking for you. We got him a doctor but he still hurts like hell. He should be in bed but instead he climbed all over and through these damned mountains to find you. So don't ever think you can't trust him."

The president turned from Miguel and looked to Hap. "You never said a word about getting shot."

"Wasn't much to say."

"You got yourself into a real mess over me."

"It's my job description."

The president smiled. "Thank you."

"Yes, sir."

The president's response—the tease, the smile, the thank-you, was everything. It meant the bond, the friendship, and the hugely necessary trust between the president and his chief protector were once again in place.

"There's something you don't know, Hap," the president said and the personal moment faded. "The vice president, secretary of defense, chief of staff, all those people present that night at Evan Byrd's house in Madrid, are planning to have the president of France and the chancellor of Germany assassinated at the Warsaw meeting. It's part of a much bigger conspiracy, one that Merriman Foxx was involved in. There has been no way for me to alert anyone without giving away my position. And you can't do it either, not now."

Hap leaned forward, "It's not Monday yet, Mr. President. My plan is to get you out of here and then down the mountain to Miguel's cousin's house where the limo is as fast as we can. Then we're gone, out of this hot surveillance area, hopefully as far as the French border by first light. At that point we can take the chance and inform the French and German governments about Warsaw. To do that we've got to deal with what comes next.

"When they break Hector and Amado, and they will," Hap glanced at Miguel. "We had to do something, Miguel, I'm sorry."

He looked back to the president. "Once they break them, they'll know for certain you're down here and alive. It won't make any difference if they find out I'm with you or not. They'll come through all these tunnels loaded for bear. Outside will be the same. More bodies brought in, more equipment. In an hour there'll be a traffic jam of air and satellite surveillance like no one on this planet has ever seen. Every road for fifty miles around will be blocked."

"And you still think we can get out."

"We have a little time before they'll know for certain and the full assault begins, that's what we bought with the boys. Still, there's a major force out there right now. The thing is, they're scattered all over and concentrating on what's going on underground. With care and luck and José knowing the way, in the dark we might have a chance to slip past them. Except for one thing."

"What do you mean?"

"By now they'll have a big surveillance satellite right over us. The digital-photo aspect won't be of much use at night, but the thermal imaging will. As soon as we're out of these tunnels and on the surface we become a heat source they will immediately identify."

"Then what makes you think we can get away at all?"

"It's more hope than think, Mr. President, but it's why these," Hap pulled one of the small, folded survival blankets from his jacket. "Open it up and you've got a thin blanket the size of a small tent. One side is Mylar, cut a couple of eyeholes, put it over your head and belt it around you, with luck it should reflect back 'cold' to the bird's thermal sensor. If we stay low to the ground and find brush and hillsides with trees to give us cover, we might just get away with it."

Miguel grinned. "You are a very smart fellow."

"Only if it works."

The president glanced at Marten and then looked to Miguel. "How far is the Aragon resort overland from where we are?"

"Ten, twelve miles. There are trails but mostly it's rough country."

"Can we reach it on foot by daybreak?"

"Maybe. José would know how to do it."

"The Aragon resort?" Hap was incredulous. "Over mountain trails in the dark. It would take four or five hours, maybe more.

Even if these blankets do work, that's too much time. There will be too many people out there, too much equipment. The chances of us getting even halfway there without being caught don't exist."

"The other way's no better, Hap," the president said. "Those roads leading to the French border are all known and, as you said, will be blocked. If we get stopped out there we have no place to go at all and no matter what I say I'll soon be in the custody of my 'friends' and Warsaw will go on as planned. We go overland by foot in wild country and in the dark, we have at least some kind of chance.

"Moreover, Aragon is more than a refuge. As you well know I was to address the New World congregation at tomorrow's sunrise service, I still plan to. No one is going to take me away in front of all those people, especially a group like that. Once I tell them the truth, the situation at Warsaw will take care of itself."

"Mr. President, the security for that convention is huge. I know, I helped set it up. Even if we get that far, we wouldn't get past it. We try and everyone who wants you out of the way will know exactly where you are. They'll order security to get you out right then. You don't know this but Chief of Staff has a CIA jet waiting at a private airstrip outside Barcelona. They get you on that plane, you're finished."

For a long moment the president said nothing and it was clear he was turning everything over in his mind; finally he looked to Hap. "We're going to try for Aragon. I know you don't like it but it's my decision. As for the security. You know the layout there—the land, the buildings, the church where I was to speak. You scouted it all in advance."

"Yes, sir."

"Then somehow we'll find a way in. I will be the surprise speaker as planned. And it will be a surprise, for everyone."

There was a noise from above and José eased around the corner. He looked to Miguel. "There are patrols," he said in Spanish, "but they have passed. I don't know if there are more. For the moment it is safe."

Miguel translated and the president looked to each man in turn—Marten, Hap, Miguel, and José.

"Let's go," he said.

SUNDAY

APRIL 9

128

Demi paced what was little more than a cell trying not to think of the horror Luciana had promised for "tomorrow," which, with the turn of the clock, was already here.

In front of her a small stainless-steel bunk was covered with a thin mattress and single blanket. As if she could sleep, or even try to. Next to it was a washbasin and next to that a toilet. And then there was the chapel. Set into the wall in the center of the room and lighted with what seemed a hundred votive candles. Little more than three feet wide and two deep, a small marble altar was at the back and on it sat something that at first appeared to be a piece of bronze sculpture. But when she looked at it closely she saw it was not a sculpture as much as a welding together of two letters.

א μ

Then she realized they were what Giacomo Gela had spoken of—a Hebrew *A* followed by the Greek *M*. It wasn't a sculpture, it was an idol, the sign of *Aradia Minor,* the secretive order inside the already secretive *boschetto* of the Aldebaran. It meant everything he had warned her of was true and told her they had known who she was all along and had simply stepped back and watched her, wanting to see how much she knew and who else might be involved. It was why Beck had invited her to Barcelona after the incident between Foxx and Nicholas Marten on Malta, a deliberate plan to see who, if anyone, would follow. And Marten had. The trip to the cathedral with Beck and Luciana had not been for Luciana to arrange a meeting with Foxx at Montserrat but for the same reason, to see who would follow. Again Marten had. It was why, too, Beck had agreed to bring her to the church to witness the coven's rituals in return for delivering Marten to Foxx. In delivering Marten she had also delivered herself and in the process seen in the fiery death of the ox, her own horrific fate. Afterward they'd simply brought her here and locked the door.

Just what the ancient cult of *Aradia Minor* was she had no idea, but she was certain Gela had been purposely mutilated and left to live as an example of what awaited anyone who might try to find out. Clearly they had watched Gela for years for that very reason, to see who was interested enough to find him, and then to learn who that person was and why they had come, and who else they might have told. It made her wonder how many others there had been over the centuries who had pursued the same course as she and fallen prey to the same unspeakable horror.

The same terrible burning horror that would soon be hers. The same horror that had been her mother's and that of twenty-six other women in her family. The same as it had been for the mothers, daughters, aunts, sisters, and cousins of other Italian families selected over the centuries. The same as it would be today, and not just for her but for Cristina.

Abruptly Demi stopped her pacing and crossed back to the altar. Before, in the church and under Luciana's gaze, the monks had stripped her of her cameras, then blindfolded her and led her down an extraordinarily long flight of steps. Soon afterward they'd put her onto some kind of open-air transport that moved quickly forward on a ride she was certain had been underground. After that they'd brought her to the cell where she was now, locking her in and leaving without a word.

But that had been all. They had not bothered to search her, either in the church or here when they brought her in and removed the blindfold. It meant she still had the hidden smart phone/camera she had used to transmit photos to her Web site in Paris. It was something that gave her hope because she still had communication out—although two unsuccessful tries here told her she was too far underground for the signal to escape whatever was above her. Still, she had both phone and camera. The phone she would do everything in her power to use later, when hopefully they brought her to an area where she would have connectivity and could somehow steal a moment alone to call the Pan-European emergency number 112 and ask for the police. The camera she would use now to help her keep what little sanity she had left, to prevent her from dwelling on the horrifying certainty of what was to come in the next few hours.

Demi knelt before the altar and began to photograph the idol, the symbol of *Aradia Minor*. She took pictures aggressively and passionately and from every angle. As she worked she began to realize that what she was doing was more than a deliberate distraction; it was a last desperate hope that in one way or another she might find a bridge to the Other Side and somehow touch her mother. To make contact with the spirit of who she had been, and to Demi, still was, even in death. In doing so, she would not only fulfill her promise to her but also to find everlasting love and salvation.

129

12:07 A.M.

Hector and Amado stood in the bright light of the command post. They were dirty and scraped and afraid, but so far they hadn't broken. Not to the Secret Service and Spanish CNP officers that had caught them in the tunnel. Not to the CIA investigators who had talked to them next. Or the half dozen Secret Service and CNP troops that had brought them back up through the chimneys and walked them through the rain to the command post. Both had stood by their story: they had simply come up that morning to explore the tunnels and become lost.

"What time?" Captain Diaz asked in Spanish.

"Nine thirty, about," was their agreed-upon answer, the one they had decided on in the seconds before the troops were first upon them.

"Where do you live?" Captain Diaz continued.

Bill Strait and National Security Adviser James Marshall stood behind her; each man fully intent on the proceedings.

"El Borràs, by the river," Amado answered.

"Just you two. Alone. No one else with you."

"Yes. I mean, no. I mean just us."

Captain Diaz studied the boys for a moment and walked over to a CNP officer. "Let's talk to the them separately," she said, then walked back to the boys.

"Which one is Hector?"

Hector raised his hand.

"Good. You stay with me. Amado is going to talk to some people on the far side of the tent."

Hector watched as Amado went off with two CNP officers.

"Now, Hector," Captain Diaz said, "you live in El Borràs."

"Yes."

"Tell me how you got here. From the river to this mountaintop."

12:12 A.M.

Hector watched as Captain Diaz left him and crossed the tent to talk with one of the CNP officers who had gone off with Amado. Nervously he glanced at Bill Strait and the exceedingly tall and distinguished man with him. Both were clearly American. For the first time he was aware of the people and equipment around him. He had seen radios and computer setups in movies but they had been nothing like this. Nor had he ever heard anything like the constant crackle of communication between the operators here and the people they were talking with outside. And nothing ever like the absolute seriousness of the atmosphere.

He took a breath as he saw Captain Diaz come back, stopping midway to say something to Bill Strait and the man with him, and then all three came toward him.

"There seems to be a conflict here, Hector," Captain Diaz said calmly. "You told me you hiked up from the river. Amado seems to remember you riding up on motorcycles."

"Hector," Bill Strait was looking at him directly, "we know you and Amado weren't the only people down there." He paused for Captain Diaz to translate.

"Yes, we were," Hector protested. "Who else would be with us?"

"The president of the United States."

"No," Hector said defiantly. He needed no translation. "No."

"Hector, listen to me carefully. When we find the president we will know you were lying and you will go to prison for a very, very long time."

Captain Diaz's translation was delivered as if what Bill Strait had said was already a given, a twenty- or thirty-year prison sentence handed down by a judge.

"No," he said, "we were alone. Amado and me. Nobody else. Ask your men. They looked, they found nothing."

Suddenly Hector felt a presence and looked up. Amado came toward him accompanied by two CNP officers. His complexion was white, his eyes filled with tears. There was no need for words. What had happened was all too clear.

He had told them.

130

12:18 A.M.

The ascent from the lower chimney to the main tunnel had been done with relative ease. The next, the hundred-yard marching along it, had been made quickly and without incident even in the dark. Then José had found the opening to the upper chimney, the one Hap, Miguel, he, Amado, and Hector had come down in what felt like days, even weeks earlier.

They were in it and climbing when Hap suddenly grunted and

stopped. Miguel put a narrow flashlight beam on him and they could see the color had drained from him and that he was sweating heavily. Quickly Miguel gave him water from his camel pack and insisted he take another pain pill and he had.

Now the five sat in stillness, giving him a chance to rest and wait for the medication to take effect. In another circumstance they might have left him and gone on alone with his blessing but they couldn't. He had walked the entire Aragon resort only weeks earlier in preparation for the president's visit and knew the details of its layout as only a man with his training and experience could. If they were going to make it at all, they needed Hap. Whether a short rest would be enough, there was no way to know.

12:23 A.M.

"The football, Mr. President," Marten said in the darkness and for no other reason than he'd been thinking about it, "that black satchel the public sees a military aide carrying around everywhere the president goes. I assume it really does have the codes for launching nuclear missiles."

"Yes."

"Excuse my asking but where is it now?"

"I would assume 'my friends' have it. I couldn't very well have taken it with me when I left."

"Your 'friends' have it?"

"It doesn't make any difference."

"What the hell does that mean?"

"There's more than one," Hap suddenly joined the conversation.

"What?"

"The president has one when he travels. There's another tucked away at the White House and a third is available to the vice president in the event the president is unable to function. Such as now."

"You mean they have it anyway."

"Yes, they have it anyway. . . . Any other questions?"

"Not for the moment."

"Good," Hap suddenly pushed himself to his feet. "Let's get moving before more 'rescuers' arrive."

12:32 A.M.

They stopped a dozen feet short of the chimney opening and sent José to the top as they had before.

12:36 A.M.

José climbed back down and spoke to Miguel in Spanish. Miguel listened and then turned to the others. "There are low clouds and it is raining," he translated quietly. "He heard nothing and saw no lights. When we get out, we follow him closely over open rock. Very soon there will be a steep path; it goes up for a short distance, then cuts back down through some brush and continues down through switchbacks for maybe a half mile before it ends in an arroyo. Afterward we follow the arroyo to a stream crossing. On the other side we pick up a trail through the woods that goes for at least another two miles before we hit an open space."

"Then what?" the president asked.

"We'll see when we get that far," Hap said flatly. "The weather will reduce the effectiveness of thermal imaging, but this is a game of little steps. If we cover almost three miles in the dark and rain without attracting visitors, that's huge. I hope not impossible."

"Are you up to it?" the president was genuinely concerned about Hap's condition.

"I'm ready when you are, Mr. President."

131

12:38 A.M.

It had taken Jim Marshall nearly twenty minutes to locate the vice president and have him connected to a secure phone. Word that the president had been seen alive, and in the shafts, and with a man fitting the description of Nicholas Marten within the past hour had disturbed the vice president but not enough to steer either him or Marshall off course. To both it was the same as it had been from the beginning when the president had gone missing in Madrid and then was located in Barcelona: he was either Marten's prisoner or he was mentally ill. In a way the situation now was better than it had been because they knew for certain where he was. Hundreds of people were zeroed in on the area with more on the way. It was only a matter of time, hours, maybe even minutes, before he was found. After that he would be in their custody and on his way out of Spain and to their isolated undisclosed location in Switzerland.

"You're right there on top of it, Jim. Nobody better to make sure it happens the way it needs to," the vice president reassured him.

"You'll inform the others."

"Right away. Let me know the minute you have him and are airborne."

"Done," Marshall said, and hung up. Immediately he went to find Bill Strait, who, along with Captain Diaz, was caught in the adrenaline-driven rush to coordinate the movements of people still underground while managing the setup and logistics for the wave of new forces being scrambled to come in.

Marshall pulled Strait aside to walk him through the confusion of the command post tent and out into the rain, where they could be alone.

"Once he's found, he and Marten are to be separated right away. Take Marten into our custody and fly him to the embassy in Madrid to be held there incommunicado for debriefing.

"No questions to the president by anyone, no conversation with him at all other than medical if he needs it. He's brought straight to the Chinook, the door closes, and we go, wheels up right then. That's it. Nothing else at all. Anyone questions it, it is a direct order from the vice president. Make certain everyone knows. Your people, CIA, Captain Diaz and her ops, everyone."

"Yes, sir."

132

They looked like ghosts.

Survival blankets over their heads Mylar side out and belted loosely around their bodies, eyeholes cut, the four followed José out of the fracture at the top of the chimney and then across a flat rock face to a steep narrow path between high rock formations. A few feet more and they stopped and listened. Nothing but the sound of the wind and the gentle beat of the rain on Mylar.

Miguel nodded and José led them on. Marten was second, then the president, then Hap, and then Miguel. Hap with the 9mm Sig Sauer automatic held just inside the Mylar, covering Miguel doing the same, his finger on the trigger of the Steyr machine pistol.

12:49 A.M.

They were on the far side of the rocks and descending along a steep, brush-lined path made up of gravelly sandstone. In the dark and rain it was impossible to know if they were leaving tracks that could be followed later. The other thing was the Mylar. At this point it was impossible to tell if their body heat was reading "cold" to the satellite watching from God-only-knew-how-many-miles-above-them or if their body signatures had already been read "hot" and heavily armed ops were on their way to intercept them.

Marten looked up through the rain, trying to see the ridgeline above them, his view narrowed by the eyeholes cut in the Mylar. He saw nothing but blackness and started to look away. In that second he saw a bright light swing over the hilltop.

"Everybody down!" he warned.

As one the men dropped to the ground, pulling back toward the brush. Seconds later one and then two jet helicopters passed over, their bright searchlights sliding over the hillside just above them. Then they were gone.

"The extra bodies are here," Hap said in the darkness. "There'll be a lot more. They weren't looking for us, just going in to land. Means, for the moment, they still think we're underground."

"Then these Mylars are working," Miguel said.

"Or somebody's not paying attention. Or the satellite's not working or it's out of orbit," Hap said. "Every second they give us, we'll take," abruptly he stood up. "Let's go! Move!"

12:53 A.M.

Captain Diaz touched Bill Strait's arm. He turned to look at her.

"CNP helicopter pilot coming in reported a reflection of something on the ground five kilometers before he touched down," she said. "He's not sure what it was, maybe debris of some kind or even someone camping. He didn't think much of it at the time but then thought he should report it anyway. Pilot of the second chopper saw nothing."

"You have the coordinates?"

"Yes, sir."

"Send them both back out now. See what's there. I want to know right away."

"Excuse me, sir. Night, in these mountains, in the rain. The pilots can't see. It's dangerous enough just trying to bring more troops up here."

"I appreciate that, Captain. He's our president, not yours. I still would appreciate it if you would send your pilots back out."

Captain Diaz hesitated.

"Would you feel better if the order came from your people in Madrid?"

"Yes, sir."

"So would I. Please send them anyway."

Captain Diaz nodded slowly, then turned away, giving the orders into her headset.

Christ, Strait thought, it can't be *them*. How the hell could they get out of the tunnels without us knowing?

Abruptly he crossed to the young Secret Service tech working the satellite feed. "Thermal images," he said. "What the hell is the bird reading?"

The tech moved aside so that Strait could see his computer screen. With a dozen clicks he covered the entire mountaintop search area. In each small groups of hot objects stood out brightly from the darkness. "Our own people, sir. Nothing new. Rain and length of time since darkness doesn't help but it's nothing we don't have control of."

"There's a new sector to focus on. Captain Diaz will give you the coordinates."

"Yes, sir."

"Bill," James Marshall was pushing through Secret Service and CNP techs, coming toward him. "I was with one of your agents interrogating the kid Amado, the one who broke. He didn't tell us everything. Two other people were down there too. His uncle, a limousine driver, and somebody who fits Hap's description. He's the one who sent them to us with their story about being lost."

"Hap is down there?"

"I don't know if he is or he isn't. Or what the hell is going on. I want all of his communications signals monitored, his cell, his BlackBerry, everything."

"That order is already standing, sir. I put it in the minute he went missing."

"If he is down there he can't communicate by phone with anyone until he gets on the surface. The minute he's found he's to be brought right here. I don't want him talking to anyone but me. If it is him, and the president is with him, we're home free. They're on the Chinook and on their way to the CIA jet, and finally we can shut the door on this whole damn thing."

133

Demi lay on the stainless-steel bunk, the horror of what lay ahead overwhelming her. More than anything she wanted to sleep, to make it all go away, but she knew that if she did it would be the last sleep of her life, and when she woke all that would be left would be the unspeakable: taken from this cell to the amphitheater or some other arena and burned alive, maybe even alongside Cristina, a featured part of some ancient ritual where—she wished she could laugh at the irony—it was the *witches* who did the burning.

The idea that by this time tomorrow she would no longer exist brought with it the thought that but for the few articles and photographs she had published there was nothing to mark her existence. No real accomplishments, no contributions to society, no husband, no children, nothing at all. The best she could point to was a string of lovers over the years, not one of whom she had given enough of herself of to even to be remembered, let alone wept for. Her life after the age of eight had been one of survival followed by the quest for her mother and her mother's fate, and nothing more. Now she had learned it, and that same fate had become her own.

Suddenly she thought of Nicholas Marten and President Harris, and her own fear and horror became compounded by terrible guilt. If they had fallen into the same kind of trap she had, only God could help them. It was like some biblical reckoning where the profoundly innocent paid for another's driving self-interest with their lives. And there was nothing she could do about it except to cry out "what have I done?" and ask for forgiveness.

She closed her eyes, trying to make everything go away. And for a time it did. She saw only darkness and heard the sound of her own breathing. Then, somewhere far off, she thought she heard the chanting of the monks. Little by little the voices rose. The chanting became louder, and more intense. She opened her eyes. When she did she saw what looked like a large photograph of her mother projected on the ceiling directly over her. It was the same photograph she'd found so long ago in her mother's trunk and had cherished for as long as she could remember. The one taken in the days just before she vanished. She was young and beautiful, the way she would have looked when the witches burned her to death.

In the next instant the ceiling above her erupted in fire and the photograph vanished.

Demi screamed out and leapt from the bunk in terror! Heart pounding she looked back to the ceiling but there was nothing. It was as blank as it had been before. It had been a dream, Demi knew. But if it was, why had she heard the chant of the monks? A sound and chant that still filled the tiny room.

Suddenly the icon of *Aradia Minor* glowed red in the cell's chapel. At the same time the voices of the monks grew louder, and then the entire wall beside her came alive with a video of her mother. She was seen in close-up, barefoot and wearing a clinging white dress like the one Cristina had worn and was bound to a massive stake on some surreal stage. The camera went to the floor at her feet. A ring of gas jets suddenly ignited. The camera pulled back as the flames grew higher. Slowly the lens crept in. It moved closer and closer until all that was visible were her mother's eyes. In them Demi saw not the peace that had rested in the eyes of the great ox but the pure horror of being burned alive. She saw her mother fight her bonds, saw her try to twist away. Glimpsed her mouth as it opened, then heard the terrible, ghastly shriek that came from within her. In seconds the fire overtook her and she was consumed in flame.

Demi screamed again and turned away. But there was no turning away. Every piece of wall, the floor, the ceiling, carried the images she had just seen, played over and over and over. As if to make her witness the hell of her mother's death a thousandfold. She closed her eyes and clamped her hands over her ears, spinning this way and that, doing anything she could to block the chanting. But it kept on. Becoming louder and louder until it occupied every part of her being.

It went on relentlessly. For how long? Seconds. Minutes. Hours.

Then suddenly the chanting stopped and silence took over. Slowly Demi opened her eyes, praying to God it was over.

Not quite.

In the absolute stillness came the next. Every photograph she had taken with the Canon digital since she'd first arrived in Malta and secretly transmitted to her Web site in Paris.

One after another. *Every* photograph.

Merriman Foxx. Nicholas Marten. Cristina. Reverend Beck. Luciana. Foxx's monastery office at Montserrat. Their table at the restaurant when Beck had brought Marten there. Her arrival at *The Church Within the Mountain.* The room where Cristina had come to bring her her dress. The parade of the monks to the amphitheater. The children. Their families. The animals. The owls. The death of the ox.

And then there was the last.

The photographs she had transmitted only a short while before. The photographs of the icon of *Aradia Minor* taken in the tiny chapel directly across from her. The icon she had so passionately and frantically photographed from every angle and through which she had so desperately hoped to somehow touch the soul of her mother. It was all there, each and every shot from beginning to end.

They had not only known who she was, but what she had been doing and how, all along.

134

1:22 A.M.

> Hap are you out there? Are you with the POTUS?
> This is extremely URGENT! Please respond immediately!
> Bill.

Hap clicked the BlackBerry off, powering it down as quickly as he could to avoid the electronic detection he knew Bill Strait would have ordered.

What Strait's text message meant was that they had broken the boys' story and were trying to determine if they were out of the tunnels and above ground. It was the reason for the dual helicopter flyover and spotlight surveillance in the canyon where they had been the first time the helos had come over. By that time they were at the bottom of the trail and already in the arroyo. From the sound, distant as it was, he was sure the machines had set down, meaning they had probably put more ops on the ground.

Dark or not, rain or not, they were already hard after them.

Abruptly he dropped back to Miguel. "I don't know if we've left tracks they can follow but we need to get into some water. Stream, rain runoff, anyplace where we can keep going but not leave tracks."

Miguel nodded and moved ahead to catch up with José.

1:25 A.M.

Captain Diaz turned to look at Bill Strait. "CNP detachment. They've found fresh imprints in the ground. Not clear enough to confirm if they're human."

"What do they think?" James Marshall was right there.

Diaz spoke Spanish into her headset and turned back. "Two people, maybe more. The rain's washed most all of it away. Still, it's possible they were made by animals."

"How many men are out there?" Marshall asked.

"Twenty. Two units, ten each."

Marshall turned to Bill Strait. "Quadruple that fast. Secret Service and CIA."

"Yes, sir."

"Still nothing from the satellite?"

"No, sir. 'Cold' read back only. We'd do a lot better without this rain and dark."

"We'd do a lot better without any of it."

1:44 A.M.

They were knee-deep in a fast-running wash, normally dry but now nearly a ten-foot-wide river of runoff. The darkness and uncertainty underfoot made progress slow. The Mylar survival blankets seemed to have worked so far, but they made breathing difficult, and seeing through the eyeholes would have been difficult even in daylight. Moreover, deep fatigue was beginning to take over, for the young José as well as the others.

Absently Marten reached into his jacket pocket, touching Merriman Foxx's security card and BlackBerry-like device he still carried. They were both evidence of sorts, which was why he had kept them, and he worried now about the water and electronics in the device but there was nothing he could do to protect it. Deliberately he dropped back to walk beside the president.

"Mr. President, we need to rest. All of us, José too. We lose him and we're just four guys wandering around in the dark."

The president started to respond but his words were cut off by the thundering, thudding roar of a military attack helicopter as it suddenly twisted through the canyon over the stream and came right toward them. Its twenty million candlepower searchlight swinging back and forth, illuminating the way for the pilot and at the same time lighting up the ground below in swaths as bright as day.

"Down!" Marten yelled.

The five hit the water an instant before the helo passed over.

"Did he see us?" The president lifted his head.

"Don't know," Hap cried.

"The trees!" José cried in Spanish. "There are trees on the bank to the right."

Miguel's translation was shouted.

"Go for them!" Hap yelled, and they moved fast. One after the other scrambling up a steep hillside and into the cover of conifer forest.

1:53 A.M.

"What now?" Miguel looked back at the stream, then squatted down next to the rest.

"We'll see in about twenty seconds," Hap said quietly and looked to the president. "Woody," he said.

"I know."

"Who or what is Woody?" Marten asked.

"Major George Herman Woods. Pilots *Marine One,* the presidential helicopter. Former combat officer. Thinks he's a real man's flier. And he is. Unfortunately."

Hap's twenty-second estimate took twelve. This time they heard the thudding chop of the helo's rotors before they saw the aircraft. Again it came through the canyon on the same twisting route it had taken the first time. As quickly it passed and was gone. Up and over a steep ravine, its red tail rotor light blinking as it went.

"If he saw us the first time he would have turned back and hovered," Miguel said.

"No," Hap said, "he took the same exact path as the first time. He was shooting video. Thought he saw something the first time; now they'll look at each pass and compare."

"Miguel," the president said suddenly. "What time is sunrise?"

"A little before eight. First light by seven."

The president looked to José. "How far is it to the resort now? By miles and by time?" he asked in Spanish.

"About eight miles the way we would have to go, keeping under trees and trying to stay to places we won't leave tracks. Nearly three hours more."

For a moment everything was silent. The only sound the rush of the water in the wash below and the *pit-pat* of the rain as it dripped from the trees. Then, in the darkness, Miguel spoke.

"José," he said quietly in Spanish. "The president speaks Spanish well enough. Can you lead them on your own?"

"Why?" the president asked.

"Who knows what the helicopter camera saw. Maybe nothing. Maybe everything. Maybe they can't tell. If one man leaves here and makes enough tracks for people to follow and the others go off over the rocks leaving no trail—" His voice drifted off then came back. "Who knows how many they think they are looking for but they want only one. The president. We bought time with Hector and Amado. Maybe I can buy us time this way."

"Miguel, we don't know anything," the president said.

"I think we can guess, Cousin." Abruptly Miguel stood and slipped the Steyr machine pistol from beneath his Mylar blanket. "I won't need this. They see I have a gun, they might get nervous," he handed it to Hap. "Follow José, I will see you again when it is time. Good luck to you all." Abruptly he turned, took his bearings, and walked off without another word.

They watched him go for the briefest moment then Hap looked to the president. "Mr. President, tell José to move us out."

135

2:00 A.M.

"We're starting our first run down the canyon here," U.S. Marine Corps Major George Herman "Woody" Woods, thirty-five-year-old pilot of the presidential helicopter *Marine One* and volunteer pilot of one of six attack helicopters scrambled to fly the night reconnaissance for the presidential rescue operation stood in the command post center alongside Bill Strait, National Security Advisor Marshall, and Captain Diaz watching the replay of the dual videos he had shot flying through the treacherous canyons above the fast-moving mountain stream.

"We're coming over the water, slow it please," Woods said. The Secret Service tech running the video slowed it down. "This section here, the searchlight's off a little but—stop it there, please."

The tech did. And they could see what looked like parts of some kind of reflective material in the water.

"Move it on slowly," Woods said. The tech did. "There's a tree branch. It's not moving. Neither are whatever it is in the water. That current's moving fast. If they were trash bags or some kind of plastic they'd be going with it. Second video please. Same area."

The tech touched a keyboard and Woody's second pass-over started. "Slow it, slow it," he said as the helo came in over the same area. This time the searchlight was focused on the spot where the reflective material had been seen in the first video. "Stop it, please." The tech did. The water where the reflective pieces had been was black. Nothing but water. "There was something there before, second pass it's gone."

"Enhance the video," Strait said, and looked to Woods. "What do you think?"

"I think we ought to get back out there and damn fast."

"Woody," Strait said, "something you should know. There's a good chance Hap is with the president."

"What?"

"A man fitting his description was with the POTUS underground. I tried to raise him by cell and BlackBerry. Nothing. We don't know what's going on."

"You don't think he's in on something."

"Woody, we don't know. You find them, just be damned careful. Our foremost objective is the president."

"I understand."

136

2:22 A.M.

The four were tucked under a thick blanket of trees high on a steep hillside when they saw the three attack helicopters. They came in high, then quickly dropped down and out of sight on the far side of the stream a good mile from where they were. Sixty seconds later the helos rose up again and then started slowly, one after the other, down along the stream, their searchlights swinging back and forth, covering the entire area.

"They've landed ground troops," Hap said.

Immediately the president looked to José and spoke in Spanish. "Where do we go from here?"

"Over the top of this hill and then down for about twenty minutes. After that we cross the stream again."

"That's where we hit the open space you were talking about."

"Yes."

"How open?"

"Two hundred yards. Then we are past it and back onto hard rock and through forest, going down toward the resort."

"How far then?"

"You want to go fast, yes?"

"Yes."

"Then we go down a chute between the rocks, a couloir as the French call it. It is shale rock and very steep, but we can save nearly two miles of trail and almost forty minutes of time. And because of the rock formations above, it would be hard for the helicopters."

The president looked to Marten and Hap and translated, then asked. "Do we chance this chute in the darkness, this couloir?"

"Your decision," Marten said.

The president turned to Hap. "How's the shoulder?"

"I'm alright. Go for the chute."

"Want another pain pill?"

"No," Hap said, then, "yes . . . please."

"Mr. President," Marten said quietly. "We didn't get the chance to rest before. We're getting worn down. Not just Hap, all of us. We need to take the chance and rest a little or we're not going to make it at all."

"You're right," the president looked to Hap. "You be our timetable, when you're ready, say so."

"Yes, sir."

2:32 A.M.

"Ready," Hap said, and abruptly stood. The others got up with him, ready to move.

Marten held them up. "Hap, at the risk of telling you your business. Our job is to see that the president gets to the resort and up in front of those people. Your pilot friend Woody's job and the job of everyone else they brought in is to find him and take him the hell out of here."

"What are you saying?" Hap asked.

"You have a 9mm and a machine pistol. Give me one or the other."

Hap hesitated then reached into his belt under the survival blanket, slid out the 9mm Sig Sauer, and gave it to Marten.

"Know how to use it?"

"Yeah, I know how to use it."

137

TRAIN #243, PARIS TO BERLIN, 2:48 A.M.

Victor lay back against his seat, unable to sleep. Across from him a young woman sat reading, her delicate features lit by a small overhead lamp. He glanced down the rest of the car. Save for one other reading lamp it was dark, the handful of other passengers sleeping.

The girl across from him turned the page and kept on reading, seemingly unaware he was watching her. She was blond and not particularly attractive but in her own way—how she held herself as she read, the way she turned the pages with one finger—intriguing. He thought she might be twenty-five, maybe a little older. He saw no wedding band and wondered if she was married and simply chose not to wear a ring, or if she was single, or perhaps even divorced. He watched her for a little longer then looked away to stare off vacantly into the semidarkness.

He had looked away purposely because he was afraid he would be caught staring at her and that such a thing might make her nervous. Still, he couldn't help thinking about her. The train would reach Berlin in a little over five hours. What would happen then? Did she have friends, family, someone to meet her? Or was she alone? And if she was, did she have a job or a home, at least somewhere to go?

Suddenly he felt an almost overwhelming need to protect her. As if she was his wife or his sister or even his daughter. It was then and for the first time he realized why he was here and why they had sent him. To take action to protect her and people like her *before* something happened. He was a *preventive force.*

It was why he had done what they had asked in Washington, why he had done as Richard had asked and walked through the Atocha Station terrorist bombing site in Madrid, why he had killed the jockeys in Chantilly, and why Richard had put him on this train, sending him to Berlin and then on to Warsaw, where he had promised him the most significant situation of his life. Where, if he carried out his directives properly, a major step toward halting the spread of terrorism would begin. The circumstances he knew would be complex, even dangerous, but he wasn't afraid or even nervous. Instead he was honored, knowing that if he succeeded he would be helping to protect the lives of innocent people everywhere. People like the young woman reading her book across from him now.

138

3:03 A.M.

They'd followed a slippery, dangerous trail downhill for a little over a mile in the dark before they reached the stream bank where they were now, stopped on a low rise, waiting as José went down to the water's edge trying to get some sense of the best place to cross the rushing current. So far they had seen nothing of the ground troops and assumed they were probably still in the hills behind them, though there was no way to be sure.

Ten minutes earlier the attack helicopters had abruptly pulled away from where they had been crisscrossing the area upstream and flown off to the southwest. It made them think Miguel had been found and was doing everything he could to delay them because so far they hadn't come back.

Marten moved partway down the bank, trying to pick José out in the dark. This was no time for their only guide to misstep and be swept away by the churning water. He was nearly to the young

Spaniard when the wind suddenly picked up. For the briefest moment the clouds parted and the moon shone through. As it did, Marten saw shadows coming down the hill behind them. In front of him, across the water, was the two-hundred-yard-wide unprotected area José had described. Then the clouds returned and the moonlight faded.

Quickly he went to José. "Men are coming down the hill behind us. We have to cross the water and then the open space fast, before the moon shows again."

3:07 A.M.

They clasped arms in a human chain to get across. Difficult enough under normal circumstances, next to impossible while trying to keep their balance against the force of cascading water and at the same time stay beneath the Mylar blankets. The order of alignment now, the same as it had been: José, then Marten, then the president, then Hap.

"Look," Marten said as something above the high ridge upstream caught his eye. Immediately the searchlight of an attack helicopter swung across the mountainside and started down over the stream coming right at them, its light playing on the hillside where they had been and where they could now see at least a dozen uniformed men rushing down toward the water.

"José, go, go!" the president yelled.

The teenager moved as if he had been shot. In seconds he was on the far bank and helping the others up. Then they turned and ran, crossing the open space and slipping into the trees a heartbeat before the helo reached the site where they had forded the stream. Abruptly it pulled up, swinging the searchlight over the open area and toward the trees where they were and then back across the stream and the hillside where they had been. Further up they saw the second and third helos crisscrossing the stream, their searchlights playing over it and the rugged hillsides on either side.

3:13 A.M.

They were in the thick woods, climbing through increasingly difficult and complex rock formations. José looked back, then stopped and waited for the others to catch up. All were nearly spent—their legs turning to rubber, gasping to draw in air under the thin Mylar blankets, by now fighting just to keep moving at all.

3:15 A.M.

They crouched at the base of a massive boulder, hidden in the close overhang of a long-dead tree fallen against it. Seconds later an attack helicopter made a pass directly overhead, the beam of its searchlight lighting up the rock formations and casting enormous shadows through the trees. A second helo followed in its path. And then came a third.

"¡Esta manera!" This way! José yelled as soon as it passed. In a blink they were up and moving.

3:17 A.M.

"¡Esta manera!" He yelled again, turning sharply off the trail and squeezing through a narrow slit at the base of two towering sandstone pillars. The others followed on the run, slipping through behind him.

"It is called 'The Devil's Slide'. It is very steep and very far to the bottom. Pretend this is a game and you are blindfolded. Follow my sound and just slide with it!" José said quickly in Spanish. As rapidly the president translated.

"Okay?" José asked in English.

"Go," the president said.

"Sí." Instantly the teenager stepped off into the blackness and was gone. They could hear him below, sliding on the shale as he went down. From high above came the distant thudding chop of the helos.

"You're next, Hap," the president ordered.

"Yes, sir," Hap nodded and, with a glance at Marten, stepped over the side.

Marten looked at the president and half smiled. "Promise kept. You didn't die in the tunnel."

"We're not going to die here either," now it was the president's turn to smile, "I hope."

"So do I. You're next, Cousin. Go!"

The president nodded, then abruptly turned and slid into the pitch black. Marten waited for him to clear the space beneath, then took a breath and followed.

3:19 A.M.

It was as if they had stepped into an elevator shaft. The chute was as José had said, very steep and very far to the bottom. Steeper and farther than any of them had imagined. Straight down through the blackness. Those above showered the ones below with pieces of flying shale.

José. Hap. The president. Marten. Plummeting down sightless. Standing on one foot and then the other. Each trying wildly to keep his balance while the earth slid out from under him. Each man above hoping to hell he didn't overtake the man below him.

Marten bounced off an unseen wall of rock to his right, that all but knocked the wind out of him. He pushed himself up and shifted to the left, hoping he could remain centered and not run into a wall on the other side.

He heard a heavy grunt below as the president hit something. He wanted to yell out, ask if he was alright but he was moving too fast. Suddenly he was afraid that if the president had been hurt he would slide right past him in the dark and not know it. The idea of reaching bottom and then having to climb back was no idea at all because it would be impossible. The shale would never hold. Then he heard the president cry out again as he hit something else and knew at least he was still in front of him.

A half second later his right foot caught on something and pitched him headfirst down the hill. He slid at terrifying speed, desperately flinging out one arm and then the other trying to slow himself. Then his right arm encircled a large rock. He jerked himself toward it and stopped. He was dazed and breathless. Then he saw the searchlights of the helicopters searching the forested rock formations above. It made him fear that at any moment their pilots would realize what had happened and suddenly swoop down to light up the entire area, at the same time sending a wave of troops cascading down in pursuit. Or worse, they would be waiting at the bottom when he finally got there. *If* he got there. Another breath and he stood. Then again stepped off into the dark.

139

3:24 A.M.

Miguel stood inside the command post with his arms folded over his chest. Captain Diaz stood in front of him. So did Bill Strait. So too did Dr. James Marshall. Hector and Amado were off to one side, silent, in the custody of two CNP officers. To Miguel's relief and delight, everyone seemed to be as exhausted as he was. It meant the longer he could drag this out, the longer it would be before they took action.

Hap had bought the president, Marten, and himself precious time earlier by giving up Hector and Amado. Miguel had given them a bit more by going off on his own and then watching the movement of the helicopter searchlights from the hilltop. When he'd seen the helos start downstream he'd taken off the Mylar blanket and exposed himself to the satellite's thermal imaging. It had worked almost instantly. In seconds the three helos pulled away and headed straight for him. Less than a minute later he was in the blaze of a searchlight. Then the helos touched down and armed men came running.

He'd told them his story at gunpoint, then repeated it to CNP and U.S. Secret Service agents in the helicopter on the way here. And now he was determined to tell it once more. Using up time was everything.

"Look," he said patiently in his Australian-accented Barcelonan English. "I will try and explain it to you once again. My name is

Miguel Balius. I am a limousine driver from Barcelona. I came to visit my cousin in El Borràs. When I arrived he was not there and his wife was crazy because my nephew Amado and his friend Hector were missing. Amado," he pointed at his nephew, "is that chap there. Hector is him," he gestured directly at Hector. "They were gone all day, did not come home for supper, nobody knows where they are, everybody's upset. Except I know where they are. Or I think I know. They're where they're not supposed to be. Up in the old mine tunnels looking for gold that's not there but everyone thinks there is. There is no gold in these mountains, but nobody believes it. Anyway, I tell no one, and take my cousin's motorcycle and come up here. I find their motorcycles where they always leave them. It starts to rain. I start to look. Eventually I find what I think are footprints. I follow them. It gets later. I'm wet and cold. Then, all of sudden, boom! Bright lights from the sky and in come these helicopters. Men jump out with guns. They want to know about the president of the United States. I say, 'I understand he's a nice man.' They say, 'What else do you know?' I say that I saw on the news he was taken away from Madrid in the middle of the night because of some terrorist threat. Next thing I know here I am and luckily I find Amado and Hector safe."

"You were with the president, out there on the mountain," Bill Strait said flatly.

"The president of the United States is out there on the mountain?"

"Where *is* he?"

"I came up here after Amado and Hector."

"What were you doing with a Mylar blanket?" Strait's manner was like ice, his questioning increasingly accusatory.

"I'm going into the mountains alone in the cold and rain and dark. I'm going to take something to help protect me. It's all I had."

"The protection you were looking for was from satellite surveillance."

Miguel laughed. "I'm running around in the dark and you've got a satellite looking for me? Thanks very much. I appreciate the help."

"Where is the president?" Strait pushed hard. "Who else was with him?"

"I said I came up here after Amado and Hector."

"Where *is* he?" Strait was right in Miguel's face, his eyes like stone, his stare cutting him in half.

"The president?"

"Yes."

"You mean now?"

"Yes, now."

Miguel suddenly stopped his banter and looked Bill Strait in the eye. "I have absolutely no idea."

140

3:30 A.M.

They sat on the flat of a rock-strewn trail at the bottom of the chute. They were shaking, breathless, scraped, bloodied, torn, wasted. But they'd made it. Each man accounted for. Each had said something to make sure he still had a grip on his senses. Each was enormously thankful to have made it down alive.

Far above they could see the helos still moving back and forth, playing their searchlights over the high pinnacles and the conifer forest below them. It meant that, for the moment at least, no one had found their trail or the drop into hell they had used for their escape.

The president took a deep breath and looked to José. "You are a very special person," he said in Spanish. "I thank you for myself and for all of us. I would like to call you my friend." He reached out and extended his hand.

José hesitated for the briefest moment, then looked to the others and back at the president. A shy, proud smile crept over his face as he reached out to take the president's hand.

"Gracias, sir. Usted es mi amigo," he looked to the others and nodded. "You es todos mis amigos." Thank you, sir. You are my friend. You are all my friends.

Abruptly the president stood. "Where do we go now?"

"There," José stood, nodding toward a narrow path leading through a rocky canyon. Just then the clouds parted enough for the moon to appear, lighting the entire area—from the deep canyon floor where they were to the pinnacles and mountaintops far above—like a silver moonscape. They could see the chute clearly, how deathly steep and narrow it really was and how far they had come down it. At any other time the idea of a grown man, let alone four, sliding down it out of his own choosing would have been insane if not suicidal, but this was hardly any other time.

The president looked to José. "Vamanos," he said. Let's go.

José nodded and led them off quickly toward the canyon.

141

5:20 A.M.

Nicholas Marten stood in the open doorway of a tiny tin-roof and stone outbuilding on the edge of the Aragon vineyard, a structure Hap had remembered from his walk-through of the resort site a month earlier when the Secret Service had been preparing for the president's visit. Mylar blanket finally taken off, Hap's Sig Sauer automatic stuck in his belt, he was eating a handful of dried dates they'd found in a bag on the shelf when they arrived and looking up at the sky. The weather was clear now, the moon just dipping behind the high peaks to the west. In another hour the horizon would begin to pale. In two it would be fully light. Sunup would come a half hour later.

Marten stood there a moment longer trying to visualize the steep zigzag trail they had come down after they'd left the base of the chute. So far he had seen nothing of the helicopters nor anything else to suggest that their tracks had been found and that their trail was being followed. With luck, Marine Corps Major George Herman "Woody" Woods and the other helo pilots were still confining their search to the mountains and would continue to do so until well after daybreak. What they did afterward would be of little consequence, because by then, if things worked the way Hap had outlined, they would have breached the Aragon resort's massive security force, and the president would long since have arrived at the church on the hill and given the speech of his life to the highly prestigious members of the New World Institute.

5:23 A.M.

Marten turned and went back inside. José was curled up asleep on the floor just inside the door. A few feet to his left, Hap slept the sleep of the dead, the Steyr machine pistol in the crook of his arm. Safely back from the doorway on Hap's far side, President Harris slept too.

Marten slid the Sig Sauer from his belt and sat down in the doorway. They had reached the outbuilding just before 4:30. Five minutes afterward Hap had determined that the area was secure. It was then they found a watering hose tethered to a wall outside the building and the bag of dates inside, and all four ate and drank. Almost immediately extreme weariness began to overtake them and Marten volunteered first watch. At 5:45 he was to wake Hap and then have some forty-odd minutes of sleep himself before they were up and moving at 6:30, hoping to cover the three-quarters of a mile across the vineyards and up the hill, to where the resort's maintenance buildings were, just before daybreak.

Hoping.

So far they had encountered no resistance. The reason, Hap said, was the time of day and the remoteness of the area, and that they had yet to approach the resort's security perimeter that was nearly a mile farther in—a gravel work road that cut the vineyard almost in half, with the inward side bordering the resort itself. That work road was where the first lines of security would be set up, lines that would ease out to encircle the entire Aragon complex, the size of which was staggering—the vineyards, the eighteen hole golf course, parking areas, tennis courts, forested walking trails, the eighteen resort buildings and bungalows, and finally their goal, the ancient church on the hill behind it.

The security force numbered five hundred and was made up of

local and state police and controlled, as the president had guessed, by the Spanish Secret Service. If the president had been going to speak as originally planned Hap would have supplemented that force with an additional one hundred U.S. Secret Service agents. But that plan was abandoned after what had "officially" taken place in Madrid and the president was removed to the famous "undisclosed location." That the president would not be attending the Aragon sunrise service was something Hap knew had been transmitted formally to The New World Institute's hierarchy by White House Chief of Staff Tom Curran from the U.S. embassy in Madrid. It was just that situation Hap was counting on because he knew security would stand down to a lesser level of alert and was why he had taken the approach he had.

The vineyards at this time of year and particularly on an early Sunday morning would have at best a skeleton crew, if even that. The maintenance-building complex housed not only the vineyard, golf course and groundskeeping equipment and supplies, but also the resort's sizable laundry where, among other things, employee uniforms were laundered and stored. Reaching those maintenance buildings safely and unseen became the first step in his plan. Far more difficult would be getting the president the next mile and a half, up the long forested hill behind the resort to the four-hundred-year-old church where the New World sunrise service was to be held.

If Marten marveled at Hap's inventory of logistical particulars, he shouldn't have. It was part of the job, what the Secret Service did before a presidential visit anywhere. He just hoped Hap's memory was as good as he thought it was and that in the meantime no new and unknown security measures had been implemented by the Spanish forces.

142

Five minutes more until Marten woke Hap. He knew that in his state of exhaustion, if he wasn't careful he would fall asleep where he was and if he did they all might sleep for days. Instead, he played mind games with himself; thinking of his work as a landscape architect at Fitzsimmons and Justice in Manchester and of the very pressing and yet unfinished Banfield project. Of Demi; where she was now, what her real motivation had been for delivering himself and the president to Merriman Foxx at Montserrat. Whatever it had been, one thing was certain, she could have had no idea at all about what was really going on, with Foxx, with his experiments, with any of the president's enemies. He had last seen her in the company of Foxx and Beck and Luciana at the monastery restaurant, but when he and the president had returned, Foxx had been alone. It meant she had gone somewhere with the others. But where and for what reason? All he could think was she had told the truth about her sister, and that finding her, or at least learning what had happened to her, was the most important thing in her life.

5:44 A.M.

"Cousin."

Marten started and looked up. The president stood before him, his bearded face more gaunt and drawn than ever.

"I know Hap was going to take second watch," he said quietly. "He's pretty banged up; let him sleep. Go get some yourself."

"You sure?"

"I'm sure."

"Want this?" Marten held up the Sig Sauer.

"Yes."

Marten handed it to him. "Thanks."

The president smiled, "You're wasting your precious forty winks."

"Don't fall back asleep."

"Can't. I've got a speech to practice."

143

6:30 A.M.

It was barely light enough to see when the president returned the Sig Sauer to Marten and the four left the outbuilding, starting up a long sloping hill, muddy from the rain, and lined with rows of just-budding grapevines. Marten first, then the president, then Hap, then José.

Moments earlier the president had thanked José for his courage and daring, and then told him he should turn back and go home before things got worse. But the teenager had refused, saying he wanted to stay, to be of any help that he could. Keeping José with them was something Hap wanted too. The youngster was not only a local who could speak easily to any worker they might come upon, but there was something else: if he went home Bill Strait would have the Secret Service, the CIA, or the Spanish police waiting for him, his presence in the shafts learned from Amado or Hector or both, his name and address taken. If they got him and he knew where the president was, it wouldn't be long before he told them everything, and in a blink the mountain teams would show up in full force, and that was something they couldn't have happen.

6:35 A.M.

Marten neared the crest of the hill, then suddenly stopped and dropped to one knee, motioning for the others to do the same. The maintenance buildings were just ahead. Four of them, large wooden barnlike structures built around a central courtyard. Immediately to their right and just beyond three rows of budding grape canes was the gravel work road that cut the vineyard in half and where the initial lines of security would be set up.

"What is it?" the president whispered.

"Listen." Marten had his head up and was looking toward the buildings.

"What?" Hap slid in beside them.

"Down," Marten motioned them flat on the ground.

Seconds later two uniformed policemen on motorcycles passed by, their eyes scanning the vineyards on either side, heading slowly back down the road behind them.

Marten looked to Hap, "Think there are more?"

"Don't know."

"I'll find out," José said to the president in Spanish.

Before they could stop him he was up and running toward the quadrangle of buildings. Then he disappeared from sight.

6:43 A.M.

"No one else," José said in Spanish as he came back to kneel beside them. "Come quickly."

In no time he was leading them past the grape canes and onto the gravel road. Then they ran, moving like shadows toward the buildings in pale light. Fifty yards, thirty. Then twenty, ten, and they were there. José opened a side door and they went inside.

6:46 A.M.

The room was huge, the central garage for the resort's rolling stock. There were four pick-up trucks; four full size tractors; six small flat-bedded three-wheel trucks; four large golf-course mowers, and four open electric-powered service carts, parked nose to tail in a line. Backed up against a closed sliding door at the rear was a dust-covered faded green Toyota van that looked like it hadn't been driven for months.

"Watch the door," Hap said, and went to the line of carts, hoping to find one with keys in the ignition.

"Here," Marten had opened a cabinet beside an office door. Inside, arranged neatly on pegs, were the keys to each vehicle. It took three full minutes before they were sorted out and the key for the first cart in line was found. Immediately Hap got in and tried it. The engine light glowed green, indicating a full electric charge.

Thirty seconds later they were warily crossing toward the building that housed the laundry. The sky was much lighter now. The cover of darkness they'd relied on for so long had given way to a rapidly brightening day.

They left José at the door and entered the main laundry room. Three enormous open vatlike stainless-steel washers took up the center area, while a bank of stainless-steel dryers was positioned against a far wall. Opposite both was a large window that looked out to the other buildings. Just past it were the pressing machines, and beyond them, stainless-steel clothing racks that held rows of assorted Aragon Resort uniforms, most on hangers and arranged by size: a necessary convenience for the exclusive five-star resort that Hap knew had more than two hundred employees who had to be in clean, well-pressed uniforms at all times.

"Un hombre está viniendo." A man is coming, José said from the doorway, then quickly ducked out of sight.

The president motioned to Hap and Marten, and the three slipped out of sight behind the pressing machines. Hap took a breath and slid out the Steyr machine pistol. Marten raised the Sig Sauer.

A moment later a large curly-haired man in white pants and a white T-shirt came in. He flicked on the overhead lights, then went to a control panel and pressed a series of buttons. Almost immediately the washing machines began to fill with water. The man adjusted a temperature gauge, then walked to the washers and looked in. Satisfied, he turned and left.

Hap waited a half beat then crossed the room, pressing up against the big window to look out. He saw the laundryman walk to a far building and go inside, closing the door behind him. Immediately Hap turned to the others.

"He'll be back soon enough. We need to move and fast."

144

Dr. James Marshall watched Captain Diaz and one of Bill Strait's Spanish-speaking Secret Service agents interrogating Miguel in an isolated area near the rear of the command post. The questions went from Spanish to English back to Spanish, then to English again. Handcuffed and more than a little nervous, CNP guards standing coldly alongside, Hector and Amado sat on folding chairs only feet away, deliberately made party to Miguel's grilling. If Miguel didn't break they were betting one of the boys would.

Abruptly Marshall turned and went to Bill Strait. "He's not telling them anything."

"He will, or one of the kids will tell us more, but it'll take time so I wouldn't count on a sudden revelation."

Marshall was tired and angry and frustrated. He was also becoming increasingly anxious and didn't like it. It made him feel like Jake Lowe. "We've got a Spanish limousine driver with an Australian accent and two local teenagers. Then we've got a guy who looks like Hap, or maybe *is* Hap, someplace out there with the president and this Nicholas Marten. We've got every piece of hi-tech equipment and an army of bodies and aircraft flying around and now we've got daylight, and still nobody can find them. Why?"

"Maybe it's because they're still somewhere in the tunnels," Strait said. "Or because they're not here at all."

"What the hell does that mean?"

Strait turned and walked over to a map of the area. "This," he said, sweeping a hand over the mountaintops, "is where we've been looking. Over here," he moved his hand far to the right, "is the Aragon Resort, where the president was originally to speak this morning."

Marshall perked. "You think that's where he's going?"

"I don't know. What I do know is we haven't found him here.

We know he was in the tunnels, and Hap or no Hap, if he some-how got out and into these mountains . . ." Strait hesitated, then went on. "I can't get inside his head except to think that the resort is a place to go that's real and that he knows about and where there are very important people he can talk to, a number of whom he knows. How he'd do it, I don't know. I'm just thinking out loud."

Marshall turned and walked back to Captain Diaz to pull her away from Miguel and the boys. "Would it be possible," he asked, "for the president to somehow get off these mountains and to the Aragon Resort?"

"Avoiding satellite detection?"

"What if he had a Mylar blanket like the limo driver? What if those were the things we saw in the water in the helicopter images. The president, Hap Daniels, Marten, and the driver."

"Then you're suggesting he went the rest of the way by foot, overland, and in the rain and dark."

"Yes."

Captain Diaz smiled. "It's not likely at all."

"Is-it-possible?" Marshall enunciated coldly.

"If he was crazy and if he had some idea of how to get there. I would say yes, I guess it's possible."

145

7:03 A.M.

They were dressed as groundskeepers. Dark green shirts with lighter green pants. The classic logo of *The Resort at Aragon* stitched in white italics over the left breast pocket, their old clothes hidden in a trash container near the back of the maintenance building where the rolling stock was. Of the four, only the president kept one per-sonal item with him and it was tucked safely inside his shirt. It was the one thing he had kept all along and what he would wear when he addressed The New World Institute delegation. The thing that, despite his workman's uniform and growth of beard, would make him instantly recognizable to everyone there, his toupee.

José stood at the door, peering out. Marten eased the electric cart up to it and stopped. The president sat beside him, Hap in back, machine pistol in hand, along with a contingent of necessary props—rakes, brooms, plastic trash cans, and something else Hap had picked up simply because he felt it might come in handy later: a pair of binoculars, lifted from the top of what appeared to be a supervisor's desk.

"Any sign of him yet?" the president asked in Spanish.

José shook his head, then—"Sí," he said suddenly, and looked back. "The man in white just went back into the laundry," he said in Spanish and the president translated.

"Let's go," Hap said.

José slid the front door open, Marten eased the cart out and waited for José to close it again. Ten seconds later he jumped into the cart alongside Hap, and then they were going, moving silently past the buildings and turning onto the gravel road that would take them down behind the golf course and then up a winding mile-and-a-half-long service road through deep woods to the church.

7:12 A.M.

They crested a hill and stopped under the cover of a large conifer. For the first time they could see past the vineyards to the golf course and the resort itself. In front of the elegant white-stuccoed main building were seven unmarked highly polished jet-black tour buses with heavily tinted windows. The buses that had picked up the New World group from the airport in Barcelona Friday and that would take them back at the close of the sunrise service this morning.

Nearby were a dozen large black SUVs, Spanish Secret Service vehicles that would escort them to the church and then to the airport. Farther out they could see a major force of police vehicles blocking the main road in from the highway. More were stationed every quarter mile or so along the work road that bisected the vineyard. Everything in place, as Hap knew it would be.

High above the resort itself and at the top of a long curving blacktop road, they could just make out the ancient stone and red-tile roof of the Romanesque structure that was La Iglesia de Santa Maria, the Church of Saint Mary.

"That it?" the president asked.

"Yes, sir," Hap said.

The president let out a breath. They were that close.

146

7:17 A.M.

The service road took them around the far edges of the golf course and then abruptly down into a wooded glade, then steeply up again, winding through thick conifers toward the church. Marten was just starting a turn and thinking about what they would do when they reached the rear of the church and the service entrance where they were headed when Hap suddenly intruded. He was looking uphill through the binoculars.

"Patrol vehicle coming down, get off the road," he snapped.

Marten drove another dozen yards, then abruptly turned the cart off the road and through some trees to stop behind a low rock wall.

Hap lifted the machine pistol, Marten slid out the Sig Sauer and then they sat back and watched a four-wheel-drive police car come down the hill. It slowed as it approached, then slowed even more. They could see four uniformed men inside, all looking in the direction where they were hidden.

"Nothing here, nothing here, keep going," Marten breathed.

The car slowed even more, and for the briefest moment they were certain it was going to stop. But it didn't, the driver just rolled it slowly on past and kept on.

"Good boys," Marten said.

"Give them a minute to clear," Hap put down the machine pistol and picked up the binoculars, then turned to follow the police vehicle as it drove slowly down the hill.

"This is fill," the president said abruptly and out of the blue looking at the land around them. "This dirt, this soil base. I've been watching it all along. The further up the road we get, the more obvious it becomes. It's all landfill. Look around, most of these trees are young. Fifteen, twenty years old at most."

"Mr. President," Hap was still looking through the glasses, "the resort is barely twenty years old. They probably graded everything and replanted."

"Except for one thing. The church. How do you put a four-hundred-year-old church on twenty-year-old landfill?"

"Number the stones, then tear it down and rebuild it as it was," Marten said.

"But why? And where was it before?"

"Uh-oh," Hap said abruptly.

"What is it?" The president turned to follow his gaze.

"More security."

A second police SUV had come up the road from below, and the car going down was stopped next to it, their drivers chatting.

"What do we do now?" the president asked.

"Nothing. We try to leave, they'll see us."

"You mean we stay here?"

"Yes, sir. We stay here."

147

7:25 A.M.

Four black-robed monks brought Demi from her cell and walked her down a long, barren, and dimly lit hallway. She wore only sandals and the scarlet dress Cristina had brought for her to wear during the ritual ceremonies the night before. That she had been forced to strip naked and put the dress on in front of the monks meant nothing.

How could it? They had come to take her to her death.

7:28 A.M.

The first monk slipped a security card through an electronic reader beside a steel door. The door slid open and they entered another long corridor. To both left and right doors stood open to what looked like physicians' examination rooms. They were small, identical, and had opaque glass boxes mounted on the walls, the kind used for reading X-rays and prints of scans. A stainless-steel examination table stood coldly in the center of each.

7:29 A.M.

They passed through another security door and entered a room filled with stainless-steel bunks, the same as the one in the cell she had just occupied. The only difference was that here they were stacked four high to the ceiling on either side of a center aisle and stretched to the far end of the chamber. Enough to easily accommodate two hundred people at a time.

Another corridor and she saw communal toilets and showers. Just past them was what looked like a small commercial kitchen and beyond it an area of stainless-steel tables with attached benches that might have been used for dining. These rooms, like the rooms and corridors she'd seen before it, were empty, as if the entire area had been a beehive of activity that had quickly and purposely been abandoned.

7:31 A.M.

The monks brought her through a series of five heavy security doors, one less than ten feet from the other. Then they entered a long, darkened subwaylike tunnel with a single monorail track running down its center. In front of them was a large, sledlike conveyance, completely open save for three rows of bench seats. Four more monks sat shoulder to shoulder on the rearmost bench. In front of them another monk sat alongside—Demi caught her breath as she saw her.

Cristina.

She wore the white gown of the night before and smiled pleasantly, even happily, when she saw Demi.

Immediately Demi was seated next to her. As quickly one of the monks slid in beside her. The remaining monks took the seats directly in front of them. Nine monks to escort two women into eternity.

Abruptly the sled moved off, quickly and silently picking up speed. A second passed, and then two, and then Cristina turned to Demi and smiled the most horrifying smile she had ever seen. Horrifying because it was so warm and genuine and childlike.

"We are going to join the ox," she said excitedly, as if they were about to go on some wonderful adventure.

"We mustn't," Demi whispered. "We have to find a way not to go."

"No!" Cristina suddenly pulled back, and her eyes shone with a terrible and immeasurable darkness. "We must go. Both of us. It has been written in the heavens since the beginning of time."

The sled began to slow and Demi saw they were approaching the end of the tunnel. Seconds later the sled stopped. The monks stood together and led both women onto a platform beside it. Immediately a large door slid open and they were taken into a large room. In the center of it was what appeared to be an oversized commercial furnace.

Demi felt the breath go out of her as she realized what it was— a steel-faced brick retort oven. The room was a crematory. The place where it all ended.

"The ox waits by the fire," Cristina smiled, and then four of the monks led her away.

A moment later the remaining monks took Demi into another room. A woman turned as they entered. It was Luciana. She was dressed in a long black clerical robe, her black hair the same tight bun as the night before, her dark eye makeup accentuated by the same theatrical streaks that ran like daggers from the corners of her eyes to the hollows of her ears, the same hideously long nails once again fixed to the ends of her fingers.

"Sit down," Luciana indicated a lone chair in the center of the room.

"Why?"

"So that I may do your hair and makeup."

"My hair and makeup?" Demi was incredulous.

"Yes."

"Why?"

"You must be beautiful."

"To die?"

Luciana smiled cruelly. "It is a requirement of the tradition."

148

7:48 A.M.

The Sig Sauer in his lap, Marten drove the last quarter mile cautiously, the gravel road twisting in a large S through a thick stand of conifers. Through them they could just see the church and the small wooded parking lot that served its rear entrance. Hap glanced behind them. There was nothing. They'd had to wait an extraordinarily long time for the police vehicles to leave the area below. When finally they had and Hap gave Marten the okay and then they'd started up again, he'd still kept a close watch behind. The police might have gone but this road was clearly their assignment which meant they could, and probably would, return at any time.

The first rays of the morning sun touched the mountain peaks behind them as Marten pulled into the parking lot and stopped beside three church vans.

"Those should be church staff getting ready for the service," Hap said of the vans. "They'll be inside and upstairs in the main part of the church." He glanced around quickly, then gave the okay, and the four got out of the cart, looking for all the world as if they belonged there, taking the rakes and brooms and trash cans and setting them near the rear entry door as if preparing for work.

The elevation here was higher than at the church's main entrance in the front and gave them a view of the large central parking area and the long curving road leading up to it from the rolling sprawl of the resort and vineyards below.

"Keep an eye on the door," Hap said to Marten, then took the binoculars and walked up a small hill to squat next to a large tree. Through the glasses he could see the force of uniformed police and police vehicles guarding the surrounding roads. A pan to the main parking lot and he could see the Spanish Secret Service SUVs taking positions in front of and behind the sleek black buses and the line of New World delegates boarding them. He wrinkled his forehead in puzzlement and looked back to the others.

"The people getting on the buses are dressed in evening clothes. All of them, men and women."

"What?" The president moved in, Hap handed him the glasses, and he looked through them. "Formal evening clothes for a nondenominational sunrise service?"

"Was this brought up to you in the briefing?"

"No," Hap said.

The president shook his head, "I don't get it."

"Neither do I."

7:50 A.M.

They left José outside to serve as a lookout, clearing leaves from a flower bed and guardedly entered the church through the rear door.

Hap led them down a narrow limestone hallway. To their right was a meeting room of some kind and past it another stairway leading up that the president would take to reach the church proper. Twenty feet more and Hap turned them left and down a stone stairway that led to a basement storage area where he felt it was safe for them to wait until the service began.

Partway down, the staircase made a large semi-circular turn as if it were circumventing a turret or something large and rounded on the far side of the wall. It was curious architecture for a church building as old as this one, reconstructed or not. Even the president mentioned it.

"There shouldn't be round walls inside an essentially rectangular building, not one like this," he said, almost eerily.

"Whatever it is, it's not noted on the blueprints the resort management gave us. The Spanish Secret Service made no reference to it either," Hap said.

The president studied it again and then let it pass as they

reached the bottom of the staircase and started along a hallway with doors open to rooms on both left and right and one closed with a "W/C" on the door, water closet or restroom.

"Meeting and classrooms, restroom," Hap said, then abruptly stopped at a closed door and opened it. "In here," he said, and flicked on a wall switch. The room filled with light, and they entered the small storage room he had promised. Cleaning materials and paper supplies filled shelves on either side. Everyday tools—hammers, wrenches, pliers, tin snips, screwdrivers, hand drills, plug-in work lights and several well-used flashlights—were mounted neatly on a rack above a workbench near the rear. A far corner was stacked with a dozen cardboard boxes labeled *Biblias Santas.* Holy Bibles.

Hap closed the door and looked at his watch. "It's seven fifty-six," he said, looking to the president. "I have no way to know if your friend Rabbi Aznar is still scheduled to be part of the service, but whoever is giving the convocation, it should begin about ten after eight. The Spanish Secret Service will sweep it before people come in. I don't want us going up there blindly and having to wait in the hallway before everyone is seated and the doors are closed. We might convince the Spaniards but most likely not, especially if their orders came from Madrid. They'd think what they all think, they're doing the right thing by hustling you out of here. So to wait up there is too dangerous. The Spaniards will stand down to a degree once the convocation begins. That's when we go up."

"How are we going to know when that is? We can't post someone up there, not even José."

"At the end of the hallway is the church's video room. In it are monitors for twenty automated security cameras mounted throughout the upper church and in the parking lot outside that are fed to central security at the resort. Trouble is, the room is locked. But if I can get us in, we'll be able to see everything that's going on in the church proper and the area outside it. What worries me is that it could take time to get that door open, if I can get it open at all. Somebody comes along in the meantime, sees us and alerts security, this whole thing can turn real nasty in a hurry."

"Hap," the president pressed him, "somebody comes along, I'm the same as you two fellas and José outside," he half-smiled and pointed to the resort logo on his work shirt, "just some half-bald guy who works here."

7:58 A.M.

The door to the control room was fifty feet down the hallway from the storage room, made of steel and locked. On the wall next to it was an electronic keypad and a slot for a coded security card.

Marten stood lookout, his back against the wall, the Sig Sauer held at his side. Hap put his hand on the doorknob and turned it. Nothing happened.

"Most of these devices have a master override, a special code technicians use to get inside them. You just have to find it."

He punched a code into the keypad and tried the door again. Nothing. He tried a different code. Still nothing. He tried another series of numbers, and then another series still. And then another. Still nothing. Finally he shook his head and turned to the president. "It's not going to work, and we can't break the door down. We'll have to go back to the storeroom and judge the start of services as best we can."

"Cousin," Marten looked to the president. "When we got up here to the church I looked back the way we had come. You can see way out across the valley, past the maintenance buildings to the mountains where we were last night.

"I drew an imaginary line from the big door where the monorail ended in the tunnel to here. It went across the vineyards, through the maintenance buildings, and to the church here in a line about as straight as you can get. If Foxx had that tunnel dug at the same time this resort was built, he would have had to put the dirt somewhere. That tunnel is ten miles long inside the mountain itself; it's probably another eight or more miles over here if he brought it that far. Any way you look at it, it's a lot of dirt and rock. You said this soil was all fill, maybe that's where it came from."

"I don't understand."

"If I'm right, all of this, the labs, the monorail tunnel, this church, even the resort, is Foxx's work. His idea, his design, his construction, everything."

"What if it is?"

"He might have left keypads and entry codes for others, but why would he complicate things for himself and have a dozen electronic security keys when one would do?" He took Merriman Foxx's security card from his jacket, went to the door, and slid it through the slot next to the door, as he had done to get them into Foxx's experimentation labs under the monastery.

There was a distinct click. Marten turned the knob, and the door opened.

"It seems Dr. Foxx's interests were even more encompassing than we thought."

149

8:00 A.M.

The control room was carpeted, with bunkerlike concrete walls and painted a deep metallic gray. A lone hi-tech office chair sat before a control console above which a bank of twenty closed-circuit television monitors were mounted. To one side was what looked like a narrow panel built into the wall. It was made of steel and painted the same color as the room. What it was was a door; one with flush-set hinges, two inset locks, one above the other, and nothing else. What it was for or where it led, Hap didn't know. The only information he had came from the blueprints the resort management had given to the Secret Service. The room they were in had been designated as *"video control room,"* the inset-panel door had been labeled *"emergency access to electrical panels."* Hap had been in the video room during his earlier security walk-thru but had not asked that the door be unlocked and opened. Although as a potential hiding place for bombs or persons bent on doing harm to the president it would have been checked during the final Secret Service sweep of the grounds in the hours just prior to the president's arrival.

"What would have Foxx's interest in all this been? The resort as some kind of ostentatious cover for his work?" the president asked as they turned their attention to the monitors.

"Don't know," Marten said, "I would have made no connection at all if you hadn't mentioned the composition of the hillside, and if

I hadn't drawn my imaginary line, and if his card hadn't just opened this door."

"Here come the buses." Hap was staring at the monitors, where a line of the sleek black buses could be seen coming up the road from the resort. Other monitors picked up the Spanish Secret Service's black SUVs escorting them. Others still, showed the inside of the church from a dozen or more angles.

One was focused on the central aisle just inside the main doors where a dozen black-robed monks waited. Another showed the altar. Another still, the choir bays on either side of it. There was an angle on the pulpit. One on the door behind it and to the side, where the president planned to enter. Another showed a long empty corridor somewhere. Another yet gave a view of the chapel's seating area, where the seats were not rows of pews but rather more like a theater with stadium seating.

Another monitor revealed an area to the side of the altar where a door suddenly opened and another black-robed monk entered followed by two people in clerical robes.

"Reverend Beck," the president said in surprise as they saw the first person. Then the second person came into view, a woman.

"The witch Luciana," Marten said.

"Congressional chaplain Rufus Beck?" Hap was as surprised as the president.

"Señor?" There was a sudden pounding on the door. "Señor?"

"José." Marten said.

Machine pistol in hand, Hap stepped to the door and carefully opened it.

"I couldn't find you. Helicopters are coming," Jose was talking excitedly to the president in Spanish. "Out there," he pointed off, "from the mountains."

The president snapped a quick translation.

"Christ!" Hap blurted. "They figured it out. We've got to go, Mr. President, and now. We're caught in here, we're dead, all of us."

8:06 A.M.

They could hear the thudding chop of approaching helicopters as they came out. Hap first, cautiously, machine pistol ready. Then

José, the president, and Marten with the Sig Sauer. Hap started them for the cart, then suddenly pulled them back behind the cover of one of the church vans. A police SUV was coming up the gravel work road toward them.

In the next moment the helicopters arrived. There were two of them and they were identical, painted dark green and white with the American flag just above the doors. They were United States Marine Squadron One, U.S. Marine helicopters that ferried the president and other ranking administration officials wherever they needed to go.

"Marine Two," Hap said in astonishment as the helos circled over the parking lot and then suddenly dropped down to land. *Marine One* was the designation when the president was aboard, *Marine Two* when it was the vice president.

"So much for your speech, Cousin," Marten said as the helos touched down and were instantly surrounded by shining black SUVs. Immediately the doors opened and the vice president's Secret Service detail got out. They waited for the helicopter engines to shut down, then the agents went directly to them. A half second later the doors were pulled back and those inside stepped out.

Vice President Hamilton Rogers. Secretary of Defense Terrence Langdon. Secretary of State David Chaplin. Chairman of the Joint Chiefs of Staff, United States Air Force General Chester Keaton. Presidential Chief of Staff Tom Curran. And Evan Byrd. Of the group that had faced the president in Madrid only his chief political advisor, Jake Lowe and National Security Advisor, Dr. James Marshall, were missing.

"My God," the president breathed.

"Hap," Marten warned, nodding toward the grove of trees and the approaching police SUV.

Hap glanced at it, then back at the helos and the swarm of Secret Service agents surrounding the president's "friends."

"We're going back inside, now!" Hap took the president by the arm and rushed him toward the church door they had come out only seconds before.

150

As if it were possible, the monks pulled Demi deeper into her nightmare.

The room was like a stage, semicircular and open to a darkened ceiling thirty feet or more above her. The walls reaching to it were polished steel. The floor, visible only moments before, was now knee-deep in swirling man-made fog illuminated from beneath by unseen lights in an ethereal combination of reds, greens, purples and ambers. In the center of it was a simple black throne where Cristina perched regally, her fall of magnificent black hair stark against her clinging white gown, the setting and the lighting making her the star attraction of whatever was to happen next. Clearly there was to be a show, and soon there would be an audience for it, one Demi clearly imagined would be made up of what Giacomo Gela had described as he told of the Traditions—"an annual rite performed before several hundred members of a powerful order called the *Unknowns.*"

Wordless, the monks took Demi toward the center of the stage, then stopped as slowly a great balled cross of Aldebaran rose up before them. Immediately the monks secured her feet to its base, then pulled a strap tight around her throat and lifted her arms outward, binding them to the crossbars. In seconds she had become a living crucifix fastened to a pagan icon.

Cristina looked over at her and smiled. "The ox waits."

"No."

"Yes."

At that moment a monk appeared through the fog and approached Cristina. He handed her a silver goblet filled with red wine. She took it, and smiled, and gently opened her mouth. As she did the monk laid a round wafer on her tongue. She lifted the goblet and drank, swallowing the wafer. This, Demi knew, was part of the ceremony. She also knew she had witnessed a false Eucharist. Christ and the Last Supper were not part of this rite. Nor was the wafer symbolic of his body nor the wine of his blood. The night before, the ox had stood calmly and peacefully as it was consumed by fire, no fear or pain in its eyes. Clearly it had been given some drug, and Demi was certain Cristina had been given one now. But she knew too that while the drugged beast had died peacefully, it had all been for show. For the children and the others to see and to believe Cristina would have that same peaceful journey. But it was a lie; she had seen the video of her mother's sacrificial death and knew what Cristina's death and hers would be like. Cristina might be drugged now, but the effect wouldn't last. Whoever these people were, their ritual centered on horrible, excruciating human death. She knew too that while Cristina's burning was the rite's centerpiece, it was she who was to be the very pointed political sideshow, her own torturous murder an example to any of the *Unknowns* who at some point might decide to rebel and turn against them.

There was something else as well: her clear memory of the video and how it had been presented to her. These people were not simply evil, they were profoundly cruel and vindictive. It was as if her heinous death was not enough; they had also to demonstrate their power, their oversight, their all-knowingness. Woe be to anyone in the afterlife who might be reborn and try again to challenge them.

Demi looked off, unable to bear more of her own thoughts. When she did, horror struck once more. As if from some medieval graveyard three more balled crosses rose from the fog. On each was mounted a severed human head.

151

Their retreat back into the church left only one place to go, the se-cured video control room. A location both helpful and dangerous. It was secluded and they had locked it from inside but it also meant that if they were found, there would be no further escape. The pres-ident would be dead before nightfall and so would the rest of them.

"Maybe," president sat down in the chair and studied the mon-itors, "what Foxx didn't tell us, they will."

Marten moved next to Hap to stand over the president's shoul-der and watch. He marveled at the president's ability to compart-mentalize and to turn sheer disadvantage into opportunity. For the most part the situation didn't seem to matter.

"José," the president turned to look at the teenager standing back against the door. He had come this far. Done everything that was asked and more. But now, locked in this room, he was clearly frightened. The presidential helicopters, the flock of Secret Ser-vice agents, the bank of high-tech monitors, everything was beyond him.

"It's alright," the president said gently in Spanish. "Come over here with us. You are a man. See what's going on. Maybe you can explain some—"

"The buses are here," Marten said, and the president turned back to the monitors. The string of black buses were seen arriving in the parking lot on five of the monitors. They stopped, the doors opened and the New World guests, resplendent in evening clothes, walked from them and toward the church entrance. They were smiling, pleasantly chatting among themselves, wholly comfortable in the presence of the heavy security.

"I never saw the full roster of the New World membership but I'll bet I know half those people, some of them well," the president was clearly and deeply troubled. "They represent some of the most powerful and influential institutions around the world. Do they have any idea what's going on? Or are they part of it?"

Just then the church's bells began to ring. Curiously, it was not the joyous tolling usually associated with a call to worship but instead the chiming of the Westminster Quarters, the familiar sound heard from clock towers around the world to strike the hour.

"Why the Quarters?" the president asked. "It's not on the hour. Is there some significance here? What does it mean, if anything?"

"Mr. President, Marten," Hap cut in, "monitor seven, middle row."

A parking-lot camera aimed down the road toward the main resort buildings picked up a distant line of helicopters coming in. There were four and then a fifth. The last, the U.S. Army Chinook.

"Who is it?" the president was intent on the screen.

"I'd guess Woody" Hap said, "with the CNP behind him. Probably Bill Strait in the Chinook with Dr. Marshall and Jake Lowe. We came up from Madrid in it. I didn't think things could get much worse, but suddenly they are."

8:16 A.M.

U.S. Marine Corps Major Woody Woods set the U.S. Marine Corps attack helicopter down on the Aragon Resort's ninth fairway. Seconds later three CNP helicopters landed. And then the Chinook set down. Immediately its doors were pulled back. Bill Strait came out first, followed by Dr. James Marshall and then a dozen U.S. Secret Service agents. The second, third, and fourth helos were Spanish CNP, with Captain Diaz in the lead chopper; their assignment: search the area from the vineyard's work road to the outside edge of the vineyards while other Secret Service, CIA, and CNP ground and helicopter units worked the area between the vineyards and the mountains. The route they suspected the president and anyone with him might have used; a group that would include Nicholas Marten and Hap Daniels.

By the vice president's order, the area from the vineyard road to the resort and beyond, all the way to the church, was under control of his Secret Service detail, the Spanish Secret Service, and the Spanish police already deployed. If the president was within that perimeter he would be found. The outer perimeters belonged to Bill Strait and Captain Diaz.

In between, the Chinook stood by, ready to take the president out.

152

8:24 A.M.

President Harris had seen his close friend Rabbi Aznar give a brief convocation before the assembled members of the New World Institute. Then he had shaken hands with Vice President Rogers and left the stage on the arm of Reverend Beck.

Less than thirty seconds later an exterior security camera picked him up as he was escorted out and into the parking lot by two of the monks. The Secret Service helped him into one of the black SUVs and he was driven away. Immediately afterward the monks went back inside, closing the doors behind them.

"What happened?" the president asked as the monitors suddenly lost their picture. Immediately he had his answer: a computerized listing began:

> Access one: locked. Lock confirmed.
> Access two: locked. Lock confirmed.
> Access three: locked. Lock confirmed.

The access scroll continued: numbers four to ten.
Then came the last:

> Lock confirmation completed.

"Those are the church doors, Mr. President," Hap said quietly. "There are ten in all. Door number ten is the one we came in through.

What we have here is a 'no one gets in, no one gets out' situation. Someone comes down to check on these monitors, we're done."

"Cousin," Marten abruptly turned to the president. "If I was right about what Foxx had constructed, if this church was in his plan and he ran the monorail all the way here, then it's somewhere below us. If it is and we can get to it, we have a way out.

"I want to send José to look for it. If he runs into someone all he has to do is say he works in maintenance, it's his first day on the job, and he got stuck when the doors locked. He's just trying to find another way out. Would you ask him to do that please?"

Ten seconds later Hap let José out, telling him to knock three times when he came back.

8:30 A.M.

"Now what?" The president was staring at the monitors that had suddenly gone black once again. Now they came back on and were showing various angles of the same thing. All two hundred very distinguished members of the New World Institute had left their seats and were filing to a dozen different locations, each monitored in close-up. Vice President Rogers was first, then one by one the others followed. Each person stepped forward, gave his or her name, place and date of birth, then reached up and pressed his or her left thumb against a small steel box.

Immediately a reading was superimposed over the person's face:

Member 2702. DNA taken: DNA confirmed.
Member 4481. DNA taken: DNA confirmed.
Member 3636. DNA taken: DNA confirmed.

"Whatever the hell's going on, I can guarantee you this video feed is not going out to main security," Hap said, his eyes locked on the monitors.

The parade continued. Members' ages ranged from twenty-eight to eighty-three. Places of birth were equally diverse: Basel, Switzerland; Salinas, Brazil; New York, New York; Berlin, Germany; Yokohama, Japan; Ottawa, Canada; Marseille, France; Tampico,

Mexico; Antwerp, Belgium; Cambridge, England; Brisbane, Australia.

The moment each member completed their sign-in a monk stepped in with what appeared to be a sterile swab, cleaned the mechanism, then stepped back, having made it ready for the next person.

"Jesus Lord," the president's voice caught in his throat as a woman stepped before a camera.

"Jane Dee Baker," she said, then gave the place and date of her birth and stepped forward to give a sample of her DNA.

"Chairwoman of the Subcommittee on Intelligence and Counterterrorism." Marten felt the same chilling surprise.

"Democrat from Maine, Mike Parsons's subcommittee," the president finished. "The one Merriman Foxx testified before."

"It's why Mike's dead and his son is dead, and why Caroline is dead," Marten said with no emotion at all. "Mike found out what was going on, or some of it anyway."

"Something else," the president said. "Each person is using his left thumb for the DNA signature. From this angle we can't see it but I would bet next year's congressional budget that every last one of them is tattooed with the sign of the Aldebaran."

153

8:35 A.M.

The soft, melodic chant of the monks floated across the church as the New World delegates returned to their seats. In the next moment the lights dimmed, as if the place was a theater and a performance was about to begin. And then it did.

"Cristina!" Marten blurted as they saw the floor in front of the altar abruptly slide back and a darkened hydraulic stage with swirling fog and eerie theatrical lighting rise up from below like some bizarre Las Vegas extravaganza. Cristina sat majestically in the center of it on a nearly invisible throne, a bright spotlight illuminating her from above as if she were some sort of grand goddess. Now a second spotlight came on nearer the front of the stage. In its glow were three apparent stage-prop severed heads mounted atop Aldebaran crosses.

As if preprogrammed, the automated, remote cameras began to play over the congregation as they inched forward in their seats. This was clearly why they were here, what they had come for and it shone in their faces.

"This Cristina, who is she?" the president asked quietly, clearly and unemotionally trying to understand what was going on.

"She was with Beck and Merriman Foxx in Malta," Marten said.

Just then, and again as if the entire bank of remote cameras had been preprogrammed, one of them moved off to begin a slow pan across the fog and onto the three severed heads mounted atop the Aldebaran crosses.

"My God, Mr. President," Hap said in a voice barely above a whisper. "Those heads are real."

Abruptly ten of the twenty monitors went blank, then two seconds later picked up the visual as another camera moved closer, one by one, showing the heads in extreme close-up. An explanatory caption was superimposed directly beneath each.

The first was that of a man, bald and very old.

Caption: *GIACOMO GELA. DIVULGED SECRETS OF "$\aleph\,\mu$". PURPOSE SERVED. TERMINATED.*

The second was the head of a woman. "Lorraine Stephenson," Marten breathed in horror and sheer disbelief.

Caption: *LORRAINE STEPHENSON. PHYSICIAN. UNSTABLE. SUICIDE.*

Then came the last.

"*Oh-Lord-No!*" Marten cried out as he saw the familiar thickset face, the gray hair and trimmed gray beard. Stone-dead eyes staring out at nothing.

Caption: *PETER FADDEN. JOURNALIST, WASHINGTON POST. DANGEROUS. TERMINATED.*

The voices of the monks grew louder and they saw them file onto the stage through the fog. Heads bowed, their chant continuing, there were fifty of them at least, maybe more. Whatever they were singing was directed wholly at Cristina.

The president looked to Marten. "This is your 'Machiavelli Covenant'," he said, his voice hushed and grave.

"Yes, I know," Marten rasped with anger. "Just as Demi described it. The only thing that seems changed from the sixteenth century is the technology. The elaborate sign-in process done by hand into a guarded journal with a bloody thumbprint placed alongside the personal signature has been traded for an electronic photograph and DNA sample. The participant's presence in the audience intercut with the video of the ceremony. Confirmation that you were here and took part in what happened. The formal dress is a charming addition. It means you were all too pleased to attend."

"I don't understand," Hap said, bewildered.

"These people are here to witness ritual murder."

"Murder?"

"They're going to kill the girl," the president said quietly.

"How?"

"I don't know."

"Why?" Hap was incredulous.

"This is a very exclusive organization, Hap," Marten's eyes shifted from Hap to the monitors and then back. "The rules of membership require not only wealth and power but complicity in murder so that none dares stray from the chief objective."

"Which is what?"

"The accumulation of even greater wealth and power."

"To dominate globally and in perpetuity, I think is a better way to put it," the president said, thinking out loud as he painstakingly studied each monitor in turn, putting together the people and activity he saw on the screens with what Marten had told him about the Covenant and what he had learned as a Rhodes scholar. "This is an international fraternity of widely diverse and highly influential people who routinely make far reaching agreements with one another. A great many of them, I would imagine, clandestine. It's an order that may well have been in operation for close to five hundred years and as such would have been a major force in the making of history. A group who, for no greater good than their own benefit, positioned themselves to expand empires by surreptitiously underwriting wars, assassinations, political and religious movements, and even—knowing of Dr. Foxx's involvement here—genocides."

The president turned away from the monitors to look at Hap

and Marten. "The idea of a single group being capable of things so huge and terrible and far-reaching and over so long a period, borders on the impossible if not the absurd. It's a statement I would wholly agree with if it weren't for the truth we see up there on those screens and the fact that these people, in particular the ones I know personally, are major global players in investment banking, insurance, law, transport, defense contracting, manufacturing, pharmaceuticals, energy, media, and politics—the things every society on the planet depends on for its daily life. You could argue that a great many of them are direct competitors and in total opposition to one another, but taken as a group, in one way or another they control a major part of the world's commerce.

"What I would imagine this weekend has been about—the seminars, the golf and tennis, the dinners and cocktail parties—is how best to conduct business in the coming year. Primarily how to respond to what will happen after the Warsaw assassinations and then to the catastrophe in the Middle East that will take place once Merriman Foxx's plan is executed. The ritual about to be performed there on the stage will irrevocably bind them to whatever course of action has been agreed upon." He looked back at the screens. "It's one of those great conspiracy theories every political theorist, writer, movie executive, and man and woman in the street around the world would love to believe exists. Well, it does exist and probably has for a very long time. The proof is right there in front of us."

154

8:44 A.M.

The chant of the monks abruptly stopped and the church filled with silence. Fog swirled on the stage where Cristina sat enraptured, joyfully waiting for the moment the fire would come and her journey, like that of the ox, would begin.

Suddenly a figure moved past her through the fog like some Shakespearean character. Another spotlight shone, illuminating

Reverend Beck dressed in clerical vestments. He crossed to the front of the stage and lifted a cordless microphone.

"Hamilton Rogers," he said, his eyes searching the audience, his voice resounding through the church's state-of-the-art speaker system. "Where are you, Mr. Vice President?"

8:45 A.M.

A great roar came from the crowd as five separate remote cameras picked up Vice President Hamilton Rogers getting up from his seat and moving to the aisle, where monks escorted him toward the stage. When he reached it, he bounded up to embrace Reverend Beck as if this were some kind of revival meeting.

"Hamilton Rogers," Beck said to the congregation. "The next president of the United States!"

Thunderous applause followed.

Beck and Rogers again embraced warmly, then turned, grasped hands, and lifted their arms to the crowd. Wave after wave of applause followed, the revival meeting suddenly become a political grandstand.

8:46 A.M.

Marten looked to the president. "If there was ever any question about their plans for you, there's none now."

"The thing is," the president said, "it's not just 'my friends' anymore. It's all of them. They all know what's going on. It shows how incredibly intertwined and indoctrinated they are. They're not ordinary human beings. They're another species altogether. One whose entire ideology is filled with unbridled arrogance."

8:47 A.M.

Hamilton Rogers motioned for silence. In seconds the applause stopped, Reverend Beck handed the microphone to the vice president, and Rogers stepped to the front of the stage. He looked to the congregation and began calling out names, recognizing new members. One by one they stood: a young CEO of a Taiwanese export company; a middle-aged woman who was a strong, left-of-center Central American politician; a fifty-two-year-old Australian investment banker; a sixty-seven-year-old Nobel prize–winning nuclear physicist from California; a seventy-year-old famously conservative Italian media mogul; and then another and another. Thundering applause followed each. Politically left, right, or center, the affiliation didn't seem to matter.

And then Vice President Rogers called out the rest. These were not new members but "old friends," he said, "dear, dear friends, longtime members joining us up here for this momentous occasion.

"United States congresswoman Jane Dee Baker. United States Secretary of State David Chaplin. Secretary of Defense Terrence Langdon. United States Air Force General and Chairman of the Joint Chiefs of Staff Chester Keaton. Presidential Chief of Staff Tom Curran. Presidential confidant Evan Byrd."

Again the church filled with ear-shattering applause. Applause that grew louder and louder as one by one the audience stood to proudly and patriotically salute those whom Rogers had designated.

155

8:53 A.M.

Marten whirled at the knock on the control-room door, the Sig Sauer coming up in his hand. Hap stepped in front of the president, swinging the machine pistol.

Hurriedly the knock came again. One, two, three.

"It's José," Marten said.

Hap nodded and Marten went to the door and cautiously opened it. José stood there alone. His eyes intense, his body wound tight. Marten let him in and then locked the door.

"What is it?" the president asked in Spanish.

"I went down into the church as far as I could," he said in

Spanish. "Through the door there are big wide stairs and then a big steel door. Also an elevator, I think. But everything is locked. No one is there. If there is a tunnel further down we cannot get to it."

"Gracias, José, muchas gracias," the president said gratefully, then smiled. "Está bien, relaja." It's alright, relax.

Immediately the president looked to Marten and Hap and translated.

"All we can do is wait and hope no one comes," Hap nodded at the monitors. "I'm assuming that when the ceremony is over the hydraulic stage will come back down, the original floor will slide back into place, and the monks will unlock the doors. After that everyone will go out to the buses as if nothing has happened. That's when we move. Up the stairs and out the way we came in. We don't go then we're dead in the water because the minute the guests have cleared the area the Spanish Secret Service will sweep the building and then lock it up tight."

"What about Cristina?" Marten snapped. "They're going to kill her."

Hap stared at him. "There's nothing we can do about her without endangering the president. Understand that and put her out of your mind."

"I understand it. I don't like it."

"Neither do I. It's just the way it is."

Marten stared back, then finally relented. "We get out. Then what?" he said quietly. "Where do we go? There are five hundred men out there, most of them focused on this building and the people inside it."

"We go out," Hap said calmly, "get in the cart, go back to the place we hid coming up. Security should depart the area in less than an hour after everyone leaves. After that we take it from there."

"Hap, your people are still out there with the Spanish police. They don't find us on the mountain, they'll start this way—maybe they already have. They're not going home until they have the president."

"Marten, we can't stay here."

"Woody," the president looked at Hap.

"Woody?"

"We take the chance he's not corrupted. As soon as we're out and you have a clear signal, text-message him on his cell phone. Tell him where we are and to get the hell in here fast with his chopper. Just him and the helo, nobody else. People will be leaving. It's a Marine Corps helicopter, nobody will know what's going on. He touches down in the back parking lot where we left the cart. Thirty seconds, we're on it and out of here."

"Mr. President, even if it works: he flies in and picks us up, we don't know what he'll do afterward. He could fly us straight to the waiting CIA jet. He does that and there're twenty guys under orders to get you to wherever they're supposed to take you and what you or I say won't matter."

"Hap," the president took a deliberate breath, "at some point damn soon we're going to have to trust somebody. I like Major Woods for a lot of reasons and always have. What I've given you are orders."

"Yes, sir."

Suddenly Reverend Beck's voice boomed through the speakers. They turned to see the congressional chaplain on every monitor. Speaking into the cordless microphone, red, green, and amber light playing on him from below, he crossed the darkened stage in a trail of theatrical fog. Whatever he was saying was in a language none of them had ever heard. He spoke again, as if it was a line of verse in adoration of someone or something. The New World members responded like a chorus in the same language, the way the families had the night before in the amphitheater.

Beck spoke again, then stopped and extended his hand to Cristina, still spotlighted on the darkened stage. She smiled proudly as Beck spoke again. A second spotlight followed him as he turned from Cristina and addressed the congregation, his right hand circling the stage the way he had done in the amphitheater. It was a call that demanded response from the congregation, and they did, repeating in enthusiastic unison what he had said. Abruptly the light swung from Beck and onto Luciana, her sharply pulled-back hair and daggered eye makeup radiating the power and nightmare fear of witchcraft.

In her hand was the ruby wand, and she moved behind Cristina, using it to draw a circle in the air above her head. Then her eyes found the congregation, and she called out a phrase. Everything about her was controlling and certain. She called it out once again, then turned and crossed the stage, the remote cameras following her through the fog.

Now she was on a dozen monitors, her eyes frozen on something before her. Then a half dozen cameras showed what it was.

Demi. Her body bound to a massive Aldebaran cross. Her eyes frozen in terror said everything. She was a living creature on the threshold of certain and horrific death.

"My God!" Marten blurted in shock and disbelief.

Luciana stopped before her, and the monks' chant began anew. Their voices rose to a crescendo, then fell quickly, only to rise again. Luciana stared at Demi, her posture grand and filled with contempt. Then Demi's eyes rose to meet hers and she returned the stare, defying her, giving the witch nothing. Luciana smiled cruelly and turned to the crowd.

"She would betray us as these have!" she said suddenly in English, a sweep of the ruby wand pointed at the heads on the Aldebaran crosses. In the next instant she uttered three sharp, distinctive words in the language she had spoken before. Immediately blue-red flame burst through the fog from gas jets in the floor beneath the heads. As it did a great cry went up from the congregation.

The monitors showed people leaning forward in their seats, straining to see. In seconds the heads were on fire. A half minute later their skin blistered up like meat thrown on a barbecue.

Immediately Demi's face filled a half dozen monitor screens. She screamed and kept on screaming. Four other monitors showed Cristina looking at her in alarm, as if the drugs given her before had worn off and she realized what was happening. Suddenly her eyes went wide as two monks appeared from the fog and dark and strapped her quickly and tightly to the throne. As quickly they stepped back and disappeared from view. All the while other monitors isolated on the burning heads. On Luciana and Beck. Followed in rapid succession by cuts on people in the congregation. Then the cameras moved in for close-ups of the newly introduced members of the institute.

A heartbeat later they cut to the vice president's "dear, dear friends"—Congresswoman Jane Dee Baker; Secretary of State David Chaplin; Secretary of Defense Terrence Langdon; Chairman of the Joint Chiefs of Staff General Chester Keaton; Chief of Staff Tom Curran; and presidential confidant Evan Byrd.

The president had been right when he said they were of another species altogether. No one there was merely a participant in murder or witness to an execution, there was another level to it entirely. Like Romans at the Colosseum's ancient barbaric spectacles, they were there for the show because it gave them immense and untold pleasure.

"This is just the beginning," the president said, his voice cracking in horror. An unthinkable situation made ten thousand times worse because he knew there was absolutely nothing they could do about it.

"The women will burn next."

156

"The hell they will. Neither one of them." Marten was already moving for the door.

Hap grabbed him just as he reached it and shoved him hard against the wall. "You try and help them, you expose the president. They know he's with you. They'll know he's in the building. I told you before, put it out of your mind. It's just the goddamn way it is."

"No! It's not the way it is. I'm not going to let those women be burned alive." Marten looked angrily at the president. "Tell him to let go of me! Tell him now!"

"The president doesn't have a vote here," Hap kept Marten pinned against the wall. "I have a sworn obligation to protect and maintain the continuation of the government, to protect the person who is president. No one in this room is going anywhere until I say so."

The chanting started again as the monks formed a large figure eight on the stage, then began what seemed like some carefully choreographed dance, circling first Cristina and then Demi and then repeating it, their song rising and falling in a ghostly, macabre timbre that was both emotionally powerful and wholly unnerving.

"Hap," the president said deliberately, "you know the layout of the building. The way up to the church proper, to the door behind

484 · ALLAN FOLSOM

the altar I was going to use to make my entrance. How long would it take Marten to get to that door from here?"

"Without trouble, I'd guess about forty seconds. Why?"

"The electrical panels are in there." The president indicated the locked narrow door in the wall next to them. "We give Marten those forty seconds, then shut off the power. Maybe a few emergency lights will come on, but except for the brightness of the flame from the gas jets the whole place basically goes dark. There were flashlights near a workbench in the storeroom we were first in. Marten goes there, takes two of them, puts one in his belt, uses the other to light his way to the altar door. When he gets there he goes through it and walks calmly onto the stage, flashlight in hand. He's still in his groundskeeper's uniform. It's dark. Nobody knows what's going on. He shines the light around like he's a maintenance man there to fix the problem. Then sets it on the stage, the light still on, drawing attention. Somebody questions him, he doesn't reply. He calmly walks around behind the women as if he's looking to repair something, then cuts them free, takes them back through the altar door, and uses the other flashlight to get back down the stairs to the corridor near the door where we came in. We're already there waiting and all of us go out it. The time from when Marten leaves to when we leave the building shouldn't be more than four, five minutes. Six at most."

"Cousin," Marten said, "all the doors to the outside are electronically locked."

"My guess is the minute the power is cut the door locks release. They wouldn't chance trapping all these VIPs during a power loss. If the fire brigade had to break in to free them, their whole game could be revealed." He looked to Hap. "You agree?"

"Mr. President. Just damn forget it!"

"Do you agree, Hap?" The president pressed him firmly.

"About the locks, yes. Not the rest of it, not for a second."

The president ignored his protest. "It'll be a shock when they realize the women are gone. The whole place will erupt, but it'll take more than a few minutes to figure out what happened. By then we're out, either in the cart and gone back down the hill or out of sight because Woody's coming in with the chopper."

"Mr. President, we just can't risk—"

"Hap, we have one shot," the president was still pushing and hard. It was the way he did things when he believed in something but still valued someone else's opinion. If it could be done, say so. If it couldn't, say that too. "Can Marten do it?"

"The sudden blackout. The surprise. The quick in and out. With a team, maybe. But for one man alone whose only knowledge of the target area is from the monitors and he's trying to work fast and in the dark . . . and not just any one man—the minute Marten steps into the light of those gas jets Beck is going to recognize him. Those monks rush him and suddenly he's in a one-man war and they know you're somewhere here. It's a helluva risk, Mr. President, an easy ninety-nine-to-one against."

"Marten and I were alone in the dark in the tunnels. We took a helluva risk there too and nobody was giving any odds at all. Hap, the power is off, the doors unlock, it lets us choose the time when we move and go out. All of us, the women included."

Hap glanced at Marten, then took a breath and relented. "Okay," he said, "okay," then ran a hand through his hair and turned away. His concession hadn't been because of the women or the force of the president's personality but because of the situation. He had given in for the same reason he had when the president had demanded that they alert Woody and order him to fly in for an air rescue: opportunity.

The president had been right when he said at some point "damn soon" they were going to have to trust somebody and despite his concern about trusting anyone, if he had to choose someone here and now it would be Woody, if for no other reason than his flying skills. He could come in over those treetops, set the chopper down in that small parking lot behind the church and get them the hell out of there faster and more safely than anyone he knew. In the worst-case scenario afterward, if he tried to fly them to the CIA jet, both Hap and Marten were armed and could force him to set the aircraft down wherever they chose.

The situation here was more immediate. One way or another they would soon be trying to get out to that parking lot and text-messaging Woody for rescue. By cutting the building's power, which he agreed would most probably release the electronic door locks, it would let them set their own timetable for when they would go out instead of having to wait for the ceremony to end and be at the mercy of whatever else might happen then.

Added to that was the fact that Marten's attempt to rescue the women would cause a major disruption in the church. Whatever Marten did when he went in would happen fast and mostly in the dark. Because of it the vice president, Beck, Luciana, the monks, everyone, would be taken wholly by surprise. Maybe Marten and the women would escape, maybe not, but either way confusion would rule. It was just that upheaval that Hap saw as giving him the best opportunity yet to get the president out alive.

"Me." Abruptly José stepped forward. He looked at the president and spoke in Spanish, "I understand a little of what you are saying. I will go with Mr. Marten. Together we will be Hap's 'team.'"

The president stared at him, then smiled. "Gracias," he said and quickly translated.

"What the hell is he going to do but get in the way?" Hap said.

"Be a diversion," Marten said quickly. "He's Spanish. He's dressed in a maintenance uniform. He becomes the front guy out there on the stage with a flashlight. Somebody asks him a question, he answers something like the power went out and he was told to see if he could fix it." Marten paused. "It gives me time, Hap. Thirty seconds, a minute when everyone's looking at him and I'm on the back part of the stage going for the women."

"Right," Hap agreed. It was one more card for them to play in the darkened church, giving them that much more of a complication and that much more of a chance to get the president out.

Immediately the president nodded toward the locked narrow door in the wall. "Open that up and let's look at the electrical panels. Shoot the locks off—there's no time for anything else."

Marten slid the Sig Sauer from his belt, then took off his shirt and wrapped it around the muzzle for a makeshift silencer.

At the same moment the chant of the monks rose. It was strong and deliberate and powerful, as if the immediate precursor to some event. Suddenly a wall of blue-red flame erupted through the fog. A great cry went up from the congregation as, in an instant, the flame encircled first Demi and then Cristina.

"Oh God, no!" the president breathed, his eyes locked on the monitors.

They saw Demi on a dozen screens as she fought wildly against the bonds that held her firmly to the Aldebaran cross but her struggle was impossible and she knew it. Wide-eyed in terror, she stared at the flames surrounding her then looked to Cristina.

"The ox was a lie!" she yelled. "A trick! You were betrayed! Your family was betrayed! All the families through the centuries have been betrayed! You thought this was part of a deep sacred religion! It is!" Her eyes shifted to congregation. "But it's theirs, not yours!"

They saw Luciana smile jubilantly, then step to the front of the stage and, like the grand actress she was, throw her arms wide to the congregation and call out something in their ritual tongue. En masse they repeated it. Again she spoke, her eyes luminous, her phrasing distinct and powerful, as if she were calling forth ancient gods. Then without warning she drew her arms around her and stepped back, vanishing into the fog.

Seconds later an apparition in a hooded black robe appeared from the very same spot. It crossed to the front of the stage and raised its head.

Beck.

Slowly he raised his arms to the gathering, and in his great melodious voice and in the same unknown tongue Luciana had used, he unleashed what sounded like a mighty oration. At length he finished and the congregation answered back. Again Beck preached. Again the congregation answered back. Then Beck gave them more. And then more still. With every breath intensifying his blistering salutation as if to draw down the heavens.

Each time the congregation responded. Each time Beck increased his delivery. His passion, momentum, and fervor bellowing forth like some unstoppable hell-bound train. It was a colossal, highly orchestrated performance designed to boil the blood and make unforgettable the emotion of this heavily guarded, closely shared experience. And Beck kept it going until the entire building threatened to collapse under the sheer force of it.

It might well have been ancient Rome.

Or Nazi Germany.

157

Pop! Pop!

Marten fired the Sig Sauer. The locks on the electrical-room door blasted apart. In an instant Hap ripped it open and then he and Marten and the president moved into the small room. Directly in front of them was a massive electrical panel with two dozen large circuit breakers, with an indication in Spanish of what area of the church each circuit was for. At the top were two larger switches with the words *Alimentación Exterior*—Outside Feed—lettered in bold black directly above them. Those were the ones the president wanted.

"There may be other panels in the building but those two should shut down everything."

"That door we just came through," Hap was suddenly looking around, "is not an emergency access to this room. It's the only access. Somebody wanted complete control over who got in here."

"Foxx," Marten said. Then something caught his eye: a second narrow steel door mounted into yet another solid concrete wall at the far end of the room. This door, like the first, had flush-mounted hinges but no noticeable hardware, no knob and no apparent lock. What it did have was centered in the wall just above it—the same kind of infrared sensor that had been mounted alongside the monstrous steel door at the end of the monorail tunnel.

Marten took a step closer, looking from that wall to the one next to it that separated the electrical room from the video room. The walls met at right angles, as they should. The difference was the wall here was set a good three feet farther into the room than the same wall in the room where the monitors were mounted.

Suddenly every hair stood up on his neck. He turned to the president. "All those monitors, all those cameras, the automated moves and cutaways that seem preprogrammed. I'll bet that on the other side of that door is some kind of electronic copying device, a computer, maybe something else. They're recording the whole thing: the names of the attendees, places and dates of birth, the close-ups of their faces, their DNA samples, as well the show itself. Putting everything onto a master disc or hard drive or both. Whatever it is amounts to a contemporary version of their ancient 'heavily guarded journal.' It's their protection against themselves.

"These two secured rooms are built side by side like military bunkers. This, like everything else, is Foxx's work, his brain trust. Fireproof, probably even bombproof, set up so no one would get in here without his knowledge or supervision. All the electronics are impeccably designed to make a permanent record of the proceedings without anyone ever touching it and at the same time making certain no one could get anywhere near the master controls to corrupt them. You said you had no proof, Mr. President. If I'm right, there's a treasure of information on the other side of that door."

The voices of the monks rose again, echoing though the speakers in the video room. The three went back to watch. Seconds later Beck proclaimed something. The monks' chant became stronger. Abruptly a second wall of flame rose through the fog encircling the women like fiery snakes. These were like the first outer rings that continued to burn, only they were closer. A tantalizing entertainment that was like a slow striptease, only this was no striptease but a heinously choreographed murder designed to inflict as much human pain as possible.

Now a third ring of fire exploded from below, circled, and came closer still. Cristina shrieked as the flame touched the base of her throne. She looked frantically to Demi for help. But there was no help. For either of them.

Marten glanced at José in the doorway, then looked to Hap. "Shoot the door hinges. If you can't get it open, try the sensor above it." He took Foxx's BlackBerry-like device from his jacket pocket and tossed it to him. "It was Foxx's. I tried to get it to work before, couldn't. You would've been schooled in some of this stuff, maybe you can." Immediately he looked at the president. "We're going. Forty seconds and cut the power."

"Good luck, Cousin," the president said.

For the briefest moment their eyes met and they knew that it might be for the last time. "You too."

"Marten, two things," Hap offered. "I'm giving you an extra sixty seconds."

"Why?"

"To get to the women you'll have to go through that fire. Stop at the room marked 'W/C', soak your hair and your clothes. That'll take up the extra minute. Next, I'd wager a million bucks that those monks are armed. Weapons concealed under their robes. Any one of them makes a move toward you, shoot him in the face. You'll scare the hell out of the rest."

"I hope," Marten glanced at José, then back to Hap. "Let us out."

158

ONE MINUTE, 38 SECONDS

The door clicked behind them, Marten slid the Sig Sauer from his belt, and they started down the hallway.

ONE MINUTE, 32 SECONDS

They were at the storeroom door and then inside.

ONE MINUTE, 28 SECONDS

Marten picked two flashlights from a shelf near the workbench and handed one to José, then lifted a pair of tin snips from where they hung on the board behind it.

ONE MINUTE, 24 SECONDS

Marten closed the storeroom door and they moved into the hallway, heading for the W/C, the restroom.

ONE MINUTE, 20 SECONDS

José watched the door while Marten took off his groundskeeper's uniform. Shirt first, then pants, and dunked them both in the toilet. When they were sopping wet he pulled them back on and stopped at the washbasin to drench his hair.

Sixty seconds later exactly, they left the W/C.

19 SECONDS

Now they were at the stairs and starting up, Marten first, tin snips and flashlight in his belt, Sig Sauer in his hand, his mind on the stage, the altar behind it, and the door they would go through to reach both. Thinking too, about the emergency lights that would come on as soon as the power was cut. Where they were located and how much they would illuminate.

Marten had taken the tin snips to cut the women free, but now he worried what the material was that had been used to bind them. If the snips didn't work, his only alternative would be to shoot the bindings free. Tricky under any circumstances because it would have to be done very quickly and accurately, never mind the dark. The situation with Demi was made all the worse because she was bound not only at the wrists and feet but at the throat. A missed shot there could be fatal.

14 SECONDS

They reached the top of the stairs and saw the hallway to the side that Hap had described. Marten turned José quickly down it.

10 SECONDS

The hallway ended. The door was right there. Marten suddenly worried it might be locked. He turned the knob. There was a slight click as the mechanism released. He pushed against it ever so slightly. The door gave and opened a crack. He pulled it back.

6 SECONDS

He looked at José. The teenager smiled and nodded.

"Gracias, José, gracias."

José smiled again and fisted him on the shoulder. Marten smiled and fisted him back. This kid was terrific. He could do anything and already had.

2 SECONDS

One!

The hallway went dark.

159

9:16 A.M.

Marten and José stepped through the door in the dark. Twenty feet in front of them they could see the fog-shrouded stage and in the center of it the roaring circles of fire surrounding Demi on the right and Cristina on the left. As yet, and mercifully, neither had begun to burn.

From what Marten could see there was one more ring yet to ignite, and that was directly at the feet of both women. Once the gas jets opened and they caught fire, the women would begin to burn and the screaming would start. Clearly the Covenant's hellish cabaret had been designed to create as much titillating drama as possible before the actual murder began. Heinous as it was, it was just this deliberately measured tempo that had so far kept the women alive.

"Go," Marten whispered, and they moved to the darkness to the right of the altar. From there they could just make out the members of the congregation, all talking in confusion about the sudden loss of power. They were a collection of vague figures lighted only by the spill from three stained-glass windows high above and by the soft flood of a half dozen emergency lights that illuminated the exits leading to the main doors. Everything else was dark.

Marten took José by the arm and motioned him forward, making a semicircular motion that meant he should go to the front of the stage and then come in from the side, waiting until then before turning on his flashlight and beginning his decoy act as a maintenance man.

9:17 A.M.

"What happened?" Luciana found Beck and three monks huddled in the dimness just off the stage.

"We don't know, we accessed the two main breaker panels off the nave. Everything was in order," Beck said brusquely. Abruptly he looked to one of the monks. "Cover the doors, no one in or out. Put six men on the vice president's section. We have no idea what this is."

9:18 A.M.

"Where and what, exactly?" Captain Diaz demanded in Spanish from a large curly-haired man in white pants and a white T-shirt. The two were standing nose to nose in the center of the Aragon Resort's laundry, Bill Strait, Dr. James Marshall, and three CNP officers hovering just feet away.

"Four clean groundskeeper's uniforms are missing," the laundry-man said hurriedly in Spanish. "The opening man counts inventory every morning. The closing man does the same at night. Because it's Sunday and because of all the security we have very few people on; I only came in to count them about ten minutes ago."

Immediately Diaz turned to Strait and Marshall. "Four groundskeeper's uniforms are missing. He found them gone a little after nine."

SAME TIME

Hap cursed out loud as the aging screwdriver he'd retrieved from the storage room slipped out of the slot of the final screw of eight.

By now they should have been outside, texting Woody for help. Instead they were in Merriman Foxx's inner bunker trying to remove the housing from dual interconnected computers in an effort to remove their hard drives; hard drives, the president insisted, reflecting what Marten had said, were very possibly the Covenant's own DNA and "a treasure-trove of vital information." Despite Hap's protest and the ticking clock he'd steadfastly refused to leave without doing everything possible to retrieve them. At that point Hap knew he had no choice but to go along and had given them the four-to-five minutes he'd allotted to Marten to get the women out to do it.

Breaking into the bunker had been the easy part. He'd taken two shots at the door locks with the machine pistol and made not so much as a dent in the steel. That left only Foxx's BlackBerry-like device.

Marten had been correct when he'd told Hap "You would've been schooled in some of this stuff." He had. Before joining the presidential detail he'd been in charge of the Miami field office of the Secret Service's electronic-crimes task force, where he was an expert in advanced electronic-based crime. Examining Foxx's handheld gadget he'd quickly recognized that it was more a computer than a simple communications tool. A closer look suggested it was some kind of miniature superprocessor, one that most probably utilized synthetic flawless diamonds that generate relatively no heat to enable ultrafast computations in so small a machine. He had worked with similar laboratory prototypes before and believed Foxx's device was little different. He'd been right. It had taken him only seven tries to break Foxx's encrypted code and get the bunker door open.

"Finally. Damn," he breathed as the last screw came loose and he slid the covers back. At first glance the inner workings of both machines were extremely complex, yet the hard drives of both were clearly accessible. Still, he didn't like it.

"Mr. President, I'm sure these drives are password-protected. I pull them without using it there's every probability they'll be permanently corrupted if not just blank. We're fast out of time here. I either pull them right now and take that chance or we just leave them and get the hell out of here. You decide."

"Pull them, Hap," the president said. "Pull them now."

160

José was nearly to the front of the stage. To his left and behind him he could just see Marten moving toward the women. Suddenly José froze. Beck was crossing the stage, coming directly toward him. Instantly he stepped back. At the same time Beck stopped and addressed the congregation.

"Friends," he said in English, "we have a simple power failure, nothing else. Bear with us a few moments more while we attempt to resolve the problem."

A loud uneasy murmur passed through the two hundred.

"Hey, you!" A male voice commanded in Spanish. José whirled to see two of the black-robed monks jump up on the stage and start toward him.

"Who are you?" the first monk spat in Spanish. "What're you doing here?"

José glanced to the side and saw Beck looking in his direction. Immediately he turned on his flashlight.

"Maintenance," he said in Spanish. "Here to find the trouble."

"Who sent you? How did you get into the building?"

Sig Sauer in one hand, the tin snips in the other, his hair and clothes still wet, Nicholas Marten moved like a shadow across the stage behind the fires. Two seconds, three and he reached them. Demi was less than six feet away on the far side of the flames; Cristina was the same distance to her left. The discharge of heat was horrendous and both women seemed to be in a stupor.

Marten could see José near the front of the stage talking with the monks. He saw Beck move toward them, then suddenly stop and look in the direction of the women. As quickly he looked past the flames and directly toward Marten. In the next instant their eyes met and Marten saw total surprise register on the minister's face. As quickly the emotion became recognition of what was happening. Immediately Beck turned and disappeared into the darkness.

Marten looked back to the women. He took a deep breath and held it, then threw up an arm to protect his face and stepped through the fire.

9:20 A.M.

Beck rushed off the stage and started down a hallway just off the nave, fully determined to execute a long-planned action.

"Reverend," he heard Luciana call after him.

He whirled. She was a dozen feet down the corridor behind him. "Inform the congregation the service is over," he said. "The power outage will have released the locks. Everyone is to leave the building and board the buses immediately. Make certain the monks let no one in from the outside."

"What is it?"

"One score and five," he said then turned and walked quickly down the corridor, the way he had been going.

"One score and five," Luciana knew what had happened and what was soon to happen. It would be one score and five, twenty-five years, Foxx had told them, from the day construction began—of the resort, the tunnels, the monorail, the underground labs, the church, everything—to when it would be shut down and destroyed.

Today, on this date exactly, one score and five had passed and everything would be ended. Rightly so from Luciana's view. The coming of Demi Picard had signaled it. Her undying love for her mother had been a curse. One far worse than any of them had imagined. She'd known it the moment she'd seen her.

9:21 A.M.

"Demi! Demi!" Marten commanded, trying to shake her from her stupor. He saw her eyelids flutter. "It's okay. Don't move!" he said quickly, then had the tin snips at the heavy strap that bound her throat to the Aldebaran cross. His face and hands glistening with sweat, the searing heat all but unbearable, he was trying not to breathe at all. "Don't move!" he exhaled and closed the snips. Nothing happened. He pressured the cutters again and this time the teeth caught and the material gave. Demi's head fell forward, then she recovered, and he saw her look at him in disbelief.

"Mr. Marten!" José shouted from somewhere on the far side of the flames. He looked up to see Luciana cross the front of the stage, heard her start to say something to the congregation.

Then he saw two monks coming right at him through the flames, one behind the other, machine pistols in their hands.

Boom! Boom!

Marten fired the Sig Sauer point blank. The first monk's face exploded and he slammed backward through the fog.

Boom! Boom!

Marten fired again. The second monk twisted away in the dark.

Marten heard the congregation scream as one.

"José! José!" he yelled, then cut the straps at Demi's wrists and feet. Her knees buckled as he pulled her from the cross. He got one hand under her waist trying to steady her. Then José was through the fire, his hair and groundskeeper's shirt burning.

Suddenly there was a burst of machine-pistol fire. A bullet nicked Marten's ear. A second seared his cheek. A half dozen more shot up the cross where Demi had just been.

Boom! Boom!

Marten fired blindly through the flames. The spit of the machine pistol continued. Rapid-fire hell coming through the flames.

Boom! Boom!

He fired again and the shooting stopped. He twisted around shoving Demi at José.

"Go!" he yelled. "Go! Go! Go!"

He caught the briefest glimpse of José wrestling Demi through the flames to the stage behind them, then whirled to free Cristina. As he did, the innermost gas jets ignited, and he was suddenly standing in the center of a blazing inferno. He screamed out loud and made a wild reach with the cutters, trying to find the straps that bound her.

Then he froze.

Most of Cristina's head was gone, chewed up by machine pistol fire. In the next instant her great mane of jet-black hair burst into flame. For a millisecond Marten's eyes registered sheer horror. Then, his own hair on fire, his hands and face scorched, he turned and leapt out through the conflagration.

161

The room was at the far end of a darkened hallway. Like the video and electrical rooms below, it was little more than a concrete bunker. Beck had gained access to it through two separate doors. The first was wooden and hand carved, and like other doors throughout the church required a security card used in conjunction with a code punched into an electronic keypad. The second, only feet away, was made of heavy-gauge steel and required another keypad code, which opened a singular slot above it and into which he slipped a special key Foxx had given him. Once inside he sat down in front of a six-foot-long control panel that looked like something out of NASA and incorporated a series of television monitors, switches, dials, and gauges that were like those in an industrial natural-gas-transmission plant, which was very nearly what this room was. That the power was out in the rest of the building was not evident here. Every light, monitor, switch, dial, and gauge operated perfectly, the entire system powered by Chinese-made heavy-duty polymer batteries.

Beck took a breath, then scrutinized the string of carefully labeled gauges in front of him.

Among them:

> Pressure Transducer Cylinder Pressure Distortion
> Centrifugal Surge and Pulsation Control
> Piping Vibration Control
> Piping Configuration Optimization
> Leak Detection Control
> Compressor Vibrations

Satisfied by their readings, he looked down and flipped five switches in succession. Then he took a second key, inserted it into an eyehole on the panel, and turned it. Immediately a half dozen gauges changed color from red to bright green. A digital timer started at sixty minutes. Beck ran it down to fifteen and stopped it. "One score and five," he breathed, "one score and five."

In a mechanical room in the tunnels far below a two thousand horsepower diesel engine was driving a gas, turbine-driven, centrifugal compressor. For the better part of two hours it had been pumping natural gas through massive twenty-inch pipelines and six-inch nozzles, charging the miles of old mining shafts, monorail transport tunnels, Foxx's laboratories, work areas, and holding cells with highly explosive, lethal fumes. The church itself was to have been the last charged, the filling to have begun once the hydraulic stage had been lowered to its hidden room below and the original floor was back in place, and when the services were over and the security forces had completed their sweep of the building and left.

Marten's presence changed that. In Foxx's absence, control fell to Beck as arranged by the Covenant's carefully designed rules for succession of power. While the Covenant's overall program fell this year to the U.S. in the revolving international chair of stewardship, the security of the Aragon project was, after Foxx's death, officially Beck's. Meaning its long-planned destruction was now fully in his hands.

Beck studied the gauges and monitors once more. Satisfied, he looked at the timer. Once started, it would activate the nozzles in the church's basement and the building would begin to fill with gas. In fifteen minutes it would rise to the level of the jets burning onstage. When it did the building and everything in it would explode. At the same time igniters in the tunnels would trigger, and a firestorm reaching as much as 2,500 degrees would roll through everything below. A "slow buildup of methane gas over the decades" the authorities would call it, and connect it to the explosion that the day before had rocked the ground beneath the monastery at Montserrat. It was an inferno the authorities would let burn itself out, and it would be weeks if not months before it did. In the end there would be nothing left but collapsed tunnels and a residue of super-heated dust.

Three decades earlier the membership had agreed on a far-reaching strategy for the Middle East and engaged a recently initiated member named Merriman Foxx to devise the plan for it. Three years later he had presented that plan to the membership. In it, and in precise terms, he outlined what needed to be done and where, how much it would cost and how long it would take, and what would happen to it afterward. They had agreed, and the project was put in motion. Two years after that the land had been bought and construction on what they termed "The Aragon Project" had begun. And now, twenty-five years later to the day, Beck, fully employing the authority invested in him, had taken control and moved up the hour.

"One score and five," he said once more, as if in final homage to that authority and to his own loyalty, then started the timer. Immediately he turned to a small computer beside it, slid a ThumbDrive from his pocket, and inserted it into the computer's USB port, then looked at the monitor just above it. A moment later a bar came up asking for a password. His fingers went to the keyboard, he typed in a password, then repeated it. A split second later he moved the cursor to Drive C: and clicked on, then dragged the entire contents to Drive A:. Ten seconds later he asked the computer for permission to remove the mass storage drive from the USB port. Permission was given, and he slipped the ThumbDrive from the machine and put it back in his pocket. The power outage had affected everything in the building but this room here and the backup battery supply for the master computer in the bunker below, where the Covenant's archive files were recorded and stored. Both machines were interconnected so no matter what might happen there the same information was always backed up here. It was just those files, that information, that Beck had safely copied onto the ThumbDrive.

Beck stood and took one last look around. Satisfied everything was in order, he left, securing the doors behind him. It was 9:25 A.M. At 9:40 precisely the rising gas would reach the burning jets on the stage and the inferno would begin.

162

His nerves on edge, machine pistol in hand, Hap hustled the president up the stairs and down the corridor toward the rear exit. They were already four minutes past the time he had allocated to Marten and José to get to the women and get them out, and he didn't like it. That he had the two hard drives from Foxx's master computers in his pants pocket was little solace. His sense was the same now as it had been when he'd cautioned the president at the beginning, that without entering the correct password before removing them they would be corrupted and therefore useless. Useless hard drives in exchange for the life of the president made no sense at all, but it had been done, and all they could do was move on. And they were.

Thirty feet down the corridor was the door leading out to the church's back parking lot where they had left the electric cart. Hap took out the BlackBerry he had preprogrammed with the text message he would send to Woody the moment he was free of the building and had a clear signal.

Ten feet more and he saw the president look anxiously up as they passed the stairway Marten and José would have used to get up to the church proper. It was dark and quiet and he knew what the president was thinking. That maybe they had rescued the women and were already outside waiting. But that, like the uncorrupted removal of the hard drives, was a pipe dream and he knew it. The situation in the upper church was far too complex for two men, or rather a man and a boy, to navigate successfully. By now he was certain both Marten and José were dead. The women too.

"Hap!" he heard the sharp cry of Marten's voice behind them. They whirled to see Marten and José appear at the bottom of the stairs with Demi between them. Her complexion was deadly white, her head slumped on her chest, her hair and scarlet dress burned and still smoldering. Seemingly half conscious, she sobbed uncontrollably.

"Marten, my God!" The president turned and was heading toward them. Hap caught him and turned him back.

"Dammit! No! Mr. President, we're going! Now!"

"The other girl?" The president's eyes were still on Marten.

Marten shook his head as he moved them forward. His hair was singed, his face and hands burned and blackened. José was much the same.

Now they were at the door. Hap held them up, then opened it cautiously. A half second later he stepped out alone, lifted the BlackBerry, and sent the rescue message to Woody.

163

9:30 A.M

Hap turned to go back inside, his intention was to hold them all just inside the door for the six to eight minutes it would take for Woody to arrive with the chopper. He'd barely gone two paces when he heard the unmistakable sound of a helicopter starting up at the front of the church. Immediately came the high whine of a second helo firing up. He glanced at the door, then turned back and went up on the knoll he'd climbed when they first came in for a better view. Forty yards away he saw *Marine Two* and its identical companion helicopter, their doors open, in pre-preparation for take-off. Beyond them evening-clothes-clad members of the New World Institute were streaming from the church and heading for the black buses. Spanish Secret Service were everywhere. He wished he knew what was going on in the church, if the gas jets had been shut off and the stage lowered away and out of sight in favor the building's original floor. And what about the other woman, Cristina? From Marten's expression and shake of his head she had to be dead. What happened to her body? And what role would the monks play in this now? Were the church vans parked here at the back of the church theirs? Was that how they had arrived? If so, at any moment they would be coming down the stairs inside the church toward the door where the president and the others were huddled.

Suddenly he caught sight of Roley Sandoval, special agent in charge of the vice-presidential detail, leading a group of U.S. Secret Service agents hastily escorting Vice President Rogers, the secretaries of state and defense, and the rest of Rogers's elite entourage which now included Congresswoman Jane Dee Baker toward *Marine Two*.

Whatever had happened, whatever was going on, and if it hadn't been before, time now had suddenly become everything. The monks aside, the moment the helos left and the buses were loaded, the Spanish Secret Service would sweep the building and then secure it. It meant they had nowhere to hide until Woody arrived, except maybe among the trees that surrounded the parking area.

The doors closed on both helos. There was a deafening roar as *Marine Two* lifted off, gained altitude, then flew away, heading due south. Immediately the second Marine helo followed. In seconds both machines disappeared from view.

9:34 A.M.

Hap looked to the buses. People were already boarding them. How much longer would it be before the monks came down and the Spanish Secret Service went inside and began their sweep? He wanted to keep the president inside and out of sight but that was no longer an option. He had to get them out of the building and into the cover of the trees or risk a firefight with the monks or capture by the Spanish Secret Service or both.

Decision made, he was turning to go back inside when there was a thundering roar and a Spanish CNP helicopter passed overhead at treetop level. A half second later it reversed course and came back. Hap dove for the cover of a big tree and watched the CNP helo approach and then slow. Suddenly it stopped to hover directly over the parking lot. He could see the pilot looking down and talking first with his first officer and then animatedly into his headset. Seconds later the machine pulled up to two hundred feet and held there, hovering where it was.

Hap looked up and past it. Where the hell was Woody? Did he not get the message? Or had he gotten it and alerted the CNP and that's why the police chopper was there now? Behind him he could see the string of sleek black buses begin to pull away.

"Damn it," he breathed, "damn it." There was nothing he could do without exposing himself to the CNP chopper and by doing so give away the president's location. On the other hand, he couldn't wait until either the monks or the Spanish Secret Service reached the corridor where the president and the others hid.

He looked at his watch. It was nearly 9:35. Where the hell was Woody? Was he was coming at all?

164

The timer Beck had set in the Control Room clicked down to an even five minutes.

Then to 4:59.

The gas had already filled the church's lower chambers and was quickly rising. It, like that in Foxx's dirty lab, was natural gas that was primarily methane but, by Foxx's design, did not have the organic chemical mercaptan added to give it odor. In result anyone still inside the building would be wholly unaware lethal fumes were present.

4:58

A CNP chopper lifted off from the resort's golf course, Captain Belinda Diaz riding shotgun in the copilot's seat. In seats behind her were six members of Bill Strait's U.S. Secret Service detail. Seconds later another CNP helo took off with a dozen more U.S. Secret Service agents aboard. At a hundred feet the Diaz helo spun left and flew toward the church. The second chopper followed.

"This is Captain Diaz," she said into her headset in Spanish. She was plugged into the broadcast frequency of every Spanish police unit and the security detail of the Spanish Secret Service. "Objectives believed to be at back entrance to La Iglesia de Santa Maria, (the church of Saint Mary). CNP units seven through twelve respond. Secret Service on scene respond at will and with caution."

Machine pistol concealed under his shirt, Hap left the cover of the tree and walked slowly toward the church, glancing up once at the CNP helo hovering overhead, then pausing to pick up the rake José had used to clean the leaves from the flower beds and put it in the back of the electric cart.

"You, groundskeeper!" the helo's loudspeaker hailed in Spanish. "Police! Stop where you are!"

Hap's boldness had come from the sudden realization that he, like José, Marten, and the president, still wore the resort's groundskeeper's uniforms. By now it was possible, if not probable, that the uniforms or the electric cart or both had been discovered missing from the maintenance buildings. If that were the case the CNP, and most probably Bill Strait and his hundreds of Secret Service and CIA operatives, knew about it and were frantically searching the resort's vast acreage for the cart and/or groundskeepers. If he was right, then he was purposely making it easy for them. He was also buying time. Hoping that at any second Woody would arrive in the attack helicopter and set it down in the parking lot. The action itself confusing everyone and giving them the seconds they needed to get aboard it.

Hap looked up, raised his hands, and then pointed toward the church door where the president and the others were. As quickly he lowered his hands and walked calmly to it. As he did he saw a half dozen police SUVs racing tailpipe to tailpipe up the hill toward the church.

In the control room Beck's manually set timer continued its countdown:

4:08
4:07

Hap entered the church quickly, expecting the president, Marten, José, and Demi, no matter her psychological state, to be ready to go right then. They weren't. José was on the floor, semiconscious, his shirt torn open, and Marten was over him, working on his chest;

blood was everywhere. The president held a still-sobbing, near hysterical Demi several feet away, giving Marten room to work.

"What the hell?" Hap blurted.

"José was shot. Nobody realized it until he collapsed. Somewhere in the upper chest," the president said quickly.

"Mr. President, there is no time. The Spanish police are here. Their Secret Service people are around the corner. If Woody's coming he's going to be here at any second. We have to go out now!"

"We can't leave them."

"We have to!"

"Marten," the president snapped. "Can we get José on his feet?"

"I think so."

The president looked at Hap, then Demi. "Take Demi. Demi go with Hap!" Immediately he bent to Marten, and they both helped José up then he looked to Hap.

"Go. Go out now!"

Inside the church the control room timer continued its cold countdown.
3:12
3:11

The rear door to the church flew open. Hap came out first and fast, his gold U.S. Secret Service badge pinned to his shirt collar, his right hand on the machine pistol under his shirt, his left arm around Demi half dragging, half cradling her. The president and Marten came next, José between them, his good arm thrown over Marten shoulder, the president on his other side holding him up by his belt.

"Freeze where you are! Now!" a disembodied voice commanded in Spanish over a loudspeaker. "Halt immediately!" the same voice said in English.

The Spanish police SUVs were parked directly in front of them, blocking off the parked church vans, the electric cart, and the road out itself. Twenty heavily armed uniformed police stood in front of them. The CNP chopper had now pulled up to five hundred feet and hovered there. Immediately it was joined by Captain Diaz's helo. The second CNP helo following pulled up and held position.

"I see them," Diaz said with a wave to the other chopper pilot. A half beat and her helo dropped down to two hundred feet and held.

To his left Hap could see at least twenty Spanish Secret Service agents coming over the hill from the front of the church.

"United States Secret Service!" Hap yelled. Then repeated it.

No one moved.

"What now?" the president said quietly.

"Tell them we are the U.S. Secret Service and have a wounded man here who needs immediate medical attention," Hap said quietly.

The president took a half step forward. "We are the United States Secret Service. This man is badly hurt. He needs a doctor right away!" he barked in Spanish. "Medical help immediately!"

Beck's timer continued its inexorable march toward zero.

    2:17

    2:16

    2:15

Captain Diaz looked over her shoulder to the U.S. Secret Service agent looking out the window directly behind her. "They say they are your people. Do you recognize anyone?"

"Looks like our SAIC, but from here and in that uniform he's wearing I'm not sure. The woman is a surprise. Don't recognize anyone else."

Diaz turned back and spoke into her headset. "CNP ground units to take charge."

In the next moment four of the armed CNP police started slowly forward, the leader motioning the Spanish Secret Service to hold their positions as he did.

"Damn it, Woody!" Hap breathed. "Where the hell are you, playing golf?"

As if in divine response a monstrous shadow suddenly blocked out the sun. Then with a thundering roar, its prop wash sending dust and debris flying and the Spanish police and the Spanish Secret Service ducking for cover, the huge twin-rotored U.S. Army

Chinook helicopter came in just over the treetops, slipping in under Captain Diaz's chopper and obscuring it from sight.

"Woody!" the president cried out.

"Four minutes ago that chopper was on the ground. What the hell's going on?" Captain Diaz's pilot looked to her, his eyes wide under his helmet visor. "What do I do?"

"Captain Diaz. This is Special Agent Strait," Bill Strait's voice came over her headset. "The Chinook is cleared to land. Please stand down."

For a moment Diaz said nothing, finally she did. "Hold position," she said to her pilot, then spoke into her headset. "The Chinook is cleared to land. All units hold position."

Hap stared wide-eyed as the Chinook came in, "He's never going to set that monster down here. There's no damn room!"

Counting its churning rotor blades the Chinook was one hundred feet long nose to tail. The parking area surrounded by trees might be that give or take ten feet in either direction. If Woody was going to land without incident he was going to need skill, luck, grease, and a shoehorn to do it.

Inside the church, Beck's timer continued to click down.
> *1:51*
> *1:50*
> *1:49*

The Chinook dropped lower. Now they could see Woody at the controls, looking front and aft and to the sides, judging the trees as if he were trying to park a semitrailer in a space made for a car. Suddenly there was a loud gnashing to the rear as the tail rotor sheared branches off of a large conifer and sent them flying. Then with a heavy bump the Chinook touched down.

"Go!" Hap yelled. "Go!"

Marten and the president rushed José forward. Hap followed with Demi.

The Chinook's crew door suddenly slid open and Bill Strait and two medics stood there. Five seconds, ten. And they were at the helo and being helped inside. Another ten and the crew door slid closed. Immediately there was a deafening roar as Woody pulled back on the throttle. A split second later they were off the ground and airborne. In eight seconds they had cleared the trees. Eight more and the machine turned 180 degrees and flew off to the east.

165

"This is Captain Diaz," her voice crackled through every headset. "All units stand down and return to base. Repeat, stand down and return to base."

Inside the church, the timer continued to click down.
   0:31
   0:30
   0:29

"You can look at me later," the president said to the two doctors and the medics over the roar of the Chinook's rotors. "It's him." He turned to José. "He's been shot and badly burned. Someone look at Ms. Picard too and right away. She's burned and severely traumatized. Mr. Marten also needs to be treated for burns."

"Thank God you're safe."

The president whirled at an all-too-familiar voice.

National Security Adviser Dr. James Marshall was coming toward him from the Chinook's flight deck. "I tried to stay out of the way here," he said with utmost sincerity. "You've been through some ordeal."

   0:05
   0:04
   0:03

"Why are you here?" the president asked Marshall point blank, his eyes little more than angry slits, his voice cold as death. "Why the hell aren't you with the others?"

From somewhere below and behind them came a dull heavy boom that sounded like a massive explosion.

"What was that?" Marten turned to look out the Chinook's window. In the next instant the shock wave hit. The Chinook was thrown sideways then dropped like a stone. Woody touched the controls. The rotor speed increased and the aircraft shook in response, then rose up quickly as he regained control.

The president moved to the window next to Marten. Hap came in too, so did Bill Strait. In the distance they could see flame and smoke billowing from the hilltop where the church had been.

"Woody, swing around!" the president yelled.

"Yes, sir."

The Chinook came around hard and flew back toward the billowing fiery inferno where the church had been. In that instant the rest of Foxx's destruction deployed. It was like nothing any of them had ever seen before. The maintenance buildings blew straight up, disintegrating into a million pieces. Then they saw a line of dust run the length of the vineyard as if some great underground snake had shivered. The line continued across a low expanse of foothills and then up into the mountain range where they had been the night before, racing in the direction of the monastery at Montserrat. Now and again giant puffs of flame erupted from cracks and chimneys in the rock.

"Foxx," Marten said and looked at the president. "He blew up the church, the maintenance buildings, the entire monorail tunnel, everything. The monks may even have still been inside."

"The nozzles in the monorail tunnel," the president said. "He planned it all far ahead of time. No one will find a thing. Not a trace of what he did. Nothing at all." Suddenly the president pulled away from the window to look at Marshall. "Is the monastery going up too?"

"I don't know what you're talking about."

"You don't?"

"No, sir."

"It won't get to the monastery," Marten said quietly. "It's what he blew earlier. There's nothing left there. It'll stop at the end of the monorail."

The president looked to Hap, "Have the CNP alert the monastery. At least they'll have some kind of warning if it does go."

"Yes, sir."

The president's eyes shifted to Woody. "Major, are we fully fueled?"

"Yes, sir."

"Our range is what, one thousand two hundred nautical miles?"

"A little more, sir."

"Then take us out of Spanish airspace, Major, and clear airspace to Germany."

"Sir. I have orders to fly you to an airstrip outside Barcelona. Chief of Staff has a CIA jet waiting."

Marten and Hap exchanged glances. Then Hap reached into his groundskeeper's shirt and slid out the machine pistol.

"Major, I've canceled that mission," the president said calmly. "I asked for airspace cleared to Germany; please do so. I'll tell you where exactly when we get closer."

"He can't do that, Mr. President," Marshall came toward him. "It's for your safety. It's all been planned out."

"Mr. National Security Adviser, I think you'll understand when I say the plans have changed. Very soon you and the vice president and every other one of my 'friends' will be taken into custody and charged with high treason. I'd suggest you go over there and sit down. Hap will be glad to escort you." The president stared at Marshall for a long moment. Finally he turned away and looked back to Woody.

"Major, change course now. That is a direct order from the commander-in-chief."

Woody looked at Marshall as if trying to decide what to do.

"Major," Marshall said firmly, "you have your orders. The president has been under a terrible strain. He has no idea at all what he is saying. It's our job to protect him. Hap's too. Along with Bill Strait. It's why we're all here."

Woody stared and then turned back to the controls.

"It's no good, Jim, you're done," the president said. "The Covenant is done."

"Covenant?" Marshall stared at him unbelieving.

"We know, Jim, and who was there. We saw it in operation. Hap, Mr. Marten, myself, even José. All of us."

"You're not well, Mr. President. I have no idea what you're talking about." Suddenly he looked to Woody. "You have your orders, Major. Stay the course. Stay the course."

The president and Marten looked toward the flight deck. Hap started toward it, machine pistol out.

It was all the time Marshall needed. In two steps he had crossed the aircraft's midsection. A second later he had the crew door open. There was a thundering roar and a terrible blast of air.

"Grab him!" the president yelled.

It was too late. They were at two thousand feet. The doorway was empty. Marshall was gone.

MONDAY

APRIL 10

166

Marten rolled over in a half sleep, edging over gently to avoid putting pressure on the bandages covering the burns on his left arm and neck. He had his own room in the officers' quarters just down the hall from where Hap Daniels and Bill Strait slept in an adjoining room to the president's.

They'd come to the U.S. air base at Spangdahlem unannounced. Normally they would have landed under presidential colors at Ramstein Air Base, but not this time, not under these circumstances. The base commanding officer and several of his general staff knew, but that was all. The doctors accompanying them on the Chinook had cleared the president and sent him to rest, an unrecognized, unnamed VIP under heavy guard.

José, Demi, Marten, and Hap had been taken to the base hospital. As far as Marten knew, José and Demi were still there and would remain there for at least several more days. José's family had been notified, and Miguel and José's father were on route from Barcelona and would arrive soon.

Miguel—Marten smiled as he lay there in the dark. What he'd fallen into as a simple limousine driver. And what a great man and dear friend he had become in so short a time. The boys too, all of them—Amado, Hector, and especially José, the youngster who'd been frightened to death to go farther down in the chimney toward the monorail tunnel because he thought he would be descending straight into Hell. Little had he known of the Hell he would volunteer to be part of very soon afterward. And what Hell Hector and Amado and Miguel had been put through by the

Spanish police and U.S. Secret Service, all of it to buy the president time.

The president had pretty much left Marten alone as the Chinook traversed Europe, crossing the Pyrenees into French airspace and then flying north across France to pass over Luxembourg before entering German airspace near Trier and touching down at Spangdahlem very soon afterward. Understandably he had pressing business. First, and most important, the president had spoken personally to the chancellor of Germany and the president of France and then held a three-way conference call with them both. All had agreed that the long-planned NATO meeting set for one o'clock in the afternoon today should go on as scheduled, but, for security reasons, the venue should be changed. With a mighty scrambling of foreign offices it had been, the twenty-six member countries unanimously approving the move from Warsaw to a special site chosen by the president, one that under the circumstances seemed highly appropriate: the former Nazi death camp at Auschwitz in southern Poland. It was there he would give a brief speech explaining, among other things, his abrupt disappearance from Madrid the week before and the sudden change of location from Warsaw to Auschwitz.

Second, the president informed White House press secretary Dick Greene, already on the press plane to Warsaw, of the change of venue to Auschwitz, adding that a major cabinet-level shake-up was imminent and that there was to be a total press blackout on anything pertaining to it.

Then, earlier informed by Bill Strait of Jake Lowe's "accidental" death and the vision of Dr. Jim Marshall's shocking suicide plunge from the Chinook still raw in their minds, and remembering too the poison capsule embedded in Merriman Foxx's teeth, the president had Hap call Roley Sandoval, special Secret Service agent in charge of the vice-presidential detail, and tell him without explanation to quietly assign extra agents to the vice president and to his entourage to prevent any attempt at "self-harm."

Immediately afterward he placed calls to Vice President Hamilton Rogers; Secretary of State David Chaplin; Secretary of Defense Terrence Langdon; Chairman of the Joint Chiefs of Staff Chester Keaton, and presidential Chief of Staff Tom Curran. The conversations had been terse and exceedingly brief. In them he demanded that each man present his resignation to the Speaker of the House by fax within the hour. Failing that, he would be fired immediately. Further, he demanded they present themselves at the U.S. embassy in London no later than noon tomorrow to be taken into custody and charged with high treason against the government and people of the United States. Last, he called the Director of the FBI in Washington to inform him of what had happened and directed he take United States congresswoman Jane Dee Baker, who was traveling with the vice president in Europe, and expatriate U.S. citizen Evan Byrd, residing in Madrid, quietly into custody and charge them with the same crime, urging precaution against suicide.

After that he had walked the length of the Chinook to confer with the doctors on the condition of both José and Demi, then spent a few moments with them both and come back to share a cup of coffee with Hap and Marten before moving off to a bunk, a medical litter really, to sleep. As he left he touched briefly on the speech he would give at Auschwitz. What he would say, what it would entail, he hadn't yet decided but it was something he hoped would be as fitting to what had happened and to what they had uncovered, as the hallowed ground on which he had chosen to deliver it. He had retired to his room to work on the speech almost immediately after their arrival at Spangdahlem.

Marten rolled over again. In the distance he could hear the roar and rumble of fighter jets taking off, which he gathered was an on-going situation that one got used to. Spangdahlem was the home of 52nd Fighter Wing which oversaw twenty-four-hour deployments of U.S. fighter aircraft around the world.

Demi.

She had come to him little more than an hour into their flight in the Chinook. The doctors had treated her burns and mildly sedated her, then put her in a hospital gown and suggested she sleep. Instead she had asked to sit with him and the doctors had let her. For a long time she had simply stared off at nothing. Her crying had stopped but her eyes were still filled with tears. Tears, he felt, that were no longer born out of fear and horror but rather out of sheer relief, maybe even disbelief, that it was over.

Why she had wanted to sit with him he didn't know, nor did she say. His sense was that she wanted to talk to him but didn't quite know what to say or how to put it, or that maybe at this point the physical effort itself was too great. Finally she turned and her eyes locked on his.

"It was my mother, not my sister. She disappeared from the streets of Paris when I was eight years old and my father died very soon afterward," she said in a voice barely above a whisper. "I have been trying to find out what happened to her ever since. Now I know I loved her very much and I know . . . she . . . loved . . . me . . ." The tears welled up and ran down her cheeks. He started to say something but she stopped him. "Are you alright?"

"Yes."

She tried to smile. "I'm very sorry for what I did to you. To you and to the president."

He put a hand to her face and gently wiped the tears away. "It's alright," he whispered, "it's alright. We're okay now. We're all okay."

At that moment she reached up and took his hand in hers and held it. Still holding it she leaned back, and he saw exhaustion overtake her. A moment later she closed her eyes and went to sleep.

Marten watched her for a moment and then turned away, certain that if he didn't he would start weeping himself. The feeling was not just a release of emotion from what they had been through but for something else.

Over *cava* and lunch at the Four Cats in Barcelona Demi had asked him about Caroline and why he had followed Foxx, first to Malta and then to Spain. When he'd told her she'd half smiled and said, "Then you are here because of love."

Now he realized she had been talking as much about herself and her mother as she was referring to himself and Caroline. They had both done what they had because of love.

That was the thing here as she slept beside him, physically and emotionally wounded, dressed in a hospital gown and holding his hand. The closeness, the intimacy, was an all-but-unbearable reminder of Caroline at the hospital in Washington as she slept with her hand in his during the last hours of her life.

Demi he had known for little more than a week. Caroline he had loved most all of his life.

And still did.

167

A knock on Marten's door woke him from deep sleep. A second knock brought him around.

"Yes," he said with no idea where he was.

The door opened and the president came in alone and closed the door behind him. "Sorry to wake you," he said quietly.

"What is it?" Marten got up on an elbow. "Cousin Jack" was still without his hairpiece and still wore the nonprescription eyeglasses he'd bought in Madrid to help change his appearance. To this moment no one, unless they had been alerted and were looking, would recognize him as John Henry Harris, president of the United States. That he wore a pair of borrowed, ill-fitting light blue pajamas wouldn't have done much to clue them in either.

"We're leaving for the NATO meeting at Auschwitz in an hour. Taking the Chinook."

Marten threw back the covers and got out of bed. "Then this is it, the formal good-bye."

"Not good-bye at all. I want you to come with me, to be there when I give my speech."

"Me?"

"Yes."

"Mr. President, that's your stage not mine. I was planning to go home to Manchester. I've got a lot of work to catch up on. That is, if I haven't been fired."

The president smiled. "I'll write you a note. 'Nicholas Marten couldn't come to work last week because he was saving the world.'"

"Mr. President, I . . ." He hesitated, uncomfortable with what he had to say and unsure not only how to put it, but how it would be taken. "I can't be seen with you in public. There will be too many people, too many cameras. It's not just me. I have a sister living in

Switzerland, I can't risk putting her in . . . danger . . ." his voice trailed off.

The president studied him. "Someone's trying to find you."

"Yes."

"What Foxx said about you once being a policeman. Were you?"

Marten hesitated; almost no one knew who he really was, but if he couldn't trust this man now, there was no one anywhere he could trust. "Yes," he said finally, "Los Angeles Police Department. I was a homicide investigator. I was involved in a situation where most of my squad were killed."

"Why?"

"I was asked to kill a prisoner in custody. I refused. It went against the credo of the squad. A few veteran detectives wanted to even the score. I changed my name, my identity and the name and identity of my sister. I wanted nothing more to do with law enforcement or violence. We left the U.S. and started another life."

"This would have been about six years ago."

Marten was amazed. "How would you know that?"

"The time frame fits. Red McClatchy."

"What?" Marten suddenly perked.

"Commander of the legendary 5-2 Squad. Half the population of California knew what it was and who he was. I met him once when I was a senator. The mayor invited me to his funeral."

"I was his partner when he was killed."

"The detectives blame you."

"For that and the rest of it. The 5-2 was disbanded afterward."

"So at this point none of them know your name or where you live or what you do."

"They keep trying to find me on the Internet. They have their own Web site for cops around the world. At least once a month they put out a query asking if anyone's seen me, playing it as if I was a lost friend and they want to know where I can be found. Nobody knows what they're really up to except me and them. It's bad enough for me but I don't want them going after my sister."

"You said she's in Switzerland."

"Her name is Rebecca, she works as governess to the children of a wealthy family in a town near Geneva," Marten half-smiled. "Someday I'll tell you her story, it's something else."

The president studied him for a long moment. "Come to

Auschwitz. I'll keep you out of camera range. I promise. Afterward you can go home."

"I—" Marten was hesitant.

"Cousin, you were there step by step. You saw everything that I did. If I start to falter or have doubts about what I'm saying I'll look at you and remember the truth."

"I don't understand."

"I'm going to say some things that diplomatically might be better left unsaid, all the while knowing the reaction around the world might and probably will be ugly. But I'm going to say them anyway because I think we've reached a point in time where the people elected to serve need to tell the truth to the people who elected them, whether they like what they hear or not. None of us anywhere can afford to go on with politics as usual," the president paused. "I'm not one man alone, Nicholas. Come with me, please. I want— I need—your presence, your moral support."

"It's that important."

"Yes, it's that important."

Marten smiled, "And you'll write me the note saying I missed work because I was saving the world."

"You can frame it."

"And then I can go home."

"And then we can all go home."

168

HOTEL VICTORIA WARSAW. WARSAW, POLAND. 6:20 A.M.

"Hello, Victor. Did you sleep well? Have you had breakfast?"

Victor turned off the television, then took his cell phone and began to pace the room in his boxer shorts. "Yes, Richard, at five thirty, I didn't sleep at all. You didn't call last night as you promised. I didn't know what had happened. I was afraid something had gone wrong."

"I'm sorry, Victor, I apologize. Things have been a little hectic.

That's why I was delayed in getting to you. There's been a change in our agenda."

"What change? What's going on?" The paranoia that had been working on Victor for hours shot through him. Suddenly they had reservations, he knew it. At the last minute they were concerned about his ability and decided to bring in someone else. Richard was going to fire him just like that. Tell him to go home. Then what? He had no money; they had paid for everything. He didn't even have plane fare back to the States.

"Victor, are you still there?"

"Yes, Richard, I am. What is this, this," he paused, terrified to say it, "change of agenda? You want me to leave Warsaw, don't you?"

"Yes."

"Why? I can do it. You know I can do it. I did the man in Washington. I did the jockeys, didn't I? Who else can shoot like that? Who else, Richard, tell me! No, let me tell you. No one, that's who. No one is as good as I am."

"Victor, Victor. Calm down. I have all the faith in the world in you. Yes I want you to leave Warsaw, but it's for the change of plan I was talking about. You don't need to worry. Everything is in order. When you get there, everything will be ready for you as always."

Victor let out a breath, then suddenly stood straighter, prouder. He felt better. "Where am I going?"

"It's a short train ride, less than three hours."

"First class?"

"Of course. Train number 13412 for Krakow. You will depart at 8:05 this morning and arrive at 10:54. Go directly to the taxi area and look for cab number 7121. The driver will have further instructions and take you the rest of the way, about a forty-minute ride."

"Forty-minute ride to where?"

"Auschwitz."

169

Surrounded by security and followed all the way by a dozen camera crews, the tall, somber, and distinguished president of Poland, Roman Janicki, led the twenty-six heads of NATO member countries through the grim corridors of the former World War II Nazi death camp.

Outside under a gray sky they had passed beneath Auschwitz's infamous welcoming gates and its wrought-iron sign emblazoned with the motto *Arbeit Macht Frei,* Work Shall Make You Free. Afterward Janicki had taken them past the weed-covered, rusting tracks arriving trains had used to deposit the estimated one and a half to four million Jews who were exterminated here and at nearby camps, most notably Auschwitz II and Birkenau. Moments later they walked in silence past the stilled gas chambers and the crematory, with its furnaces and iron body carts. Past the remains of the wooden barracks that housed prisoners overseen by the camp's horrific Nazi guards, the dreaded Schutzstaffel, the SS.

Toupee on, cosmetic glasses removed and dressed in a dark blue suit, and with Hap Daniels at his side, fully recognizable as president of the United States, John Henry Harris walked side by side with the chancellor of Germany, Anna Bohlen, and French president, Jacques Geroux, his thoughts on the speech he would give while standing on a hastily constructed platform outside what remained of the rows of former prisoners' barracks.

11:50 P.M.

A taxi drove past a fenced-in area containing a sea of media satellite trucks and up to the press gate. The door opened and a middle-aged man wearing a suit and tie got out, then the taxi pulled away.

Immediately he went to the highly secured press gate, where a dozen heavily armed Polish army commandos waited with members of the Polish and U.S. Secret Services.

"Victor Young, Associated Press. My name is on your list," Victor said calmly and produced an AP identification card and his United States passport.

A USSS special agent examined both IDs and handed them to a uniformed woman in a bulletproof glass enclosure. She took them, matched them against a list she had, then pressed a button and took his picture.

"Alright," she nodded and handed the IDs back along with the appropriate security press tag which Victor put around his neck.

"Hands over your head, please?" another special agent said and Victor complied. Another moment and he had been patted down for weapons.

"Go ahead, sir."

"Thank you," Victor said and unmolested went inside. In a way he amazed himself. How terribly nervous and upset he always was when he waited for Richard to call, and how calm and easygoing he was when he was face-to-face with the enemy. Of course they knew that; along with his excellent marksmanship, it was the reason they had recruited him and stayed with him.

11:52 P.M.

Nicholas Marten stood back watching as the hour drew closer to one o'clock, the scheduled time of the president's speech. Everywhere were representatives of the world press. Equally impressive was the number of invited guests who jostled with security details for space in front of the long platformlike dais where world leaders would gather to hear the president speak.

His speech, as White House press secretary Dick Greene had informed the press corps earlier, would be, among other things, an explanation of the last minute shift of venue from Warsaw to Auschwitz and an elaboration on the "terrorist threat" that had seen him removed from his hotel in Madrid by the Secret Service in the middle of the night and taken to the "undisclosed location" where he had been until earlier today.

The fact that his speech would be carried live worldwide by all of the major broadcast organizations, coupled with the promise of getting the facts on the past days from the president himself both intrigued and frightened, and put an already anxious world further on edge. In addition, something else made the moment even more immediate and compelling. Earlier that morning the president had called for "a special session of Congress" to be convened at 7:00 A.M. Washington time, where a live telecast of the Auschwitz proceedings would be shown on a large-screen television. The special session, the early hour, and the fact that what the president would say couldn't wait until he returned to Washington added a level of urgency to everything.

11:55 P.M.

Marten, like the president, was dressed in a hastily found but well-enough-fitting dark blue suit with white shirt and dark tie. Like everyone else he had been issued a security clearance badge that hung around his neck. To protect his image from the public and from accidental pickup by the hordes of media cameras, he had been given a Secret Service buzz haircut and the accompanying requisite Secret Service sunglasses, giving him the appearance, if not the authority, of a USSS special agent.

Marten crossed toward the podium, watching the final pieces being put into place. All around he could feel the intensity growing as the clock ticked down and people waited for the president and the other NATO dignitaries to arrive and take their place. He stopped near the back of the twenty or so rows of folding chairs set up in front of the podium to watch the media crews inspecting camera equipment and making sound checks on the microphones at the podium. A hundred yards away he could see the press gates and the area beyond it, where the media's satellite trucks were parked. Here and there Polish security teams patrolled with dogs.

Marten shaded his eyes from the glare of the high overcast and looked up. Nearby were several old two-story buildings. On the roof of each were two two-man sniper teams, Polish or U.S. Secret Service or maybe NATO, he couldn't tell. Security everywhere was immense.

He turned back and walked on. As he did, a troubling thought passed over him. From what he could see the dais was set up in three distinct levels: the first, the podium where the president of Poland would introduce President Harris; the second, a raised level immediately behind it where the president, the chancellor of Germany, and the president of France would stand, and then a third level behind that, where the rest of the NATO representatives would stand before a sea of waving flags of the twenty-six member nations.

All to the good, except for one thing. There would be a short period of time when the president of Poland made his opening remarks and then introduced President Harris that Harris, the chancellor of Germany, and the president of France would be standing shoulder to shoulder in a perfect line behind him. That perfect line was what troubled because it brought to mind the single-shot killings of the two jockeys at the Chantilly race track outside Paris just days before.

The president had told him the Covenant had planned to assassinate the chancellor of Germany and the president of France at the NATO meeting. More chillingly, he remembered the president's harsh words after Foxx's death—*His plan isn't dead. Neither is theirs!*

The president had survived everything to stand here today. He also knew everything. The heavy security aside, if a sharpshooter could hide in the woods and kill two jockeys on running horses from a hundred yards with one shot why couldn't he do the same here? Only instead of taking out two people he could take out three, especially if they were standing shoulder to shoulder in a line for the two or three minutes it would take for the president of Poland to make his introduction.

Marten looked quickly around. They were surrounded by old buildings and trees. And beyond those trees, more trees, like the forest bordering the Chantilly race track. Suddenly he remembered the weapon that had been used was an M14, the same type of gun used to kill the man at Union Station in Washington; both times the weapon had been left behind. The M14 was not only powerful and extremely accurate from even four hundred yards, it was probably one of the easiest weapons in the world for anyone to get ahold of. Marten looked at his watch. It was 11:54.

"Jesus God," he breathed. He needed to find Hap and right now!

170

11:56 P.M.

Marten entered the Secret Service command post and alerted Bill Strait to his fears. In seconds Strait had contacted Hap, who was with the president.

Two minutes later, Hap, Marten, and Bill Strait were deep in the Secret Service command post, surrounded by a dozen agents and tech specialists and three commanders of the Polish Secret Service. They had no idea if Marten was right or, if he was, whom they might be looking for—man, woman, young, middle-aged, old—and how that person might have been able to smuggle an M14 or other rifle past the heavy security and onto the grounds. One thing was certain: whoever that person was, if they existed at all, had to have security clearance. No one else was inside the compound. Of that they were doubly certain.

12:00 NOON

Collecting the M14 was easy. Brought onto the grounds inside a television satellite truck and hidden among literally tons of broadcast equipment inside a long black tubular case used to carry camera tripods, it had been left in a pile of other camera equipment outside the truck. Victor's AP press pass gave him easy access to the media area and to the huge gaggle of satellite vans. The tripod case holding the rifle was to the left and near the bottom of the pile and marked with a singular piece of light blue masking tape. All Victor had to do was pick up the case and retreat to the cover of nearby trees as had been explained in the instruction packet the driver of taxicab #7121 had given him when he'd picked him up from the Warsaw train in Krakow.

12:10 P.M.

Inside the Secret Service command post Marten, Hap, and Bill Strait sat in front of computer screens, scanning the photo IDs of everyone who had been given security clearance and photographed upon entry—all six hundred and seventy-two of them—and that included the heads of state themselves, their families and entourages, other invited guests, every member of the security force, every member of the media.

Marten was there because Hap had asked him to be—because he had been with the president all the way from Barcelona and in that time he might have glimpsed a face in passing he would recognize here. Maybe one of Foxx's people from Montserrat or someone he had seen with Foxx or Beck or Demi in Malta or even on the television monitors inside the church at Aragon. It was a reach at best but it was better than nothing.

"Damn it," Hap snapped in as the photos whirred by, "we have no idea who the hell we're looking for."

"I hope I'm wrong about the whole thing," Marten said. "I hope nothing comes up."

"Hap," Bill Strait said suddenly. "Everyone admitted to the grounds will have had a background check, otherwise they wouldn't have been given security credentials. Ninety percent were invited to the original summit in Warsaw which means the security checks on them would have been extensive. The remaining ten percent are here mainly because of the last minute change of location. Background checks on them would be less thorough simply because of the time factor."

"You're right. Let's isolate those sixty-seventy odd people. Go over them in particular."

12:20 P.M.

Victor moved readily past a row of old stone buildings and toward a stand of budding trees that partially concealed a long run of what looked like original death camp concrete-post-and-barbed-wire security fence.

12:30 P.M.

Photograph after photograph whirred past Hap, Marten, and Bill Strait. So far they had seen no one who would give them pause, no one at all who seemed questionable or whom they might have seen before. Still, they had no choice but to keep on. In thirty minutes the president would step to the podium. If someone was out there, they had to find him.

12:35 P.M.

Victor moved through high grass toward a small pond twenty yards away.

"Testing. One, two. Testing. One, two."

In the distance he could hear the voice of a technical engineer testing the podium's sound system.

"Testing. One, two. Testing. One, two."

Victor smiled as he reached the edge of the pond and skirted around behind it. For some reason he had felt no emotion until now. He'd been calm all the way from Warsaw. Calm through the security check. Calm as he'd walked past the satellite trucks on the way to retrieve the tripod case with the M14 inside. Calm, even when he'd been challenged by a guard dog team; readily showing his ID, even patting one of the dogs on the head. Calm as he picked up the tripod moments later and walked away with it toward the woods. It was only now as he heard them testing the sound system that he felt his adrenaline come up. It was why he had smiled. This was not only dangerous, it was fun.

171

Three large black SUVs, their windows tinted, turned off Park Lane onto Grosvenor Street and a moment later turned onto the embassy grounds on Grosvenor Square.

Immediately they were surrounded by an armed squad of United States Marines in dress uniform. A moment later the doors to the lead and tail cars opened and a half dozen special agents of the United States Secret Service stepped out. In a heartbeat they opened the doors to the third SUV. Special Agent Roland Sandoval stepped out first, followed immediately and in silence by Vice President Hamilton Rogers; Secretary of Defense Terrence Langdon; Secretary of State David Chaplin; Chairman of the Joint Chiefs of Staff Chester Keaton; and lastly by presidential Chief of Staff Tom Curran.

Surrounded by Marines and Secret Service agents the group entered the embassy building, the doors closed behind them and the SUVs drove off. The entire operation took less than a minute, beginning to end.

AUSCHWITZ, U.S. SECRET SERVICE COMMAND POST. 12:47 P.M.

"This man here," Bill Strait suddenly snapped out loud.

Both Hap and Marten turned to look at Strait's computer screen. On it he had the photograph and AP Press credentials of VICTOR YOUNG. "He was in the Ritz in Madrid the night the president vanished," Strait said. "He tried to get up to the fourth floor. It seemed to be a mistake, he said he was just a tourist waiting for friends. We had him on security cameras and studied him later and decided he was no risk."

"You sure it's him?" Hap said.

"Not exactly but pretty damn close."

"I've seen him too," Marten was staring at the screen. "He passed me in a car in Washington the night Dr. Stephenson shot herself."

"You sure?"

"Yes, I'm sure."

"Get this photo to every security team!" Hap snapped at a special agent standing behind him. "We're going out, now!"

12:48 P.M.

Unnoticed by the invited guests or the media, two hundred Secret Service agents from Poland, the U.S., Germany, and France fanned out as unobtrusively as possible searching for one Victor Young, a possible phantom sniper carrying an M14.

12:50 P.M.

President Harris, German Chancellor Bohlen, French President Geroux and Polish President Roman Janicki huddled with the leaders of the other twenty-three NATO countries in the large tent from which they would make their public entrance in less than seven minutes.

"Mr. President," Hap came in fast, "May I see you for a moment please?"

The president excused himself and stepped away.

"Mr. President, we have a security breach. A lone man. We think he's a sniper. I want to postpone the event."

"Sniper?"

"Yes, sir."

"But you're not sure."

"A hundred percent, no."

"Hap, we've got the world watching on television. We have the Congress in special session waiting for us. We've already changed venue because of security concerns. We postpone this now, we show the entire world how vulnerable we are even under a security blanket as tight as this. Hap, we can't do it. I'll have to trust that you'll find your man or you'll find you've made a mistake and there's no one at all." The president looked at his watch. "We go out in four minutes, Hap."

"Mr. President, let me ask you for a compromise. Live television coverage has already begun. At 12:55 let me put out the word there has been an equipment problem and there will be a short delay until it's fixed. In the meantime the TV anchors can ad-lib or play video of your earlier tour through the camp. Give us a little time, please."

"Then you do think this person is out there."

"Yes, sir, I do."

"You have your compromise."

12:55 P.M.

Victor moved on his stomach to edge up through the high grass at the edge of the pond, then lifted the rifle and sighted down it. Four hundred yards away through trees he saw the podium. Just as his instructions had said he would.

From them he knew too that the president of Poland would speak for three minutes and that during that time the chancellor of Germany, the president of the United States, and the president of France would line up shoulder to shoulder behind him—and in that order, which was fortunate because the chancellor was shorter than the men. From his ground angle his shot would be elevated and would strike Anna Bohlen in the lower jaw before hitting President Harris just below his right ear, and then carry through his skull and into that of the president of France.

He inched forward to make his view a little clearer, then waited. It was only minutes now—seconds, really—before they came out and took their places. One shot and he was done. Afterward he would simply leave the weapon and walk away, then rejoin the press corps in the chaos. He would linger there in the crowd, then slip out through the media gate and walk down the road past a long line of parked cars to where the taxi would be waiting.

Dogs. Why did he hear dogs?

172

His heart pounding, Victor slid back in the grass. The dogs were barking, coming in his direction from the far side of the pond. Over the
loudspeakers he heard someone speak in English and then Polish:

*"There is a short delay because of technical problems. Please bear
with us for a few moments."*

Technical problems? Oh Lord! He'd been found out!

Panicked, he looked behind him. All he saw was the old security fencing and the trees behind it. The barking got louder. In front
of him was the pond; to his right, more fencing that melded into
the trees and seemed to go on forever. To his left was the old cre-
matorium. In between was a hundred yards of open land. He had
no option but to go to his right. Then he remembered a secondary
plan that had been in the instructions the taxi driver had given him.
A quarter mile beyond the high grass on the far side of the pond
were the ruins of old barracks that were now little more than a
graveyard of concrete foundations and still-standing chimneys.
Among those was a dilapidated stone-and-wood building where the
Nazis had stored wagons to haul the dead to the crematory. Hidden
in a back corner under some old planking would be food and water,
a cell phone, and an automatic pistol. If all things failed, that was
where he had been directed to hide and where he would be contacted.

The barking was louder and more intense—the dogs were closing. Somewhere off he heard the sound of a helicopter starting up.

"Leave the rifle. Get rid of your scent. Get rid of your clothes,"
he said out loud, and in a burst stood up and ran low through tall
grass for the cover of the pond.

Then he was at the water's edge. A pudgy, white middle-aged
man, pulling off his shoes and socks and throwing off the rest of his
clothes. His AP identification and security passes went with them.

In seconds he was in the water swimming for the far bank. Where was Richard? *Who* was Richard? It made no difference. This was the end, he knew it. He didn't have a chance.

1:03 P.M.

"We've got the weapon and his clothes," a special agent's voice crackled simultaneously over Secret Service headsets.

Marten was running with the other agents, a 9mm Sig Sauer that Hap had tossed him as they left the command post in his hand. Ahead they saw the pond and the barking, howling dogs stopped at the edge of it. Bill Strait was in front of him gripping a machine pistol and running flat out. Suddenly he cut right toward the far side of the pond and what looked like the ruins of old barracks some distance behind it.

Marten veered right, following Strait and away from the agents running in front of him. Strait was alone. If he got into trouble he was by himself.

Fifty yards ahead Strait jumped a small stream and kept on. Lungs on fire, Marten followed. In seconds he was at the stream and over it. For a moment he lost Strait, didn't know where he had gone. Then he saw him, charging down an overgrown gravel path toward the ruined barracks.

Strait glanced back, then said something into his headset, and ran on with a renewed burst of speed.

Marten hit the gravel pathway still fifty yards behind him. As he did, his feet slid out from under him and he went down. As quickly he recovered and was up and running. Closing now, forty yards, thirty.

Ahead he saw Strait stop at a dilapidated stone-and-wood building. Then, machine pistol up, carefully move to a partially open door.

"Bill, wait!" Marten yelled.

Strait either didn't hear him or ignored him, because in the next instant he slipped through the door and disappeared from sight.

Two seconds, three, and Marten was there, right outside. There was an abrupt, very brief exchange of voices inside, then came the dull, sharp spit of machine-pistol fire.

"Christ," Marten breathed. Sig Sauer up, he ducked low and went in through the door.

Strait swung the machine pistol in reaction as he came in.

"Don't shoot!" Marten yelled.

Sweating, breathing hard, Strait stared at him for the longest moment, then lowered the gun and nodded toward the rear of the building. The body of a naked middle-aged man lay against the old stone foundation. A .45 automatic was in one hand, the rest of him a bullet-riddled composite of flesh, blood, and bone.

"Victor Young," Strait said. "He the man you saw in Washington?"

Marten walked over and knelt down just as a half dozen special agents came through the door. Marten studied him for a moment, then stood and looked at Strait.

"Yeah," he said. "Yeah, it's him."

Strait nodded, then made an adjustment on his headset. "Hap, it's Bill," he said into it. "We got him. I think it's safe to let the show go on."

173

Marten handed the Sig Sauer to Bill Strait, then moved past the other agents and went back outside. Sun had broken through the clouds here and there, painting the land and buildings with an extraordinary soft white light. It seemed a terrible thing to use the word "beautiful" to describe a place like this, but for the moment it was, and Marten had the sense that despite what had just happened, with the gathering of so many divergent people here that perhaps, and once and for all, a healing had begun.

In the distance he heard the voice of the Polish president resonate through the loudspeakers as he began his welcoming speech and then introduced President Harris.

Abruptly he pushed past a wave of Polish and U.S. Secret Service agents and walked toward the seating area in front of the podium. The president had wanted him there and close by where he could see him. He picked up his pace. Crossing near the pond, he was suddenly aware of the miles of still-standing barbed-wire fence that despite the beauty of the day seemed as ominous now as it must have been seventy years earlier. Maybe he was wrong, maybe the healing had not begun at all.

"President Janicki, Madam Chancellor, Mr. President," President Harris's amplified voice floated across the land, *"my fellow NATO representatives, honored guests and members of the United States Congress in Washington, and those watching on television around the world. I have come here today as one of you, a citizen of this planet, and as such feel it my duty as both that citizen and president of the United States to share with you some facts that have come to light in the last few days and hours.*

"As you know, this convening of the leaders of NATO member countries was to have taken place in Warsaw. Because of a raised security threat it was suggested the meeting be postponed entirely. After discussion with the member countries it was decided we would meet as planned. The change of location was my idea, and after further dialogue the membership concurred. The choice of Auschwitz was not made at random. It is where millions of people were brought against their will and summarily slaughtered by one of the most heinous, genocidal terrorist organizations in modern history."

Marten turned a corner to walk between aging stone buildings. Ahead he could see the president at the podium, while the NATO leaders stood on the platform behind him, the flags of their twenty-six countries fluttering in the breeze. The sniper teams were still clearly in view on the rooftops. Polish commandos wearing flak jackets and carrying automatic weapons stood guarding the area's perimeter, while inside it hundreds of plainclothes Secret Service agents circulated and watched the crowd.

"In the past week," the president continued, his voice exceedingly clear through the banks of loudspeakers, *"the existence of another terrorist organization, as heinous and genocidal as the one*

under Adolf Hitler, has been exposed and its leadership crushed."

Marten reached the gathering and moved to stand under a tree near the front. As he did he saw the president pause and glance his way and nod ever so slightly. Marten nodded back.

"This group, which we have temporarily and simply called 'The Covenant' represents no single nation, nor religion, nor race, except their own. They are a membership of highly privileged criminals embedded in political, military, and economic institutions around the world, and, if allegations prove true, have been for centuries. This may sound impossible, something out of fantasy, even absurd. I assure you it is not. In the past days I have personally witnessed their terror firsthand. I have seen the results of their human experiments. I have seen bodies and body parts hidden away in secret laboratories in old mining tunnels in Spain. I have seen them take a people's deepest religious beliefs and manipulate them to serve their own ideals in the form of heinous rituals where human beings are burned alive like witches at the stake in an elaborate ceremony that is the highlight of their so-called 'annual meeting.'

"Last week I was thought to have been spirited out of a hotel in Madrid and taken to an 'undisclosed location' for my own safety because of a 'very credible terrorist threat.' In a way that is true, it was a terrorist threat, but it came from members of my own inner circle. People at the highest levels of power in the American government, people I have known as my best friends and advisers for years. These people demanded I break the laws of the United States and the oath of office of the presidency. I refused to do so. I was not taken to an undisclosed location, I fled those people. I fled them not only because they threatened my life, but because they and their cohorts in Europe and elsewhere around the world were preparing to unleash a massive genocide against the Middle Eastern states, the scope of which has never before been seen in history.

"Yesterday I asked for and received the resignations of the following: Vice President of the United States Hamilton Rogers; Secretary of State David Chaplin; Secretary of Defense Terrence Langdon; Chairman of the Joint Chiefs of Staff, United States Air Force General Chester Keaton; White House Chief of Staff Tom Curran. I have been informed that in the past hour they all have been taken into federal custody at the United States embassy in London. They have been

charged with suspicion of membership in a terrorist organization and with high treason against the people and government of the United States.

"Concurrently I have been informed that similar arrests are underway in Germany and France. It is too early in our investigations to say more except that we anticipate that the detention of prominent persons in other countries will follow.

"To all of us this has been a thunderclap of surprise, horror, and revulsion. For myself and for the chancellor of Germany and the president of France it is also a personal and deeply felt wound of betrayal by close and long-trusted friends.

"Bad news does not travel well. Truth of this nature is both painful and ugly, but the same truth hidden away is far worse. In the coming days and weeks we will know more, and you will be kept informed. In the meantime we can only thank providence that we were fortunate enough to have found the beast and killed it before it began its slaughter.

"We need only look around us here at Auschwitz to be reminded of the terrible, harrowing price of fanaticism. We owe it to those who perished here, to ourselves, to our children and theirs, to make this cancer a disease of the past. It is something that together we can do.

"Thank you and good afternoon."

The president stared out at the audience for several seconds before turning to take the handshakes of Anna Bohlen of Germany and Jacques Geroux of France and then of the president of Poland, Roman Janicki. And then of the leaders of the NATO countries who came down one by one to greet him and say a few words and to solemnly take his hand.

For the longest moment Marten, like nearly everyone else—the guests, the security personnel, the media—stood silent. The president's speech had been no self-serving discourse, no political glad hand; he had spoken the truth as he had promised Marten he would. How and when and where the fallout would come—a firestorm of protest and outrage in the Middle East and in Muslim enclaves around the world, charges the president was mentally unbalanced and incapable of serving, furious denials and counterattacks by those arrested or revealed as they rallied their people behind them—was impossible to say. But it would come as the president had known it would from the beginning.

"I'm going to say some things that diplomatically might be better left unsaid," he had told Marten, "all the while knowing the reaction around the world might and probably will be ugly. But I'm going to say them anyway because I think we've reached a point in time where the people elected to serve need to tell the truth to the people who elected them, whether they like what they hear or not. None of us anywhere can afford to go on with politics as usual."

The president had asked Marten to come to supply moral support, but he hadn't needed it. He had his own clear vision of who he was and of the grave responsibility of his office. His "friends" had made him president because he had never made an enemy of anyone. It made them think he was soft and they could mold him any way they wished. The trouble was, they'd misjudged him greatly.

Marten took one last glance at the president and the leaders surrounding him. That was his world, where he belonged. It was time Marten got back to his. He was turning, starting to walk away, when he heard a familiar voice call his name. He looked up and saw Hap Daniels coming toward him.

"We're leaving. *Marine One,* wheels up from here in ten minutes," he said. "*Air Force One,* wheels up from Krakow in fifty. The president asked us to file a flight plan through Manchester. Drop you off there," he smiled "kind of like a personal shuttle."

Marten grinned. "I've already booked a commercial flight, Hap. Tell the president thanks but I don't need the publicity. He'll know what I'm talking about. Tell him maybe sometime we can all sit down someplace for a steak and a beer. You and him and me and Miguel. The boys too, José especially."

"Be careful, he just might do it."

Marten smiled, then extended his hand. "I'll be waiting."

They shook hands and then Hap was called away. Marten watched him go, then turned and headed for the gate. A minute later he passed between the columns and looked back at the ancient wrought-iron sign above it.

Arbeit Macht Frei, Work Shall Make You Free

The slogan had been the Nazis' idea of graveyard humor, yet

aside from them, no one who saw it smiled much. But in his exhausted state the words crept through and touched Marten in an entirely unintended way, making him smile inwardly and shake his head at the irony of it.

It made him wonder if he still had a job.

EPILOGUE

PART ONE

It had been two months to the day when Marten had told Hap good-bye and walked out of Auschwitz. If he'd been worried about keeping his job at Fitzsimmons and Justice, he needn't have bothered. By the time he had returned to Manchester that evening he had a half-dozen very recent calls backed up on his voice mail. Four were from his manager Ian Graff asking him to call him the moment he got in. The others were, respectively, from Robert Fitzsimmons and Horace Justice. Fitzsimmons he knew well from the workplace. Horace Justice, the founder of the company, eighty-seven years old and retired and living in the south of France, he'd never met. Still, he had messages from all three wishing him well and hoping he would be at work first thing the next morning.

The primary reason?

The president, it seemed, had placed direct calls to each man from *Air Force One* telling them how grateful he was for Marten's personal assistance during the last days and trusting that his unreported absence wouldn't be held against him. Indeed it wasn't. He was put immediately and full-time back onto the Banfield job, which between the arguments and changes of mind between Mr. and Mrs. Banfield, seemed to have been filled with more minefields than anything he'd encountered with the president. Still, he'd eagerly jumped back in and pressed on. Now, finally and at last, things were coming together. The grading had been done, the irrigation was in, the planting was beginning, and the Banfields were at peace. Chiefly because Mrs. Banfield was happily pregnant with twins and hence had shifted her time, opinions, and energy to preparing the house for their arrival. Happily too, Mr. Banfield, when he wasn't following his career as a professional soccer star, followed her indoors. All of which left Marten to supervise the remainder of the landscape work. Which was what he did while the world hung upside down in massive reaction to the president's speech.

The president had been right when he'd said things "might and probably will be ugly." They were from outset and still were.

The United States, Washington in particular, was an on-going typhoon of round-the-clock media chaos. Political talk shows owned television, radio, magazines, and newspapers. The Internet was overrun with bloggers saying the president had gone off the deep end and was a nutcase, that he should be hospitalized or impeached or both. Conspiracy theorists everywhere were rife with their trademark *"I told you so."* Right, left, and center everyone wanted to know what this mysterious *"Covenant"* was and who belonged to it; what religion the president had been referring to; who had been burned to death in ceremonial rituals; how could the very distinguished members of the New World Institute have been involved with anything like the accusations he had made; where was the proof of any of it?

In the Middle East and throughout Muslim enclaves in Europe and the Pacific, things were no different. People and governments wanted details about this "genocide." In which countries and when was it to have taken place? How many deaths would have resulted? Who was to have occupied their lands? What else would've happened? What was the reasoning, the goal behind it? What had the members of this organization hoped to gain? Was the threat of it truly over? And finally, was this another arrogant move by an American president designed to provoke untold fear in the Islamic world, countering terrorist strikes against the U.S., Europe, and the Pacific with the nightmare threat of all-out annihilation?

Without answers, Islam responded quickly. Massive, violent anti-American and anti-Europe demonstrations took place across the Middle East. Equally violent street clashes and car burnings broke out across France, perpetrated by young, mostly poor Muslims whipped into rage by radical clerics for what authorities termed "dubious purpose." Less violent demonstrations took place in England, the Netherlands, Germany, Italy, and Spain. Demands were made in the United Nations for further explanation and specific details. None of which were forthcoming because, as of yet, no particulars of Foxx's master plan had been found.

Nor had the interrogations of Vice President Hamilton Rogers, Secretary of State David Chaplin, Secretary of Defense Terrence Langdon, Chairman of the Joint Chiefs of Staff, General Chester Keaton, and White House Chief of Staff Tom Curran—who proclaimed their innocence after being returned to Washington and arraigned by a federal magistrate and were now being held in the custody of United States marshals at Andrews Air Force Base—turned up new information.

Nor had the interrogations of the members of the New World Institute present at the Aragon meeting—now arrested and being held at various locations around the world, charged with suspicion of membership in a terrorist organization and conspiracy to commit mass murder—revealed facts not already known.

Nor had anything official come from the Secret Service ECSAP unit (Electronic Crimes Special Agent Program) charged with examining the hard drives Hap and the president had taken from the master computer at the Aragon church. Understandably this was a snail's-pace investigation and being done with extreme care, not only for the recovery of information contained within but because whatever was there might well be crucial evidence that would be used in federal court.

Still, and quietly, international security agencies were working in close cooperation to piece together information that would lead to a clear trail of conspiracy. Particularly targeted were political parties in France and Germany where, as Jake Lowe had told the president in Evan Byrd's home in Madrid, "before, our people were not yet in place. Now they are. We have been assured of this by friends of trust. Friends who are in a position to know."

"What friends?" the president had shot back. "Who are you talking about?"

Those "friends" were precisely the people being sought worldwide. In Germany, a minor political party called *Das Demokratische Bündnis,* the Democratic Alliance, the party of Marten's Salt and Pepper Barcelona shadow, the civil engineer Klaus Melzer, was covertly targeted; its entire membership put under heavy surveillance that included electronic monitoring of phone calls, e-mails, bank accounts, as well as travel records. It was an investigation that quickly turned up a sister organization in France; *Nouveau Français Libre,* the New Free French party, with headquarters in Lyon, and branches as far north as Calais on the English Channel, and south, to Marseilles on the Mediterranean.

The great explosion and fire in the church and in the miles of old mining tunnels leading beneath and away from the Aragon resort to an ancient church on the far side of the mountains called *La iglesia dentro de la Montaña,* the Church Within the Mountain, and nearly all the way to the monastery at Montserrat, still burned.

Authorities and mine experts had agreed it would be weeks if not months longer before it burned itself out and cooled enough to be safe for crews to explore. The source of the explosions, like the one barely a day earlier near the monastery at Montserrat, had been attributed to a decades-old-buildup of deadly methane gas in the long-sealed tunnels. It was a declaration that immediately raised eyebrows and brought up the question of how anyone could have purposely planned this kind of massive destruction.

Yet, for all of it, there was evidence. The president and Nicholas Marten had been deposed in secret on what they had seen in the tunnels and laboratories and in the church and elsewhere. So had Demi Picard, Hap Daniels, Miguel Balius, and the Spanish teenagers José, Hector, and Amado. Others deposed— USSS Special Agent Bill Strait, U.S. Marine Corps helicopter pilot Major George Herman "Woody" Woods and the medical team and air crew aboard the Chinook—confirmed the death of National Security Adviser Dr. James Marshall, publicly pronounced a tragic accident, as suicide. The death of political adviser Jake Lowe was presented as a possible homicide, especially after secret testimony by Spanish CNP captain Belinda Diaz and further questioning of Agent Strait concerning Dr. Marshall's reporting of the incident.

At the same time constitutional lawyers for the vice president, the secretary of state, the secretary of defense and the others—despite the posturing of outrage and claims of complete innocence—were already trying to plead the case down from high treason to "threats against the president."

All of which gave the president hope that the truth he had told in his address at Auschwitz was not the political suicide many had thought but simply the right thing to do by a man who believed in telling the people "what was what" and "who was who" because he felt that at this fragile point in history there was no other way to do it.

Careful to keep his distance and his name and face from public view, Marten kept his eyes on the news and his attention on the Banfield project.

Then, on Friday morning, May 21st, Robert Fitzsimmons summoned him to his office and asked him to fly to London to meet with a special client, a prominent London surgeon named Dr. Norbert Holmgren, who lived just off Hyde Park and who had a large estate in the Manchester countryside where he wanted to make considerable landscape modifications.

Dr. Holmgren was not at home when Marten arrived but he was shown into the sitting room anyway. When he entered he found two people waiting, Hap Daniels and President Harris, who was quietly in London for private talks with British prime minister Jack Randolph. Marten's immediate response was to grin broadly and to joyfully bear-hug each man in turn. Then, as quickly, a caution bell rang through him and he pulled back.

"Now what?" he asked.

The "now what" was top secret information the president had wanted to share with him.

"*Aradia Minor,*" the president had said, explaining Demi had been debriefed by the FBI in Paris and had told of her decades-long search for her mother and what she had learned about the ancient and secretive coven of Italian female witches called *Aradia,* which used as its identifying mark the balled cross of Aldebaran, and what Giacomo Gela had revealed about the more secretive order hidden within it called *Aradia Minor.* An order referred to in writing simply as the letter *A* followed by the letter *M* and written in a combination of Hebrew and Greek alphabets as "א μ." It was *Aradia Minor,* a deeply religious cult of true believers that over the centuries had been manipulated into providing the Covenant with their sacrificial "witches."

Later Demi had told of her captivity and of the terrible, torturous videos they had played over and over of her mother's death by fire. Lastly she had told of what she had seen underground when they had brought her via the monorail to the church: the empty experimental medical chambers, the long-abandoned barrackslike rooms, and finally, beneath the church itself and at the end of the monorail track, the large crematory oven.

"That's how Foxx got rid of the bodies." Marten felt the hair stand up on his neck as he said it.

"Yes," the president said. "Look at this," he nodded to Hap who opened a laptop.

"The Secret Service is still working with the hard drives, but already some information has been salvaged. Take a look."

Marten looked at the computer screen. What he saw was a series of still photographs taken in a room in one of Montserrat's tall buildings that overlooked the large plaza in front of the basilica. Apparently taken of Foxx by Foxx with a remote camera, they showed a small office-sized room, a telescope, and a video recorder. Next came photos taken with a telescopic lens, as if through the telescope itself, and showing a number of close-ups of people in the plaza.

"It was how he selected his 'patients,'" the president said, "a never-ending supply. It was the 'general populace' he was looking for. Photographed handwritten notes suggest he pointed out those he'd selected to the monks, who took it from there. Not right away, but following the victims back to wherever they'd come from and later kidnapping them."

"The bastard thought everything through," Marten said angrily, and looked at them both. "Nothing on his plan for the Middle East or notes on his experiments?"

"No, at least not yet."

"What about Beck and Luciana?"

"Not a trace. They either got away or were trapped when the church went up. They are still on the list of those to be apprehended."

"So that's it? Until more of what the hard drives hold are uncovered or what the ongoing investigations might reveal."

"Sort of," Hap said quietly and looked to the president.

"A simple listing in a separate journal that was kept by my

friend and adviser Jake Lowe," the president said, then he hesitated and Marten could see a wave of emotion come over him.

"What is it?"

"You knew my wife was Jewish."

"Yes."

"You knew too that she died of brain cancer in the weeks just before the presidential election."

"Yes."

"They wanted the Jewish vote. They didn't want a Jew in the White House. They thought if she died I would gain a huge boost in the polls not just in sympathy from the Jews but from the general public."

Again Marten felt the hair rise up on his neck. "Foxx killed her with something that mimicked brain cancer."

"Yes," the president nodded and then trembled and tried to blink the tears from his eyes. "It seems," he said with great difficulty, "we both lost someone we loved immeasurably."

Marten went to the president and embraced him, and for the longest moment the two men stood there in each other's arms. Each knowing to his soul what the other was feeling.

"Mr. President, we have to go," Hap said finally.

"I know," he said, "I know."

The men looked at each other and the president smiled. "When this all calms down you'll come to my ranch in California and we'll have that steak and beer. Everyone. You, Hap, Demi, Miguel, and the boys."

Marten grinned, "Hap told you."

Now it was Hap's turn. "I started to but he told me first."

Marten put out his hand. "Good luck, Mr. President."

The president took it, then hugged him once more and stepped back. "Good luck to you too, Cousin, and God bless."

Then he turned and was gone. Hap took Marten's hand and nodded in a way only men who have shared battle and lived can. Then he winked and smiled and followed the president out.

PART TWO

Marten lay in the dark in his loft apartment that overlooked the River Irwell. Occasionally lights from passing cars below played across the ceiling. Now and again came the voices of people passing on the sidewalks. But for the most part it was quiet, the end of a long summer's day.

Deliberately he turned his thoughts from the Banfield project and from memories of "The Covenant." He wanted to fall asleep, not rekindle thoughts that he knew would pump him up and keep him awake.

For a moment he thought back to when he'd first come to England from Los Angeles, changing his name from John Barron to Nicholas Marten and trying very hard to find a place where he could fade from sight and from anyone from the LAPD who might be hunting him while at the same time help his sister Rebecca recover from a devastating mental trauma. Her recovery and relocation to Switzerland and her story afterward, as he had briefly hinted to the president, had been truly remarkable, if not fantastic. A great deal of it had been made possible by the most inimitable person he'd ever known; the sexy, bawdy, blue-blooded "Lady Clem," Lady Clementine Simpson, the only child of the Earl of Prestbury, who he had seriously considered marrying, but who had abruptly shown up one day to tell him she had just become engaged to the newly appointed British ambassador to Japan and in result would be moving from Manchester to Tokyo forthwith. And she had. As far as he knew she was still married and still there because in nearly six years he hadn't had so much as a postcard or e-mail from her.

Rebecca's experience in recovering her own mental health and her sensitivity to what recovery meant made her volunteer to spend time with Demi, who, as Marten had told her, had experienced enormous psychological trauma that specialists in Paris had told him might take years to recuperate from. With a leave of absence from her position at *Agence France-Presse,* she had gone to Switzerland to live with Rebecca, where she was now assisting her in her job as governess to three rapidly growing children and ever so slowly letting go of the memories of her mother and of Merriman Foxx, Luciana, Reverend Beck, and of Cristina and the fire.

TUESDAY, JUNE 13, 1:20 A.M.

Marten was still awake. And he knew why. A vivid portrait burned in his mind, that of a naked middle-aged man lying against the old stone foundation of a shed in Auschwitz, a .45 automatic in one hand, the rest of him shot to pieces. Victor Young, the man he had seen briefly as he'd driven past in a car in Washington, D.C., as Marten had waited for Dr. Lorraine Stephenson to come home the night she committed suicide on the sidewalk in front of him, the same man he later remembered as having seen two nights earlier when Marten had so emotionally and tearfully walked the rainy streets near the White House in the hours after Caroline had died. Young, or whatever his real name was, had been driving the car that had slowly passed him on a darkened, near-empty boulevard. Marten had seen him clearly twice. It made him wonder if even then, Foxx or Beck or both had been concerned about him because of Caroline and had sent someone to watch him.

But that wasn't all.

The Secret Service had traced Victor's whereabouts from Washington to Berlin, to Madrid, to Paris, and then to Chantilly, where he'd taken a hotel room the night before the jockeys had been killed. After that he'd gone back to Paris and then taken a train to Warsaw, where the NATO meeting was originally to have been held. Then, with the location switched to Auschwitz, he'd taken a train there, arriving at the Auschwitz press gate an hour before the president's scheduled speech with the proper AP press credentials, his name on the Secret Service's approved list, and an M14 rifle hidden in a tripod case brought in in a media satellite truck.

How he had heard of the change of venue from Warsaw to Auschwitz in time to change locations himself, how he had gotten his press credentials and been put on the approved list, how and by whom the rifle had been smuggled in, was unclear and still under investigation. What was clear was that from Berlin on he had been clearly stalking the president at nearly every stop along the way during his European tour, even to the point of testing the Secret Service's security at the Hotel Ritz in Madrid.

And that was the thing keeping Marten awake. The thing that had been gnawing at him for some time but that had only now begun to come together. Whether Victor was working alone or for "The Covenant" or for someone else entirely made little difference. With the presence of the M14, it was obvious he had meant to kill the president wherever he spoke either at Warsaw or at Auschwitz. He may well have been planning to kill the chancellor of Germany and the president of France as well, and that was just the problem. In retrospect it was too obvious. Too deliberate. He'd left too perfect a trail.

As good a marksman as Victor was, he was not a professional, and if "The Covenant" with all their resources and connections—from the military to the Secretary of Defense to the National Security Advisor—had meant to kill one or all three, and it seemed they had, at least until their undoing at Aragon, then they would unquestionably have used a professional or a team of professionals. Victor, Marten knew, was their fall guy. Somebody's Lee Harvey Oswald. If he took the shots and made the kill, fine; if not, fine too. He'd left a stalking trail and in doing so he'd left himself wide open to be killed if anything went wrong. And it had, not just because of the fiasco at Aragon, but because Marten had remembered the killings in Washington and at the Chantilly racetrack and sounded the alarm.

And that was the thing that disturbed him now and kept him from sleep. The whole thing had seemingly been put to bed. The Covenant was stopped, every piece of it was being investigated and if the information on the hard drives continued to deliver, they would have complete annual records of the events and the identities of members attending, potentially blockbuster revelations that might go back years, even decades, maybe even centuries, depending on what was there.

When Marten had come through London on his way home to Manchester, he'd taken a few hours between connecting flights to go into the city. There he'd heard Big Ben chime out the hour, the same way the hour was chimed out in cities and towns around the globe, by chimes that played the Westminster Quarters, a striking of familiar notes half the world's population knew by heart. The same Westminster Quarters that had chimed—and seemed so out of place—at the Aragon church as the members of the New World Institute entered. It made him wonder if that was a universal signal from The Covenant to its secretive members everywhere, that no matter what happened it was alive and well. And had been. And would continue to be for centuries to come. If so, The Covenant was not stopped at all, but like Foxx's planned destruction of Aragon, had simply chosen to go underground for a time, decades maybe. If that were the case it meant people still existed inside it that no one else knew about or could even imagine.

It was why he remembered now what had happened at Auschwitz after he'd alerted Hap to the possibility of a sniper. Never mind the press credentials or the Secret Service–approved list or the hidden gun. Victor had been fingered by someone else. Bill Strait had been the one who pulled up his press picture on the video screen to identify him as the man who had tested their security in Madrid. Moments later when they were out chasing him, running with the other agents following the dogs and dog handlers, it had been Strait who had suddenly veered to the side of the pond ahead of Marten and away from everyone else, running almost directly to the place where Victor was hiding, as if he knew exactly where he would be.

And when Marten had given chase and shouted for Strait to wait to go into the building until he got there, Strait had ignored him and gone in alone. It was when Marten finally reached the building that he'd heard their very brief exchange inside, just two words spoken between the men.

"Victor," Strait had said clearly.

"Richard?" Victor had asked, as if suddenly surprised by some-one he knew by voice but had never seen.

Immediately after that had come the dull, sharp spit of Strait's machine pistol.

Eyes wide, Marten rolled over again. Bill Strait. Hap's trusted deputy—or for a time in Barcelona not trusted at all when Hap, like the president, could afford to place his faith in no one. What if Strait was "The Covenant's" man inside the Secret Service and posted to the presidential detail? A perfect cover for access to all kinds of things that went on deep within the executive branch.

Marten wondered if anyone else knew or even had the suspicion he had. Probably not, because he was the only one who had been there at the end. Had seen the direct route Strait had taken. Had heard him say Victor's name and heard Victor say "Richard?"

If he was right, it meant that only he knew, or suspected. Which also meant that in time, maybe sooner than later, Bill Strait would figure it out too.

2:22 A.M.

Marten lay back and closed his eyes. He'd worked in close liaison with people from the U.S. Secret Service off and on for years when he'd been a member of the LAPD. He knew their motto of "Worthy of Trust and Confidence" was not taken lightly and that all of its agents had top secret clearances, and most were cleared beyond that level. Furthermore the organization was far too respected, far too professional, and far too much of a close knit brotherhood for someone to infiltrate it like that.

So maybe, even probably, he was wrong about Bill Strait. Maybe, even probably, he was just thinking too much. Maybe he—

Suddenly there was a sharp knock on his door.

EDITOR'S NOTE

If you would care to know more about Nicholas Marten, his story, and that of his sister Rebecca, Lady Clementine Simpson, and of the LAPD's infamous 5-2 squad, it is told at length in *The Exile*.

ACKNOWLEDGMENTS

For technical information and advice I am especially grateful to Anthony Chapa; and to Ron Nessen, former White House Press Secretary and fellow writer; Emma Casanova and Josep Maria Cañadell, Policia—Mossos d'Esquadra, Barcelona, Spain; Paul Tippin, former Los Angeles Police Department homicide investigator; Colonel John R. Power, U.S. Army—retired; Kirk Stapp, U.S. Army Special Forces; Alan Landsburg; Andrew Robart; Stanley Mendes; and Norton Kristy, Ph.D.

For suggestions and corrections to the manuscript I am particularly thankful to Robert Gleason. I am also indebted to Robert Gottlieb and John Silbersack for their counsel and guidance, and to Tom Doherty and Linda Quinton for their support and faith in the project.

Finally, a very special thanks to my friends in the United States Secret Service.